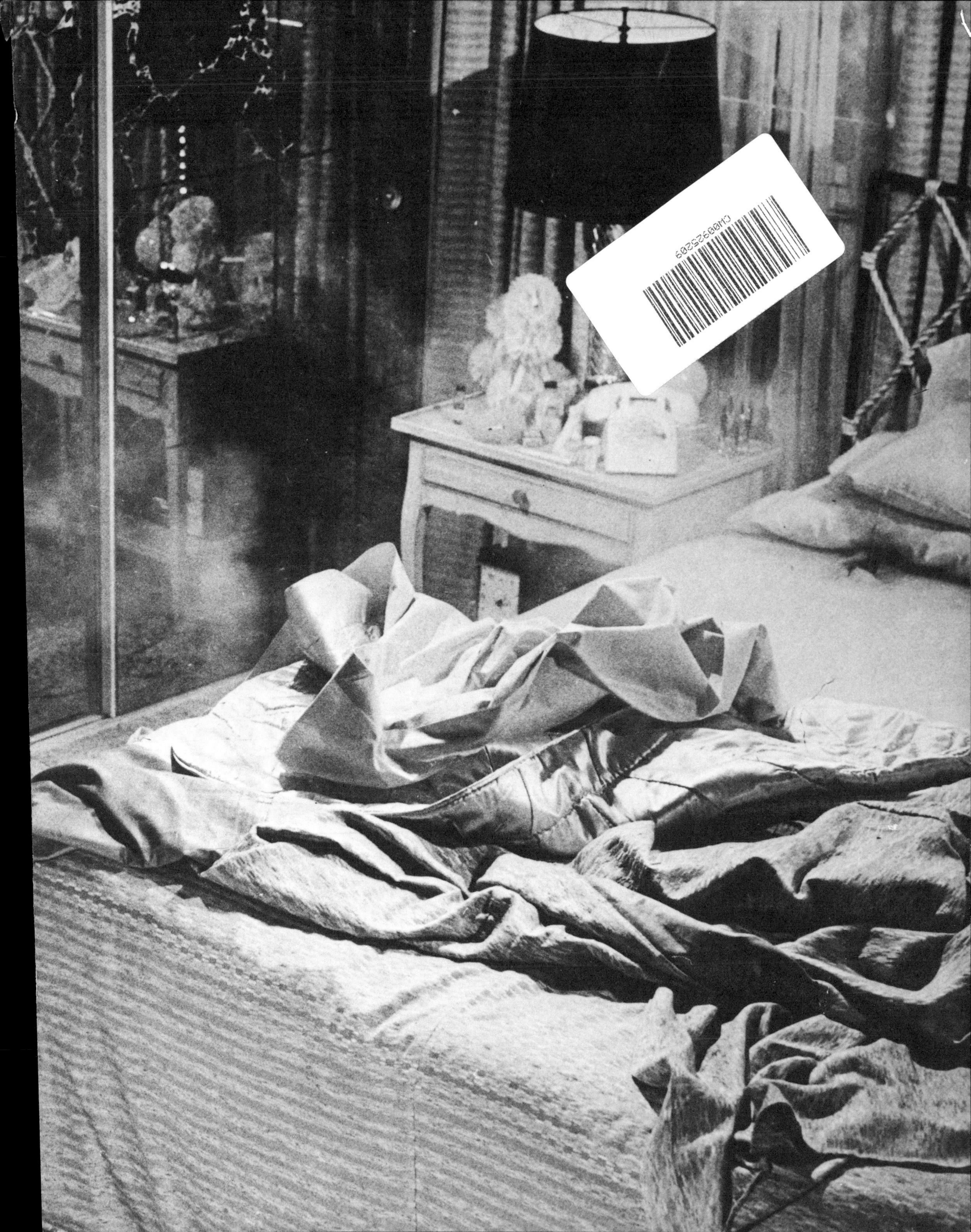

Endpapers Lee Marvin in *Point Blank*.
Ned Beatty, Burt Reynolds, Jon Voight and Ronny Cox in *Deliverance*.

Michel Ciment

John Boorman

Translated by Gilbert Adair

faber and faber
LONDON · BOSTON

First published in Great Britain in 1986
by Faber and Faber Limited
3 Queen Square London WC1N 3AU

Photoset by Parker Typesetting Service, Leicester

Printed in France

British Library Cataloguing in Publication Data
Ciment, Michel
John Boorman.
1. Boorman, John, *1933–* 2. Moving-picture
producers and directors—Biography
I. Title II. John Boorman. *English*
791.43'0233'0924 PN1998.A3B6

ISBN 0–571–13831–4

For my mother

Contents

Foreword

I cannot conceive of such a critical study not proceeding from a basic *shock*, from a revelation; followed by the wish to know better, to understand better, the better to admire. Sometimes it will happen that subsequent works temper such an urge. Sometimes not – on the contrary, they become part of the cinéphile's life, enriching and, as it were, legitimizing his initial enthusiasm. The advantage, too, of writing about a modern artist – and one's own immediate contemporary – is that one comes to his work without preconceptions, without the cultural 'security blanket' of pre-programmed admiration.

I remember, for instance, in the spring of 1968, at the request of Metro-Goldwyn-Mayer, making my way to the company's Paris screening room in the rue Condorcet to see a new gangster film, *Point Blank*, directed by an unknown. All I knew was that its star was Lee Marvin, then at the very height of his fame, and that his name and talent were associated, for me as for all of us, with Ford and Lang, and more recently with Brooks and Aldrich. From the opening shots I had the revelation of an astonishing visual power, the shock of images which contrived to be both realistic and dreamlike – an impact undiminished during the ninety minutes that followed. I learned the name of its director, John Boorman; and, as the years passed, with a series of no less powerful and startling films, I took pleasure in recognizing the 'figure in the carpet', the living signs of an aesthetic and intellectual universe. I also rediscovered on each occasion the enchantment of a cinema whose sense of spectacle was never allowed to degenerate into futile escapism, a cinema whose reflections on contemporary life were never drily demonstrative.

In this book I should like to retrace the steps of my discovery: by recounting Boorman's life and exploring his poetic world; examining each of his nine films in turn and interviewing him on them; collating the recollections of his collaborators – scenarists, designers, actors, cinematographers and editors – as the best means of analysing his personality.

Since, as a visionary, he is essentially a visual director, such a book could hardly exist without illustrations. For even when, as here, they are bereft of movement, they succeed in evoking the romanticism and the rigour, the sense of space and the physical intensity, the variety and the originality of invention, the intermingled presence of dreams and topicality, which are characteristic of the work, no less than of the life, of John Boorman.

John Boorman directing *The Heretic* on the 34th floor of the Warner building in New York.

Each of Boorman's films is a variation on a cinematic genre.
Point Blank and the gangster movie (John Vernon, Sharon Acker and Lee Marvin).

From Reality to Fantasy

When one considers the nine films directed by John Boorman, what strikes one most forcefully at first glance is their sheer diversity; it is as though, determined to astonish his public, he has on each occasion set himself a new and different challenge. In the English-speaking world, he is currently, with Robert Altman, Francis Ford Coppola and Stanley Kubrick, the film-maker whose temperament is most clearly that of a gambler and experimenter. Like them, too, he expresses himself exclusively through codified cinematic genres, whose strict formal parameters he will subsequently be free to subvert or enrich. In this sense, one can detect a kind of classical-romantic opposition which informs other aspects of his work and personality. Classical in that he exploits a traditional fund of material, one rich in populist resonances, as the subject-matter of his films; romantic in that, at the same time, he endeavours to reshape it so that it might become the vehicle of his own personal vision. There is a risk attached to such a contradiction; that of dis-

1

2

1 *Hell in the Pacific* and the war film (Lee Marvin and Toshiro Mifune).
2 *Catch Us If You Can* and the musical (Dave Clark and Barbara Ferris).

orienting the general public, accustomed as it is to genre stereotypes, without ever quite satisfying the connoisseurs of ultra-modernity and of the immediately recognizable 'signature'. Yet it's precisely such a hackneyed conception of modernity – the iconoclastic mania for originality at whatever the cost – that Boorman would appear to be challenging. As was noted by Octavio Paz, the tradition of discontinuity implies not only the negation of tradition but that of discontinuity itself.[2*] Boorman is aware that each genre creates its own tradition; and that from such a tradition, and the narrative codes which circumscribe it, derives the possibility of communicating with a mass audience and fulfilling its expectations. Hans Robert Jauss wrote that 'even when, as a pure creation of language, the work of art disappoints or exceeds one's expectations, it continues to assume the existence either of pre-established givens or of an orientation of expectation against which its originality and novelty can be measured – a horizon which (for the spectator) incorporates an already familiar tradition or series of works as well as the specific state of mind engendered by the appearance of the new work, by its genre and its organizing principles.'[202]

The notion of a 'horizon of expectation' proposed by Jauss is necessarily related to one's previous knowledge of the art form in question. Every spectator of a genre film experiences a phenomenon of *re*-cognition. The more extensive his cinematic culture, the greater are the resonances which any new work will arouse in him. Boorman – like many of his generation, a ciné-literate director – appeared on the scene at a moment of film history when it had become possible to avail oneself of that vast cultural backlog. Each of his films, therefore, uses the whole deck of cards belonging to its respective genre, only to reshuffle them and declare them trumps. *Catch Us If You Can*, a musical comedy made in the wake of Richard Lester's *A Hard Day's Night*, eventually chooses to focus on the picaresque peregrinations of a couple rather than perform some filmic variation on the Dave Clark Five. *Point Blank*, a gangster film in the vein of *Underworld USA*, exposes the kind of anonymous power that is endemic to a violent society. *Hell in the Pacific* is a war film in which war is absent and the American-Japanese conflict reduced to the confrontation of two men, a beach, the sea and the jungle. *Leo the Last*, a philosophical fable, also contains a subtle analysis of the state of the Western world. *Deliverance*, an adventure movie, inverts the clichés of the ecological movement. *Zardoz*, a science-fiction film, prefers to the high-tech charms of special effects those of the fairy-tale and the *fantastique*. *The Heretic*, a horror

movie, substitutes for the crude effects of *The Exorcist* (of which it was intended to be the sequel) the complexity of a 'metaphysical thriller'. *Excalibur*, a costume film, reinvents a mythical past in which a bewildering variety of styles and periods together conspire to revive the Arthurian cycle. *The Emerald Forest*, finally, a western, reworks the theme of the child abducted by Indians in the context of contemporary Brazil and the opposition between a rational, technocractic society and a tribal existence founded on an occult relationship with nature. This teasing of the conventions has not been without its risks for Boorman's career. There has been scant public support for any too extreme form of narrative originality or distortion *vis-à-vis* the accepted genre schemas (*Leo the Last*, *Zardoz*), even less for a work (*The Heretic*)which bore only a faint resemblance to its ostensible model.

Boorman is perfectly conscious of the power of classical story-telling, its appeal to the public and the energy with which its recharges the cinema, an art, after all, of duration; but he also recognizes its tyranny, of a type that all but encourages mindlessness and too often limits the possibilities of any real moral and aesthetic distancing on the part of the spectator. However, the fact that, like Altman, Coppola or Kubrick again

*Superior figures refer to the bibliography at the end of the book.

1 *Leo the Last* and the philosophical fable (Marcello Mastroianni).
2 *Deliverance* and the adventure film (Burt Reynolds).

1 *Zardoz* and science fiction.
2 *The Heretic* and horror (Richard Burton).

(though one could as easily cite Buñuel, Fellini and Resnais), his primary concern has been to escape the categorical imperatives of 'plot' has not prevented him from exploiting its power of seduction and its capacity to structure a narrative. The means adopted to solve this problem have been as numerous as they are varied: most notably mixing genres, as in *Leo the Last*, *Zardoz* and even *Excalibur* (e.g. the character of Merlin), with humour providing a kind of mordant commentary on the more serious aspects of the theme and thereby creating an alienation effect; interlacing the real with the imaginary through mental flashbacks (*Point Blank*) or dream sequences (*The Heretic* and *The Emerald Forest*); and rejecting the kind of psychology which might frustrate a spectator's identification with his characters. Even the use made by Boorman of certain mythic actors contributes to this subtle effect of displacement: the ultimate capitulation of Lee Marvin to a hostile environment (*Point Blank*, *Hell in the Pacific*); the acquisition of superior intellect by the Brutal played by Sean Connery (*Zardoz*); and the symbolic injury inflicted on the hyper-virile Burt Reynolds (*Deliverance*). In this way, Boorman's intelligence – even, on occasion, his irony – reinforces as it fragments the expression of feeling; and his intellectuality is constantly enriched by a

Excalibur and the historical film.

The Emerald Forest and the Western (Charley Boorman and Rui Polonah).

more poetic strain. The 'problematics' of his themes therefore never stifles the lyricism of his films – *pace* the poet René Char: 'No bird has the heart to sing in a bushful of question marks.'[198]

However varied the settings of Boorman's films and the cinematic genres to which they belong, all of them are based on the notion of a quest. Each is the story of a journey – a journey undertaken by a hero who, at the conclusion of a series of tests and ordeals, finds himself radically transformed. As in Jung, a crucial influence on the film-maker, the hero personifies the evolutionary urge and the power of the mind; his first victory – sometimes his only victory – is that which he wins over himself. We know that, from his earliest reading, Boorman has been haunted by the cycle of the Grail, symbolizing as it does the inner richness to which every human being aspires. Each of his protagonists might have been named 'Walker', like Lee Marvin in *Point Blank*. Boorman's heroes are literally 'walkers', from Steve and Dinah in *Catch Us If You Can* to Bill Markham and his son Tomme in search of each other in *The Emerald Forest*, from Father Lamont in the depths of Africa (*The Heretic*) to the quartet of urbanites braving the rapids of the Chattooga River (*Deliverance*), from Zed infiltrating the Vortex (*Zardoz*) to the Japanese and the American steering their flimsy craft towards a desert island (*Hell in the Pacific*), and, of course, the Knights of the Round Table (*Excalibur*).

For the traveller, what lies at the end of his journey is his own rebirth; and it's worth noting that, as a symbol of regeneration, water is present everywhere in Boorman's films. Plunging into the ocean means drawing new strength from it, since it represents an infinity of possibilities, as also the very flux of human existence.[199] Before departing for the Devon coast, Steven and Dinah dive into a swimming pool (*Catch Us If You Can*), just as Leo does during a collective therapy session (*Leo the Last*), before rediscovering the reality of the world. Walker crosses the sound which takes him from Alcatraz to the mainland (*Point Blank*), Ed and a corpse sink into the depths of the river (*Deliverance*) and, before reaching the Grail, Perceval must replenish his strength in the Lake. Finally, it's the rainwater conjured up by Tomme, with the attendant storm, that causes the dam to burst in *The Emerald Forest* and makes a landscape, which had been turned into a desert, grow fertile again. But if the rites of passage which Boorman's heroes undergo resemble each other, the understanding which they acquire of their destiny may vary considerably. To be sure, a recurrent motif can be detected in each of his films: the capacity of a human being to deceive himself, to feed off fantasies, to live in a fool's paradise, to refuse to confront reality head on – Boorman being thus the first critic of his own romanticism. But Alain Garsault has indicated to what degree *Zardoz*, when it appeared, represented a turning-point in his work. In it, Zed knows absolutely what he is about, which could not have been claimed for either Walker in *Point Blank* or the American soldier in *Hell in the Pacific*. Leo, for his part, gropes towards understanding; and Ed, brutally awakened by it, learns in the last shot of *Deliverance* the cost of his odyssey.[128] Such self-awareness, after being attained by Zed, will be confirmed by the conduct of Father Lamont, Arthur and Perceval, as well as that of Bill and Tomme in *The Emerald Forest*.

An identical, correlative evolution is visible in the conception of the omniscient individual present in all of Boorman's fictions. Before *Zardoz*, his protagonists were manipulated, their every movement directed, by a puppeteer whose identity would be revealed to them only at the end of their search. This secondary, malevolent figure, the character who 'pulls the strings', might be Zissell, the director of the advertising agency in *Catch Us If You Can*, or Yost, alias Fairfax, the head of the Organization in *Point Blank*, or Laszlo, in *Leo the Last*, who reminds one of Eliot's verse in 'Prufrock':

> And I have seen the eternal Footman hold my coat, and snicker,
> And in short, I was afraid

or Arthur Frayn in *Zardoz*. Except that, to the latter, Zed is finally able to reply: 'It's I who have conquered the power which put this idea into your head, for you too have been

The Boorman hero on the rising trajectory of his quest. Father Merrin scales a corridor more than a hundred metres high towards the Ethiopian churches (Joey Green and Max von Sydow in *The Heretic*).
Ed in search of Drew's killer (Jon Voight in *Deliverance*), page 15 .

The Exterminator Zed leads a group of Brutals into the mountains of the Outlands (Sean Connery in *Zardoz*).

created and controlled.' After *Zardoz*, the magician – whether it be Merlin in *Excalibur*, Kokumo in *The Heretic* or Wanadi in *The Emerald Forest* – becomes a benevolent creature assisting the hero in his quest for illumination.

The initiatory journey, a physical undertaking, is therefore also the spatial transcription of a mental pilgrimage. For the director, the film shoot itself would seem to mirror those ordeals with which his characters' paths are strewn. An essentially insular person (he has lived for many years in the Wicklow hills in Ireland), Boorman becomes a nomad when filming, travelling all over the world in search of striking similarities and differences among peoples of different cultures. His travels have acquainted him with an earthquake in Los Angeles, a typhoon in the Pacific and the inside of a volcano in Tahiti. Filming on the island of Palau (*Hell in the Pacific*), on the rivers of Georgia (*Deliverance*) or in the Amazonian jungle (*The Emerald Forest*) has meant experiencing, in conjunction with his artistic and intellectual restlessness, a number of physical hardships, hardships which he has actively sought in order that the shoot might become an element of the film. And the film itself may be said to play the role of a manipulator, a guide, to the unwitting film-maker. As his regular collaborator, Bill Stair, has written: 'He will invariably choose the most arduous path and advance along it by a series of unpredictable intuitions, a risky procedure in that it necessarily entails some physical or financial risk. I have the feeling that, with him, it's sheer will-power which takes precedence over everything else. The fact that he is always working under pressure means that an

1

2

1 Years later, Father Lamont retraces Father Merrin's footsteps (Richard Burton in *The Heretic*).
2 Tommy climbs up the wall of the building in which his father lives (Charley Boorman in *The Emerald Forest*).

amazing degree of energy is being expended. He surrounds himself with workaholics like himself, he drives all of them, himself included, to breaking point – then he films the results.'[192]

A predilection for genres, a fondness for the theme of the hero and the quest, and frequent recourse to a symbolic nexus which I intend to analyse in his films (water, already mentioned, as well as the other elements; also the crystal, the sword, the forest, the bow-and-arrow, the island, the dragon, the tree and, finally, a rich and colourful bestiary): we can see how attuned Boorman is to mythic thought. But the comparative study of myths and genres reveals a number of striking correspondences. The disclosure, through a set of fictional structures, of a series of recurrent motifs and constants, recalls the type of analysis to which Lévi-Strauss has subjected myths, by

1

2

The elements play an essential role in Boorman's symbolism, with its close links to the cosmos. The idea of levitation is associated with air.

3

studying a corpus of folk tales collected by ethnographers and anthropologists. The value of any given term in a mythical narrative can only be determined by the study of its function in a sequence of polarized connections. But the constituent units of the myth are not isolated: only a network of such connections will render the myth intelligible. Lévi-Strauss has stressed the importance of polarized thought. Polarization is at the base of every mechanism of thought and language, insofar as it represents a classification and a systematization of the world around us. It reflects the essential nature of myths: the repetitive, obsessive conceptualization of a dilemma or a contradiction. Boorman is a dialectical film-maker, in whose work can be found just such an interaction of opposites, and also a deployment of archetypes which recalls Jung yet again (whereas Kubrick, an analytical director, fundamentally pessimistic and fiercely individualistic, is overtly Freudian) – Jung, for whom they constitute the very basis of our collective unconscious. These archetypes determine our sensibilities, our perception of things, our instincts, and so condition our actions and patterns of behaviour. As Rosemary Gordon Montagnon has written: 'What impressed Jung in these two fields of research – psychopathology and mythology – was the repetition and universality of a few themes and a few images all over the world, and through very different periods and cultures.'[209] For the archetype to assume a form, it must become manifest in an image, an emotion, a dream – images which might equally be of a hero or a magician, or else an element of the cosmos, or a collective ritual, or even a geometrical figure. Far from being estranged from his fellow creatures and from the universe, man therefore will find his freedom in adherence to a cosmic order which escapes his understanding.

One of the distinctive characteristics of a myth, then, is its

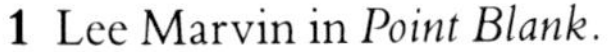

1 Lee Marvin in *Point Blank*.
2 Linda Blair in *The Heretic*.
3 Calvin Lockhart in *Leo the Last*.

a-historical nature. But if Boorman takes his inspiration from mythic thought, his films are strongly rooted in our own period, being set for the most part in the present. The resonance possessed by a film like *Deliverance* derives from the fact that it interweaves the most timeless of phantasms with the contemporary preoccupations of the ecological ideal, 'that tranquil weekend of fear', as the film's Italian title has it. *Point Blank* glitteringly metaphorizes the position of the individual in American society. *The Heretic* raises the question of parapsychology and the limitations of rational thinking. *The Emerald Forest* describes a return to the origins of those primitive thought processes which have so fascinated modern man and the modern artist. As for *Leo the Last* and *Zardoz*,

ambitious fables if ever there were any, they attempt nothing less than to encompass the whole of society, with its rich and poor, strong and weak, castes and classes. Boorman is a man of his time; and that is why, as I believe, he has been so adept at revitalizing the cinematic genres to which he has been attracted.

Genre is intimately related to History. One might even say that it can undergo a transformation only insofar as it participates in History. It can generate living works of art only if they retain a symbiotic relationship to contemporary evolution; otherwise, it atrophies and produces dead, formalistic commonplaces. The roots of a genre are implanted, not only in film history, but in the history of society itself. *Point Blank*, *Hell in the Pacific*, *Deliverance* and *The Emerald Forest* articulate both historical and archetypical elements; and what makes

Earth.

1 The Japanese officer (Toshiro Mifune) in front of the rocky precipice of the island on which he is marooned (*Hell in the Pacific*).

2 The clay village in Africa (*The Heretic*).

Merlin the magician (Nicol Williamson) and the standing stones of Stonehenge (*Excalibur*).

1

these films so rich and multilayered is their evolution and mutual interaction. It is in his position with regard to the concept of Utopia that we can best understand Boorman's claim of a historical evolution. The Vortex in *Zardoz*, like the Camelot of the Knights of the Round Table, begins as a dream of purity and perfection before declining into boredom and sterility. In his book, *Utopia and Civilization*, Gilles Lapouge distinguishes three classes of mentality which might be defined by their relation to logic: the counter-Utopian, who is ignorant of logic, who considers it a point of honour to belittle common sense, reality and reason, and whose mentality can be found, for example, in the American counterculture movements; the Utopian, wholly devoid of the ability to think dialectically, a pure logician who believes in order and stability, and whose contemporary avatar, curiously, might be some high-powered technocrat; because both Utopian and counter-Utopian reject history, in a sense, they find themselves in opposition to the Historical man, the dialectician, the man of metamorphoses, 'less concerned by the pattern of structures than by the interaction of events along the course of evolution.'[205] It is in the third class that one recognizes Boorman's approach, since he always clearly indicates the distance – in every sense of the word – which has been covered between the first and last images of his films. If, by the end, both man and the world

2

Water as the hero's rite of passage.
1 Lee Marvin (*Point Blank*).
2 Jon Voight (*Deliverance*).

3 Lee Marvin (*Hell in the Pacific*).
4 Charley Boorman (*The Emerald Forest*).

Water.
1 Marcello Mastroianni with Billie Whitelaw (*Leo the Last*).
2 King Arthur (Nigel Terry) and the hand (belonging, in fact, to Telsche Boorman) of the Lady of the Lake (*Excalibur*).

Inside the Tabernacle, the Eternals heal their wounds by floating (*Zardoz*).

Fire.
1 Pursuing Zed, the Eternals burn the village (Charlotte Rampling in *Zardoz*).
2 In Brazil, the young madwoman immolates herself (Rose Portillo in *The Heretic*).

3 Merlin (Nicol Williamson) and the Knights of the Round Table taking the oath (*Excalibur*).
4 Tomme (Charley Boorman) with his tribe (*The Emerald Forest*).

have changed, it is because the hero has been forced to enter into conflict with his social environment.

For, if Boorman's protagonists strive, in effect, to achieve harmony with the cosmos, they not infrequently find themselves in a position of revolt *vis-à-vis* that same social environment. While the metaphysical and the poetic tend towards osmosis, the social generates conflict. The Boormanian hero is a 'heretic' like Father Lamont, who disobeys the Vatican and seeks the truth at the heart of the Golden City. Dinah flees the advertising agency which merchandizes her image (*Catch Us If You Can*), Walker single-handedly confronts the omnipotent Organization (*Point Blank*), Leo reduces his own house to ashes as a protest against the inequitable order which it represents (*Leo the Last*), Zed slays his god and unlawfully invades the sanctum of the Eternals (*Zardoz*). Though the director of *Excalibur* has shown undeniable spiritualist tendencies, these have always been accompanied by a distrust of religion in its institutionalized form, as though to endorse Valéry's remark: 'Every mystic is a receptacle of anarchy. The anarchist is the observer who sees what he sees and not what it is customary to see.'[216] However vigorously he reflects the spirit of his own period, Boorman's personality necessarily sets him at odds with that period in a relationship that one might term culturally Oedipal. Symbolically, on the only occasion on which the director made an appearance in one of his own films, he played, in the space of a single shot, a Brutal executed by an Exterminator in the Outlands of *Zardoz*.

No doubt the film which most clearly illustrates the pressures exerted by society on the individual is (paradoxically) *Hell in the Pacific*, in which not the slightest material trace of civilization remains. From their initial encounter, and because of the culture and education by which they have been conditioned, the 'instinct' of both the Japanese and the American is to kill each other. Gradually displaced from their social contexts, they arrive at a mutual understanding – until, on the second of their island homes, a handful of culturally determined objects first threaten, then destroy, the fragile *modus vivendi* which they had contrived to establish.

It's significant that one of the principal elements of Boorman's personal cosmogony should be that reduced, and simplified, model of the world, the image of the island. In every civilization,[199] the island has been designated the symbol of an atavistic spiritual centre, an 'other world', a haven from the assaults of life. But this dream of isolation incorporates its own

The body of a Brutal (John Boorman) executed by an Exterminator (Sean Connery) in *Zardoz*.

destruction: as an enclosed space, it becomes a prison for those who take shelter on it. The island which Dinah hopes to purchase in *Catch Us If You Can*; the island of Alcatraz, where Walker almost died and where, at the end of *Point Blank*, he once more finds himself trapped; the island as an enclosure of confrontation in *Hell in the Pacific*; the isolated cul-de-sac in which Leo wastes away; that region cut off from the rest of the world in which moronic hillbillies live and which four city dudes come to violate (*Deliverance*); the Vortex (*Zardoz*); the castle of Camelot (*Excalibur*): in all of these, man languishes in self-delusion.

And yet there is in Boorman's work a perennial nostalgia for the communal life, as witness his fondness for parties, for collective festivities, for gatherings at a round table (the Knights of *Excalibur*, the Eternals of *Zardoz*, the members of the secret society presided over by Laszlo in *Leo the Last*, the Invisible People and their ritual ceremonies in *The Emerald Forest*). Since the fancy-dress ball of *Catch Us If You Can*, these party scenes, these songs and dances, have been a constant in his films; but they cannot quite camouflage the solitude of the individual. On two occasions – in *Point Blank* and *Leo the Last* – the protagonist will find himself, during a party, separated by the crowd of guests from the acquaintance who is waving to him. There again, one notes the tension, felt by the artist, between a need for communion and a desire to cultivate one's singularity and one's difference.

Nothing better typifies Boorman's feelings about his own period than this movement of attraction and repulsion between the self and the world. If he was able, in the late sixties and early seventies, when the fashion for a 'politicized' cinema was at its height, to make films as relevant to the society in which he lived as *Point Blank*, *Leo the Last* and *Zardoz*, it was because his sense of period could never be criticized as over-calculated; which is to say, the works which it inspired were never schematic, didactic or moralistic. Without forfeiting his own individuality, he exposed the fundamental configurations of society in a manner comparable to that of T. S. Eliot, who, in *The Waste Land*, also poeticized the absence of values, the anxieties of the twentieth century, and the sterility of human intercourse. Similarly, for Kierkegaard, 'culture is the cycle traversed by the individual in order that he might attain self-knowledge'. The 'cures' undergone by Zed in the Tabernacle (*Zardoz*) and Regan in the 'synchronizer' (*The Heretic*) follow precisely that course. When man is alienated by neurosis from his cultural heritage (neurosis being a partial deculturation), psychoanalysis delivers him up to desire and the capacity to

1

3

2

4
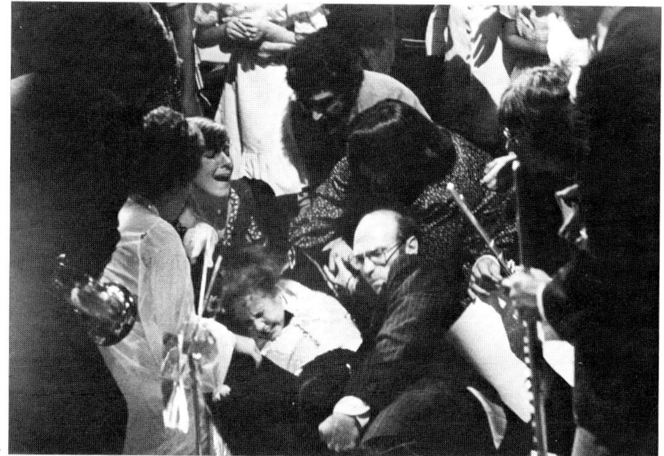

A predilection for parties and the tensions they generate.
1 The fancy-dress ball in *Catch Us If You Can* (Barbara Ferris).
2 The party in *Point Blank* (Lee Marvin) . . .
3 . . . and in *Leo the Last* (Marcello Mastroianni).
4 Panic interrupts a musical show (Kitty Winn and Linda Blair in *The Heretic*).

1 The dance of the Renegades (*Zardoz*).
2 The ritual ceremony of the Invisible People (Dira Paes and Charley Boorman in *The Emerald Forest*).

The party in *Leo the Last* (Marcello Mastroianni and Billie Whitelaw).

effect choice. *Zardoz* may therefore be regarded as a general inventory of knowledge and the Vortex as a cultural kaleidoscope. Boorman's own relation to the cinema (from his admiration for Griffith, the medium's founding father, to his subversion of genre forms) may be comparably described: each of his films is inscribed in an historical evolution; it can be created only in relation to the films which preceded it, to the society on which it depends and to the public for whom it is destined. The artist therefore contemplates the past as it fades from view while conjuring up the landscapes of the future. In that, too, Boorman is a Romantic: for him, it is necessary to establish a link with the past in order to light the lamp which will illuminate the future.

This reflection on culture also, of course, implies a reflection on the cinema, the medium through which Boorman expresses himself. In his films, the importance of the eye, of its scrutiny, of the still shot or moving image, is too evident not to have the value of a sign. In *Catch Us If You Can*, Dinah observes her boss's henchmen through a telescope before encountering a man who collects film projectors, while Zissell projects her image in the offices of his advertising agency. In *Point Blank*, Walker brawls in a nightclub on whose walls slides of paintings by Rembrandt and Botticelli alternate with gigantic pin-ups. Later, he scrutinizes the hotel through a pair of binoculars, as the Japanese officer scrutinizes the horizon in *Hell in the Pacific*. *Leo the Last* is constructed on the principle of a lived experience viewed as a silent film, with Leo 'directing' the lives of his neighbours through his telescope. The 'synchronizer' of *The Heretic*, enabling Father Lamont, Dr Tuskin and Regan to journey through time and space, cannot help but remind one of the experience of cinema-going. Finally, the characters of *Point Blank*, *Excalibur* and *Zardoz* relive fragments of their lives as though in a film. In the Vortex, Zed sees the rape which he has committed projected on a screen. The weapon-camera-rape equation, proposed on a quite literal level by Michael Powell in *Peeping Tom*, can also be detected in Boorman's films. In *Zardoz*, at the end of the prologue, Zed fires at the spectator and the motif of the observing eye is transformed into that of the bow-and-arrow and its target (*Deliverance*, *The Emerald Forest*). For Ed, the narrator of James Dickey's novel, *Deliverance*: 'Nothing mattered outside of the frame, and what was inside it existed in a terribly alive and coherent way: it was as if the target had been created by the eye that observed it.'[88] One could hardly imagine a more accurate definition of Boorman's directorial style, a style which creates its own autonomous space, while granting the spectator the illusion of a transparent reality. Gérard Legrand observed that, in Boorman's films, 'armed with his desire, and with the violence which is inseparable from it, the watcher penetrates the world from which an injustice originally excluded him.'[26] The hero's trajectory is described by images of penetration, emphasized by the ubiquitous weapons (a rifle, a revolver, a knife, a sword, arrows): Walker penetrates the Organization (*Point Blank*), as Zed penetrates the Vortex (*Zardoz*), as the urbanites of *Deliverance* violate a forbidden region before one of them is violated in his turn, as Lamont penetrates Kokumo's sanctuary (*The Heretic*), and Markham the space of the Invisible People (*The Emerald Forest*). Boorman's vision of mankind is therefore purely dynamic, founded on a process of evolution and transformation, underscored by images of emergence and intrusion. The gesture with which Zed, a revolver in his hand, slowly emerges from a mountain of grain (*Zardoz*) is mirrored in that of Walker, also armed, raising the curtain of Reese's bedroom and catching him making love with Chris (*Point Blank*). The frequent presence of mirrors, masks, crystals and water reflections make even more potent this reference to the world of the image and the imaginary.

For Boorman, as for the Surrealists ('It is at the cinema that the one absolutely modern mystery is celebrated' – André Breton), film enjoys a privileged relation with dreams: in the dark auditorium, the spectator's experience has obvious affinities with that of the sleeper. Working in the field of television

1 Billie Whitelaw (*Leo the Last*).
2 Linda Blair (*The Heretic*).
3 Sharon Acker (*Point Blank*).

documentary, Boorman was soon made aware of the limitations of a strictly realistic approach. If, in the late fifties, Free Cinema was a reaction to an academic national cinema divorced from national realities, Boorman's films in their turn represented an advance beyond a primarily social and psychological approach to the 'real'. He wanted them to possess the freedom of dreams, without disdaining the power of persuasion which we associate with documentaries. There, too, his point of view was an eminently dialectical one, the union of opposites appearing yet again as the governing force of the creative act. To underscore the limitations of rational thought is not necessarily to restrict oneself of the instruments of intelligence and analysis, nor slavishly surrender oneself to some shapeless poetic 'trance'. It means, rather, ending the antagonism between the kind of rational, progressive thinking which proposes a logical explanation for every phenomenon and the kind of irrationality, too often confused with religion, which is more concerned to live than to analyse.

What surprises one is not so much Boorman's approach but the fact that so few film directors take account, as he does, of modern man's discovery of new patterns of thinking and feeling, patterns which mobilize the more latent regions of our personalities. The interest which has been aroused since the turn of the century in primitive art, the development of ethnology, the birth of psychoanalysis and the reacquired taste for the occult tradition testifies to a readiness to admit dreams and imagination as essential factors of the human personality. It is, perhaps, an attitude not untinged by nostalgia, albeit as a defence against the excessive rationalization of our industrial and post-industrial eras. And what Boorman's films demonstrate is the desire to reforge the link between man and nature, to return to mythological roots without abandoning the dictates of reason. Scientic knowledge and initiatory knowledge together ought to be able to follow such a path, the path, as Picasso said, 'that intelligence must take to lend a concrete form to dreams'. Among the closed societies created by Boor-

Like masks (see pp.58–9), or the reflections created by water, the mirror shows Boorman's fascination for the double and the deceptive quality of appearances. Sean Connery in *Zardoz*.

1

2

The presence of the past and its culture.
1 The paintings in the Coptic churches of Ethiopia (Max von Sydow in *The Heretic*).
2 Antique statuary (Sean Connery, John Alderton and Sara Kestelman in *Zardoz*).

Mantegna's 'Crucifixion' (Paul Henreid and Richard Burton in *The Heretic*).

man, only those willing to admit the magical attributes of mankind (the African tribes of *The Heretic* and the Amazonian tribes of *The Emerald Forest*) have attained a genuine stability. And, in his films, the director has followed the same path: burrowing into his dreams and trusting to his intuition, but also exploiting the hitherto unsuspected resources of modern technology and the gift of reason.

The artist, in Boorman's conception, is therefore someone capable of reconciling emotion and rationality. One has often wondered, while watching certain sequences of his films, whether they were tragic or comic. The puppeteer and the magician who lend an ironic distance to works like *Leo the Last*, *Zardoz* and *Excalibur* are in a sense the director's *alter egos*, his representatives on the screen. If, as Horace Walpole claimed, 'life is a comedy for those who think and a tragedy for those who feel', one begins to understand that some critics might be reticent about a body of work in which feeling and intelligence are so intimately fused. It is, in any case, certain that creating is for Boorman the only possible response to the anguish of living. As proof, consider *Zardoz*, an important departure in the director's work: its final shot reveals the trace of a hand on the wall of a cave, a sign that creativity was already present in some distant past. Previously, Boorman's films invariably ended on a pessimistic note, on an acknowledgement of failure. *Zardoz*, in which the feminine characters acquire a new significance in his work, also shows us for the first time the triumph of love – love as a means of access to self-revelation. (Zed tells Consuella: 'You gave me love, and that no one else had done; and if I live, we'll live together.') The fear of death seems to have been dispelled in this film in which, precisely, it finds acceptance after having been banned by the Eternals for three hundred years. Here again, Boorman affirms the unity of opposites: to confront death when alive is to have death inserted into life. *Zardoz*, in a sense, ending as it does on the spectacle of a man and woman ageing in successsive stages (and to the accompaniment of Beethoven's Seventh Symphony), until they are no more than skeletons, prefigures the original ending of *The Heretic*, in which Lamont departed with Regan; or the idyll of Guinevere and Arthur; or even the blissful marriage of Tomme and Kachiri in *The Emerald Forest*. Art makes immortal; the artist's imagination wards off the despair of the world; and creation affords man the possibility of inventing his own future, of imagining his own world and, particularly in the cinema, of celebrating a ritual which brings him close to the collective unconscious. The revelation of the film-maker as shaman occurred to Boorman when, in *Zardoz*, he let us witness the death of God and the collapse of religion. For, as Octavio Paz has indicated, 'the religious experience and poetry have a common origin. But religion interprets, channels and systematizes this experience within a theology and the churches confiscate its produce. Poetry opens up a possibility of being which every human birth closes: it recreates man as a totality: life and death in a single instant of incandescence.'[211] It's just this kind of totality that is embraced by Boorman's films. A Protestant raised by Jesuits, what he has retained from his mentors was a taste for baroque flamboyance and sensuality, qualities evident in his work to a far greater degree than the austerity of the Reformed Church.

Boorman appears to ascribe a *formal* vocation to the manifestations of nature: the foaming rivers of *Deliverance*; the stifling, clotted jungle of *The Emerald Forest*; the stony crags of *The Heretic*; the storms of *Hell in the Pacific*; and the rebirth of spring in *Excalibur*. The director, we feel, has given himself up to the sheer sensual gratification of filming, of deploying, with a kind of Dionysiac energy, the whole chromatic and gestual palette available to him. There is, in his work, what might be called an 'overfiguration', an excess of perception, though one which is never exaggerated. Yet the reservations sometimes expressed about his films no doubt derive from that quality. Flaubert wrote in these terms to Louise Collet: 'There is a permanent conspiracy against anything that is original, that's what you have to get inside your head. The more colour you have, the more drama, then the more opposition you will meet' (20 June 1853).[201] Few contemporary film-makers are capable of recreating a truly cosmic space; and it's revealing that among his earliest devotees in France – Pierre Rissient, Marc Bernard, Gérard Legrand – were included the 'MacMahonites', admirers in their time of Walsh, Losey and Lang, in whose work decor and human gesture were organically linked, as were a lyrical impulse and a rigorous sense of form.

I admit to admiring Boorman for his tendency towards ever greater control over his work, for his desire to encompass both the individual and the collective, the material and the spiritual, fantasy and reality. Whatever degree of success one is willing to grant him, he seems to me to respond to Valéry's appreciation: 'What I call "great art" is simply art which demands that *all the faculties* of one man are engaged upon it, and whose works are such that *all the faculties* of another man are invoked in his concern to understand them.'[215]

The presence of the past and its culture.
The projection of a Botticelli painting in the nightclub of *Point Blank* (Lee Marvin).

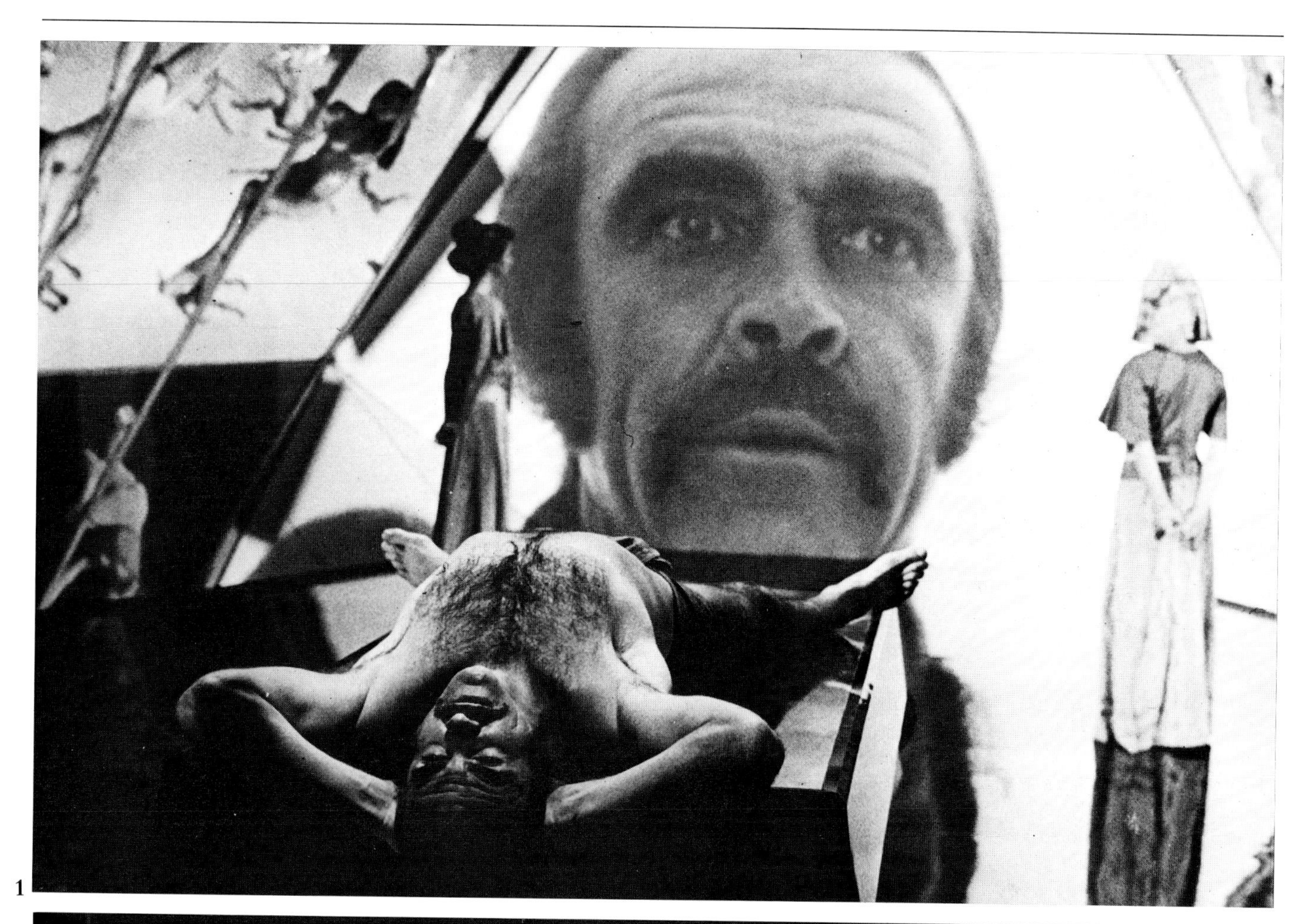

1

2

The image is also a reflection on the cinema. **1** Zed revisits his past on the screen of the Vortex (Sean Connery, Charlotte Rampling and Sara Kestelman in *Zardoz*). **2** The synchronizer allows Regan to relive the film of her childhood (Linda Blair, Richard Burton, Louise Fletcher and Kitty Winn in *The Heretic*).

Pictorial influences. **1** Kokumo and his locust mask (James Earl Jones in *The Heretic*).
2 William Blake: *The Ghost of a Flea*, distemper on wood, *circa* 1819–20. (The Tate Gallery)
3 John Everett Millais: *Ophelia*, 1851–2. (The Tate Gallery)

1 Nicholas Clay in *Excalibur*.
2 Sally Anne Newton in *Zardoz*.
3 Arthur Rackham: illustration for *The Romance of King Arthur*, 1917.

Photographed in 1973, the Boorman family in their Irish home (a former presbytery in the Wicklow hills). From left to right: Daisy, Katrine, Jonn, Christel, Telsche, Charley.

From Shepperton to Griffith

Childhood and Adolescence (1933–55)

John Boorman was born in Epsom on 18 January 1933. His maternal grandfather, whose name was Chapman, had married a Miss MacDonald of Scottish origin and was the landlord of several pubs and gin palaces in London's East End. He was relatively prosperous and owned, in Shepperton, a wooden, colonial-style bungalow with a verandah, Chinese lanterns and a lawn bordered by the Thames. It was in this house that the Boorman family took refuge during the Second World War after their own had been destroyed in the Blitz. 'It was in that bungalow,' Boorman recalls, 'that my mother had spent the weekends and holidays of her childhood. She was always very fond of the river.'*

His paternal grandfather, of Dutch origin, had married an Irishwoman named Fitzpatrick. A few generations earlier, the Boormans had come from the Netherlands to build dikes on the west coast of England and had finally settled in Kent, where, in the nineteenth century, they owned a reputable local newspaper, the *Kent Messenger*. Boorman was greatly influenced by his grandfather. 'He was an inventor, an extraordinary man. He made and lost several fortunes; he was very generous with his money. He'd inherited a washhouse where women would immerse their laundry in tubs. He then invented the very first washing-machine. I've seen the prototype. It was a large, octagonal wooden drum which you turned with a handle; and it was so successful that my grandfather was able to mass-produce it. He also had an enormous stable with about sixty horses to draw the carts on which washing was collected in the streets of London. My father adored those horses and spent hours every day with them.' When he was seventeen, at the onset of the First World War, Boorman's father enlisted in the army and left for India, where he served as a lieutenant, then a captain. He commanded a battalion of Gurkhas who, with sabres drawn, attacked the Turks on horseback. 'I've always been intrigued by the fact that a man who lived through that was also around to see the first astronauts land on the moon,' Boorman says. 'But, in fact, unknown to my father, the Turks had already withdrawn from their positions when he attacked, so that he never actually had his baptism of fire. Most of his time was taken up with polo, pig-sticking and tiger hunts.' He returned to England during the Depression to find that his father had yet again been declared a bankrupt. The old man still had numerous contacts, however – including Joseph Kennedy, at that time American ambassador in London (Boorman can remember owning in his childhood a pair of boxing-gloves inscribed with the initials of the Kennedy sons) and, especially, Michael Abraham, who had just founded the Shell company in Britain. He recommended his son; and so it was that, without any particular interest in petrol, Boorman's father became Abraham's assistant and remained so until the Second World War.

The war was Boorman's first vivid memory: 'I was nearly evacuated from England when hostilities broke out. There was a plan to send children to Canada and Australia, and my mother had an aunt in Australia. My sister and I were supposed to leave, except that we got no further than the railway station. There were thousands of weeping children there. My mother simply couldn't bear the thought and led us both back home.' In 1940, Boorman was seven years old and he recalls, very clearly and with evident satisfaction, the Battle of Britain: 'For a child, it was a wonderful experience. I'd stand in the garden of our house watching Messerschmitts and Spitfires battling it out in the sky. Our school was bombed over and over again and, half-way through a lesson, we'd have to scurry to the shelters. We sat on two rows of wooden benches inside a bunker and we'd recite the multiplication tables from inside our gas masks. At night, my friends and I would go looting through the bombed houses – what treasures we unearthed!'

Shortly after the war, in 1947, the wooden house in Shepperton in which the Boormans had lived for several years was destroyed by fire. It was a period of rationing and economic austerity; the family found itself without material possessions, without clothes, without anything. Boorman never forgot the experience. It was at that moment that his father, backed by his maternal grandfather, became the landlord of a pub. 'I was never too close to my father, though we were both mad about sport. But I was always a disappointment to him as he believed I ought to have played cricket or football for England. Nothing I've accomplished since ever compensated for the fact that I didn't turn out to be a sports champion.'

Boorman was rather more influenced by the women in his family. If his two grandfathers were Anglo-Saxon in origin, his grandmothers belonged to the Celtic race, whose mythology has had such an enduring influence on the director. Though Boorman feels he was not close enough to his mother in his childhood, their relationship grew increasingly affectionate in later years. 'My mother still has three sisters. They've all buried their husbands and now live together. As for me, I have two sisters – one of whom is eight years my senior, the other two years my junior – but no brother. I have three daughters

*All comments attributed to John Boorman in this chapter were made to the author during hitherto unpublished conversations. As for the numbers which follow other quotations, they refer to the bibliography at the end of the book.

and one son. My father had one sister and no brother. In December 1981, I gave a dinner for my mother's eightieth birthday. Of the forty people present there were just six men: my son Charley and I, and four others who belonged to the family only by marriage! My mother and her sisters all married somewhat weak-willed men. Their own father had had such a strong personality that I think it might have been a kind of reaction against him: they'd become afraid of domineering men. I grew up surrounded by women and I'm glad I did. The exclusive company of men, in school and the army, always struck me as quite terrifying. I think the way in which women have moderated, even changed, my outlook on things is exactly what I need.'

The major influence in his childhood was doubtless that of Father John McGuire, his schoolmaster, whom Boorman describes as 'almost a second father'. Though the family was Protestant, Boorman's mother had him attend a Jesuit school in the belief that, if teachers were sent off to the war, Catholic priests at least would remain in England. It was Father McGuire who, appreciating the young boy's original cast of mind, encouraged him to write and acquainted him with the culture which he could not find in his family.

In his childhood, Boorman was an avid reader of comics. Apart from his school textbooks, the first literary work he can recall having read was Shaw's *Man and Superman*. One of his aunts had given it to him, believing, because of its title, that it was another comic strip. 'I read the play with amazement and, for years to come, I was enormously influenced by Shaw and got to know all of his plays.' In fact, one of the most memorable artistic experiences of his youth was a production of *Man and Superman*, with John Clements, which he saw when he was eighteen.

He also regularly visited the cinema, having an especial fondness for serials. Though he cannot actually remember the first film he ever saw, he has not forgotten the circumstances. 'It was a Saturday matinée show for children. I was seven and absolutely petrified at the sight of all those kids crying, screaming and throwing things at each other. I told myself that, if I ever got out of it alive, I'd have nothing more to do with the cinema!' Oddly enough, it was the radio which caught his attention and acquired a real importance in his early life. 'Listening to plays on the radio and staging them in my imagination taught me, in a way, how to create, how to bring my mental universe to life.' Though Father McGuire hoped that he would continue his studies, the young Boorman had not the slightest intention of doing so. The matter was not even discussed at home, since a university education had never been part of the family tradition. And, by the time he was sixteen, he was already chafing under the educational system.

'What I wanted was to work in the cinema. Having grown up in Shepperton, I would often visit the studios, which were quite close to our home. I remember saying to myself, as I watched a scene being shot, "What a good idea to reorganize the world!" David Young, my best friend at the time, and I both wanted to become clapper-boys. It was the most prestigious and elevated position to which we could aspire. David's brother was a lighting cameraman; we'd listen to all his anecdotes and he was a kind of hero to us. David succeeded in becoming a clapper-boy. Not I. Later, when I was directing the scene in *Leo the Last* when the house collapses, we had eight separate teams for the photography and, in one of them, there was David, with whom I'd lost contact. He was still a clapper-boy!' When he was seventeen, and while his friend David was temporarily unemployed, Boorman asked his paternal grandfather to help him set himself up on his own. The latter suggested that money might be made in laundromats. With David, he founded a company: in the first year, they owned three or four laundromats and as many vans. Thereafter, David continued running the business while Boorman, with his profits, settled in a London bedsitter and, between the ages of eighteen and twenty, earned his living by writing for women's magazines and broadcasting on a weekly radio programme for young people, which required him to review a book, a film, a play and an art exhibition.

He was then invited to join the BBC at the request of a radio producer, Richard Keen, who was to be of considerable assistance to him in his career. During his National Service years, he also worked on a weekly documentary programme. One series took the cinema as its theme; every week, Boorman would visit the studios and deal with some film-related job: continuity girl, editor, lighting cameraman, etc. As a National Service conscript, he served in the infantry and became a map-reading instructor: 'I can never find my way around, I'm constantly losing my way and maps have always fascinated me as a key to understanding the world.'

When demobbed, he continued his radio work and began temporarily managing laundromats again. 'Having been in business was later of great service to me. My parents' generation had been that of the Depression. They'd lived in permanent dread of poverty and unemployment. That left an impression on me; and I always said that the first thing I wanted for myself was enough money to pay for my independence. When making films, my initial concern is to find the necessary financing and become directly involved in drawing up the budget. I'd be less harassed if I had a producer to take care of such things and leave me more time for the strictly artistic aspects of film-making. But I have inside me a kind of self-assertion which drives me to assume every possible responsibility; it can, I suppose, be traced back to my youth. If you delegate responsibilities to others – lawyers, accountants and so on – you lose something. And one reason why I find the cinema so appealing is that it touches upon so many different realms of activity: all the known forms of art, of course, but also finance, technology, human relationships and manual crafts. And all the thoughts and deeds you invest in these various spheres are to be found, bizarrely reunited, in the finished film.'

The Experience of Television (1956–64)

In 1956, Boorman was offered the post of apprentice editor at ITN. He worked with Brian Lewis: 'Lewis was a clever man who'd received a traditional editor's training. He really taught me everything I know though he almost despaired of me, since I wasn't very gifted to start with. Finally, I acquired this new language and became an editor six months later.' Curiously, his daily sessions at the editing-table led to his abandoning journalism. Boorman had, in fact, never stopped writing during these years. In the *Manchester Guardian* he had published an article on the problems facing small businessmen ('Enterprise'); another on a German village and the conversion of cabbage into sauerkraut ('The Cabbage Kings'), following a trip to his wife Christel's native country; and another on a group of children visiting the City of London one Sunday morning, an excursion he watched from Fore Street, where his father kept a public house ('In the City, on Sundays'). Written in a highly allusive style, these articles furnished evidence of Boorman's gift for observation as well as his grasp of the current economic situation. 'I would write almost every day, but I stopped shortly after entering television, as I felt that they were two antithetical occupations, two diametrically opposed ways of thinking.' What ITN produced were essentially documentaries and news bulletins; and Boorman edited a weekly series, *Roving Report*, which, thanks to Brian Lewis, attained a remarkably high technical standard.

Commercial television stations were, at that period, being established not only in London but in the provinces, in Manchester and Birmingham. In 1957, Southampton acquired its first station, Southern TV, for which Boorman now went to work. During that year, he became adept in various capacities – from shooting to editing, from scoring a film to dramatizing a non-fictional situation – and was employed on a widely varied range of programmes. He directed several documentaries and began to make a name for himself. In 1958, the company invited him to take over its top weekly current events programme, *Southern Affairs*: he became its producer, editor and, on occasion, director. After a few months, however, he felt cramped and persuaded Southern to entrust him with a daily programme, *Day By Day*. With a hundred and fifty people taking orders from him, Boorman turned out a five-days-a-week, 45-minute programme, interchanging portraits of well-known personalities with items on the lives of ordinary people, satire, landscape studies and discussions on those problems with which he felt particularly concerned: poverty, apathy, one's confidence (or not) in life. Though it went out live, the programme also included filmed material and dealt with local, national and international matters. 'I knew what I wanted – in particular, I was eager to get away from a purely journalistic approach. I was a director of documentaries and knew how to get out into the street and see the world. I'd choose colleagues who had a personal vision of things – some of them, in later years, were to make their own reputations in television, men like Julian Pettifer and Richard Davis – and I'd send them out in search of interesting subject-matter. It was very exciting, very stimulating; we portrayed reality such as it appeared to the group of young people that we were.' Such a flurry of production and coordination left Boorman little time to direct much himself. He did sometimes succeed, however: in 1959, for example, he made *Come Sailing With Uffa Fox*, a filmed portrait of the celebrated seaman, eccentric and friend of Prince Philip, which created quite a stir in its day. But Boorman felt increasingly hemmed in by the growing success of *Day By Day*: 'In television, there's no worse failure than success. You're forced by viewing figures to retain the same format and viewers will write in to complain if you should so much as alter a detail. I was determined to avoid that trap.'

The BBC (in the person of Desmond Hawkins, Head of Programmes), impressed by the popularity of *Day By Day*, offered him a job at Bristol, starting on 1 January 1962. Since his ultimate goal was to direct both documentaries and fiction films, Boorman accepted.

His first assignment, however, was to relaunch the station's flagship programme, *View*, a half-hour weekly regional magazine. Instead of building up a mosaic of items, as he had done in *Day By Day*, Boorman decided that each programme – he himself directed one in three – should focus on a particular theme: the British Airways factory in Bristol, which was then starting to build the first Concordes; the rhythm of a single day in and around Salisbury Cathedral; and, especially, a series of personal portraits, such as that of the Mayor of Glastonbury.

Later, in 1963, Boorman supervised a weekly half-hour series, *Arena*, an offshoot of *View*, which set up debates on current affairs (the cost of living, central government, housing, the world of high finance, etc.). The matter under debate was put before a court of justice. A pair of reporters, one of them presenting the case for the defence, the other for the prosecution, would call witnesses to the stand and develop their arguments with the aid of photographs and extracts from films. Each programme was presided over by Anthony Wedgwood Benn, now, of course, the *enfant terrible* of the Labour Party. 'At the time,' says Boorman, 'he was very conservative and considered my ideas too extreme!' It was Boorman's intention, with such a format, to move beyond conventional interviewing techniques, so that the various problems besetting the contemporary citizen might be aired in a more direct and vigorous fashion. In a sense, *Arena*, like the productions which followed it, demonstrated his interest in a more dramatic structure, even if one still contingent on documentary. Such innovations tended to meet with criticism, however, and it was only through strength and nerve that Boorman was able to impose them. 'Before the advent of commercial television, the BBC was a somewhat fusty organization. In the evening, after seven o'clock, the announcers would wear dinner jackets and bow ties. When I arrived in Bristol, I was the first producer there not to have a university degree. The others all behaved like university dons in some cosy and exclusive club. They were absolutely horrified. It was the beginning of the end, and they were extremely hostile towards me when I accepted the challenge issued by commercial television and tried to change the working methods then in force. To get what I wanted, I founded my own production unit with a group of like-minded and equally motivated technicians, which was indispensable, and cut myself off from the rest of the BBC.'

Thus it was that he managed to set up his most ambitious project to date, *Citizen 63*. Boorman was determined to break new ground, given how little of the BBC's output he then admired. The exceptions, which were rare, included the impressionistic documentaries made by the Manchester-based Dennis Mitchell, notably *Morning in the Streets*; and *Monitor*, the weekly series on the arts produced by Huw Wheldon, a series which gave such film-makers as Ken Russell and John Schlesinger their first chance. What Boorman wanted for *Citizen 63* was to focus on average English men and women; but, conscious as he was of the abyss which separated the Corporation's officially approved vision of British society and what it was in reality, he decided against a traditional journalistic format. He went to see Donald Baverstock, who was then head of BBC Current Affairs and deviser of the programme *Tonight*. Totally committed to the journalistic approach, Baverstock could not see the point of spending half an hour on some young schoolgirl whom, in any case, he did not find 'typical'. The untypical, however, was precisely what interested Boorman, and it was thanks to Huw Wheldon, who had been named Head of Documentaries, that *Citizen 63* got off the ground. 'The series affected a lot of people, since they were suddenly confronted in their living-rooms with fellow-countrymen and ways of life and attitudes about which they knew nothing. I was asked, at a press conference, how I'd found such extraordinary individuals and Wheldon replied: "He didn't find them, he recognized them."' *Citizen 63* portrayed six men and women at a decisive moment in their lives and in relation to their environment. Three of them were filmed by Boorman himself (the others by Michael Croucher): Barry Langford, a Jew from Brighton who, when he wasn't selling silverware, acted as a manager for pop singers; Marion Knight, an eighteen-year-old schoolgirl in rebellion against her family and her religion; and Frank George, an electronics and computer scientist with an ability to predict the future, who nevertheless contrived to lead a completely conventional life. That was what fascinated Boorman: 'Our minds have been propelled into the most complex and futuristic universes, but emotionally we're rooted in a distant past.'

Though a novelty for British television, these programmes employed a number of cinematic practices introduced a few years before in the United States by such directors as Drew, Leacock and the Maysles brothers: filming an individual without burdening him with one's own personal thesis; using, for the most part, a light, hand-held camera and natural sound. A brief introduction, with photographs, presented the subject of the programme; then followed the main portrait, encompassing his daily life, his background, his most prominent behavioural traits. The sound was sometimes synchronous with the image, sometimes commented on it and sometimes served to counterpoint it. At the end, the still shots were screened again, much more tellingly, however, since they were now weighted with everything the viewer had learned during the intervening half-hour.

The portraits were notable for their vivacity, their density

Frank George, the scientist of *Citizen 63*.

Marion Knight, the schoolgirl of *Citizen 63*.

Anthony Smith in *The Newcomers*.

John Boorman during the period when he worked in Bristol.

and their invention, as was remarked by the novelist Anthony Burgess when reviewing the programme on Barry Langford.[35] Quite justifiably, Boorman rejected the epithet 'cinéma-vérité'. These films were stylized artefacts, reconstructed and re-interpreted by the director in the light of his research into his subjects' lives. Barry Langford's contradictions, Marion Knight's confusion, the dichotomy in Frank George's life, all tended to coincide with Boorman's thoughts on his own pre-occupations. Yet, at the same time, it might be said that his subjects were 'writing' their autobiographies with the director's help. 'Documentary is always equally compounded of preparation and chance. There's always a conflict between your original project and those accidents which may subsequently occur and which you have to integrate into the film. Events can overwhelm you and cause you to lose sight of your structure, with all the muddle which that would imply. It's important in documentary to have a rhythm and a clear narrative line; if not, your work becomes shapeless. What also interested me in *Citizen 63* was exploring the space between what people say about themselves and what they really are.' The Marion Knight episode, in particular, caused a sensation. The headmaster of her school was dismissed and the young girl – an adopted child – was so distressed by her new celebrity that she moved in with the Boormans. It was after *Citizen 63* that Boorman lost faith in documentary: 'First of all, I'd become aware of its limitations. There were aspects of my subjects' personalities that I found awkward to deal with in documentary terms. And I realized that it could be dangerous for them to suffer this kind of exposure. You have the choice between a general, and therefore superficial, approach or a more personal and truthful point of view – but, in the latter case, you usually end up by hurting someone.'

From that point on, Boorman started to gravitate towards a style more rooted in fiction. For the launching of BBC 2 in 1964, Huw Wheldon, now Programme Controller, offered him *carte blanche*. Boorman suggested *The Newcomers*, an idea similar to that of *Citizen 63* – recounting the life of a Bristol couple – but stylistically more radical. In six half-hour episodes, each filmed in a different style, Boorman (and his brilliant cinematographer, James Saunders) filmed the four last months of Alison Smith's pregnancy, the professional activities of her husband Anthony (a Bristol-based journalist), and their social life together. The first episode, an 'objective' portrait of their day-to-day existence, came closest to *Citizen 63*. The second dealt with their fantasies: dream sequences in which the Smiths were shown together with their favourite movie stars – Alison dancing with Sinatra, for example, or Anthony playing cricket while Boorman crosscut shots of Alan Ladd in a fight sequence from *Shane*. The third juxtaposed a nocturnal excursion into Bristol by Anthony Smith and his friends (in search of photographs for a magazine they hoped to publish) with shots of Alison at home reciting Louis MacNeice's poem 'To the

Unborn Child'. The fourth revolved around a party (one of many in Boorman's films) hosted by the Smiths in their Clifton flat on the top floor of a Georgian house overlooking the docks, the green Somerset hills and half the city. Among their guests were such writers, friends of both the Smiths and the Boormans, as Tom Stoppard, Peter Nichols and Charles Wood, as well as John Hale, an Old Vic director. They too, like the Smiths, like the Boormans, were 'newcomers', transforming the social and intellectual landscape of a country which was then in the laborious process of acquiring a new identity. Notwithstanding its five hundred thousand inhabitants, Bristol could be compared to a village in which all the artists knew each other well. 'In Bristol, we were constantly aware of the country's problems. In London, everyone is part of a "set" and most of one's impressions are false. As Peter Nichols said to me the other day, there we all were, sitting in a Bristol pub, inventing "Swinging London"!' The two final episodes centred on Alison's confinement. While she was giving birth to twins, Boorman had eighteen cameras disposed around the city, covering the urban bustle in a manner reminiscent of Dos Passos. 'It was fascinating. In journalistic terms, nothing much was happening; yet the film abounded in quirky observations. With *The Newcomers*, I was trying to extend the boundaries of documentary, by dramatizing the material as much as possible in order to come up with some deeper truth about the country and its inhabitants.' After producing and directing hundreds of documentaries, Boorman endeavoured to revitalize a format which he had come to regard as outmoded, and, as it were, film the private diary of a city and a couple. Alas, it was not the success he had hoped for: the public was alienated by the way in which it switched styles from one episode to the next.

In the same year, with *The Quarry*, Boorman broached the world of fiction for the first time in his career, though retaining a number of documentary elements. BBC West in Bristol having decided to launch a series of programmes on the arts, Boorman agreed to direct one on a sculptor if he were allowed to give it a dramatic form. He nevertheless had to respect the limitations of time and money imposed by documentary: two weeks to write the screenplay, two weeks for the film's prepa-

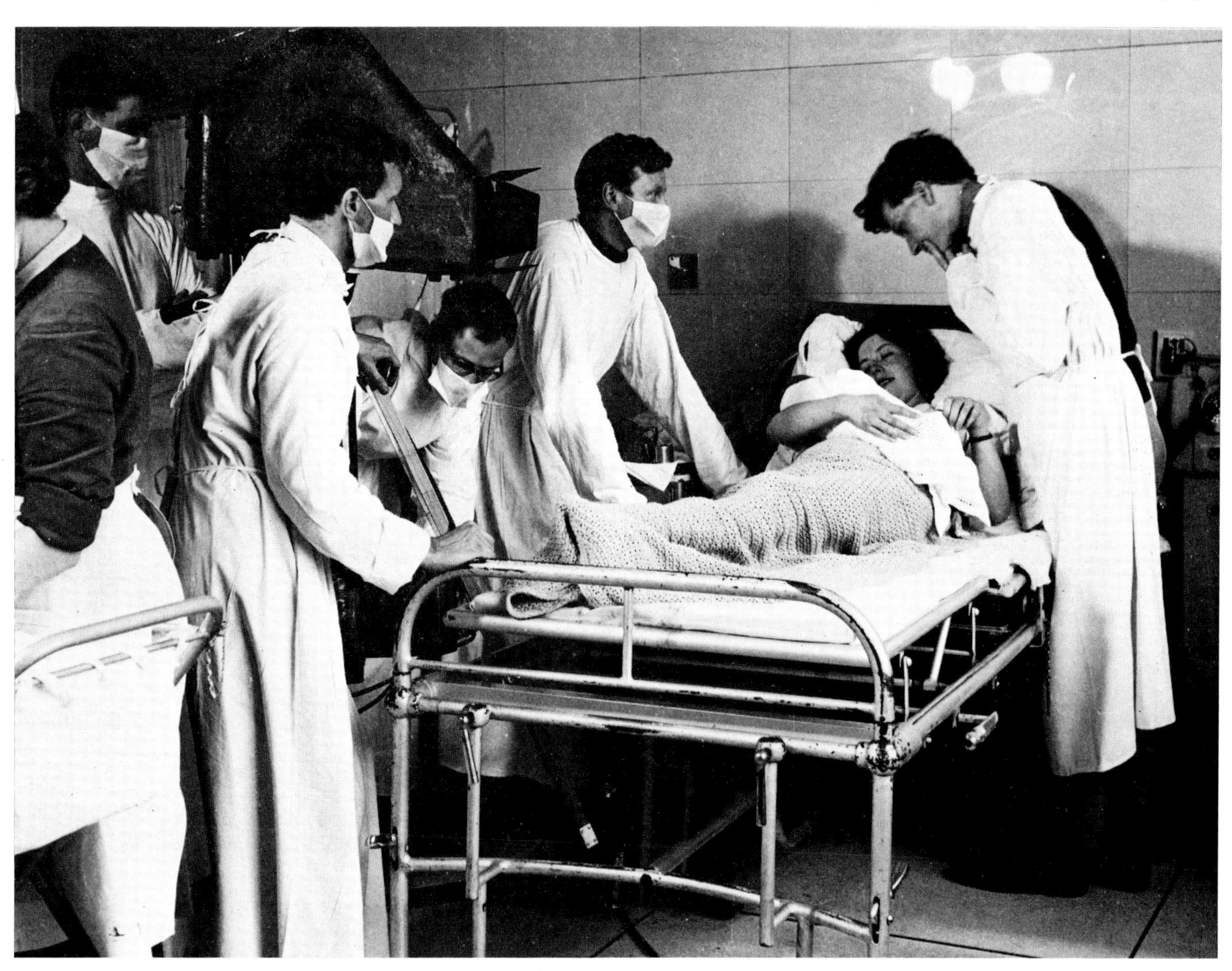

Alison Smith after the birth of one of her twins. Right, her husband Anthony. Left, the BBC West television crew: R. E. Robinson (assistant), Jim Saunders (cameraman), Peter Heeley (assistant cameraman), John Boorman (shooting *The Newcomers*).

ration, four weeks for both shooting and editing. The theme of *The Quarry*, that of an artist in crisis, was developed within the iconographic framework of the quest for the Grail, a legend with which Boorman was already obsessed. 'I was impatient to tackle a fictional subject and probably overloaded *The Quarry* with too many themes and ideas.' His protagonist, Arthur King, is also the Fisher King (as would later be the case in *Excalibur*); and, like Leo in *Leo the Last*, he not only suffers from a creative block but is regularly prey to morbid bouts of ennui. Though a giant slab of stone awaits him in his studio for a commission which he has accepted, it is only in the film's final shot that we actually see him working on it. King is the leader of a little clan of artists in a provincial town; and, as is proper to the genre of fictionalized documentary, Boorman used genuine artists as well as professional actors. As was noted by Bill Stair, the film's co-scenarist (who would subsequently collaborate with Boorman on the scripts of *Leo the Last* and *Zardoz*): 'The film was remarkable from several points of view, independently of the boldness of both project and theme. I'm thinking above all of its vision of a restless wanderer and his eternally elusive prey, who need each other for each to be able to play his own role.'[192] Arthur King is also suffering a crisis in marriage: he cannot leave his wife, and his mistress is indifferent to his problems. The dialogue of *The Quarry* (a title denoting, of course, both an excavation and a hunter's prey) contains an explicit reference to Jung: 'I was trying to interpret the Arthurian legend in order to understand the spell it had cast over me,' says Boorman. 'And it was Jung, whom I was reading at the time, who enabled me to comprehend the power and importance of myth. I'd been watching the world change around me and trying to interpret it, and Jung helped me see things more clearly.' Another Jungian feature of the film was its division of womanhood into three archetypes: the wife, the mistress and the ideal woman. With its density of texture, it was unquestionably Boorman's most personal work to date and offered an intriguing foretaste of the films to come. Specifically cinematic, for example, was the idea of the hero reliving his life through a succession of images; in another sequence, King projects for his mistress a series of reproductions summarizing the history of art. The references to Merlin, 'symbol of the forest and its mystery, offspring of a virgin and the Devil', the evocation of a waste land, the allusion to destruction as integral to the creative process, the belief in 'a community possessing some great psychic energy' – all of these are currents which would run through his subsequent work.

Symbolically, *The Quarry* brought Boorman's television work to a close. Shortly after, he made his first feature film, *Catch Us If You Can*, and took temporary leave of television. Temporary in that a brief parenthesis was later opened: his film on D. W. Griffith, *The Great Director*, a homage to the founding-father of the American cinema, made for the BBC just before Boorman crossed the Atlantic to shoot *Point Blank* and therefore before he himself had been tested in Hollywood. 'I've always hugely admired Griffith. The film which I devoted to him took much longer than I thought it would, more than a year. I had, to start with, enormous difficulties securing authorization to use extracts from his films. I saw everything by him that was still extant and made *The Great Director* with nothing but footage from his own work. If, for example, I wished to show what America looked like in Griffith's time, I used his images of the country. You also know that he went to France during the First World War with his cameraman Billy Bitzer and shot a lot of material for *Hearts of the World*, material which now constitutes one of the finest documents we possess on the war. In addition, I found movie theatre programmes from the period and used the same music, and respected the same orchestration, for the soundtrack of my film. My idea was that Griffith conceived film to be the universal language promised in the Bible and a harbinger of the Millennium. It must, after all, have seemed a new, universal language. For me, Griffith was the very source of the cinema; and one of the problems of the medium is that it tends to feed off itself: films are imitated and the imitations are imitated in their turn. Griffith was imitated, but the original impulse, the original vitality, were lost.' It was precisely that vitality, that faith in the power of the image, that Boorman was about to exploit in *Point Blank* just after having returned to the origins of his chosen art.

D. W. Griffith (*The Great Director*).

Twenty Years of Cinema (1965–85)

John Boorman's cinematic career represents the continuation of his work in television, reinforced by an ever tighter control over the parameters of his vision. Characterized by their energy and their readiness to take risks, his nine films, whether commissions (*Hell in the Pacific*, *Deliverance*, *The Heretic*) or original projects (*Leo the Last*, *Zardoz*, *Excalibur*, *The Emerald Forest*), are all, by virtue of his courage and tenacity, equally personal works. To be sure, the precise context of the British film industry played a determinant role in his development, as witness his first two films. He was able to make *Catch Us If You Can* (1965) not only because of his reputation at the BBC, a nursery of sixties' talents (Schlesinger, Russell), but also because of the flourishing state of the domestic industry during the period of 'Swinging London'. As for *Point Blank* (1967), it was a further example of the irresistible appeal which Hollywood has always had for English directors, from Hitchcock and Korda to Karel Reisz, Tony Richardson, John Schlesinger and Ken Russell, without forgetting David Lean and Alexander MacKendrick. Boorman's specific originality is doubtless to have alternated the films he has made in America (*Point Blank*, *Deliverance*, *The Heretic*) with those made in Ireland (*Zardoz*, *Excalibur*), in England (*Catch Us If You Can*, *Leo the Last*) and even Polynesia (*Hell in the Pacific*) and Amazonia (*The Emerald Forest*). A fervent traveller, a tireless tracker of images, he carries his personal universe with him wherever he goes and is willing to subject himself to severe physical hardships if, in these different countries, there might exist the possibility of reconstructing his inner world – then regularly replenishes himself at the fountain of his own culture.

John Boorman directs his daughter Katrine (Igraine) in *Excalibur*.

Similarly, in the sixties, when past experience had made

American companies reluctant to finance *films d'auteur* in Europe, Boorman succeeded in persuading them to back a number of commercially dubious projects. These were, in order, MGM (*Point Blank*), Selmur (*Hell in the Pacific*), United Artists (*Leo the Last*), Warner Bros (*Deliverance*), Twentieth Century-Fox (*Zardoz*), Warners again (*The Heretic*), Orion (*Excalibur*) and, most recently, Embassy (*The Emerald Forest*).

While so many directors lack the means of their ambition, and just as many others possess the means but lack the ambition, Boorman, through his energy and enthusiasm, and in spite of difficulties and compromises, has remained true to his original purpose: to defend the universality of the cinema, to reject all forms of elitism, to ignore the shibboleths of class and race and to work for the largest possible audience without ever offering it anything less than an intelligent, adult work of art. It was for that reason that he decided to 'work within the system while attempting on every possible occasion to expand its boundaries'.

Deliverance (1971) was therefore a significant departure in his career since, with it, Boorman became his own producer. *Zardoz*, which succeeded it, was no less pivotal, the director working for the first time from original material. He decided, early in 1972, to write alone, to confront his own dreams and his own universe, after having expressed himself – no less eloquently, to be sure – through adaptations. Never so happy as when *sharing* an adventure, fond of galvanizing a film crew into the closest possible collaboration with him, Boorman found in the solitary act of writing a challenge to his perseverance and self-confidence. Even if the experience were never to have been repeated, it influenced his development and would probably not have happened at all had Boorman not settled shortly before in Ireland, the country where, to all intents and purposes, he has lived ever since. While he was filming *Point Blank*, the Boormans – his wife Christel, who would later design the costumes for *Zardoz*, his daughters Telsche (born in 1959), Katrine (born in 1960), who would act in *Excalibur*, Daisy (born in 1966) and his son Charley (Daisy's twin), who would play Ed's son in *Deliverance*, Mordred as a child in *Excalibur* and the 'wild child' in *The Emerald Forest* – were foreign residents in California. But the director was unhappy with the idea that his children might grow up there. For tax reasons, *Leo the Last* was edited in Ireland and Boor-

John Boorman directs his son Charley (Tomme) in *The Emerald Forest*.

man, as he himself puts it, fell in love with the country. 'It got to something inside me, it seemed to correspond to my own inner landscape. Ireland escaped the Industrial Revolution, it has a medieval side to it, the countryside hasn't been spoiled and pillaged as it has elsewhere. We were looking for a holiday cottage. One Saturday, my wife visited a former presbytery in the Wicklow area, which was to be auctioned off the following Monday. We went to the auction out of curiosity and returned from it owners of the house. For me, it's become a sanctuary from the ravages of the film industry; and, when I'm not filming, that's where I'm to be found. Ireland is, in fact, an extremely dangerous drug. It's hard to live without it, even if you have to pay the price (the telephone, for example, doesn't work awfully well) for such a journey into the past. But it's a country which, for the last fifteen years, has meant a great deal to me, and I enjoyed exploring its landscapes in *Zardoz* and *Excalibur*.'

Boorman also supervised the management of the film studios at Ardmore; and when the government nationalized them in 1975, he became their executive director as a means of fostering the development of an indigenous Irish cinema. In that capacity, he encouraged the training of new directors, helped find untapped sources of funding, involved himself in the problem of print conservation and, by his very presence, attracted several film crews to Ireland. Under his aegis, a number of first films were completed, notably Neil Jordan's *Angel* and Michael Dryhurst's *The Hard Way*. In 1982, he gave up running Ardmore Studios. Complementing his more personal projects with such local involvement, Boorman demonstrates yet again his conception of the artist as both artisan and businessman, his feet on the ground and his head in the clouds, his ambition to be the kind of person of whom it may be said that nothing concerning the cinema is alien to him.

For him, too, the film-making process itself already articulates those personal preoccupations which the completed work will only confirm. 'Making films is converting money into light, with all of us hoping that the light on the screen will in its turn be converted into money. As such, it isn't so far removed from myth, which represents an endeavour to escape the material world in order to attain a more spiritual sphere. In the cinema, too, we employ all the resources of an industrial and technological society to create a dream, a luminous cone which, when projected on a wall, will also project a little of our soul.'

Charley Boorman in *Deliverance* (Ed's son).

Excalibur (Mordred as a child).

The Emerald Forest (Tomme).

1965

Dinah and her image (Barbara Ferris in *Catch Us If You Can*).

Catch Us If You Can

Interplay of Illusion and Reality

In the case of a film-maker with a strongly defined personality, it is always instructive to return to his very first work, especially if it should happen to have been the product of circumstances, the result of a compromise; for what, at an initial viewing, may have appeared to pertain primarily to some prevailing artistic climate tends subsequently to be subsumed by the already tangible presence of the future artist. *Catch Us If You Can* is no exception to the rule. The film, to be sure, was well received on its release. It was praised, and justly so, not only for its sense of fantasy, humour and visual invention but also for the light touch with which it handled serious matters – the problem, notably, of alienation through advertising. At the very height of the sixties, John Boorman became part of the cinema of 'Swinging London' which, with a few Bristol friends (including the dramatist Peter Nichols, who wrote the film's screenplay), he had helped to create. From his documentary experience, he retained the art of filming a landscape, the streets of London or the architecture of Bath; also intact was his social awareness, his very personal view of English society and its various strata.

Yet Boorman was already distancing himself from such a superficial approach. Though the realism with which he was all the more familiar for having mastered it in television seemed to him an essential foundation for his work in the cinema, it alone could not instil in his films the kind of resonance he wished them to possess. *Catch Us If You Can* actually takes pleasure in playing with illusion and reality, in poking fun at a world in which it is difficult to distinguish the bogus from the genuine article. A TV commercial, the classic example of contemporary artifice, may well be filmed in a meat hangar of startling authenticity. The charred tanks and gutted houses glimpsed in the countryside are not, as we soon learn, the signs of a nuclear holocaust but the humdrum 'props' of military manoeuvres; nevertheless, when a group of hippies is surrounded by soldiers in training, the spectator, even if forewarned, cannot help but be struck by an undercurrent of real violence, the frontier between life and its representation being a difficult one to situate with any exactitude. On a more humorous level, at a fancy-dress ball in Bath, the film's performers disguise themselves as cinema icons – Charlie Chaplin, Harpo Marx, Frankenstein's monster, Sabu, Al Jolson, Jean Harlow, Laurel and Hardy . . . all those Hollywood myths on which Boorman was weaned and which he would set about subverting in his subsequent works. And, later, Steve and Dinah, the film's protagonists, take refuge in a farm run by Louis, the former director of a London youth club frequented by Steve. Louis amuses himself by recreating the atmosphere of a western ranch, turning the stable into a saloon and letting his horses roam at liberty through the west of England. It is, therefore, a whole populist imagery, one generated by the cinema, that is being conjured up by the director; and it should be noted that one of the film's themes is a cover girl's refusal to continue working for an advertising agency, for a factory of lies . . . She goes so far as to scrawl a pair of glasses and a moustache on a poster of her own face.

Louis and his 'ranch' in the west of England (David Lodge in *Catch Us If You Can*).

Catch Us If You Can, like all of Boorman's films, is the story of a quest. Two young people flee the synthetic glitter of the world in search of an 'elsewhere' which will finally prove inaccessible. Dinah dreams of owning an island off the Devon coast, only to discover, too late, that this uninhabited spot with its abandoned old hotel is, at low tide, connected to the mainland. Yet she had already found this 'island for myself alone', the object of her dreams, in the heart of London: namely, the 'wonderful tropical isle' of Kew Gardens, complete with hot-house oranges.

Not only is Utopia out of reach, it has been deployed as bait by those in authority. From the beginning of their journey, Zissell, Dinah's boss, has been organizing their pursuit; and, with the help of his henchmen, he has contrived to turn into a publicity exercise what originally derived from a desperate craving to escape. Thus the flight represents, in fact, the ultimate stage in a gradual process of disillusionment: not merely for Steve, who sees in Louis, the hero of his youth, a man now obsessed with his own social position, but for Dinah, to whom the sterility of marital relationships is revealed by a middle-class couple from Bath. 'No one can stand reality,' she is told by the elderly husband, whose hobby is collecting Victoriana, history's pop art, preserving the past under glass, incapable as

he is of relating to it more directly. In this, his first film, Boorman develops, in a playfully allusive manner, the ideas on culture which had already been set forth in *The Quarry*. Guy and Nan, the aforementioned couple, who take in the young runaways (though not without an ulterior motive), are fetishists of a dead past: she preserves old clothes, he collects film projectors. Though quite harmless in themselves, they represent that same adult world which manipulates the young and whose most sinister agent is Zissell, with his dark glasses and his equally dark suits.

During the race-cum-chase, Boorman crosscuts between shots of a wintry, if liberating, landscape and the functional office of the advertising agency, whose geometric asceticism prefigures the metallic sets of *Point Blank*. Similarly, the warmth of Steve, his friends and the hippies is contrasted with the 'deep freeze' of human relations induced either by domestic routine (the married couple) or by monetary greed (Zissell's company). And, symbolically, the director begins his film with a shot of men sleeping (a recurrent image in his work) inside a deconsecrated church, its organ serving as their alarm-clock –

1 Shooting a TV commercial in a meat hangar (Barbara Ferris and Dave Clark in *Catch Us If You Can*).
2 The coldly functional office of the advertising agency prefigures the metallic sets of *Point Blank* (in the centre, David de Keyser in *Catch Us If You Can*).

an ironic commentary on the absence of spirituality. *Catch Us If You Can* is therefore the prelude and fugue (in a minor key) of the films which were to succeed it. And, as though to underline its status, Boorman progressively abandons the giddy, syncopated, staccato pyrotechnics of the opening scenes, which might almost be said to endorse the advertising and television world of his heroine, in favour of the more fluid, if no less dynamic, style of his later films.

Interview

How did you happen to direct your first film, Catch Us If You Can?

David Deutsch, who was working for both Anglo-Amalgamated and Hammer, admired what I'd done for television and suggested that I make a musical with a pop group, the Dave Clark Five. I wasn't sure that I'd be able to, or that I had anything to say. I discussed the matter with a friend of mine from Bristol, the dramatist Peter Nichols, and our reply was that we were incapable of writing a 'pop' movie. So David left us completely free, and the opportunity was simply too tempting. We began to work together and came up with a story in which characters, settings and events I had noted in my years of working on documentaries would reappear. The young schoolgirl from *Citizen 63*, for instance, appears in the 'beat' sequence. And the young husband from *The Newcomers* is the photographer who turns up at the end of the film. I prepared *Catch Us If You Can* in the same way as the documentaries: I sketched out a rough draft of the plot and the locations I wanted; then Pete Nichols wrote the dialogue, which was often first-rate, and I might later modify it during the shoot. The various landscapes in the film were also ones I had already explored while working at the BBC: Bath, the west coast of England, the Mendip hills and Salisbury Plain. The choice of settings was made much less consciously than in my subsequent films, since they were, in a way, already part of my life. It's what Griffith said: I want to photograph thoughts and emotions. Everyone since Griffith has tried to do the same, and one way of doing it is to use landscape as a means of

John Boorman directs Barbara Ferris in *Catch Us If You Can.*

conveying emotion. It's become a cliché. The whole thing was more instinctive in *Catch Us If You Can* than in *Point Blank*, where I had a character with a certain state of mind and so was much more precise in choosing locations which would evoke a feeling of desolation, emptiness, loneliness and betrayal. *Catch Us If You Can* was shot in winter; I was attracted to the idea of a deserted seaside resort, since I find the English countryside melancholic in that season. The subject really arose out of its setting. In the hotel, I was struck by the lifelessness of a place that no longer fulfilled its function: it's what, in a sense, has happened to England. It's like those farms that are no longer farms but parks for strolling about in. They seem almost asleep, like waste lands . . .

Was it the first time you had used a screenwriter?

For my television films, it's true, I was my own screenwriter, but I was working in the field of documentary, in terms of structure and architecture, sketching out scenes and letting the actors supply the dialogue. I think, in contemporary cinema, the performers ought to work on their own dialogue, so that it takes definitive shape only when the scene is being rehearsed.

Pete Nichols is a persistent pessimist. Every morning, while he was waiting for me to arrive, he'd write out an adverse review of the film in the styles of all the English critics! We worked day and night on the script; and when we'd completed it, he typed on the fly-leaf: 'To Valium, without which this film could not have been written'!

Like The Quarry, *it's a mélange of documentary and fiction. The first section is more fragmented, with a more staccato style. The second is more fluid.*

It's a picaresque film, a sort of trip for the two characters, a means for them of coming to terms with the English soil and landscape and customs. Each episode has both a personal meaning for me and is linked to some aspect of English life in general. And each sequence has its own unity, as was the case in the longer version of *The Newcomers*. The scene in Bath, with Yootha Joyce and Robin Bailey, is like some weird comedy of manners, whereas the fancy-dress ball, which is full of all kinds of movie characters, becomes a farcical chase in a much more exuberant style. For me, the film represented both an exploration of cinematic possibilities and an opportunity to express certain personal ideas.

You very quickly abandon the other four members of the pop group in order to concentrate on the young couple.

What enabled us to make the film was the success of Richard Lester's *A Hard Day's Night* with the Beatles. In a way, the pop group was just a point of departure. I was also obliged to begin with them as that was what the public expected. What I wanted was not to disappoint their fans, but gradually to engage them in something quite different. I think that what I really hoped to convey was my conflict with English society and the class system I'd encountered at the BBC. On the one hand, I'm tremendously fond of many aspects of my native country; on the other hand, I feel as though I'm almost a foreigner in it. Sir Walter Raleigh, one of my heroes, found himself at odds with the fusty, snobbish, hopelessly conservative side of English society and he believed one should confront it and try to get the better of it. I feel the same way, and I think that emerges in the stories I film.

Didn't it worry the producers that the film's ending was so downbeat – the young girl going off with the photographers and her boyfriend leaving her?

When we started filming, I didn't know exactly how the film was going to end, as I was shooting more or less in chronological order. David Deutsch – a wonderful man, by the way – wanted it to end with the boy and girl leaving together; but I felt that that would betray the spirit of the film. David was in an extremely awkward position. On the one hand, he was gifted with taste and intelligence; on the other, he worked for Anglo-Amalgamated. If he'd taken a stronger line, he would have insisted on a more populist style for *Catch Us If You Can*, one that would have corresponded to the company's house-style. His influence eventually began to wane, since he wanted to produce quality films – none of which was commercially successful.

1 'I find the English countryside magnificent in that season' (Barbara Ferris and Dave Clark in *Catch Us If You Can*).
2 The hippie community (Barbara Ferris and Dave Clark in *Catch Us If You Can*).

Though, in the film, the island is a romantic idea, it turns out to be just as hostile as the rest of the world. Would you call yourself a disenchanted romantic?

Let's say 'disappointed'. According to my wife, it's because I refuse to see things as they are, and she's probably right. I've always been attracted to whatever is romantic and lyrical in life, and in the end I invariably feel betrayed.

The film's narrative is that of a journey. But making a film is in itself a journey, an exploration. I never know where it's going to take me; and, if I did know, I couldn't bear the idea of all the effort in store for me. What motivates me is the process of discovery. When I begin shooting, I don't really know what my theme will be. Once the film is completed, I look back on it all, everything that's happened to me becomes clearer, and it's then that I understand the true meaning of what I've achieved.

1 The ferry to the island (Barbara Ferris and Dave Clark in *Catch Us If You Can*).
2 The 'Hollywood' fancy-dress ball prefigures the masks of plaster, mud and gold, and the body paint in Boorman's subsequent films.

1

2

3

1 The Exterminators of *Zardoz*.
2 Lee Marvin in *Hell in the Pacific*.

Robert Addie in *Exalibur*.

1967

Sharon Acker, Lee Marvin and John Vernon (*Point Blank*).

Point Blank

An American Dream

Though belonging to the unexpected revival of the Hollywood thriller in the mid-sixties, a gangster film like *Point Blank* is easily distinguishable from the concurrent 'private eye' cycle, represented by such titles as *P.J.*, *Harper*, *Tony Rome* and *Peter Gunn*. It is, in a sense, the extreme – and, to this day, unsurpassed – culmination of a phenomenon first seen in Don Siegel's *The Killers* (which also co-starred Lee Marvin and Angie Dickinson and whose French title, *A bout portant*, is, oddly enough, a literal translation of 'point blank'): the apparition of the ice-cold, robotic killer, of whom Johnny Cool (in William Asher's film of that name) was yet another incarnation. The world of the private eye, latterly illustrated by Jack Smight and Gordon Douglas, Blake Edwards and John Guillermin, engendered a return to 'psychology', to social satire and the picturesque, to a brand of story-telling in which the intricacy of human relationships was rivalled only by the complication of the plot. *Point Blank*, by contrast, plays down both characterization and psychology, reduces motivation to the absolute essential and dispenses with labyrinthine subplots, thereby, quite naturally, acquiring the stark linearity of a fable. And if Boorman's use of flashbacks was criticized in certain quarters as gratuitous and too patently 'European' in influence, we can now see how integral they are to the overall narrative thrust. In fact, they serve a wholly different function from those found in traditional thrillers. Their expository value is virtually nil: the information which they contain might just as well have been conveyed in two or three lines of dialogue. What they do possess, however, is a visual immediacy that is as poetic as it is sheerly physical.

Superficially, *Point Blank* would appear to be just a story of vengeance. And it is that, certainly, from beginning to end. But it's also possible to interpret it as a more complex allegory, as a symbolic portrait of the United States, such as was attempted by Arthur Penn in *Mickey One*, albeit with, in his case, recourse to a whole literary tradition. Walker (Lee Marvin), denied his share of the loot and left for dead by the wife and best friend who have betrayed him, will not rest until he has recovered his 93,000 dollars and measured himself against the omnipotent Organization. One of the living dead, insensitive to everything and everybody, obsessed by his betrayal and by the point-blank shots which almost killed him, he finds himself sucked into an unending quest whose original motive he may well have forgotten. For the money itself has ceased to be important: more significantly, Walker's ambition is now to reach the very source of *power*, that mysterious entity to which no one is allowed access. When he believes that he has attained his goal, after liquidating all the intermediate figures (his for-

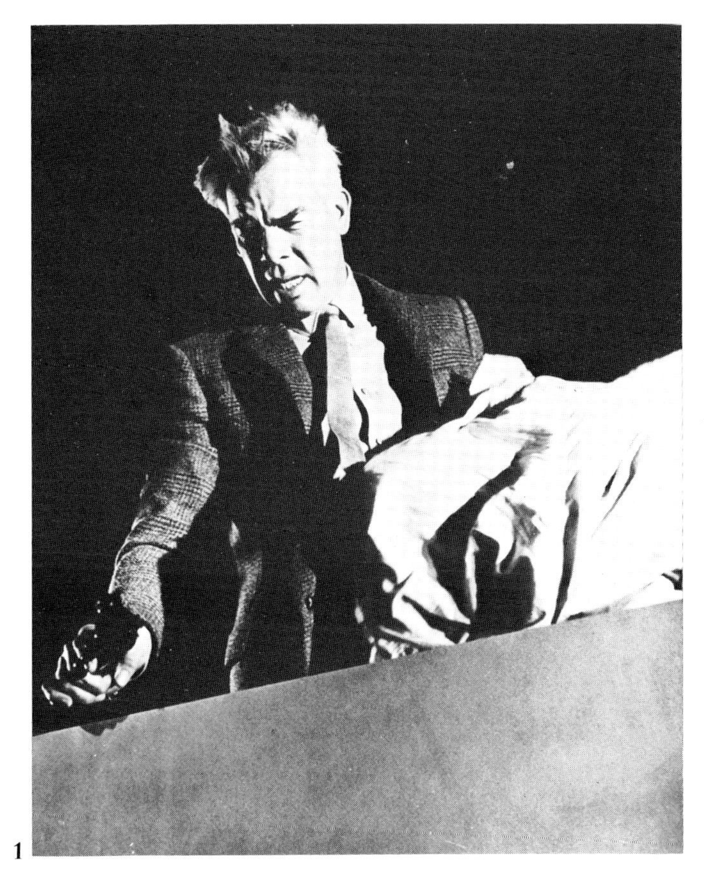

1 One of the living dead, indifferent to everyone around him, obsessed with this betrayal: Lee Marvin (*Point Blank*).
2 Angie Dickinson and Lee Marvin (*Point Blank*).

1 The nightclub (Lee Marvin in *Point Blank*).
2 The dried-up canal (Lee Marvin in *Point Blank*).

3

Lynne's apartment (Sharon Acker and Lee Marvin in *Point Blank*).

mer friend Reese, now a mere cog in the machine; the car salesman Stegman; finally, Carter and Brewster), it's only to discover that it continues to elude him, that it cannot ever be pinned down and that Fairfax has been using him in the same way as Mr Arkadin used Van Stratten in Orson Welles' *Confidential Report*: as a means of ridding himself of undesirable witnesses and accomplices. Walker has been nothing but an agent, manipulated by Fairfax to restructure the Organization internally, even if, externally, it remains unchanged. And, at the end, as Fairfax emerges from the shadows, Walker returns to the darkness of a cell in Alcatraz from which he had emerged two years before only to plunge headlong into a nightmare. The circular construction of the narrative, moreover, eventually lends the whole film an aura of unreality, or of reality filtered through dreams, of lighting suffused by memories – as is suggested by certain gauzy images of Lee Marvin. Its closing shots – of the abandoned prison and its stone walls, the water of the river and the lights twinkling in the night sky – would appear to confirm the words spoken by the guide on a sightseeing steamer: that the treacherous currents encircling the island preclude all possibility of escape. Caught in the whirlwind of a storm which he himself has raised, Walker can no more easily escape from his nightmare.

This dreamlike atmosphere is reinforced by the doubling of Walker's wife Lynne, who appears to have been reincarnated in her sister Chris (and the casting of Sharon Acker and Angie Dickinson, who physically resemble each other, was a deliberate ploy on Boorman's part). Walker drives his sister-in-law into the arms of his betrayer, Reese; he forces her to prostitute herself, humiliating her as though he might settle the score with his wife by catching them in bed together, just as he himself was caught by Reese while kissing Lynne in Alcatraz. Later, too, he will enjoy a relaxed moment with Chris in a bar, thereby doubling his one happy memory of Lynne on the beach.

As also in a dream, the events of the narrative will always

The gestures of a ruthless killer who never kills.
Above Michael Strong and Lee Marvin (*Point Blank*).
Opposite Lee Marvin, Rico Cattani and Carroll O'Connor (*Point Blank*).

elude those who live through them. For though his gestures and attitudes may suggest those of some ruthless killer, Walker in fact never does kill. He is only a pawn, to be played with by a monolithic corporation which manages even to exploit its adversaries. The Organization is a 'parallel' society which, though illegal, respects all the outward signs of legality. The men who run it have very Wasp-ish names, being neither Jewish nor Italian. They are respectable and anonymous representatives of corporate America; and, as such, they hold Walker's methods in distaste, regarding them as brutal, outmoded and uncivilized. When one of them dies, his pockets will contain a few credit cards and maybe eleven dollars in cash. Ensconced in the inner sanctum of power, they have their enemies quietly disappear at the end of long-range rifles; they commit perfect, motiveless murders and, when business is bad, they simply bribe the police. Theirs is the world of Raoul Walsh's *The Enforcer*, except that, here, the underworld has become a codified American institution: its bosses stay in plush hotels, attend charity receptions and own elegant country estates, even as they exert an almost occult influence over the country. Ironically, if the police intervene, it is only to serve Walker's aims. Otherwise, they are absent, just as the 'feel' of any particular city is absent: here, Los Angeles is The City, modern, anonymous and indifferent. The characters are alive, their context is abstract.

So the fable unfolds; and, should any doubts remain as to the director's intentions, one has only to read Richard Stark's somewhat tedious novel, *The Hunter*, on which the film is based. (Stark's work also served as a point of departure for Alain Cavalier's *Mise à sac* and, another essay in symbolic transcription, Godard's *Made in USA*, adapted from *The Juggler*.) Though retaining the basic structure of the narrative, Boorman and his scenarists have turned it completely inside out: by introducing a second female character as well as the mysterious Yost; by establishing the cyclical construction (whereas, in the novel, Walker recovers his money); and, above all, by eliminating police intervention, any sense of a

The man caught *in flagrante delicto* who becomes entangled in his own bedclothes . . . John Vernon and Lee Marvin (*Point Blank*).

. . . and the man who left Walker for dead in an Alcatraz cell. John Vernon, Sharon Acker and Lee Marvin (*Point Blank*).

The penitentiary of Alcatraz from which sinister helicopters come and go (*Point Blank*).

precise locale (whereas the novel was set in New York), and the gunfights with which the original was punctated. If 'private eye' movies, whether adapted from Chandler, Hammett or Ross MacDonald, are – by their analytic and realistic nature – directly contingent on their screenplay and dialogue, the fascination of *Point Blank* derives exclusively from the treatment to which these have been subjected by its director. Boorman's mastery is evident. First, in the choice of settings, each of them vividly evoked, none of them originating in Stark's novel: the penitentiary of Alcatraz, from which sinister helicopters come and go; the psychedelic nightclub, or Movie-House, in which a Botticelli Madonna will succeed a pin-up of Rita Hayworth, image will succeed image, in a manner that would have delighted MacLuhan; and a dried-up canal, its surface as white and arid as a desert. Second, in the profusion of startling narrative ideas: the notion of ordeal by stock-car, for example, or that of a man caught *in flagrante delicto* who becomes so entangled in his own bedsheets that he hurtles from the twentieth floor of a skyscraper. Finally, in a style subtly attuned to both action and location and far removed from that, trite even in its vulgarity, of Richard Stark.

For his first American movie, the Englishman Boorman retained all the modish brilliance, the razzle-dazzle, of which the film-makers of his native country were so fond in the sixties; yet he also managed to purify it, to invest it with a seamless fluidity, an all-American gloss. Though often intolerably pretentious in Hollywood films, the narrative devices inherited from Resnais (among others) are extraordinarily well integrated. It cannot have been easy to get away with superimposing shots of a beauty parlour over a sound collage of footsteps resounding along a corridor; yet the effect is thrilling and, like the film as a whole, impresses us with its well-nigh supernatural vision of an America which is nevertheless concrete enough. Boorman's lyrical portrait of a country with, apparently, no other outlet but that of violence corresponds to Robert Aldrich's in *Kiss Me Deadly*: there, too, an apocalyptic fable grew out of an extremely lightweight original. The 'thing' in Aldrich's thriller has been replaced by a secret

Yost, alias Fairfax, the omniscient manipulator of *Point Blank*, is as evil a character as Zissell and Laszlo, his alter egos from Boorman's early work. In *Zardoz*, Arthur Frayn proves to be rather more ambiguous before being replaced by the benevolent guardians of the recent works (Keenan Wynn and Lee Marvin in *Point Blank*).

1

2

3

1 Zissell, the director of the advertising agency (Dave Clark, Barbara Ferris and David de Keyser in *Catch Us If You Can*).
2 Arthur Frayn, the magician (Niall Buggy in *Zardoz*).
3 Kokumo, the witch-doctor (James Earl Jones in *The Heretic*).

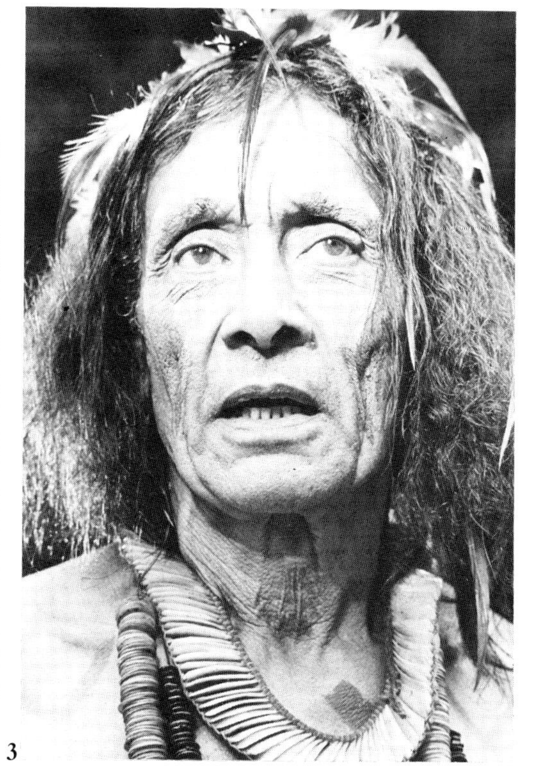

1 Laszlo, the major-domo (Vladek Sheybal and Marcello Mastroianni in *Leo the Last*).
2 Merlin, the enchanter (Nicol Williamson in *Excalibur*).
3 Wanadi, the shaman (Rui Polonah in *The Emerald Forest*).

society, its climactic destruction by an unshakeable stability; but Walker, like Mike Hammer before him, surrounded by the same obscurely evil forces, the same images of fear and death, is a hunter of shadows in search of an inaccessible Grail. And it is to Boorman's credit that he was able to remain so allusive that, even as he unveiled it, the enigma of his twentieth-century fable remained intact. Morality has been vandalized, corruption reigns over these smooth, gleaming surfaces and an orgy of violence can only culminate in the darkness of a prison cell which no longer has need of its guards.

How did you come to direct Point Blank*?*

I was doing some research in Los Angeles for my film on Griffith, and I met the producer, Judd Bernard; he showed me a script which was dreadful, but whose hero fascinated me. He'd also given it to Lee Marvin. A few months later, I met Marvin in London, where he was filming *The Dirty Dozen*. He felt as I did about the script and, though he'd seen none of my films, he asked me if I'd like to make this one with him.

He was totally supportive – always ready to back up my most offbeat ideas. He's a man of instinct, very intuitive and impulsive. Whenever I meet ciné-literate directors like Brian De Palma, they invariably ask me how I filmed the scene in which Walker returns to his wife's apartment and, in the following scenes, all the furniture has disappeared. It's so strange and mysterious, it couldn't have been written into the script. In fact, it was while Lee and I were talking, during the shoot, that the idea came to us. He suddenly sat down in a corner of the empty room, as though he were back in his cell in Alcatraz. It's in that sense that, for me, the set is not 'realistic': I changed it so that it would correspond to the character's state

John Boorman, a copy of the script under his arm, with his daughters Telsche and Katrine on the set of *Point Blank*.

of mind. But it had to be done without the spectator feeling aware of what was happening: the editing had to be fluid and seamless.

The shoot was both difficult and exhilarating, since we were inventing new ideas all the time. For instance, I wasn't happy with the Carroll O'Connor scene in the luxury house, as it was in the script. Since I'd be working with the actors every week-end, preparing the following week's shoot, I discussed the problem with Carroll, who's a very inventive actor, and we conceived the scene where he turns to Marvin and tells him that he's a crook and that he can't pay him, as he's only got four dollars in his pocket. When the MGM executives viewed the rushes, they were furious, as that scene hadn't been in the script. The next day, in the afternoon, my assistant, Al Jennings, came looking for me on the set: the studio wanted us to stop filming, they thought I'd gone crazy and wanted me to see a psychiatrist!

How did you work with your screenwriter, Alexander Jacobs?

Alex had been production assistant on *Catch Us If You Can.* He'd been of great assistance on the construction of the film: he's very clever at condensing a scene, he's a good critic, he's able to tell you where to cut. He's not really a writer, but someone who writes directly for the screen. I asked him to join me in Hollywood and for a month we worked on the script together. Then he left, and the script changed a lot more before shooting began. He also worked with me on *Hell in the Pacific* – though less effectively, as he didn't feel as much affinity with the subject-matter.

In Film Quarterly, *Alexander Jacobs said that he would have liked to invest the characters of* Point Blank *with greater psychological depth, with greater warmth. The film, as it stands, is quite cold, almost a fable. Were you affected by these divergent views?*

I haven't read that interview. I supppose that, up to a point, we saw things from a different angle. But it's not an easy thing to speak about. When you write a script, you try to convince the people you're working with, you try to satisfy the producers, so that less pressure is exerted on you. What I have in my head and what I get down on paper tend to differ more and more. In any event, Alexander Jacobs was of great help to me during the preparation of *Point Blank.*

Wasn't it your original intention to make the film in San Francisco?

Now there's a point on which Alex and I disagreed. Originally, the film was set entirely in San Francisco. I'd never been there; but when I saw the city, I realized it wasn't at all the kind of setting I was looking for. It was all in soft, romantic, pastel shades – a very beautiful place – but the complete opposite of what I wanted for the film. I wanted my setting to be hard, cold and, in a sense, futuristic. I wanted an empty, sterile world, for which Los Angeles was absolutely right. I had to fight to get my way, against the studio, against the producers and even against Alex. I finally won because filming in Los Angeles was less expensive. For me, it was an absolutely crucial battle, as the film would have been completely different if I hadn't won.

How did you find the dried-up canal?

To make *Point Blank,* I had first of all to establish the emotional climate of each scene, then seek the appropriate location by helicopter. People who have worked for years in Hollywood ask me where I found all those locations. In fact, all I did was look, but I knew what I was looking for. At which point, however, the system – Metro-Goldwyn-Mayer – intervened and said: 'Tell us what you want and we'll find it for you. If you want a house, we have a department for that sort of thing and it'll find it for you. A photographer will take photographs of ten different houses and you can choose the one you want.' That was of no use to me at all, since I couldn't know what I was looking for until I saw and recognized it, and I certainly couldn't describe it in advance. That's why they seldom use their own natural environment. Everything is filtered through the 'location department' and its archives. They always use the same locations, the ones they know to be practical because the police will facilitate shooting by blocking off such and such a street. They prevented me from finding locations by myself because the union was against it. People were paid for that kind of thing. So I set off with seven people at my heels in order to respect the union's rules. They followed me in four separate cars. I drove my own, which was already contrary to the rules: they have someone to drive you. My driver followed me. Behind him came the photographer, the location manager, the production manager and the assistants. I accelerated, I managed to lose them and, at last, I was alone.

The canal you're referring to is on the river bank; it takes the overflow whenever there's a major flood. As soon as I saw it, I knew it would be one of the settings in *Point Blank.* Do you remember the scene in the cemetery where Walker is standing at his wife's grave and all around the city the freeways are swarming as though covered with ants? I shot that late in the afternoon, just at the moment when the light creates precisely

Stegman, the car salesman, the first link in the chain (Michael Strong and Lee Marvin in *Point Blank*).

that impression of swarming. And while I was out location-hunting, I discovered the excavator, an incredible machine used for digging graves. It used to be that, no matter how useless your life had been, it would at least give a gravedigger a day's work to dig your grave. For me, that summed up American life. It struck me as the greatest of all betrayals: digging a grave in ten minutes with a mechanical spade.

As for the nightmarish atmosphere of the discothèque, what I wanted it to express was all that violence seething inside his head. I visited just such a club in San Francisco where I saw similar images flashing past on a screen and met the singer Stu Gardner. I brought him to Hollywood and I reconstructed everything in the studio. It was, technically, a very complex sequence to direct, because of the wall projections. I was fascinated by this man screaming and making others scream; for them, in their despair, it was an immense relief to be given the right to scream. I didn't have enough time to develop the scene, but I remember these women shrieking and sobbing as though the desolation of their lives could be contained in a scream. Though one doesn't often have the right to cry, every one of us feels the urge.

What was MGM's attitude before, during and after the shoot?

I was extremely lucky. In his contract, Marvin had the right of approval over the script, the cast and the technical crew. Lee told MGM that he was transferring his approvals to me. You know that Margaret Booth used to be head of MGM's editing department. She had worked for the studio for more than fifty years; she had been involved with Stroheim's *Greed* and everybody was terribly afraid of her. But she was very pleased with the film's rushes. She's very modern in her outlook; she became my ally, in a way, and insisted that I be allowed to work as I wished. It was thanks to her that I had complete control over the editing.

I'd decided to make each scene monochromatic. One day, the head of the art department called a meeting to let it be known that he declined all responsibility for the film. He announced: 'There's one scene in a green office with green furniture and seven men wearing green suits, green ties and green shoes. I haven't seen anything like it since *The Wizard of*

Above 'The nightmarish atmosphere of the discothèque' (Lee Marvin in *Point Blank*).
Opposite Angie Dickinson in *Point Blank*.

Oz. The film will be unreleasable and we're going to make fools of ourselves.' Yet he was a fine painter with a very wide knowledge of his craft. I was amazed he did not understand how film emulsion reacts to tones of the same colour, or the relation between reality and the cinema. When you film this kind of scene, certain greens turn yellowish, others brownish. Artists have been applying the phenomenon for years: when you employ all the shades of a given colour, you give the illusion of the complete spectrum. The film was very stylized, each scene with its own colour; we ran the whole gamut of colours from beginning to end, moving from cool ones to warmer ones.

The film is very different from Richard Stark's book, The Hunter.

You know, I've never read the book! The first script adapted from Stark's novel was the work of David and Rafe Newhouse. They'd turned it into a somewhat dated and slightly nostalgic gangster story in the style of Raymond Chandler – another *Harper*, if you like. What intrigued me about the subject-matter was something else entirely. It was the leading character and the situations, which were very contemporary – they struck me as very relevant to modern America. But though I made drastic alterations to their script, the Newhouses liked the film!

You understand, I'm very fond of the films based on Chandler, particularly Hawks' *The Big Sleep*. But when you see them again, you notice how much they depend on dialogue. Though you think of them as fast-paced thrillers. they are in fact rather slow, unlike those of Hitchcock, who all but dispensed with dialogue. And I agree with Hitchcock that dialogue is often unnecessary in this kind of narrative and serves only to create atmosphere. The plot is always the awkward element of a thriller. You need it, but not overmuch. Another curious feature of thrillers is that the rhythm within a shot can afford to be much slower than in any other type of film as the tension has already been created. A man looks out of a window: you can focus on his face for a long, long time if the spectator knows that someone wants to kill him. In another context, you couldn't allow yourself such freedom.

In Point Blank, *Lee Marvin conforms to his public image even if, in fact, he does not kill anyone.*

What I wanted to say in the film (and, no doubt, it's a cliché) is that American society is killing itself; it's on a course of self-destruction. In the film, Walker is a catalyst. The decadence of American society makes it very vulnerable to more primitive forces. In fact, by the end, the public believes he has killed a lot of people – yet is isn't so. One critic, comparing *Point Blank* to *Bonnie and Clyde*, said that, though Bonnie and Clyde do a lot of killing, they don't give the impression of being killers, whereas one regards Marvin as a killer even if he doesn't kill anyone. I didn't want my characters to look like gangsters; I wanted them to look like businessmen and I cast neither Jews nor Italians. They've all got blue eyes.

The film has been criticized for its use of flashbacks in the manner of

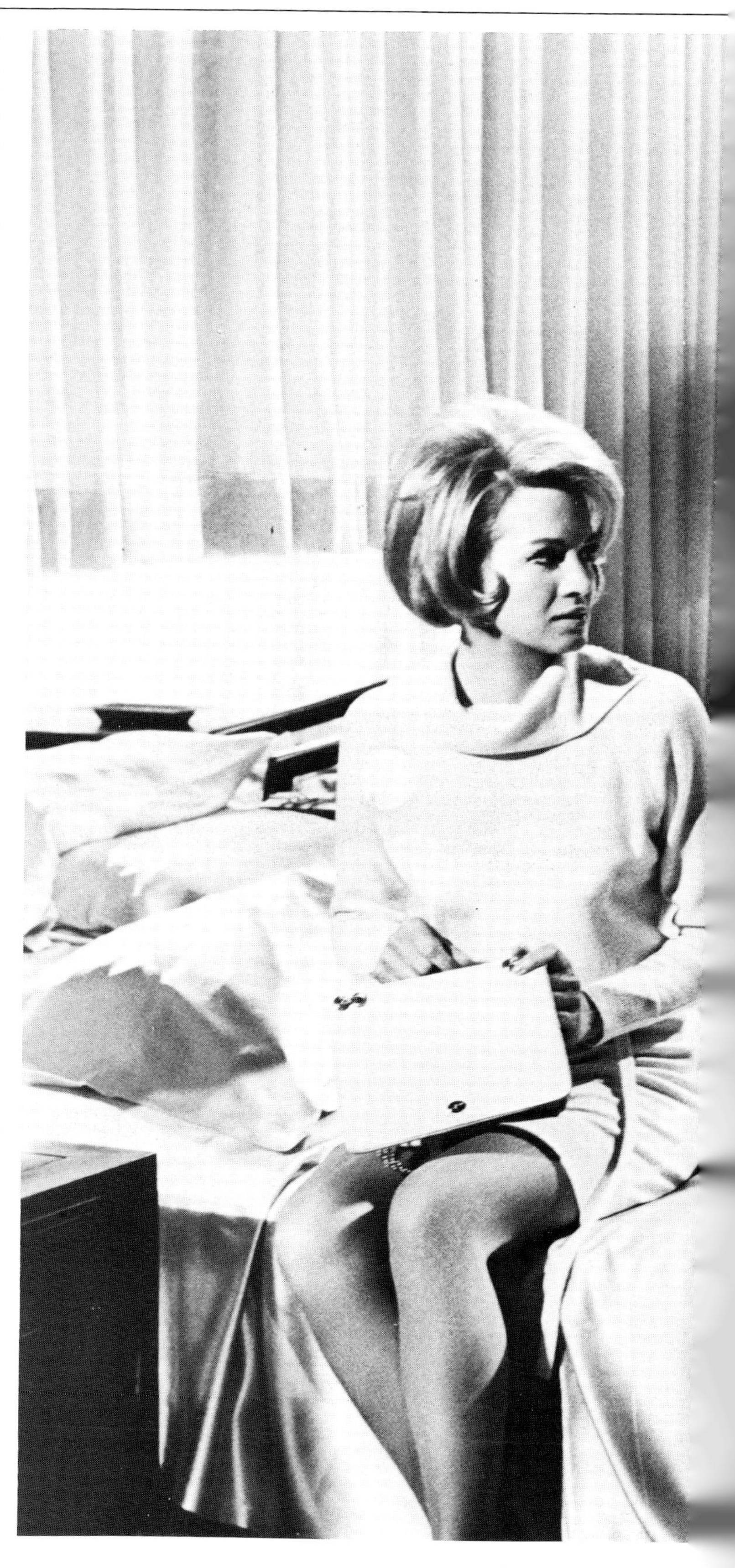

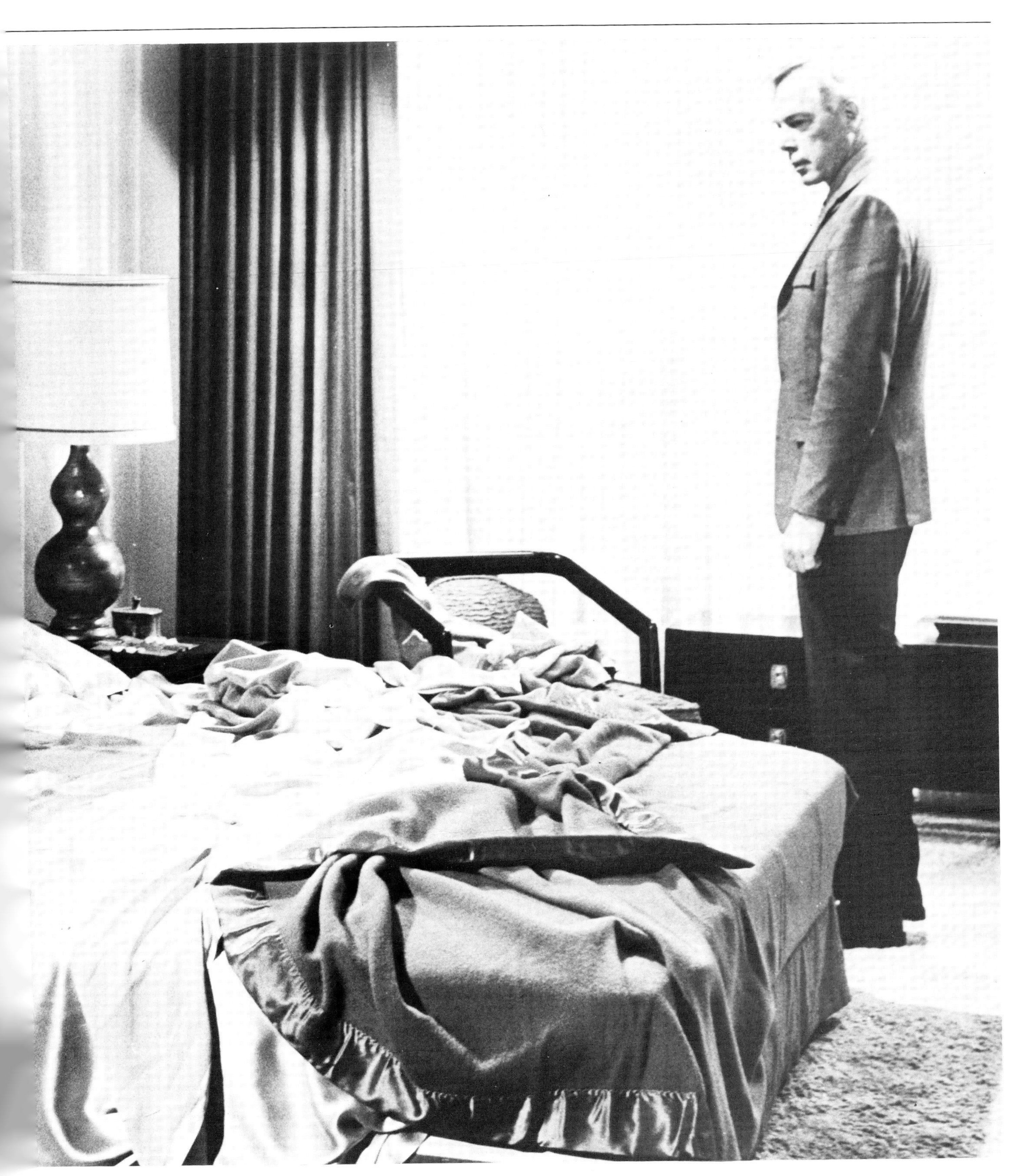

Walker is very vulnerable (Angie Dickinson and Lee Marvin in *Point Blank*).

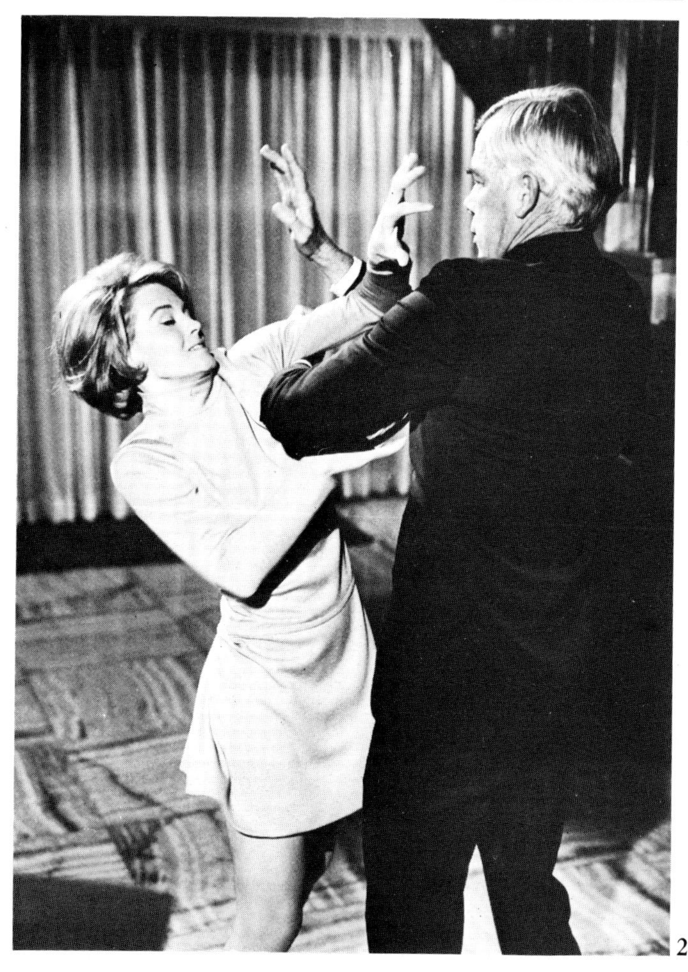

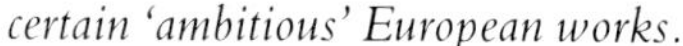

certain 'ambitious' European works.

What's important in the film is the feeling of repetition, of *déjà vu*. Everything that happens to Walker has happened to him before. There are two parallel stories: that of his wife and that of his sister-in-law. Everything that happens to him with his wife, ending with his betrayal when he is shot, happens to him all over again. His wife dies from an overdose of sleeping pills; and when he goes to see his sister-in-law, he finds her asleep, with sleeping pills beside her bed. I wanted increasingly to create the feeling of a nightmare, the impression that he is caught in a revolving door, that his life is repeating itself. For that it seemed to me necessary to use flashbacks. Overall, it isn't a very easy film, and this device enabled me to convey what was happening inside his head. And, after all, though we associate the effect with Resnais, I suppose, it's an editing style which has always existed. Griffith used it a lot in his films. In *The Birth of a Nation*, during the battle, the young boy is never without a photograph of Lillian Gish; and when he looks at it, Griffith cuts away to show us the young girl herself in order to illustrate the boy's thoughts. What Resnais did was make the device more subtle. Critics are very fond of displaying their erudition. If they're hostile to a film, they maintain that this or that was stolen from Antonioni; if they like it, they point out the wonderful allusion or homage to René Clair, etc. The cinema is a living language and once a technical process has been used successfully it becomes part of the medium's vocabulary. The public has merely to be able to understand and interpret it. Audiences were quite prepared to accept the flashbacks in *Point Blank*. They were disturbed, even 'drained', by the film. And, speaking of the editing, I'm reminded of a scene in particular, the one in which Angie Dickinson slaps Lee Marvin. Originally, it was much longer. I wanted the audience's reaction gradually to change. The scene begins by being amusing, then it becomes unpleasant and finally terrifying. When I saw it in a cinema, the audience began by laughing, almost out of relief, and I realized that I could have kept everything I'd shot – the scene could have been longer, because it worked very well.

One problem I have in writing a script without any external pressure is that, if I shoot it in the same way, there's a risk the public won't understand it. So I end by simplifying it, by making it more 'conventional'. With *Point Blank*, I was at the beginning of my career; and, particularly in the opening sequences, when Walker is injured in Alcatraz, when he attempts to swim to freedom, when he walks along the endless corridor and, at the same time, we see him shooting at the bed, I didn't hold back at all. There was, however, an exchange of dialogue between him and his wife with which I wasn't too

'His only motivation, the one thing that keeps him alive, is his quest.'
1 Lee Marvin in *Point Blank*.
2 Angie Dickinson and Lee Marvin in *Point Blank*.

happy. In the script, Marvin asks her where Reese is and whether he's sent him any money. I said to Lee: 'You aim at the bed, you empty the barrel and then you sit down, dazed, exhausted. It's a very sexual scene.' But, subsequently, Lee felt incapable of posing the initial question. Sharon Acker meanwhile replied, while Lee remained silent throughout. And it was then that I realized what the scene must become: the woman answering questions she hadn't been asked.

A situation which frequently recurs in your films is that of betrayal; for instance, in the mysterious party scene when Walker says to Reese: 'Trust me, trust me.'

The woman's betrayal is, of course, the story of Lancelot, Arthur and Guinevere. There again, the scene had been written differently. We gradually realized that it was a love scene between two men, as in those reunions of soldiers or sportsmen where everyone is a bit drunk. It could have been sentimental and stupid. Then I got the idea of having them separated by a crowd of guests; we have the impression they're slowly swimming towards each other; then they meet up, and it ends with one of them lying on top of the other.

Like many of your protagonists, Walker is a marginal.

His only motivation, the one thing that keeps him alive, is his quest. When it's completed, he ceases to exist. Seeing the film, one should be able to imagine that this whole story of vengeance is taking place inside his head at the moment of his death. In any case, that's a possible interpretation. He's powerful, he can destroy the whole world, because his values aren't those of the gangsters; he isn't afraid of the same things, he isn't afraid of dying. He exposes their weaknesses. He's a catalyst who exposes the corruption of their world.

'He isn't afraid of what they're afraid of: death', Lee Marvin in Alcatraz (*Point Blank*).

1968

A fable reduced to its essential: two men on an island, neither speaking the other's language (Lee Marvin and Toshiro Mifune in *Hell in the Pacific*).

Hell in the Pacific

No Man is an Island

Hell in the Pacific is, in every sense, an elemental film. It is as though, before undertaking a complex and multi-levelled fable such as *Leo the Last*, Boorman wished to make a clean sweep by creating a different kind of fable, one in which narrative would be reduced to the bare minimum: two men on an island, neither speaking the other's language. Elemental, too, in the sense that here, Boorman, a cosmic film-maker, plays with water, fire, air and earth, to the point where they become almost complementary characters to his ascetic pair of leading men. When, on the beach, with his back to the sea, and beneath a dazzling blue sky, Mifune sets fire to the forest, all four elements have been symbolically convened. For the first time, after the urban desert of *Point Blank*, and before the claustrophobic cul-de-sac of *Leo the Last*, the director assigns to nature the fundamental role which it will never forfeit in his work, from *Deliverance* to *The Emerald Forest*. It isn't difficult to see the major risk run by *Hell in the Pacific*: that of being no more than a stylistic exercise or simplistic allegory. What permits Boorman to avoid such a double trap is the sheer sensuousness of his direction, which makes us *feel* the rustling of leaves on his characters' bodies, the relief instilled by a torrential downpour, the sun's rays glinting through the treetops, the mud mask that turns a mere man into a terrifyingly outlandish creature. His humour, too: the sardonic tone adopted by the director contrives to distance the spectator from the evolution of the relationship between the two enemies. As he would later do with Sean Connery, disguised as a blushing bride in *Zardoz*, Boorman has Lee Marvin, that emblem of cinematic virility, play the role of a little wife 'fed up with cooking for her husband' or of a dog scurrying off to fetch a stick when Toshiro Mifune, pretending not to understand, has refused to play his master's game.

But the strength of *Hell in the Pacific* no doubt also derives from the fact that he has managed to preserve the truth behind the fable, the man behind the symbol. The American and the Japanese represent, to be sure, their respective cultures (which accounts for the casting of two 'larger-than-life' stars, archetypical images of their countries of origin); but the actors playing them are, in a sense, reliving their own former experiences (Mifune was a non-commissioned officer in the Japanese army and Marvin a Marine at Saipan during the Second World War) on the very locations on which some of the war's bloodiest battles were fought. The ruined buildings in which the two men take shelter at the end of the film once housed the Japanese naval communications centre for the Pacific, receiving messages from Midway and Guadalcanal. Thus, if the director has claimed that *Point Blank* was, in part, a documentary on Lee Marvin, *Hell in the Pacific* is its continuation; and the first words spoken by the sleeping American pilot: 'I told you to go. Why did you marry me?' are uncannily reminiscent of the opening shots of Walker in his cell in Alcatraz.

The film is constructed in three movements. The first sets the two men face to face; the second establishes their solidarity in building a raft and sailing it; and the third separates them again when, coming into contact with the flotsam of their respective civilizations, they allow national stereotypes to reassert themselves and, with them, the original antagonism. The first, and longest, movement has itself a tripartite structure, corresponding, as Gérard Legrand has noted, to the dialectics of master and slave as described by Hegel and subsequently analysed by Alexandre Kojève. By failing to kill the American when the opportunity presented itself, the Japanese lays the foundation for a process of reciprocal gratitude, com-

The basic confrontation of *Hell in the Pacific* sums up all such conflicts at the heart of Boorman's films (Lee Marvin and Toshiro Mifune).

1 Walker confronting one of the Organization's henchmen (Lee Marvin in *Point Blank*).
2 The hillbillies versus the dudes (Herbert 'Cowboy' Coward, Jon Voight, Ned Beatty and Billy McKinney in *Deliverance*).

Arthur face to face with his son Mordred (Nigel Terry and Robert Addie in *Excalibur*).

pleted in his turn by the American when he designates him his slave. 'The Japanese calculates that he can free himself by initially, and only apparently, "agreeing" to work in the presence of an idle *master*.'[69] Though this lethal tug-of-war ends by driving them all but insane – one of them will run screaming down the beach to the ocean, the other will obsessively hum military marches and explode his now useless ammunition – it also has its comic side (as, for example, when the American urinates on the Japanese). It shows, too, in spite – or perhaps because – of the subtlety of the torments which they inflict on each other, to what degree each needs the other for his own survival; and their mutual dependence ends, moreover, by gradually shading into sympathy and solidarity. Finally, their incapacity to kill each other is conveyed through the mental images which punctuate their initial confrontation, as each fantasizes the death of *the enemy* (the film's original title) in accordance with the most characteristic military technique of his race: for the Japanese, a bamboo stalk sharpened into a sword; for the American, a 'close combat' knife.

It's possible to compare the film to Defoe's *Robinson Crusoe*, except that, here, each becomes in turn the Man Friday of the other. In addition, where the novelist illustrated *homo economicus* by making his hero the incarnation of economic individualism, enjoying total freedom in the role ascribed to him, the film-maker opts for a more pluralistic conception of humanity, one in which mental, physical and even mythic attributes play as significant a role as purely economic ones and ineluctably force their subject into a state of dependence. And if

Defoe's masterpiece recorded the triumph of Western man, *Hell in the Pacific* demonstrates, on the contrary, the Oriental's superior ability to adjust to his environment and domesticate nature in order to ensure that he himself will stay alive. It is he who collects the rainwater, invents a fish-trap, plants a garden and protects himself with a system of miniature bells. Even with all his training manuals, the American pilot proves far less adaptable.

In *Hell in the Pacific*, we also return to the theme of the voyage. The tranquil lyricism of the journey by raft (filmed in superb monochromatic images by Conrad Hall) evokes the rediscovery of freedom and friendship on the part of its two passengers – until, that is, they once more find themselves surrounded precisely by the trappings of the war which they

Mutual dependence: Lee Marvin and Toshiro Mifune (*Hell in the Pacific*).

The Japanese adapts more easily to his surroundings (Toshiro Mifune and Lee Marvin in *Hell in the Pacific*).

had sought to escape. And the disenchanted irony of such a conclusion, typical of Boorman, is equalled by the manner in which the film portrays the extraordinary ingenuity with which men reshape their environment – whatever it might happen to be – only to set about destroying it again in the wake of some idiotic quarrel. Thus the brilliance of Boorman's *mise en scène* (which, though it could hardly be more physical, paradoxically never strays far from abstraction) is placed yet again at the service of his ideas – ideas on the relationship of nature and culture, on man's capacity equally to ensure his pre-eminence in a hostile world and engineer his own downfall.

I believe Hell in the Pacific *began as a Broadway play.*

It had a rather peculiar gestation. Marvin had always admired Mifune and was keen to make a film with him. The producer Reuben Bercovitch brought us a short story, which was how it all started. When I said I'd like to adapt it for the screen, I was told there existed a play with the same theme – a play I didn't know and still don't know. The author of the play sued and won damages. According to Bercovitch, any resemblance between the play and the short story he had written in collaboration with a screenwriter from Toho Films was purely coincidental. In any event, the situation was virtually the same: a Japanese and an American alone on a desert island.

What attracted you to the subject-matter of Hell in the Pacific?

Among other things, the notion of playing a trick on the movie

John Boorman directs Lee Marvin and Toshiro Mifune (shooting *Hell in the Pacific*).

industry by making a silent film – or, at least, seeing if I could. There is a little dialogue, of course, but it's unimportant. What interested me, too, was the relationship of the individual with the society to which he belongs. To what extent can a man exist outside his own society? In particular, men who have been trained as soldiers. How do they behave when they're no longer directly influenced by that society? The question of killing is also raised. These men were trained to kill; but outside the context of war, outside the ritual of murder which is what war represents, they were incapable of killing. I do think that's true. One of the obscene aspects of war is the way in which it legalizes crime and makes it respectable. That strikes me as fundamentally contrary to human nature – and it's society which is its cause.

The racial aspect also interested me – the relationship between a Japanese and an American, both of them from a military background but separated by so many factors. I would have liked to develop that element even further, but it was a very difficult film to make. Most of the resources on which one can depend in a normal film no longer applied to *Hell in the Pacific*: the juxtaposition of various types of action, the use of dialogue, the possibility of different settings. What I was able to achieve was very limited; and the film became simpler and simpler to the point where, by the end, I began to wonder if it really existed – in particular, because I had shot the whole film with an Ariflex camera and without sound. When I edited it, I found myself with two hours of silent cinema, two hours of foliage!

How long did you stay on the island?

Four months. Two or three weeks of preparation, two weeks of rehearsals with the actors. I discovered at the end that, for this kind of film, a written script is practically useless. Its only value is informative. What really counts is working with the actors, having fun, 'trying out' scenes. So I took notes, I sketched out scenes – I made nearly six hundred drawings. And these became the real script, the basis of the film. First of all, to be sure, there had been the short story. Alexander Jacobs and I worked on an adaptation for two weeks, a version which the producers rejected. The film was going to be abandoned. But Marvin read that first version and liked it a lot. So we were told to continue working on it, except that the production company requested that another screenwriter join us – this was Eric Bercovici. The three of us then worked in rather uneasy collaboration. I also wanted a Japanese scenarist to flesh out the details of Mifune's character. That's why I called on Hashimoto, a charming man who had written the scripts of Kurosawa's *Rashomon* and *The Seven Samurai*. We discussed scenes together, and I sketched out a treatment which I gave to Bercovici , to Jacobs and, in a translated version, to Hashimoto. Each of them would then add his own observations, which we collated; at this point, the scene would become definitive. It was exhausting, and at the end the scenario was nothing but a description of events: how do you write a script without dialogue? It can never be anything but a point of departure, a guide – all the same, it's a crucial stage in the preparation of a film.

After two or three weeks' work at the Goldwyn studios, Hashimoto came to me with a proposal for a different version of the story and requested a week to write it. When he presented me with it, I realized that he'd turned it into a comedy in the style of *Yojimbo*; he'd treated everything farcically. It wasn't bad in itself, but it bore no relation to what I wanted. So we continued working on the script and shooting began. Mifune immediately created dreadful problems. He was very proud of what he had prepared, but he invariably missed the point of the scenes he was playing. I'd have a word with him and advise him, but he'd make the same mistakes all over again. After three or four days, I realized that Hashimoto had given him the script which I'd rejected.

'They were trained to kill but outside the context of war they were incapable of it' (Lee Marvin and Toshiro Mifune in *Hell in the Pacific*).

Was, for example, the scene in which Marvin sends Mifune to fetch the piece of wood written in advance?

No, I got the idea while rehearsing with the actors. There were several scenes of the same kind. But I was looking for just one which would encapsulate them all. I had the idea of the piece of wood which, on Marvin's orders, Mifune would fetch like a dog. We began to rehearse it; but, as it was a new idea, Mifune didn't understand what we wanted from him. Lee threw the piece of wood and asked him to run after it. Mifune didn't move. So Lee went to fetch it, and I thought it would be funnier to keep the idea of Mifune pretending not to understand and Marvin finally fetching the wood himself. The scene was much stronger: it showed that the man being tormented was the master, not the slave. When Mifune is master, he's depressed and neurotic; when he's the slave, he's much more relaxed – and the same is true of Marvin. What each of them found most difficult to accept was being responsible for the other.

In the film, the American copes with the situation far less well than the Japanese. Marvin never stops insulting Mifune and treating him like an idiot, though it's the Japanese who knows how to fish and find water. It's Marvin, rather, who is helpless.

That's very true of relations between Americans and Japanese. It's what happened during the last war: the Americans always had the feeling they were fighting hordes of little monkeys. They had the same attitude towards blacks. When I screened the film for a black audience, they completely identified with Mifune. In the scene where Marvin urinates on Mifune, a black stood up and shouted: 'And they're still pissing on everybody!'

The two men land on the island with everything that 'civilization' has given them. Little by little, they shed these influences and arrive at a modus vivendi. *With* Life *magazine, the world reappears and they become just as hostile to each other as before.*

People of different cultures and races can only live together, can only coexist, if they have a common objective. In this case, for example, building a raft. Once the job is finished, there's no further contact. It's pointless to say 'people ought to try and get on with each other' or 'they ought to understand the need for mutual respect'. What they need is a shared objective. Business is an obvious example. The people who get on best with each other are businessmen. If you have to sell something to somebody, you treat him well, since you have a mutual need. If not, the differences between you can only increase. Marvin and Mifune wanted their relationship to continue as before. It was an illegitimate relationship, almost an erotic one, if you like. In a sense, both of them were married men . . . married to the societies which produced them. But society couldn't accept their illegitimate relationship and so it was destroyed. When, at the end, Marvin speaks of God, we can see the hypocrisy of the American system, which is founded on the Christian faith, on belief in God. It's part of the Constitution. But, in fact, it's a de-Christianized country, a godless country. What I wanted to show was that they were trying to find a reason for separating, they were making up reasons. They were piling up all the clichés of their civilization, one of which is language: the only scene in the film where they speak to each other, where they have a conversation, is the one just before their separation. Marvin asks: 'Are you married?', which is, in fact, the first thing any two soldiers would say when they meet. Here, however, it happens at the last moment. As soon as they begin to spout clichés, received ideas on God and society, they themselves become clichés. They are reintegrated into their society.

The mental images, which are wholly justified in Point Blank, *are less so here in the beach scene, where each of them imagines killing the other. It's out of key with the style of the film.*

I'd love to cut them. I put them in partly because of the pressure that was exerted on me. The producers wanted some violence since there were two violent men in the film. There was also a tension in this scene with the two men face to face: the audience knew they weren't going to kill each other. I wanted to lessen that tension by showing them something they felt certain they weren't going to see, but which was beginning to obsess them. I didn't want them to feel conditioned. All the same, it would be a better film if there weren't these shots.

What was your relationship with Marvin?

One of my reasons for making the film was Lee Marvin. Probably it comes from my training in documentary, but I've always been interested in Marvin's personality. *Hell in the Pacific* is very close to him. His formative years were those in which he fought the Japanese in the Pacific. He comes from a middle-class background, his parents were very creative people and he himself was extremely well educated, with a genuinely artistic sensibility. When he was seventeen, he enlisted in the Marines; and, from what one can gather, he felt compelled to conceal and repress his interest in the arts and be a 'tough guy' like his buddies. From the start of his career in the film industry, it was the role he found himself playing; and he has emphasized that side of his character ever since. When I met him, he was forty-seven, and the sensitivity which he had repressed since his youth was aching to find expression, to become once more part of his personality. There's a feminine side to him which I used and developed in *Hell in the Pacific.*

Reliving that period of his life provoked a kind of crisis in him. The producers wanted him to kill Mifune in the end. And perhaps that's also what the public wanted. But I refused. Everything that Lee was – his violence, his killer's instinct – made him want to kill Mifune. While we were shooting, Lee would say to me: 'Don't let me get too close to him or I'll kill that sonofabitch.' I always kept him in check, as I wanted the ending to refer, like the structure of the whole film, to T. S. Eliot's poem 'The Hollow Men', whose closing lines are:

> *This is the way the world ends*
> *Not with a bang but a whimper.*

The fact that we were able to film that ending was a kind of catharsis for Marvin. He said to me: 'I'm sick of killing people to gratify millions of spectators. From now on they can kill each other.' You understand, then, why it upsets me to think that they imposed another ending on the American and English version: the island is bombed out of existence. It was the worst thing that could have happened to the film; it doesn't make sense by ending it with a 'bang'. At first, my version was screened in the United States, but it was changed for distribution nationwide.

Did you think of Defoe's Robinson Crusoe, *and have you read Michel Tournier's novel* Friday, or The Other Island, *which bears an odd resemblance to the film.*

No, I don't know Tournier's book. I saw Buñuel's film of *Robinson Crusoe* a long time ago and I found it very interesting. Of course, I reread the book while preparing the film. Oddly enough, it wasn't terribly useful, even if one can't help being struck by immediate comparisons. I wanted to go much further in the scenes where they retrogress, where they begin to behave like animals, but I couldn't persuade Mifune to do it. He believed he was defending the honour of Japan. Just as Marvin wanted to relive his personal experience, so Mifune wanted to relive the war – with Japan on the winning side. He refused to do anything that might have been considered uncouth; he was determined to retain his honour. In a way, he was right: in that kind of situation, the Japanese are probably far more resourceful and far less likely to go to pieces. That

'Mifune wanted to relive the war – with Japan on the winning side' (*Hell in the Pacific*).

apart, like all Japanese, he has a highly developed sense of honour and no sense of honesty. That's because their written language is so different from their spoken language that they don't feel that one constrains the other. I'd rehearse with him until five in the morning to persuade him to perform one little piece of business. By the end, he had accepted my arguments. Then, on the set, he would revert to his original idea and would refuse to be budged. Despite his unconditional acceptance of my ideas, he was capable of undoing a whole night's work. And he simply wouldn't give way. But when I was hospitalized during the shoot, and the producers considered engaging another director, Mifune announced that he would refuse to continue the film with someone else. I have to say, too, that he didn't speak a word of English. Marvin, however, taught him a few choice expressions; and, when we finished shooting, his vocabulary consisted of a dozen or so of the most obscene words in the English language.

What is the line of dialogue he speaks at the end of their conversation about building the boat?

I really shouldn't tell you. To see the film, one ought to be able to understand either English or Japanese, but not both. In Japan, there were no subtitles for Marvin's dialogue: there are, to be sure, perhaps more spectators there capable of understanding English than there are in the United States and England capable of understanding Japanese. Anyway, at that point, Mifune says: 'We're going to die if we stay here, I'm sure of it.'

Which lenses did you use, and what shooting method, for the chase through the jungle?

I used the anamorphic 200 or 300mm, which corresponds to a normal 100 or 150mm. It was very dark in the jungle, which required extensive lighting. And when it rains, there's simply nothing to be done. Sometimes we had to wait three days for the rain to stop; sometimes we'd find ourselves shooting scenes with artificial rain. Shooting in a jungle really creates havoc: twenty people were employed to replant it! We made the film on the island of Palau, between New Guinea and the Philippines.

Lee Marvin and Toshiro Mifune (*Hell in the Pacific*).

For the chase, I used two classic methods for filming westerns: on the one hand, what is called the 'western dolly'; on the other, a camera that pivots on a stand while the actor moves around it – it's used in westerns for conversations on horseback.

You've often spoken of your interest in stylization. Here you had an extreme case of location shooting.

I wanted the island to appear both hostile and nightmarish. I crossed the whole of the Pacific to find it. It would have been more practical to film in Hawaii and we did begin our search in that area of the Pacific, since it boasts every possible type of landscape. But it just wasn't suitable. The camera possesses an extraordinary ability to bring out the spirit of a place, and Hawaii has been domesticated by its tourists. Besides which, as soon as you have palm trees on the screen, it becomes impossible to suggest that life is anything but pleasant! So we found this island of Palau, which looks both inhospitable and strangely beautiful – the coconut palms had been destroyed by disease, the rocks had been eroded and the jungle is overgrown and descends right to the beach. The shoot was very difficult because we were miles from anywhere. An ancient DC4 would land every two weeks, which meant that I couldn't fire anyone as we'd have had him on our hands for a fortnight! We chose our settings very carefully in order to achieve a formal unity, a visual coherence, the kind of autonomous universe I try to obtain for all my films – even this one, which was shot entirely on location. Like *Point Blank*, *Hell in the Pacific* could conceivably be narrated from the viewpoint of a man about to die. As he leaps from his aircraft, the pilot (Marvin) might be thinking of what would happen to him if he found himself stranded on a desert island. As I recall, other than Eliot's 'The Hollow Men', my reference was William Golding's novel *Pincher Martin*, which I got Lee to read. It's the story of a pilot who plummets into the ocean, reaches an island, breaks his ankle and clings on to a rock. It's an extraordinary tale of man's instinct for self-preservation. At the end, a fisherman discovers his body: in reality, he was dead from the moment he touched the water. *Hell in the Pacific* was also a film about the power of nature and, in that sense, it was a preparation for *Deliverance*.

1970

Leo's affinity with birds reflects his two contradictory impulses: to aspire towards the Other or else curl up within himself (Marcello Mastroianni in *Leo the Last*).

Leo the Last

The Melancholic Observer

Leo is, for a long time, defined by his eyes. And Boorman's film, to begin with, is the story of those eyes, the sole link between their owner and the outside world. Leo is an impatient, feverish observer, sensitive to the slightest tremor, lying in wait for something, *anything*, to happen, like a huntsman stalking his prey. But seeing is essentially a form of defeat. There is in Leo's attitude a possessive violence which will always be frustrated: all he will be left with is the sense of his own irresolution and impotence – the same impotence from which his voyeurism derives. From within his huge, sumptuously appointed house he contemplates the poverty of the street outside, inhabited as it is by blacks and poor whites. Jean Starobinski has described this function of sight: 'Of all the senses, it is sight which is most clearly governed by impatience. A magical impulse, never wholly effective, never quite discouraged, accompanies each of one's glances: seizing, undressing, petrifying, penetrating. The eye is an excess: it guarantees one's conscience an exit from the space occupied by one's body.'[213] With his telescope, Leo endeavours to escape from the body in which he is enclosed, from the insensitive, indifferent self. But he is, at the same time, afraid of venturing forth, of accepting the risk of becoming emotionally involved, of communicating, of living.

An affinity with birds reflects his two contradictory impulses: to aspire towards the Other or else curl up within himself. The bird represents winged movement, the dissolution of car-

The excessive eye: optical games in Boorman's films (Marcello Mastroianni in *Leo the Last*).

Barbara Ferris (*Catch Us If You Can*).
Lee Marvin and Toshiro Mifune (*Hell in the Pacific*).

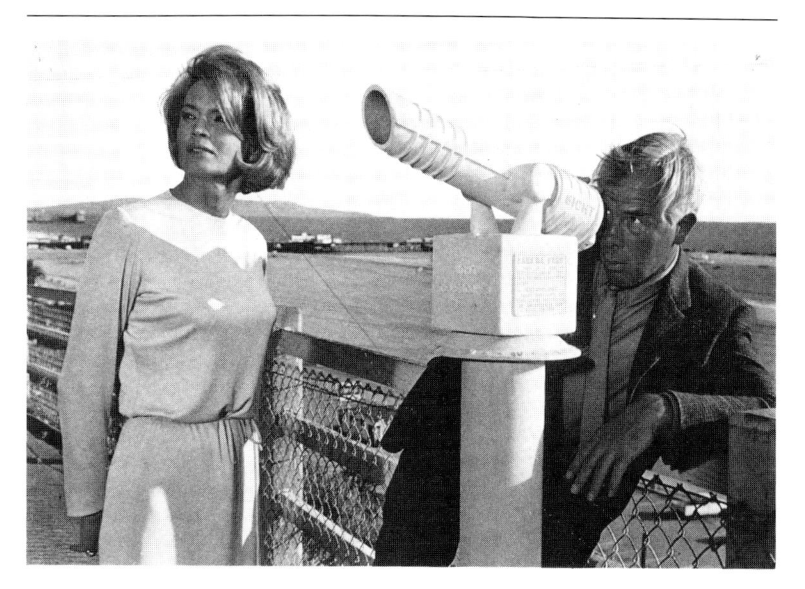

Angie Dickinson and Lee Marvin (*Point Blank*).
Powers Boothe and William Rodriguez (*The Emerald Forest*).

nality, the withdrawal from materiality, the desire to leave behind the squalid inadequacy of the earth. But also, for Bachelard, 'the bird, an almost completely spherical creature, is certainly the highest, most sublime, most divine point of living concentration. It is impossible to find, or even imagine, a higher degree of unity. However, if such an excess of concentration invests the bird with great personal strength, it also implies its extreme individuality, its isolation, its social weakness.'[193] For Leo, a bird is both what he would like to become and what he is. In a revealing slip of the tongue, he thanks the Companions of Saragossa for having welcomed him into their *womb*. His nostalgia for the seamless circularity of a protective cocoon is no less strong than his desire to escape. But the perfection and sphericity so admired by Leo have as their corollary the isolation and social weakness from which he suffers. Life cannot be contained in a ball and the melancholic observer gradually begins to discover, from the bird-infested rooftops, the existence of his fellow men. The discovery disturbs him; he sees others without being able to reach them, just as he sees himself without being able to reach himself. What he fears most, as he is the first to admit, is *being seen*: 'Seeing without being seen'.

Leo resembles Walker, the hero of *Point Blank*, in his isolation – except that *he* has not sought it. Distrusting emotions, regretting his lack of knowledge and experience, he is, beneath his whimsical exterior, a touching figure. Though not unaware of the beauty underlying the humdrum surface of life, and painfully groping towards an understanding of human sympathy, he remains trammelled by his incapacity to grasp them. The theme of water, introduced in the credit titles by shots of some unspecified, fog-swathed liquid, attests to that impotence (which is also sexual in connotation, as witness his relations with Margaret, Salambo and the bird, the latter a common phallic symbol). Water, often the sign of purification or fertility, is here the insidious leitmotif of an ash-grey, death-obsessed world: the persistent rain; the ludicrous scene in the

Confrontations in the laundromat, the café and the street: Marcello Mastroianni, Glenna Forster Jones and Calvin Lockhart (*Leo the Last*).

public baths with everyone feeling regenerated except Leo, who feels only wet and embarrassed; the scene in the laundry. Leo dreams, rather, of the sun (and of other islands, the Galapagos); and if he prefers the black race above all, it's doubtless because it originated in those lands which the sun 'warms up'. It's through his admiration for the black Roscoe – who, in his attempts to capture a bird, seems to be taking flight himself – that Leo starts to communicate with the world. His ambiguous friendship with Roscoe (he will later confess to having kept Salambo for him until he should be released from prison) specifically illustrates the evolution of his emotional life.

From being a story of observation, *Leo the Last* becomes one of discovery, of a movement out of isolation into contact with the world. Initially incapable of mastering his experience, the victim of some unexplained trauma or failure, Leo will gradually undergo his transformation, without the dubious assistance of an entourage whose only reason for wishing him to lead a normal life is that they might exert a tighter control over

1 Bernard Boston, Marcello Mastroianni, Roy Stewart and Keefe West (*Leo the Last*).
2 Billie Whitelaw, Calvin Lockhart and Glenna Forster Jones (*Leo the Last*).

The absence of sentimentality and despondency: Thomas Buson and Kenneth J. Warren (*Leo the Last*).

him and who will attempt to have him confined when he flees their influence. Boorman's fourth film can therefore be seen as a decisive departure in relation to those preceding it, all of which ended in the tragedy of total isolation. Before, the island was viewed as a haven which invariably turned into a prison. Here, on the contrary, the cul-de-sac becomes a peninsula, and self-indulgent absurdism gives way to socially motivated revolt. But such a revolt can only be collective: the failures recorded in the first two films were the inevitable outcome of an individual's struggle against a well-organized society of virtually unlimited power. Leo, the representative of the governing classes, assumes in turn every conceivable attitude *vis-à-vis* those whom he exploits, before defecting to their cause. He begins by living off the rents paid by the blacks without even suspecting the source of his income (in blissful ignorance himself, his own conscience undisturbed, he lets his underlings deal with this neo-colonialist racket); he then becomes vaguely, apathetically aware of their wretchedness; charity fleetingly tempts him but, as with Buñuel's *Nazarin*, it rebounds against him (killing the person to whom it is offered); finally, he is spurred into action, with the destruction of the master's house as apparently the only solution. The fire next time, Boorman is telling us; but also that revolt, like charity, must begin at home and not in flight. It isn't, of course, enough simply to sweep the pavement in front of one's own doorstep; but, to change the world, one must also change one's own life and world.

The danger of such an analysis is that one reduces the fable

Glenna Forster Jones (*Leo the Last*).

to mere words, whereas its strength derives precisely from its concreteness. The director's lucidity, the absence of sentimentality and despondency (with a subject which lends itself to them), no less than the directorial style, distinguishes *Leo the Last* from certain allegories *à la* Capra or de Sica (e.g. *Miracle in Milan*) to which it has been compared. If an affinity can be detected, it might rather be with the contemporary English theatre. Boorman, a friend of Peter Nichols and Charles Wood, an admirer of Arden and Wesker, is as concerned as they are to expose the violence inherent in every society, the underlying conflicts, and to devise a form of realism capable of accommodating both stylization and poetic lyricism, 'at an equal distance from naturalism and Expressionism'.[210] John Arden's *The Waters of Babylon* took as its theme the comparable situation of a Polish émigré in London, the landlord of an insalubrious block of flats whose black tenants he exploits. One of his acquaintances, a political agitator, manufactures bombs to be used during state visits by socialist politicians. Racism, prostitution and housing exploitation are as closely bound up as in *Leo the Last*; and Boorman's film contains numerous references to a whole period of English life, the wave of black immigrants in the 1950s coinciding with the arrival of Hungarian émigrés in 1956, then Czech in 1968, and the frequent racial disturbances which resulted. In this context, the neo-fascist group which rallies to the Shakespearian evocation of national grandeur, 'This sceptred isle . . .', and actively prepares to defend the country by military means, is rather less 'symbolic' than might at first appear.

The tiny cross-section of humanity, then, on which the film-maker has focused his attention is not only a microcosm, an emblematic representation of the world at large; it also depicts a slice of lived experience, which a poet's eye has somehow rendered surreal. Boorman's originality lies in the way he succeeds in constantly playing off realism and stylization: his film is a fable, but one which parodies itself. Leo may be the Fisher King, ruined and physically debilitated, and his native soil may have become a waste land which it will be for him to restore, but the Knights of the Round Table are just a

The journey becomes an inner adventure. Brinsley Forde and Marcello Mastroianni (*Leo the Last*).

collection of nonentities living in dank basements and the Grail itself nothing but a sugar-bowl topped by a silver strawberry. Yet the quest is a poignant one, for all that it may seem absurd. A man travels towards an uncertain goal and, like all of Boorman's heroes, suffers adversity as the goal begins to elude him. His journey is transformed into an inner adventure and, for the first time, anxiety gives way to exaltation. As we have seen, moreover, the fable is not without its own sardonic annotation; reality itself is undermined by a narrative form which juxtaposes realistic dialogue and songs, a voice-off commentary honeycombed with quotations and a highly theatrical conception of décor.

Though the film can therefore be read on several levels, these are unified by a wholly personal sensibility which never compromises its more formal, more deliberately distancing parameters. Boorman's brilliance is such that he is able to assimilate an extraordinary variety of styles and approaches (irony, lyricism, symbolism, realism) without ever impairing the unity of his personal vision. If he is fond of referring to T. S. Eliot – and, in this instance, specifically to 'The Love Song of J. Alfred Prufrock' – it is, of course, because of obvious thematic analogies (Prufrock, the prisoner of his own dispassion, is the man who does not dare, who thinks of having 'squeezed the universe into a ball', who from a distance watches men at windows in their short-sleeves, who is finally, like the evening, 'a patient anaesthetized on a table')[200] but even more, it strikes me, because both the poet and he are concerned to fuse emotion and thought, to expose the presence of the idea in the image. Nor are such preoccupations dissimilar to those of Losey, from *Eva* to *Secret Ceremony*, with their formalization of reality and interplay of metaphorical relationships. From the banality of the everyday Boorman extracts those myths embedded in the collective unconscious, but he never attempts to address us by way of some abstract discourse or pre-

1

2

Diverse moods (ironic, lyric, symbolic, realistic).
1 Marcello Mastroianni (*Leo the Last*).
2 Ram John Holder, Marcello Mastroianni (*Leo the Last*).

programmed declaration of intentions. We are not invited to provide a purely intellectual response, but to *feel* the thought as a physical experience. It would appear that, in *Leo the Last*, Boorman was determined to find out just how much elegance and subtlety he could deploy without the spectator ever losing touch with his characters, and without their ever being less than 'natural' in language and gesture. The primary task he set himself was that of avoiding the trap of realism without forfeiting its thematic richness; and if, on occasion, one might criticize a hint of self-indulgence (in the meal and orgy scenes, for example), the sense of balance, precarious as it must have been, is almost always brilliantly sustained.

Faced with the chaos around him, the modern artist finds two paths open to him: depicting that chaos complacently and adding to the general confusion the particular confusion of his own style; or proposing a few potential solutions only after unequivocally setting forth the problems besetting the world in

3

4

3 Marcello Mastroianni, Alba, Billie Whitelaw and Graham Crowden (*Leo the Last*).
4 Graham Crowden, Billie Whitelaw (*Leo the Last*).

which he lives. By choosing the second path, by avoiding demagoguery and over-simplification, and by seamlessly interlacing ideas and emotions, Boorman has composed a deeply affecting hymn to despair and eventual liberation (a liberation, however, not untainted by bitterness: for Leo is alone at the end, while his former tenants stroll cheerfully away). An incantatory work, basing its rhythm on the blues which comment on the narrative, *Leo the Last* advances from rejection to acceptance and, by the sheer power of its *mise en scène* – of, in other words, those *eyes* which are at the centre of the film – lays bare that which exists beyond action and appearance.

Interview

What was the origin of Leo the Last*?*

It began as a one-act play by George Tabori, *The Prince*, which was set in New York and had as its protagonist a man observing his neighbours from the opposite side of the street. Tabori translated Brecht and was influenced by him. Perhaps traces of that influence can be detected in the film, but his play also bore a resemblance to Greek tragedy: in fact, at the end, Leo blinded himself by gouging his eyes out because they had offended him. It interested me because I had just spent two years in America and the problem of an atrophied emotional life – here, that of someone incapable of communicating with his fellow men – seemed to me what was affecting the American middle classes. I wanted to remove the subject from a particularized social situation; if I had shot it in Harlem, the social environment would have inhibited what I was trying to say. It would have overwhelmed the film's content. I therefore wanted to create a totally artificial world, though one that would possess its own reality.

I began by exploring the theme. To start with, for instance, Laszlo didn't exist, but I was looking for some Iago-like character to articulate Leo's story, to articulate what was going through his mind. He's a character from the underworld who

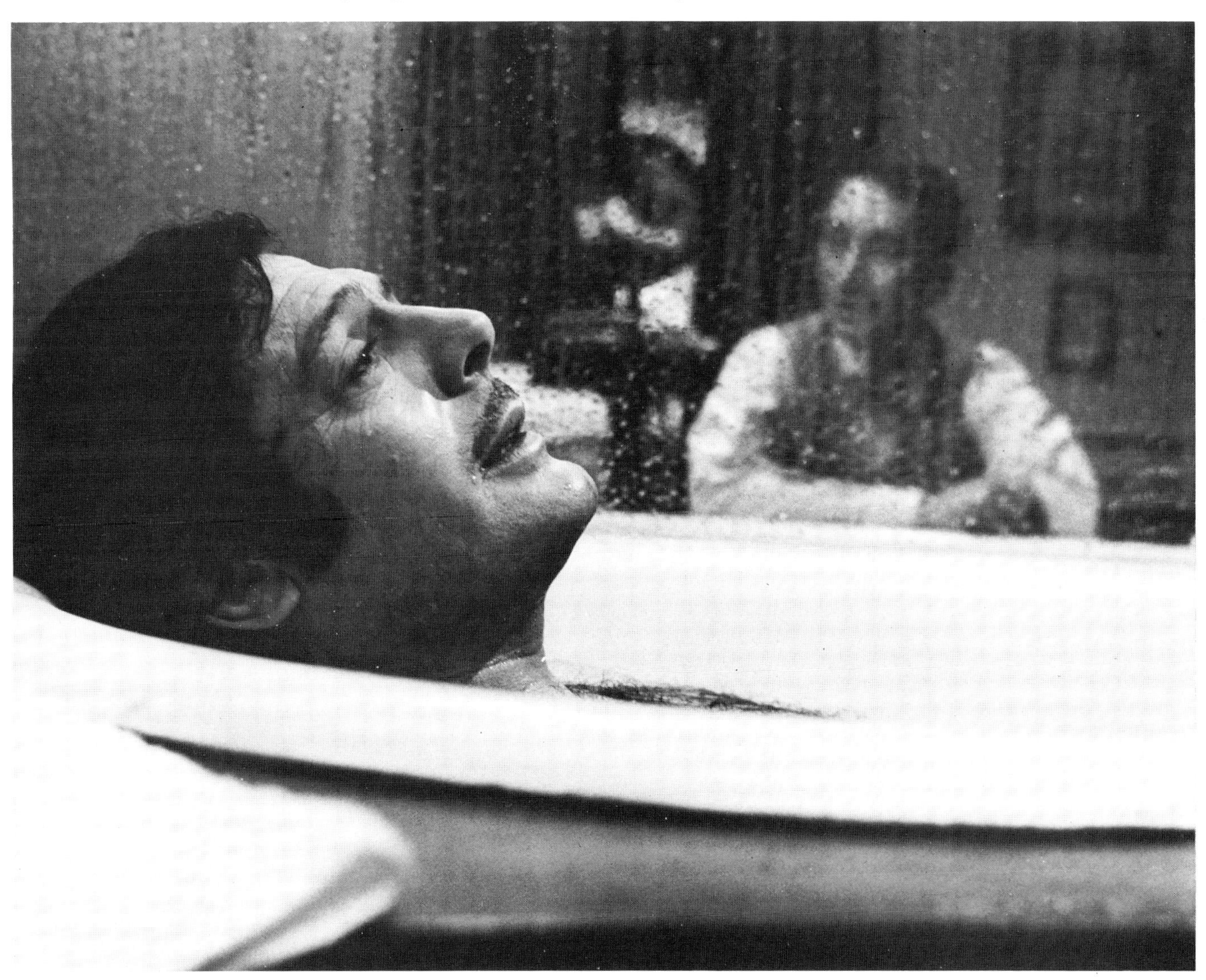

Opposite John Boorman (shooting *Leo the Last*).
Above 'What was going through his mind?' (Marcello Mastroianni and Vladek Sheybal in *Leo the Last*).

constantly rises to the surface . . . and for the role I immediately thought of Vladeck Sheybal, who plays the piano in Wajda's *Kanal* and whom I greatly admired. Without his participation, the character would never have existed, as I couldn't imagine any other actor in the role. We both thought of Saragossa, the country of exiles, which is the setting of Potocki's novel, *The Manuscript Found at Saragossa*. Everyone in the film has his own Saragossa – they're all foreigners, exiles, people who, in one way or another, have been dispossessed of their nationality.

Little by little, the film took shape, and it was the first time I had the opportunity of working without outside interference. United Artists left me completely free and I was very relaxed. I was able to experiment, to go my own way, to reject all kinds of limitations, to blend allegory with social comment and psychological study, and see whether I could switch from one to the other and still follow a narrative line. The film exploits the audience's own cinematic experience: it's a series of quotations. Someone mentioned to me Dylan Thomas's poem 'Go gently . . .', etc., which he wrote on the occasion of his father's death and which I quote in the film. Thomas couldn't get over the fact that his father died without saying a word, whereas, in his opinion, after the ghastly life he'd led as a miner, he ought to have been screaming at the approach of death. Leo dreams of his own death, he imagines himself dying, he decides to act and completely changes his attitude to life. The film is therefore made up of references, like an intellectual crossword; but I hope it can also be received directly, on a less cerebral level.

The casting of Mastroianni already acts as a reference.

I thought at once of Mastroianni for the role as I remembered his performance in Monicelli's *I Campagni* (*The Organizer*), an excellent film. He played a very passive character who contrived, at the same time, to attract all kinds of trouble to himself. An English actor would have given the film a precise class context, allowing the spectator to identify with him too easily. I'm no longer satisfied with the notion of picking up a camera and filming in the streets. The public has seen too many things in the cinema, even more on television: it's become blasé. I've no desire now to see New York's shops on the screen. I've seen New York; and even if there can be something very beautiful about the sun setting at the end of the street, it no longer holds any surprise for me. It can only get in the way of the story. The cinema would appear to be going in two directions: in the one case, *cinéma vérité*; in the other, abstraction or allegory. Both are valid, but I'm more attracted to the latter.

How did you work on the colour?

It was my intention to invest the world I was creating with a different, unique quality, but I was working with very ordinary equipment. There were, in the film, many disparate elements and I wanted them to be unified. That's why I decided to paint everything black. All the props and costumes were black, grey or white. There were a few lapses – for example, a yellow bottle label in the pub scene which, every time I see it, makes me ill. Since *Point Blank*, I've always tried to establish a unity in the treatment of colour, as it creates all sorts of problems during editing when you jump from one colour to another.

There's a difference in tone between the scenes with the whites, which are rather grotesque, and those with the blacks, which are warmer and more lyrical.

I'm not sure the two elements coexist perfectly. The blacks are seen through Leo's telescope: they express the romantic view which he has of them. It's a subjective view. By contrast, the society of the whites, of which he is the focal point, reflects his sense of the absurdity of humanity and of life itself. The fact that he went to the Galapagos Islands links him with the idea of

'The society of the whites, of which he is the focal point, reflects his sense of the absurdity of humanity and of life itself.'

1 David de Keyser and Marcello Mastroianni (*Leo the Last*).

2 Billie Whitelaw (*Leo the Last*). **3** Marcello Mastroianni (*Leo the Last*).

human evolution. And that was the advice I gave my white actors: that we were observing animal patterns of behaviour. Perhaps, as a reaction, I exaggerated that aspect, for it's usually out of prejudice that black patterns of behaviour are compared to animal life.

Did you do any research on the Jamaican community?

It's a community I've known since I was eighteen. I used to frequent the Sunset Club, where West Indian music was played. *Leo the Last* has an interesting sociological source, in the relationship between Laszlo and the blacks, since Notting Hill Gate has always been an immigrant area. One wave has succeeded another. Before the war, fleeing Nazi persecution, numerous Poles settled there. Then there were the Free Forces. They bought houses and rented them to Jamaicans when they arrived in the early 1950s. The character of Laszlo was inspired by a Pole who had caused a scandal because of the exorbitant rents he charged. I also based him on a Hungarian I'd known, a doctor who arrived after the war in the wake of the fall of Budapest. He was a brilliant scientist and, at the same time, a fervent Nazi, with all his romantic notions of the purity of blood and the vestiges of pre-First World War Europe.

'A bluesy quality' (Princess Patience, Glenna Forster Jones and Tina Solomon in *Leo the Last*).

All the same, *Leo the Last* is not a solemn drama. It's a comedy whose primary aim is to make the public laugh, and the plot has been handled with a certain detachment. It was originally to have been called *Black Comedy*, but that was already the title of a play by Peter Shaffer. In many respects, I find it the most interesting of all my films, even if it's not perhaps completely successful. I like the way it juggles several balls in the air without dropping any of them, and also the idea of variations on a theme with different interlocking and mutually influential elements. You think it's going to sink beneath its own weight and yet it remains light and airy throughout, without ever betraying its intentions. And it's impossible to imagine it as anything but a film, since it's also a film about the cinema.

What was Bill Stair's role?

He's an old friend, a painter, with whom I'd already worked in television. He has lots of ideas, he invents games, he designs furniture. He's also written a play about Brecht's American trial, when one of his prosecutors was Richard Nixon. He was with me all the time I was writing the script; and he'd try to find equivalents for the emotional content of each scene –

'It was originally to have been called *Black Comedy*' (Phyllis McMahon, Glenna Forster Jones and Keefe West in *Leo the Last*).

snipping items out of newspapers, making sketches, preparing a file on every character, on their attitudes, etc. . . . On this occasion he wrote the script with me; for *Point Blank*, he was one of the people responsible for sets and costumes; and, subsequently, he would collaborate on the script of *Zardoz*. In *Leo the Last*, the dialogue was considerably rewritten during rehearsals, since the actors really participated in the making of the film. If an actor feels at ease in his role, he can very easily write his own dialogue.

How did you use the soundtrack?

I wanted Orff and Berio for the music. Berio employs vocal collages, a little like switching from one foreign radio station to the next, where you hear one language, then another. It's as though you were entering another dimension: you can *hear* the human race. Seven languages are spoken in the film. 'Prufrock' was my constant inspiration, just as 'The Hollow Men' had been for *Hell in the Pacific*. Leo is Prufrock in the sense that he observes others without implicating himself. It's partly a Babel of voices, partly a series of quotations from poetry and song (we hear some Beatles lyrics), partly Leo's own conscience, partly the observations of spectators watching the film, and partly myself. There's one member of the public who says: 'What kind of film is this?', and at that moment I explain it. Originally, at the end of the film, someone said, 'This is the end', and you heard the editor, Tom Priestley, saying, 'What a ridiculous film!', and someone replying, 'It's a typical introduction to a depraved society.' Another voice said, 'It's a masterpiece,' and my wife cried 'Oh, Marcello!' But I cut all of that. The voices aren't important in themselves, they simply create an atmosphere, a musical context.

In Hell in the Pacific, *you had already dealt with the theme of relations between different races.*

It's more the fact of establishing any relationship with others that interest me: you remember in *Point Blank* when Angie is on the telephone and we have the impression of a total absence of emotion in Marvin. Poverty is more important than race in *Leo the Last*. And, unlike Leo, the blacks possess an inner vitality. Yet, within the community, there are those who – like the pimp – work with the whites. Formerly, in Africa, there were slave traders already hustling for white men. Since the pimp collects money for the landlord, he opposes any change in the system from which he profits. That's why we find him in the house at the end. It's he who says to Leo: 'You – you can afford to have principles and choose poverty.' For him, anything goes if it means escaping poverty. As Shaw said, there's nothing moral about poverty, it's the only sin there is. And I couldn't agree more.

Where did you get the idea of the silver strawberry?

I tried to find a story which would express Laszlo's conception of nobility and honour. The silver strawberry is one of those things which become so ritual and decadent that a man like Leo can fall victim to them. It was Vladeck Sheybal who told me the story, which happened to one of his ancestors. The absurd romanticism of a silver strawberry perfectly expressed that state of mind.

Though you have said that you are not really interested in contemporary subjects, most of your films are set in the present.

Yes, but not directly. The problem is that the real world is too strong and I don't want to be drowned in the images which surround me. Len Lye said that, if you enter an office and see a man sitting on a chair, after speaking to him you no longer remember what the chair was like. In the cinema, however, the chair becomes as important as the man sitting on it. That's the trouble with films: everything you put in a scene has a meaning. A film is short and the only way of saying what one has to say is to remove things. I'm beginning to realize that I remove

more and more elements from my films.

What problems were created by the scenes in which Leo looks out of the window?

I had to convey a narrative line without any dialogue. I wasn't at all certain in which direction I was going; and if I thought yet again of Griffith, whom I admire enormously, it's because everything had to be expressed through gesture. I employed a shooting method which he devised, having the scenes played at first behind different windows by other actors while I observed them with the real actors of the film. That's also how I'd worked with Toshiro Mifune.

The final sequence of *Leo the Last* (with Marcello Mastroianni).

1, **2** Marcello Mastroianni (*Leo the Last*).
3 Keefe West, Glenna Forster Jones and Roy Stewart (*Leo the Last*).
4 Glenna Forster Jones (*Leo the Last*).

Billie Whitelaw (*Leo the Last*).

1972

A society whose code of violence recalls that of the nineteenth-century West. Herbert 'Cowboy' Coward and Jon Voight (*Deliverance*).

Deliverance

Journey to the End of Night

As a result of the commercial failure of *Leo the Last*, Boorman was obliged to postpone one of his dearest projects ('dearest' in both senses of the word), a film version of Tolkien's mythological trilogy, *The Lord of the Rings*, and adapt another bestseller, of an unimpeachable literary quality, James Dickey's *Deliverance*. It was a new experience for a director who, previously, had been only very loosely inspired by his source material. *Deliverance*, by contrast, strikes one – on the surface, at least – as totally faithful to its model, an impression corroborated by the designation, in the credit titles, of the author of the novel as its sole scenarist. In fact, viewing the film and reading Dickey's book, one is soon made aware of just how much the latter has been adapted, not only by the extremely intelligent manner in which it has been condensed (the book's quite lengthy introduction, for example, is reduced to a single voice-off conversation heard over the credits) but also because certain crucial details, not to mention the moral and philosophical perspectives of the narrative, have been radically modified. Like *Point Blank*, *Hell in the Pacific* and *Leo the Last*, *Deliverance* centres on the quest of an individual for his own identity, which he eventually finds, albeit transformed and no less solitary than before. The theme of the journey, too, is foregrounded in this canoe excursion by four middle-class American males down the turbulent rivers of North Georgia.

Burt Reynolds (*Deliverance*).

1 Ned Beatty, Herbert 'Cowboy' Coward, Burt Reynolds and Jon Voight (*Deliverance*).
2 Jon Voight (*Deliverance*).
3 Burt Reynolds, Billy McKinney and Ned Beatty (*Deliverance*).

Burt Reynolds, Billy McKinney, Ronny Cox, Jon Voight and Ned Beatty (*Deliverance*).

Ed, an average guy, subjected to a series of ordeals (Ned Beatty and Jon Voight in *Deliverance*).

But though Boorman has omitted the novel's first-person narration, he has emphasized the role of Ed (Dickey's narrator) to the point where he can almost be compared to the Everyman of mediaeval mystery plays – an average, fairly anonymous man subjected to a series of ordeals. With him are his companions: Lewis, the 'philosopher', fascinated to a near-fascist degree by notions of survival and courage and physical culture; Bobby, the pragmatic nice guy, fond of life's simple pleasures; and Drew, the artist, the advocate of law and democracy, values which in the course of their shared adventure will be exposed as only the veneer of a society whose code of violence recalls that of the nineteenth-century West. Each of them will receive retribution in accordance with his initial choices. The badly wounded Lewis will find his macho self-image irretrievably tarnished. Bobby will be sodomized by a hillbilly and forced to imitate the squeals of a sow on heat. (Similarly, Stu Gardner, the nightclub singer in *Point Blank*, forced a baby-faced client to shriek along with him.) And Drew, having watched his friends pervert the course of justice after committing a murder and felt bound to endorse their decision, will jettison his lifebelt and allow himself to be drowned. Each of these four men – no matter how emblematic they might superficially appear – nevertheless manages to avoid the snare of allegory and retain all his human complexity. But it is Ed who – because

Like Boorman's other films, *Deliverance* centres on the quest of an individual for his own identity (Jon Voight).

1 Barbara Ferris and Dave Clark (*Catch Us If You Can*).
2 Nigel Terry (*Excalibur*).
3 Lee Marvin (*Point Blank*).
4 Linda Blair and Richard Burton (*The Heretic*).

1

2

1 Sean Connery (*Zardoz*).
2 Charley Boorman and Powers Boothe (*The Emerald Forest*).

he has agreed, under the possessive influence of Lewis, to exchange the tranquillity of a charmed life for the unruliness of nature – is transformed from a law-abiding citizen into a ruthless killer and subjected to the medieval test of ordeal by water, a rite of passage from which he is apparently the only one to emerge unscathed but which has, in truth, definitively scarred him. Already it was said that no one could swim his way out of Alcatraz; and if Walker did succeed, it was to find himself hardly less of a prisoner on the far side of the bay. Leo, too, unable to share the physical and mental well-being of his fellow-bathers in the swimming pool, was seized with anxiety and panic. As for the American soldier and his Japanese counterpart, their journey by raft only brought them closer to renewed antagonism and final estrangement. Deliverance: the word signifies both itself and its opposite. Whatever is referred to by this ambiguous title – the legal consequences (the guilty men are certain to remain above suspicion), a sense of social liberation (the expedition as an escape from the routine of their daily existence) or a more metaphysical salvation (Ed's belated self-discovery) – in Boorman's film, at least, it cannot be read other than in the light of the director's sardonic irony.

In Dickey's novel, however, prominence is given to Ed's discovery of his skill and strength, as is the idea that he who *kills* survives. In this sense the film is irremediably pessimistic, stranding its leading character – like Walker, like the Japanese officer and the American pilot, like the exiled prince – in a state of clammy alienation, a hermetically sealed, damned universe.

As always in Boorman's work, the social analysis of *Deliverance* is filtered through a specific cinematic genre: in this instance, an updated Western in which the director turns a number of American myths on their head. The Garden of Eden is a poisonous jungle; and if Lewis is thinking of the euphoric adventurism of the frontiersmen (who included another Lewis, celebrated for his expedition with Clark), he is soon to be disabused: his wish to improve his 'image' among his social equals – an archetypal American trait – ends in total, devastating ignominy. In addition, Robert Ardrey's theory (subscribed to by a fair proportion of American artists and intellectuals) of the 'territorial imperative', according to which the invader will almost always be repulsed, since 'the protection of his home invests its owner with a mysterious energy and resolution', is overturned: here it is the two locals who are murdered by the visiting 'dudes', the former, by an ironic twist, bearing firearms, the latter only bows and arrows. But what the film most eloquently denounces is the notion of violence as an initiation, as the acquisition of a technical skill. Unlike certain

Above Deliverance: the word signifies both itself and its opposite (Jon Voight, Burt Reynolds, Ned Beatty and James Dickey).
Opposite The 'territorial imperative' is overturned (Jon Voight, Herbert 'Cowboy' Coward and Billy McKinney in *Deliverance*).

of Sam Peckinpah's heroes, Ed does not regard himself as more of a 'man' after the slaughter. The myth of regeneration through violence, a myth fundamental to American civilization, is portrayed as a pathetic delusion. By killing an innocent man (one who was, in all likelihood, a stranger to the incident; and Drew, in any case, was not shot), Ed is caught up in a vicious circle of reprisals, goaded into acts of violence whose first victim is his own peace of mind. The deserted hospital corridor is reminiscent of the atmosphere of Alcatraz established in the opening shots of *Point Blank*. Like that film, *Deliverance* depicts a crumbling, decadent society, its harmony merely superficial, as, indeed, is that of the four men who, as we are informed by the song which Drew sings, 'want red meat when they're hungry, liquor when they're thirsty, dollars when they're broke, religion when they're dead'. What deeper harmony once existed has been lost for ever, as is clear from a haunting scene in which Drew and a retarded youth play a lively duet for guitar and banjo whose melody will serve as a leitmotif as their sense of security is eroded by both the current of the river and that of the narrative. But violence, here, is also linked to pollution, that other major obsession of a country in crisis. The film opens with shots of a dam in construction; Lewis remarks, 'They're going to rape this whole country,' and Bobby is disturbed by his companion's premonition. The river becomes the enemy, the incarnation of those primitive forces of which the director has spoken; it sets the scene for the decisive encounter which the film's protagonists are fated to have with themselves; and it is the trap which will destroy the fragile state of equilibrium which they have contrived to establish. No one was better qualified than Boorman to illustrate such a dialogue between man and nature.

In one of the most beautiful scenes, Ed clambers up a rockface by moonlight, the river far below him, the night sky looming far over his head. This physical intimacy with the cosmos, admirably captured by the director, reminds one (not only because of the tormented hero) of the art of Anthony Mann (in particular, of *The Naked Spur*) or, better still, Raoul Walsh and his dynamic sense of space: Boorman appears to have preserved intact the secret – a secret one thought to have been lost – of a *physical* cinema. It would be interesting to study the articulation of space by artists whose emotional and intellectual relationship with the universe is founded on what one can only term a metaphysic – from the dramatic, essentially scenic space of Losey (*Boom*) and that, closed and claustrophobic, of Lang (*Moonfleet*, *The Tiger of Bengal*) to the greater expansiveness of Walsh (*Colorado Territory*, *Distant Drums*). But it is surely no longer necessary to insist on these preoccupations in Boorman's work: they are tangible, here, in the meticulous realism of the extraordinarily evocative soundtrack, in the acute sense of spatial homogeneity and the total mastery of location shooting.

As far as his handling of violence is concerned, he belongs to a classic American tradition. Where some film-makers – most notably, Peckinpah – have had recourse to staccato editing or slow motion to render palatable a series of complacent shock effects, the unbearable tension of Boorman's *mise en scène* is generated, rather, through an impression of continuity (e.g.

A deeper harmony is lost for ever . . . (Ronny Cox, Jon Voight and Burt Reynolds in *Deliverance*).

the rape scene filmed mostly in long shot, the second murder encompassed within a vertiginous circular movement).

Like Leo and Walker, Ed is a man living out a bad dream. And one of the most powerful ideas in *Deliverance*, made very real by Boorman in the concise framing of the film's closing shots, is that of the river which has ceased to exist, but continues to flow on through the darkest, deepest recesses of Ed's nightmares, while his pregnant wife – awaiting, as it were, her own deliverance – cradles him back to sleep. In the way it calls the values of American society into question, and beyond the purely topographical journey which it records, *Deliverance* is therefore, literally, a return to sources, with American man reawakening in a cold sweat to the most elemental impulses of his civilization.

Interview

This is the first of your films in which you remain more or less faithful to the original novel.

I made *Deliverance* as a result of a confluence of circumstances. I found myself offered the opportunity of adapting Dickey's novel by Warner Bros. Following a change of management in the company, a young man, Barry Beckman, who'd been

1

2

. . . as is clear from the scene in which Drew and a retarded child play a duet on banjo and guitar.
1 Hoyt T. Pollard (*Deliverance*). **2** Ronny Cox (*Deliverance*).

Dickey's pupil and also admired my films, had become story editor. Even before Dickey had finished writing his novel, Beckman managed to persuade Warners to purchase the rights and allow me to adapt it, which they did. The book greatly interested me, as it seemed ideal material for a film, with a whole series of themes which could be expressed through action. At the same time, however, I was worried by the fact that, for the first time, I was starting from a literary work which I felt I had to respect. I met Dickey, we got on well together, we got drunk together, we told each other stories; even so, face to face, we never really got down to discussing the book, which was probably due to the fact that James Dickey is a mass of paradoxes, paradoxes which can be found in the novel and are also those of the American South.

Our work together was carried on by correspondence. I drafted an adaptation of the novel which I sent to him and he replied with a long letter full of comments. From then on, we often exchanged letters; and though, orally, he tends to be rather self-indulgent, he is, by contrast, very precise and disciplined where the written word is concerned. I felt that I was going to be ill-at-ease with such a strong personality; that, in the end, I myself would have to find *filmic* solutions to the problem of adaptation – solutions which took me off in a different direction. Philosophically, we had little in common. Dickey's beliefs are not unlike Hemingway's, especially the idea that one attains manhood through some initiatory act of violence. For me, the contrary is true: violence doesn't make you a better person – instead, it degrades you. That was one essential difference between us; and that idea was closely related to another theme which I hoped to emphasize at the beginning of the film: that the journey of these urbanites is also a journey through time, through America's history, in search of its beauty, its power, its resources and its wealth. When they arrive at the village, they come into contact with people who live by the old frontier values, in an autonomous society in which they themselves build their houses, cultivate their land and defend themselves against outsiders, yet who are at the same time degenerates. In a sense, these four men are seeing their own history in a distorted mirror. The river itself has been tamed, contained, transformed into a placid lake. It's therefore a re-evaluation of American myths.

Why did you decide to exclude from the film the introductory scenes in the city?

I think that, from the structural point of view, it would have made for a much weaker film: for me, the context had to be defined by the landscape. I also think that, for the American public, the four men are very familiar figures. They're already known to them, Lewis less than the others – though his obsession with survival, with physical fitness, etc., is quite well-known. Using up time with descriptions of where they lived, what they did for a living, struck me as rather futile; these were things the spectator could deduce for himself and which he'd also come to divine as the film advanced. When Ed, for example, makes a little speech at Drew's burial, we understand that they were close friends.

James Dickey is the only screenwriter credited in the titles.

In the first place, most of the dialogue was his, except for what we improvised during the shoot. What's more, the story is his and there was no question of my appropriating it. My own contribution centred much more on structure and organization. In fact, I wrote the script, it wasn't he who actually drafted it; but, as I said before, we corresponded at great length and everything I wanted to do, I discussed point by point with him. So he was very closely involved with the film's preparation.

The hand emerging from the river in the last shot doesn't appear in the novel.

No, that was an idea of mine. What interested me in Ed's evolution was that he becomes a wild animal, acquiring an extraordinary instinct for self-preservation and a paranoid manner towards Bobby. Lewis, too, is different in the book. It always seemed to me that, when he breaks his leg, it was a flaw in the narrative, an author's 'device' to allow Ed to take charge of the group. But when I met the friend of Dickey who inspired the character, I realized that his desire to become one with nature, his mistrust of civilization, betrayed a neurotic, insecure personality. In fact, he didn't have a genuine relationship with nature, it was by force of will that he tried to establish such a relationship; and that explains his accident. No one in harmony with nature is injured in that fashion. I was therefore able to understand why he had broken his leg.

Warners felt that the film's ending was weak and anti-dramatic. It seemed to me on the contrary that, up to that point, it had been so powerful that the public would let itself be borne along by the final, calmer scenes. When Ed, who's now a killer, returns to civilization, haunted by his experience, we realize that he won't be able to pick up his humdrum life where he left off.

What exactly did you mean when you said that Dickey's paradoxes could be found in the book?

The four characters represent four facets of Dickey's personality; and, in a way, one might interpret the story as an attempt on his part to reunite these four fragments in one. Dickey was an athlete, an archer: that's the Lewis, vaguely fascistic, side of his personality. He plays the guitar, he has, like Drew, something of the artist and the moralist in him. And, like Bobby, he's also a bit of a coward: there are certain dangers he's afraid of, as is often true of men with imagination. Now the problem of violence is as central to the book as to the film. The English and American censors wanted me to cut the film, but I refused, as it would have altered its meaning. What I wanted was not to show violence in itself – you don't see too much blood in the film – but to confront both characters and spectators with the reality of violence. It's very important for me, for example, that the victim takes a long time to die: it was intended as an antidote to the kind of death one normally sees on the screen, happening so quickly, so banal as to be hypocritical. In the same way, I admired in the novel the ambiguity

John Boorman directs Burt Reynolds (shooting *Deliverance*).

which surrounded the identity of the hillbilly who is killed. In effect, the public participates in the manhunt, it acquires the taste for blood; then it discovers that it's perhaps an innocent man who's been killed. The action is suddenly separated from its motive and we see it in a different light.

Given the physical problems posed by the film, it's quite close to Hell in the Pacific.

It's true that several members of the crew had worked on the earlier film and one of them said to me: 'I didn't think it was possible to find a tougher shoot than the one we had, but you've found it!'

What was the work of the second unit?

Relatively unimportant, as it happens. You know that American unions are subdivided into three sections: the East, out of New York; the Middle West, out of Chicago; and the West, out of Los Angeles. The Chattooga River, where we were filming, is on the state line between Georgia, whose union is based in Chicago, and North Carolina, whose union is based in New York. The two unions were therefore in contention as to which ought to be working on the film and we were forced to compromise. Bill Butler, who had worked for Jack Nicholson on *Drive, He Said*, filmed several shots for me, including that of the fish being caught and a handful of night shots.

For the scenes on the river, though, there was no question of having a second unit – we didn't even have room for a second camera. One of the reasons why the landscape is completely unspoiled is that it's practically inaccessible. Every day it would take us between an hour and an hour-and-a-half by jeep to transport the canoes to the river. There were eight of us – four actors, the cameraman, two technicians and myself – sharing four canoes; and we'd spend the day shooting in and on the water, then in the late afternoon we'd be picked up a little further downstream.

How exactly did you work on the colour?

I spent three months in Los Angeles working at Technicolor. Overall, the film was desaturated of colour, and we used a new system which had been perfected by the laboratories in conjunction with our lighting cameraman, Vilmos Zsigmond. In my opinion, we achieved wonderful results, except that, in some prints, the colour has a tendency to go off, especially in the first reels, where there's so little of it. I prefer the colours to remain within a limited range, since strong colour contrasts create problems during editing. Desaturation not only lent the landscape a greater reality, but it gave the dreamlike, nightmarish quality I wanted.

When I saw Huston's experiments with colour desaturation – in *Moby Dick*, for example, or *Reflections in a Golden Eye* – their failure seemed to me to lie in the fact that different colours desaturate in different degrees: primary colours, and particularly strong colours, tend to stay the same, whereas mid-tones shade into black-and-white. The danger, then, is to have bright blobs of colour on a black-and-white background. That's why I tried to eliminate primary colours from the settings and keep only mid-tones, to achieve a more balanced desaturation. The snag is that, during colour grading, when you desaturate, you often alter colour values. So the problems posed by the density and balance of colours, as well as by desaturation, can become extremely complex – which explains the three months I spent in Los Angeles!

The music is used discreetly, but much more effectively than in Hell in the Pacific.

I have to say, frankly, that my decisions concerning the music were mostly practical ones. To begin with, I had financial problems. Then, I wanted to finish the film (editing, sound-mixing) in Ireland, which I did. But American unions insist that the music for an American film should be composed *in* America. I took a musical theme I was fond of and asked two first-class musicians, a banjo player and a guitarist, to come to the studio with me before filming began and play the theme for

two hours in every possible style. I subsequently used these variations throughout the film: it was very useful for me, as the scene between Drew and the little boy, a musical scene, is in fact the key to the film. The music sometimes expresses harmony, sometimes disharmony.

It's true that in *Hell in the Pacific* the music went against the film, since it should have been as unconventional as the film itself – but I was to blame, not Lalo Schifrin, perhaps because I lacked confidence in the film and hoped to 'help it along' a little with the musical score. I've always believed that music ought to be organically related to a film; it ought to arise out of the film and not be imposed upon it; and I was going against my own theory. In *Leo the Last*, by contrast, the music and the film were as one. In *Point Blank*, for the first time, I used a Moog electronic synthesizer in order to make slight modifications to the music. I used it again in *Hell in the Pacific* to produce certain sound effects, as in the scene where the rain begins to fall on the leaves and the music was artificially created by this method.

In *Deliverance*, I used it with a precise purpose: as you know, optical sound has a very narrow dynamic range and it's difficult to obtain particularly low-pitched sounds. But I needed to catch the characteristic roaring sound of cataracts and rapids.

Ed's climb (Jon Voight in *Deliverance*).

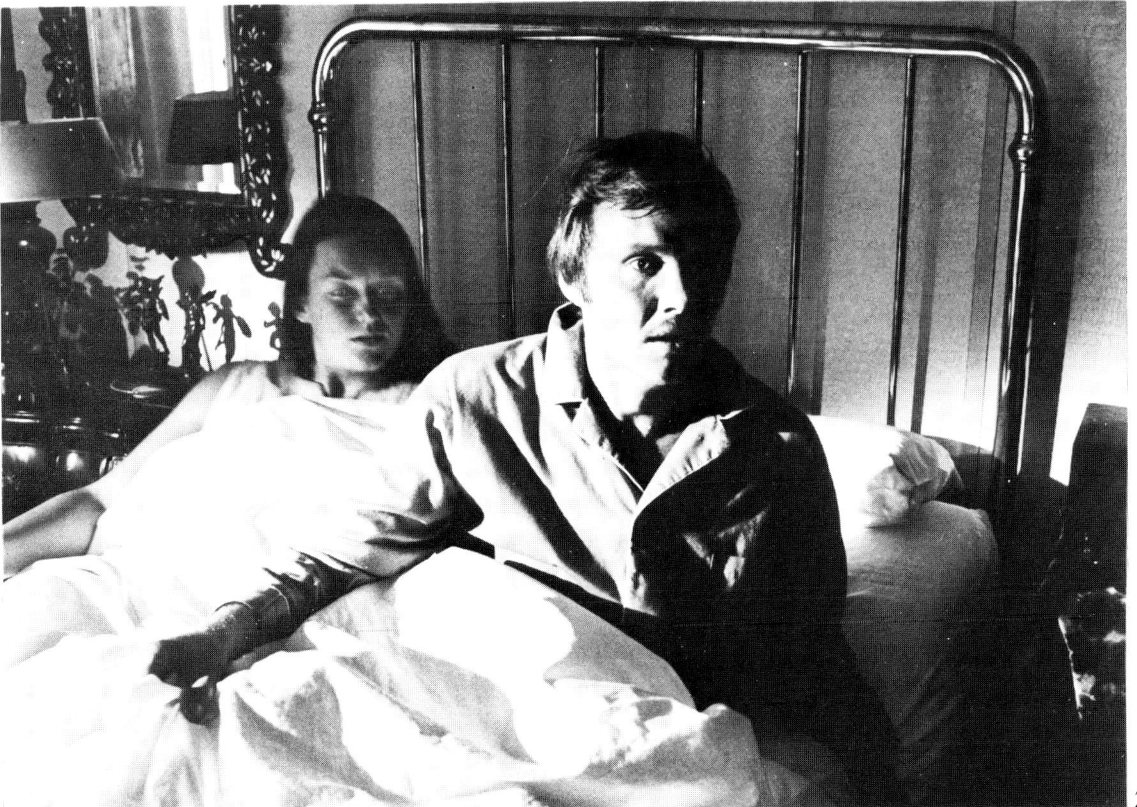

1 'To confront both characters and spectators with the reality of violence' (Herbert 'Cowboy' Coward and Jon Voight in *Deliverance*).
2 Waking up in a cold sweat (Belinha Beatty and Jon Voight in *Deliverance*).

When you record natural sound, it contains many variations; but, once you transfer it to film, the high and low 'crests' are cut, which makes it sound weak. So I created this sound with the Moog synthesizer and I set it at the lowest possible level that the soundtrack would record; I was therefore able to obtain a coherent continuity, a roaring sound that makes a much stronger impression. It's a problem encountered by all film-makers – the disappointment produced by transferring magnetic sound on to optical sound.

The idea of the retarded boy watching the four men from the top of the bridge is not in the novel.

I'm very fond of Dickey, even if our relationship was rather chequered. Sometimes he was jealous and hated me for, as he imagined, stealing his story from him. Then, another day, he'd congratulate me on one of my ideas and regret that it hadn't occurred to him when writing the book! He's a fascinating man, very mature and yet somehow childlike. All his defects and qualities are exaggerated. In a way, just as *Hell in the Pacific* was a film about Lee Marvin, and grew out of my knowledge of him, so *Deliverance* was inspired as much by the time I spent with Dickey as by his novel.

However, to return to the idea of the little boy on the bridge, I wanted, as a means of thinning out the narrative, to summarize a whole passage in the novel by a single shot. In the book, they leave Oree for the head waters in order to reach the river, then come back down and cross the village. I wanted to use certain rather tempting settings, such as the chicken-conditioning factory, with lots of feathers around it, but the lack of time at my disposal made it very complicated. So I thought of this shot, which might serve as a kind of warning. Similarly, towards the end, I wanted an image that would give the impression that the village was about to be submerged. One day I saw a house being physically transported and I thought of a church in the same situation – which would add the final touch to the shot of the graves being dug. We associate a church with the idea of stability so that, when it begins to move, it's like a nightmare, a hallucination, something solid becoming fluid.

In the work of T. S. Eliot, a poet you admire, water plays a regenerative role. In Deliverance*, it's a threat.*

Yes and no. In effect, what I prefer whenever I see the film are the underwater shots, when the bodies are sinking. The corpse seems to come to life again and I have the same idea about America: beneath the surface, America's dreams and memories do not die, they remain alive.

The four characters represent four facets of Dickey's personality (Billy McKinney, Jon Voight, Burt Reynolds, Ned Beatty and Ronny Cox in *Deliverance*).

1973

Zed discovers *The (Wi)zard(of)oz* (Sean Connery in *Zardoz*).

Zardoz

The Dreaming Crystal

In line with the alternating principle by which the linear simplicity of *Hell in the Pacific* was followed by the structural complexity of *Leo the Last*, the multifaceted kaleidoscope of *Zardoz* succeeded the classical narrative of *Deliverance*. If, in the latter film, four civilized men were confronted with a world of barbarians, in *Zardoz* a primitive being finds himself pitted against a hyper-civilized society. But whereas the half-witted hillbillies of the Appalachians were circumscribed by virtually unlimited space, the Eternals are housed within the closed structure of the Vortex and the Brutals inhabit the neighbouring territories, or Outlands. Jacques Goimard has noted the manner in which the film posits three classic parameters of any Utopia: the invisible wall which, for those within it, guarantees protection from the pollution of the Outlands and the life of their inhabitants; the antidote to old age which permits them to arrest the ageing process in the mid-twenties; and the transmitter which records their experiences and enables them to communicate with the Tabernacle.[130]

In reality, *Zardoz* is a Dystopia, a pessimistic view of just one of many possible futures, a cautionary tale coloured by Boorman's concern for the evolution of humanity. Like the urbanites of *Deliverance*, the Eternals have attempted to flee their problems and, by extension, themselves. There is, however, no such thing as perfection and no other solution for mankind than that of assuming its contradictions. As already in *Leo the Last*, Boorman quotes from Eliot's 'The Love Song of J. Alfred Prufrock', a poem which repudiates perfection such as it is embodied in sphericity:

> Would it have been worthwhile,
> To have bitten off the matter with a smile,
> To have squeezed the universe into a ball
> To roll it towards some overwhelming question,
> To say: 'I'm Lazarus, come from the dead'.

He might equally, in a solemn register, have quoted Eliot's contemporary, Paul Valéry: 'We now know that our civilization too is mortal'. What Boorman rejects in *Zardoz* is not only the twentieth-century cult of science as a panacea, but the notion of an existence without goals, as it is without limits; of a life without desires, as it is without needs. It will be for Zed the Exterminator (following Ed in *Deliverance* as the model of a Boormanian hero) to disrupt this false tranquillity, to reintroduce the love and violence which the world of the film has been denied. Merely by tasting his sweat, the Apathetics reanimate their sexual energies; by pursuing him, by setting fire to the houses of the village, the Eternals revert to a kind of physical violence which, previously, had been the sole preserve of the Brutals; by these acts, the inhabitants of the Vortex prepare for the destruction of their system.

1 Zed emerges from a mountain of grain in the flying head (Sean Connery in *Zardoz*).
2 Zed and an Apathetic in the Vortex (Sean Connery and Jessica Swift in *Zardoz*).

This 'ideal' society is seen to be, as its founder, a Renegade, admits with his dying breath, 'an offence against nature, for we have forced the hand of evolution'. Having reached its pinnacle, but petrified in its very immobility, it can only expect – even yearn for – its own annihilation. Inside the Vortex – in which, passing through a cultural kaleidoscope, a collage of images and quotations, Zed becomes a superior being and learns to dominate his former master – Boorman presents us with one of the keys to his universe when he alludes to 'the law of the unity of opposites'. A dialectical film-maker such as he is, he cannot conceive of a society as fossilized, as 'crystallized',

as that of the Eternals.

Zardoz is therefore open to a philosophical interpretation (can one isolate oneself from the real world? Does life have any meaning when death no longer exists?), as also to a political interpretation relating it to the allegory of *Leo the Last*. It is, after all, a tendency of the West (and primarily of the United States) to evacuate the very image of death and draw pleasure, profit and privilege from resources extorted from the wretched populations of the Third World which it maintains in a state of dependence and exploitation. But Boorman's vision is too rich, the structure of his fable too open-ended, to be exhausted by such a narrow reading. Apart from its incisive denunciation of imperialism, the film bears witness to the director's suspicion of all Utopias (and how can any revolutionary project exist without the concept of Utopia?) as well as his acknowledgment of the life force (interpreted by some critics as a new kind of machismo) personified by Sean Connery. It is, at the very least, difficult not to read *Zardoz* as an indictment of institutionalized religion. When, inside God's head, Zed kills the 'puppeteer' Arthur Frayn, who ruled both him and the other Exterminators, one is at first tempted to regard his gesture as merely mindless and brutish, whereas it proves to be, as one subsequently learns, the first stage of his liberation. Zardoz is, in effect, a god whom the Eternals invented to retain their authority over the Brutals by oppression and mystification.

In a sense, as Marsha Kinder pointed out, the crystal is the

From the Apathetics of the Vortex to the Brutals of the Outlands (*Zardoz*).

A whirligig of images (Sean Connery in *Zardoz*).

point of convergence of the film's themes. It represents the sum total of all the inhabitants of the Vortex, as it itself declares to Zed: it reunites the Eternals as in the Tabernacle; it is simultaneously receiver and transmitter, the link between the inside and the outside world, the body and the spirit, the individual and his culture, nature and art. But it is also 'a source of conformism and sterility, precluding all possibility of change. The crystal, like the society of the Eternals, is only waiting to be infiltrated and violated.'[135] That, indeed, is what happens to it through the agency of Zed – an invasion which prefigures the climactic holocaust.

The crystal is also, with its prismatic structure, the film's own mirror image. *Zardoz* is the most baroque of Boorman's films, the one in which he deploys colour most flamboyantly (as in the opposition between the dark, mournful shades of the Outlands, the pastel chromaticism of the lush green valley and the garish hues of the Vortex); the one in which he accumulates reflections, projections and the fragments of broken mirrors to create a whirligig of images – images not infrequently alluding to the history of the cinema, from its earliest days (*Méliès*) to its latest (*2001*), from *Flash Gordon* to *The Lady From Shanghai* – hardly surprising for a film which constitutes both a reflection on and homage to culture itself, and is as much a fairy-tale as an essay in science fiction. Such, at least, is the interpretation implied by its title, an explicit reference to J. Frank Baum's *(Wi)zard (of) Oz*, the story of an old man who terrorizes his fellow creatures, who wears a mask and speaks in a stentorian voice, until the day dawns when the inhabitants of his village

peep behind the mask and discover the truth. Both complex and naive (and sometimes let down by its relatively low budget), *Zardoz* has been the least loved of all Boorman's films. Yet it contains some ravishingly beautiful moments and its 'overload' of meaning is essential for a fuller understanding of its maker's universe.

What relation is there between Zardoz *and one of your earliest projects, an adaptation of* The Lord of the Rings?

What interested me in *The Lord of the Rings* was its mythic content. As you know, Tolkien was an expert in mythology who, in his work, combined several fundamental myths, and it's that amalgam which, in my opinion, gives his saga its extraordinary power. *Zardoz* is also a mythic story. My frustration at having to abandon the Tolkien project had left me in an extreme state of tension – a tension that had to be resolved in my next film. Another resemblance is that *The Lord of the Rings* is set in Middle-earth, in a world familiar to us, of a supposedly prehistorical era; and yet it seems to unfold in a time continuum different from our own. Good and evil represent two diametrically opposed poles; but when, at the end of the book, the evil is vanquished, it doesn't disappear but is diluted, or dissipated, in the good, which creates a complex condition, one again with which we're familiar, the two being inextricably linked. Though *Zardoz* takes place in the future, we also have the impression that it's another time continuum, that it could be happening in our own period, if, formerly, the world had taken another direction. The essence of *Zardoz* came to me in a dream; and since I believe, as Jung claimed, that these myths exist inside us, I was waiting for them to be released, to emerge into the light.

John Boorman directs Sean Connery (shooting *Zardoz*).

Given that you're attracted to the past, and in particular to the legend of the Grail, why did you prefer to set this fable in the future?

I didn't feel quite ready to tackle an adaptation of the Arthurian cycle. To start with, I wanted to show how emotions remain more or less the same, while living conditions never stop changing. We live in a universe which is becoming both more and more complex and more and more cut off from the natural world; our emotions, however, have hardly changed in a thousand years.

To emphasize that, and underline the separation, I decided to set the action in the future. It began as the story of a scientist whose hobby was futurology, the study of the future in terms of structures. But there existed a gulf between these preoccupations and his emotional life. I started to do some research; I went to North California and visited communes to see how the alternative society of the counterculture was progressing, to see where it was headed. And I read lots of books on futurology.

Then, gradually, a new idea began to evolve, a different one from my original project, the idea of a semi-mystical, semi-scientific community which has survived a holocaust or, if you like, the end of the world. A group of scientists, who continue to possess the technology of space, find the means of isolating themselves with all the treasures of civilization, all its accumulated knowledge, as happened with monasteries during the Middle Ages. One of the problems posed by the conquest of space, for example, is that journeys through the cosmos are too long in relation to the length of a man's life – which leads to the desire to prolong it. These scientists, therefore, live on earth as though in a spaceship, with a closed economy; and they're immortal.

As they've no further need of procreation, their sexual activity atrophies. They communicate by means of a single brain, a fact that invests them with unparalleled power. Since highly elaborate computers satisfy all their needs, machines have ceased to operate; they have, in fact, advanced beyond the era of the machine into that of a kind of mystical technology. In a sense, it's already here: when there's a power failure, the telephone continues to work, because it needs only a six-volt battery. Following Lewis's prediction in *Deliverance*, I imagine existence in cities as having become both impossible and unnecessary, since the means of communication, not only oral but visual – computers, for example – would have reached such a degree of perfection that anyone could be contacted immediately.

My community, the Vortex, is completely democratic. All decisions are put to the vote and every member can offer his opinion on any problem that arises. I then began to think about relationships within the group and a system of penalties. Instead of people being put in prison, they're condemned to be aged several months or years in proportion to the seriousness of the offence which they've committed against the community. I spent a lot of time visualizing such a situation – their way of life, their clothes and their patterns of behaviour. But since the situation was, by its very nature, static, I thought of the story of an outsider who succeeds in penetrating the com-

The beautiful Eternals of the Vortex (Charlotte Rampling *above* in *Zardoz*).

1

2

Closed societies and circular forms.
1 The Eternals of the Vortex (*Zardoz*).
2 The Companions of Saragossa (Vladek Sheybal and Marcello Mastroianni in *Leo the Last*).

1

2

1 The Knights of the Round Table (Nigel Terry, Cherie Lunghi and Nicholas Clay in *Excalibur*).
2 The shabona of the Invisible People (*The Emerald Forest*).

munity. He's been chosen for just such a mission – like Arthur in the legend of the Grail – and he enters mysteriously, becoming the catalyst who triggers off both destruction and evolution.

In imagining the future, it's always necessary to refer to cultural elements which already exist. What determined your choice of a visual style?

Because they no longer possess machines, these people weave their own clothes and make their own bread. They do so not only from necessity, but also deliberately, because they've learned how important it is to remain in contact with the soil, with nature. In many science-fiction stories, it's very difficult to identify with the characters, because their experience is so different from our own. In fact, in *Zardoz*, the characters share our experiences; and since the world has been destroyed, and though it all takes place three hundred years from now, there have been no major changes in relation to the present day. There are, as I said, no new industries, no new buildings. In the Vortex, the objects are like those of our own world, but with slight differences which make them appear rather strange. The clothes are of extremely fine quality, such as was the case in ancient Egypt; both women and men have become very delicate creatures, finally resembling each other and wearing the same clothes. The fact that the clothing style is so consistent isn't explained in the film, but it was arrived at after several different stages of research and it does carry an historical weight: they're not just pretty costumes.

Do you read a lot of science fiction?

I'm fond of Bradbury and, above all, John Wyndham, particularly *The Day of the Triffids*, *The Midwich Cuckoos* and *The Kraken Wakes*. These are books which had a great influence on me. I've also been influenced by Frank Herbert's *Dune*, and feel a certain affinity with Kurt Vonnegut Jr, particularly *Mother Night*.

Did you think of the title Zardoz *and the allusion to* The Wizard of Oz *from the very beginning?*

No, that came later. The character of Arthur Frayn became more and more important – he's the Merlin of the story. I developed the idea of controlling the Outlands by means of religion. Then it occurred to me that, with his terrifying voice, he resembled the Wizard of Oz. I also wanted the film to have a title that wouldn't give too much away, and would be more of a sound than a meaning. Since the film itself doesn't offer any rational meaning, it was important that the title not suggest one.

Like Leo the Last, Zardoz *demonstrates the impossibility of isolation, and how it can lead to sterility.*

The way a community functions has always interested me: in fact, it's something that amazes me. Most people are surprised when something goes wrong. For me, it's rather the contrary: it's what works that intrigues me, given what we know about

The surviving Renegades of the Vortex head for the silver lake (*Zardoz*).

The destiny of Zed and Consuella (Sean Connery and Charlotte Rampling in the final sequence of *Zardoz*).

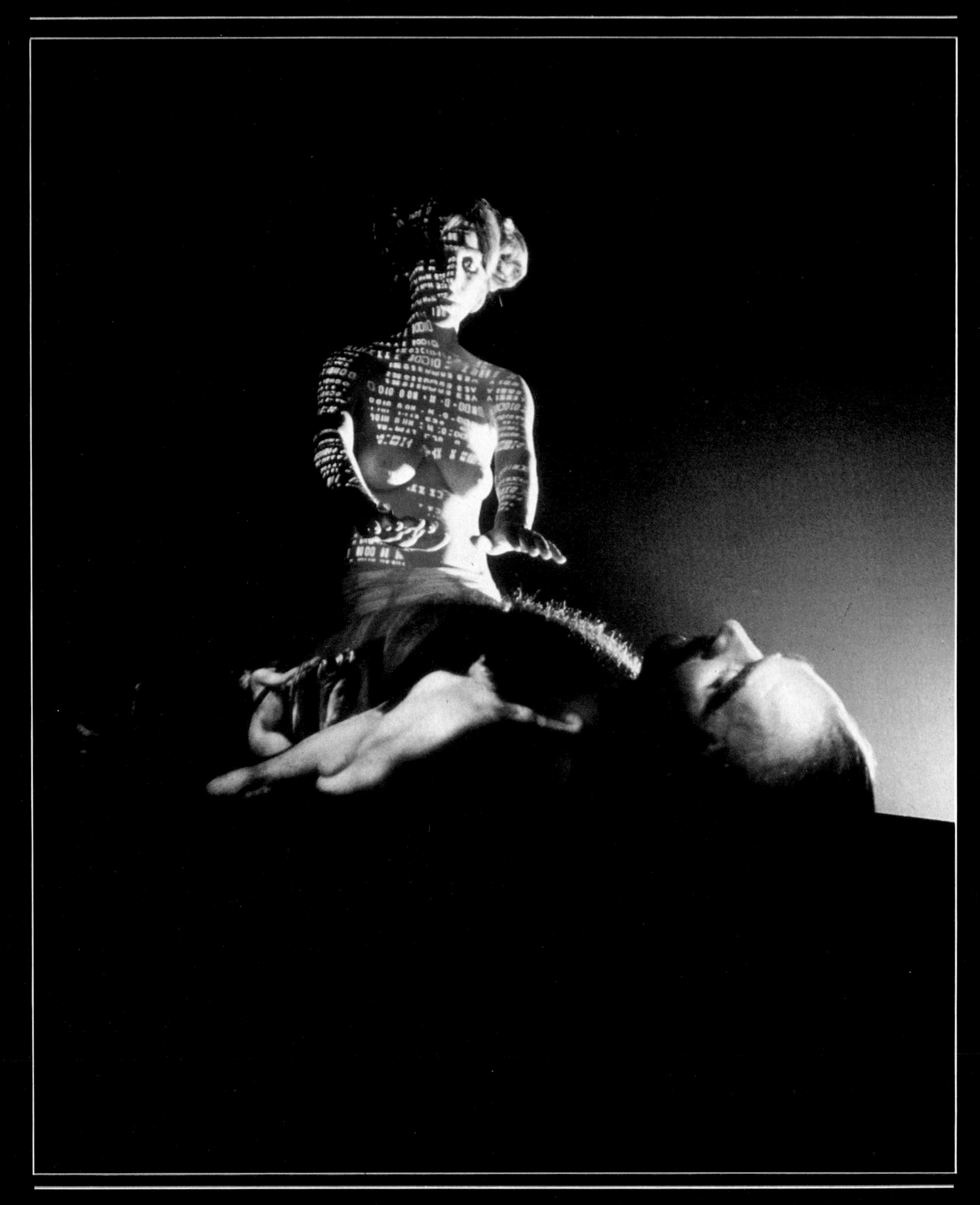

Above The transformation of Zed in the Tabernacle of the Vortex. Sally Anne Newton and Sean Connery (*Zardoz*).
Opposite Charlotte Rampling and Sean Connery (*Zardoz*).

human nature and the organization of society. It's how precarious the world is that strikes me most forcefully, the way in which groups are formed and close themselves off from other groups. In *Zardoz*, though the motives and the objectives of the Eternals – like those of Leo (in *Leo the Last*) – might be considered noble, their security, their innocence and their purity have been purchased at the expense of the Brutals in the Outlands. They regard Zed and his memories the way Leo regards the blacks in the street, the way we tend to watch the news on television: without any real feeling. Like Leo, they're conscious of their dominance in a general context, but not of their responsibility in these particular circumstances. They prefer to isolate themselves, and such isolation is destructive since, if society is to advance, it has need of a certain dynamic. In every man there's an inclination to inertia and an inclination to action, and these divide him in two: I feel it very strongly in myself. When I'm in the city, I dream of the kind of calm which I get in Ireland for my work; and when I'm in Ireland, I dream of the bustle of the city.

The more complex a work of art is, the more difficult it is to judge it as either optimistic or pessimistic. From this point of view, Leo the Last *and* Zardoz, *in which one can find the widest possible gamut of emotions and ideas, are less easily definable than* Point Blank *and* Deliverance, *both of which are overtly pessimistic. And if one senses a greater optimism in* Zardoz *than in* Leo the Last, *it's perhaps because Roscoe, the rebellious black, is not the film's protagonist, whereas Zed the rebel is the hero of* Zardoz.

That's true. But at the end of *Leo the Last* there's a sense of liberation, which comes from the destruction of the sterile house. In *Zardoz*, the Vortex is destroyed, but from its destruction is born the possibility of another life. What makes it a more positive film is that Zed's objective is to destroy a place which has become an insult to nature, and to life, by its very quiescence. In death, there is a beginning. Before shooting started, I was very much struck by a newspaper article I read. It dealt with an experiment conducted on a colony of mice. Living in ideal conditions, they began to behave like the inhabitants of the Vortex such as I had imagined them. Some of them became apathetic; the females began to dominate the males, who stopped working and played all day long. Others became aggressive – genuine Renegades. And they ceased to reproduce. The article helped me in my discussions with the cast of the film, who were very concerned about their roles, about the sexuality of the characters – for it wasn't an easy film for the actors.

How did you choose your actors and work with them?

From the beginning, the film posed a problem: that of diction and behaviour. I decided on a language that would be simple, as unidiomatic as possible, cold and neutral. I merely used

Above The flight of the Eternals (Sara Kestelman in *Zardoz*) . . .
Opposite . . . after the destruction of the Vortex by the Exterminators (*Zardoz*).

The social groups of *Zardoz*.
Above The Apathetics.
Below The Renegades (Sean Connery and John Alderton).

The Exterminators in front of the stone mask.
The Eternals (from behind, Sally Anne Newton).

The end of a society at the edge of the silver lake (*Zardoz*).

certain archaic words and neologisms to create a sense of strangeness and rhythm. It sounded almost like free verse. I was looking for actors and actresses who, though young, already had signs of maturity on their faces. Charlotte Rampling and Sara Kestelman fulfilled these conditions; both of them, in addition, have beautiful voices. Actually, I spent more time choosing the extras: what I needed were young faces with malicious, prematurely ageing expressions, wide eyes and thin lips.

I have lots of discussions with the actors about their characters before shooting begins, but I tell them that it's for them to feel at ease with these characters so that they might be capable of confronting a situation which wasn't in the script but added by me at the last moment. If an actor can do that, he brings ideas to the film you yourself wouldn't have thought of, which is a very enriching experience. When an actor isn't in a scene and he asks you what he's supposed to be doing during it, it shows that he has his character's point of view in the whole story, and that's extremely enlightening for a director. Sara Kestelman, a Shakespearian actress whose first film role this was, wanted me to explain everything to her, but it was I who asked the questions. I'd tell her: 'You come in here and I'm telling you this because it's what I need for my camera movement, but it's up to you to tell me where you're coming from!' Connery is also a very intelligent actor, which is a great help. He understood Zed from the beginning and his performance was a revelation. He's half Irish and half Scottish – there's something mystical about him which was just waiting to be brought to the surface. He's very instinctive, and one of his strong points as an actor is that he has a very direct approach to each scene.

May might represent the Mother, Consuella the Wife and Avalow the Daughter.

That's probably true! But, at the start, as I hadn't ever really created feminine characters, I was afraid that all three women would resemble each other. I took a great interest in studying them – in the first scene, for example, when May and Consuella inspect Zed, there are hints of their former relationship, a lesbian one, and the way in which they've since grown apart from each other. The least successful character is Avalow, a prophetess, a good fairy, an 'anima', a totally mythic being whom I perhaps didn't truly 'feel', and whose role I allowed to become purely functional.

You tended in your previous films to aim for a more monochromatic effect. Here, the range of colours is much wider.

I've always been interested in the relationship between dreams and the cinema, which was linked for me with that monochromatic effect. For this film, which is more dreamlike than the others, I felt curiously freer in my use of colours, much more at ease in its fantastic universe. If you're dealing with the contemporary world, you have to be less realistic, you have to avoid a sense of recognition. Here, on the contrary, I felt liberated, I could let my imagination roam freely, whereas in those films of mine which take place in perfectly familiar settings, I have to simplify, I have to eliminate the kind of inessential detail that gets in the way.

Which brings us back to your question about the direction of actors. When I shoot, I'm incapable of speaking to actors about their motivations, because at that stage I'm interested in images, in the juxtaposition of shots, in surfaces rather than depths. The cinema becomes a two-dimensional means of expression. What matters to me then is the position of the actor in the shot, his movement within the frame, the sound of his voice. Instead of telling an actor to become angrier or more nervous, I tell him to raise his voice or turn his head so that it's the light on his eyes that creates the impression of anger or fear. At that stage, one works the way a painter does. Oddly enough, when I write a script, most of the time I don't see it in terms of shots, except for a handful of scenes, like the one at the beginning of *Zardoz* where there aren't any acted exchanges. In my first films, I decided in advance what kind of shots I'd be using; not now, though, not before I'm actually on the set. The problem is knowing which shot of a scene I'm going to film first. Usually I shoot the most important one first, whereas, according to Geoffrey Unsworth, Kubrick always begins with insert shots or secondary shots, something I quite understand: it's one way of putting yourself at ease. The evening before filming a shot, I walk through the set and I think about all the shots which have already been filmed, then I act out the scene for myself and visualize it on film. In this act of concentration, what I'm looking for is not so much the composition I'm going to choose as the rhythm of the shot, the weight I intend to give it in relation to the film as a whole. Then, the next day, the first shot I film is the one which contains the energy of the whole scene. The number of places where you can set your camera is, in theory, infinite; but, in reality, there is, more often than not, only one place; and the better I come to know a scene, the fewer problems I have in placing the camera.

In your films, the role of the image seems to interest you: binoculars, mirrors, screens, telescopes, etc.

One of the film's motifs is the crystal in which images are reflected and fragmented. The Vortex itself is like a block of crystal which Zed enters. For me, the mirror is an enigma, as

The destruction of the Vortex: an Exterminator and a Renegade (*Zardoz*).

are double images. In two dimensions, a reflected image has the same value as a genuine image, which isn't the case in life. Geoffrey Unsworth, who shot *A Night to Remember*, about the sinking of the *Titanic*, told me that the half of the ship which, for economic reasons, they filmed in a mirror was more lifelike on the screen than the other half!

You devote a great deal of time to editing.

I prefer editing to shooting, since, during the shoot, one is constantly under the pressure of time, especially nowadays. And, as I try to get the most out of a film, I set up difficulties for myself which I later have to overcome. This was particularly true of *Zardoz*, which I agreed to undertake on a very tight, unalterable budget. In effect, the distributors were afraid of the subject and their faith in me was circumscribed by extremely precise financial limits – which, I have to say, I perfectly understand. On the other hand, while editing, you're master of your own time. In addition, I love working on the soundtrack, directing the spectator by means of sounds and music. Each stage of a film represents a kind of torment, one that's created precisely by abandoning the previous stage and by the feeling that there's a gulf between the script and the shooting, then between the shooting and the editing. When you are shooting, the script becomes a kind of dead skin; then, at the end of the shoot, you finally have some footage, to be sure, but it's a clumsy, shapeless monster which unfolds before you. What upsets me during the shooting is that I have the impression that each shot represents a kind of defeat. John Ford would never view rushes, something I'm beginning to understand: I know, without there being any sense of surprise, exactly what I'm going to see and what I'm not going to see. It's only on the editing table that one suddenly has the feeling that the film exists. Each stage is a struggle against the preceding one: the shoot against the script, the editing against the shoot. When I direct, I have neither indulgence nor respect for the screenwriter that I am, then the editor in me becomes very critical with regard to myself as director. My editors are always having to hold me back because I'm ready to cut shots which took the greatest effort to film. I don't know what that means, but it's a fact.

Zed and Consuella (Sean Connery and Charlotte Rampling in *Zardoz*).

1977

Father Lamont in the cavern of the witchdoctor Kokumo (Richard Burton in *The Heretic*).

The Heretic

Trembling Reflections of the Future

The Story Behind the Film

The story behind *The Heretic* bears a curious resemblance to the scenario of another of its director's films, *Point Blank*: a man sets himself a challenge, deploys all the resources of his talent and intelligence to meet it, overcomes one by one every obstacle in his path without ever allowing himself to be distracted from it, then discovers at the end of his adventure that he has been engulfed by the system he had hoped to defeat.

By agreeing to film the sequel to William Friedkin's *The Exorcist*, one of the most commercially successful films in the history of the cinema (indeed, *the* most successful in its day), Boorman saw the possibility of articulating his own preoccupations through an original screenplay by William Goodhart, while disposing not only of an enormous budget (eighteen million dollars) but of guaranteed support from a public which would, as he believed, be willing to follow him off the beaten track. Warner Bros, the production company, authorized his visionary ambitions; and, by virtue of energy and calculation, in spite of all the inherent difficulties, he succeeded in imposing

The splitting of Regan in the Georgetown house (Linda Blair and Richard Burton in *The Heretic*).

his personality on a super-production, in wresting a *film d'auteur* out of the least 'noble' of Hollywood genres: the horror movie.

Boorman, however, had neglected one essential question: can a film-maker with impunity run counter to a colossal success and so disappoint the expectations of its unforgiving fans? Yet, like his own protagonists – who, in each film, painfully emerge from self-delusion into self-knowledge – he coolly and dispassionately faced the consequences of the whole unhappy affair. Savaged by the American critics (who, though prepared on occasion to praise his films – cf. *Deliverance* and *The Emerald Forest* – have rarely been equal to the dimension of his talent and originality), and violently rejected by audiences (who were no doubt hoping for effects even more gruesome than those of *The Exorcist*), he could only acknowledge the total failure of *The Heretic* and undertake, *himself*, a few days after its initial release, a second, scrupulously re-edited version. This version was, in fact, never screened in America (except for the new ending, a shot of Father Lamont and the young girl together beneath a radiant sun, and the explanatory prologue) and was exclusively reserved for foreign distribution.

Reading the original screenplay, one can see in detail the nature of the changes which were effected.[141] But after being privileged to view both versions of the film (which might usefully be designated *The Heretic I* and *The Heretic II*, i.e. the first American version, with its original epilogue, and the version distributed in Europe), I can state that, apart from the question of the ending, the differences are minimal: in short, no major scene is missing from *The Heretic II*. There was, to be sure, a further development of the theological aspects in *The Heretic I*, through the conversations with Cardinal Jaros (the two scenes in the Vatican, somewhat abridged in *The Heretic II*), thereby better explaining Father Lamont's crisis and loss of faith. Similarly, his conflict with Dr Tuskin and the latent sexuality which draws him to Regan were lent greater emphasis. These cuts are certainly regrettable, as is that of the

A permanent counterpoint between Africa and America: Father Lamont and the dealer in religious trinkets (Richard Burton and Ned Beatty in *The Heretic*).

scene in which Regan rehearses her tap-dancing act (originally, the film's second scene), which made more comprehensible the director's decision to crosscut between the musical show and the stoning of Lamont in Ethiopia. On the other hand, Boorman took the opportunity of adding the beautiful opening shots of Lamont climbing a hill and of tightening up the final chase from New York to the Georgetown house, so that one might almost envisage some ideal synthesis, *The Heretic III*, combining the respective qualities of both versions.

There remains the problem of the ending, which was what appeared most to infuriate the American public. In *The Heretic I*, the sacrilegious union of the priest and the young girl unambiguously established the triumph of good over evil and brought the film to as positive a conclusion as that of *Zardoz*. In *The Heretic II*, the supposed death of Father Lamont (even if his voice over the prologue would seem to imply that he is still alive; but *Sunset Boulevard*, after all, had given voice to a dead man from the depths of a swimming pool) leaves victory with Regan alone, inviting us to question the implications of that victory and ending the film on the same note of tempered optimism as *Leo the Last* (in which a house is also destroyed). If this version is, in certain respects, more faithful to the conventions of the genre (the notion of the priest, as in *The Exorcist*, sacrificing himself to 'save' his young charge), it might nevertheless be defended as in keeping with the personality and performance of Burton, who strikes one, even while he seeks the truth, as crushed by the weight of his own failure. And it can, in addition, be situated squarely within the parameters of Boorman's thematics. Lamont's 'death' corresponds to the doomed quest for the Grail, whether it be the Grail of *Point Blank* or that of *Deliverance*; and Regan's conciliatory gesture mirrors the serenity rediscovered by Leo, who also kept company with doves.

The excitement surrounding the release of *The Heretic*, not to mention the publicity which it received, exposed to the world's beady eye the various transformations it had under-

The New York clinic (Linda Blair and Louise Fletcher in *The Heretic*).

gone. Boorman himself publicly claimed the right to revise a film which had never been 'previewed' (as most Hollywood films are) and openly derided the Romantic myth of the 'untouchable' work of art. And, even if one should always defend the artist's right to total control over his work, it's nevertheless possible to recognize as authentically his own the different versions which Boorman was induced to make of his film. Who now remembers that Kubrick cut eighteen minutes from *2001 – A Space Odyssey*, between its frosty reception in Washington and its subsequent New York release? As for *Greed*, *La Règle du jeu*, *The Magnificent Ambersons*, *A Star Is Born*, *Eva*, *The Private Life of Sherlock Holmes* and so many

other films subjected to infinitely more pernicious indignities than *The Heretic* (indignities often inflicted against their directors' wishes), they have no less continued to exert their influence and retain their expressive power. As Boorman himself has said: 'If a film is truly of value, then it possesses a soul which will resist any compromise.'

The Film Behind the Story

The Heretic, like all of Boorman's films, is the product of a poeticism – a fact which no doubt explains why it is still so misunderstood. 'The bourgeois is willing to be "epaté" on condition that there should appear to be no risk attached – which is to say, as long as it remains within the framework of the rational. Within the limits of rationality, he will sanction every hypertrophied form of ugliness. It becomes, for him, a kind of Grand Guignol: something, in short, acceptable as

Sharon (Kitty Winn), followed by Father Lamont (Richard Burton), explores the Georgetown house (*The Heretic*).

Father Lamont in front of the golden city (Richard Burton in *The Heretic*).

legitimately romantic. But what he rejects as the worst of all horrors is the irrational in itself.' (Hermann Brock).[196] Psychology no longer has any control over a universe placed under the sign of analogy; and never, probably, has any film used analogical crosscutting as systematically as *The Heretic*: not merely to generate tension – as in the breathtaking dash to Washington, a 'last-minute rescue' quite worthy of Boorman's master, D. W. Griffith – but also in the organization of the central narrative, oscillating as it does between shots of New York and of Africa. Yet, just as Boorman refuses to sacrifice the autonomous power and visual splendour of a composition to either movement or duration (or vice versa), but strives, instead to develop them in tandem, so his poetic sensibility is never allowed to weaken the narrative continuity. To paraphrase Freud, a plane is not only, in *The Heretic*, a phallic symbol (or a sinister insect), it's also, prosaically, a means of transport from Ethiopia to New York. The metaphysical fable, the mythological tale: these, already in themselves a constant source of fascination to the director of *Zardoz*, have given him the thread with which to weave his poetic reveries and philosophical reflections.

Which means that *The Heretic* is not – as some of its fiercest defenders will doubtless claim – a great film *in spite of* its screenplay. Its pivotal idea – the therapy of the synchronizer and the visions which it engenders – is, on the contrary, rich in thematic possibilities and wholly consistent with the film-maker's obsessions. As the link between two separate worlds, and therefore a metaphor for the cinema itself, the synchronizer could hardly fail to captivate Boorman. The situation of the spectator, thrust into the darkness of the auditorium, ready to live out his fantasies and gradually abandoning his rationality, can be compared to that of Regan in the hands of Dr Tuskin and Father Lamont. And the cinema, a medium half technical and half poetic, can no less be compared to the kind of synthesis which is sought in *The Heretic*.

In the same way, psychoanalysis has been described as the combination of two categories of knowledge: the scientific and the initiatory. If Dr Tuskin, the psychiatrist who is treating Regan, restricts her professional function to one of practical therapy, it's from a desire to understand *in fine* the necessary synthesis. For his part, Father Lamont, associated as a priest with the notion of a spiritual renaissance, discovers the extraordinary potential of science. But it is in Africa – and on making contact with Kokumo, magician and sage, who has found the means of defeating evil by isolating the 'good' locust – that Lamont learns the secret of dialectical progression. For Boorman, as for Blake, without opposites there can be no advance. Good and evil coexist in Regan; science and religion are mutually exclusive until capable of overcoming their opposition; and, faced with the concurrent crises of materialism and faith, man restlessly pursues the unity which has been lost. *The Heretic* therefore enabled Boorman to develop his thoughts on the relationship of a civilization with its own past; and the objects of his study were, naturally, science and religion, the only two means of knowing the world that have been offered mankind since the beginning of time.

This interrogation of culture, this descent into the history of a civilization, is yet another avatar of the primal drama which all of Boorman's heroes have enacted. Like Regan, Walker (*Point Blank*), Leo (*Leo the Last*) and Zed (*Zardoz*) have to liberate themselves from a secret buried deep in the past. And one might almost claim that the individual undergoes a process of evolution similar to that of humanity. Regan's recovery prefigures the renewal of mankind; the New York clinic, the Georgetown house, become the microcosm of revolution on a planetary scale. The young girl is liberated from her neurosis as civilization might still be from its malaise – a liberation which, in her case, is accomplished through a transference (and also union) with the figure of the father (which makes all the more regrettable the excision of the original ending, the *logical* culmination of the narrative), insofar as Lamont represents the absent father whom Regan has been seeking (and the final scene of the synchronizer in the hotel is explicit in this regard). If, in *Puzzle of a Downfall Child*, another admirable descent into the abyss of the unconscious, Schatzberg focused on the patient rather than the listener, Boorman in *The Heretic* analyses equally the crises of carer and cared-for (given that the Jesuit 'relieves' the doctor). Lamont is affected by the current of transference which passes between psychoanalyst and patient; and, in the help he offers another, he ends by knowing himself. It's when he genuinely agrees to become the heretic, to follow Regan on her African journey, to fly with her and Pazuzu, the demon of evil, to yield to his repressed impulses and to suffer the attendant anguish, that Lamont is able to mark out a path towards a personal liberation and a global comprehension of reality. By killing the bad Regan in the climactic apocalypse, he rediscovers the identity which attaches him to the good Regan. Burton's somnambulistic performance, moreover, dovetails with Regan's hypnosis and her *oneiric* adventures. Their waking dream is suggested by the narrative's repetitions (two visits to the Vatican, to the Museum of Natural History, to Kokumo, to Georgetown; also, the mirrored sets). Like the hero of *Point Blank*, Lamont is propelled into a voyage of discovery from which there can be no return; he enters a labyrinth whose centre is Kokumo's home; but, unlike Walker, he learns the secret before it is too late. Each of Boorman's films is the confrontation of two spaces, the story of a conquest and an aggression. In *The Heretic*, that confrontation is accompanied by an exploration, a more extreme one than ever before, of the dimension of time – thereby exploiting all of the cinema's powers of expression. By abolishing the frontiers between the past and the present, between the inside and the outside, Boorman attains that sphere of thought desired by André Breton, in which 'the imaginary and the real will cease to be perceived as contradictions'.[195] We can measure his success by the fact that he does so without a hint of intellectual aridity but with a totally consummate artistry. Like the English metaphysical poets, he renders the idea tangible by a style which invests each image with the highest possible degree of physical presence.

It was, again, Breton who said: 'The value of a work of art depends on the degree to which it is traversed by the trembling reflections of the future.'[195] *The Heretic*, a speculation on the individual and his place in history, an interrogation into the

The journey to the churches in the Ethiopian mountains (Richard Burton in *The Heretic*).

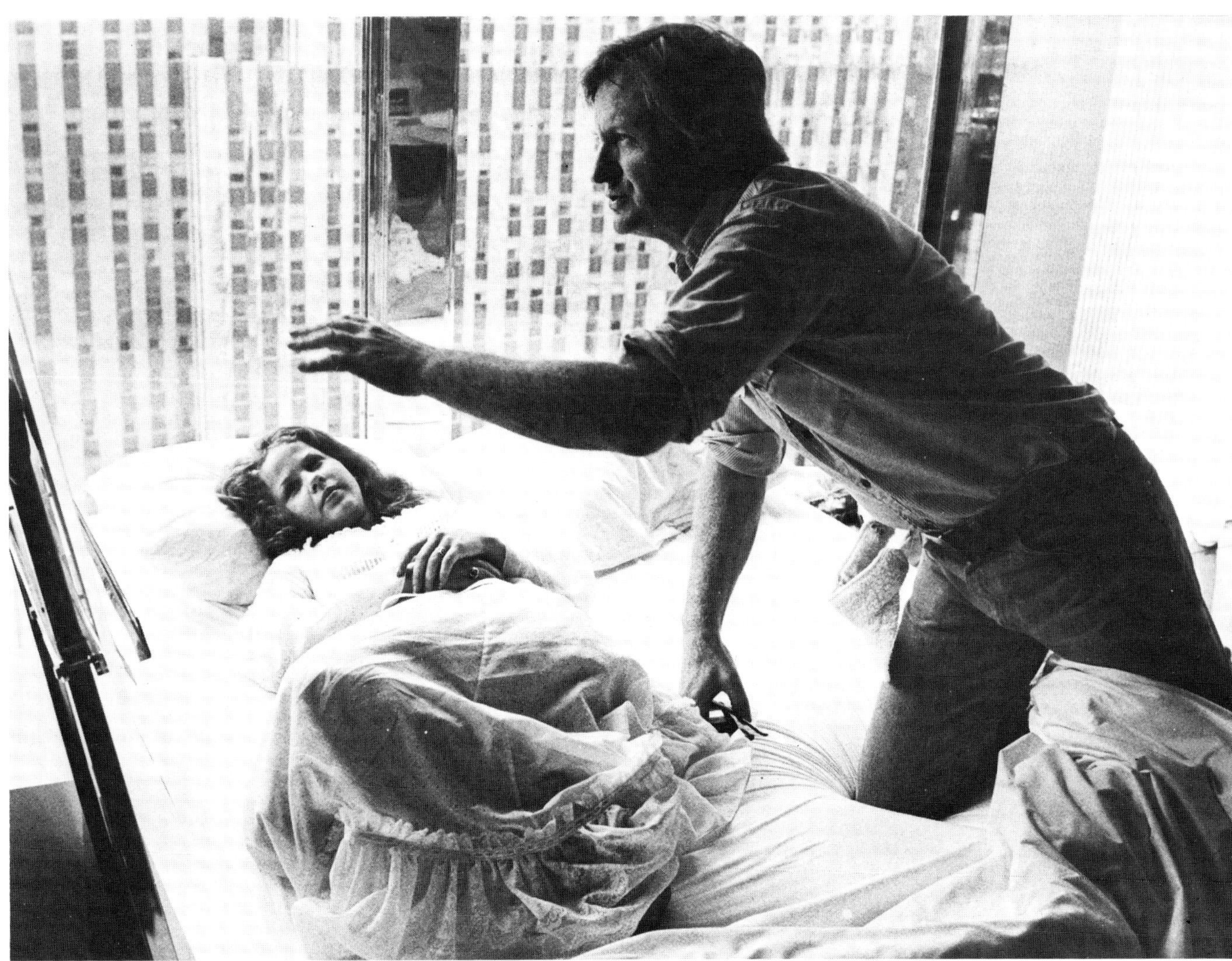

meaning of the future, is confirmation of his phrase. Anti-religious by conviction (the subject of *Zardoz*, his previous film, was the death of God and the tyranny of cultism), but preoccupied by metaphysics and conscious of the impasse in which an unhealthy society has found itself, Boorman offers us in *The Heretic* a new image of his personal cosmogony in which are blended the songs of innocence and experience, in which are united Heaven and Hell.

Weren't you originally offered the chance to film The Exorcist?

After *Deliverance*, John Calley, an executive at Warners, asked me to read the proofs of the book and give him an immediate answer as he was thinking of buying the rights. At the same time, he suggested that I might direct it. I replied that not only would I refuse, but that I didn't think Warners should produce it. It seemed to me a very difficult film to make, since everything depended on the performance of a twelve-year-old child. The problem of rendering the story credible was enormous. And, as a father, I found the book extremely tasteless, cruel and sadistic towards children. But Warners informed me that my advice had come too late, as they'd bought the rights the day before! And, later, I admired Friedkin for having handled the technical side of it so well.

Subsequently, after *Zardoz*, I worked on two projects, neither of which got off the ground. It was at that point that Calley asked me to read Goodhart's script of *The Heretic*, the sequel to *The Exorcist*. I was very impressed. It struck me as technically very difficult, but I was stimulated by the idea of a metaphysical thriller, and also by the theme of spiritual evolution. In addition, far from being destructive, the story was an optimistic one, which reinforced one's faith in life. I was therefore tempted by it, and by the fact that I'd have practically unlimited financial and technical means to do what I wanted. There was also the frustration of having two scripts which, for various reasons, I'd had to abandon. So I decided to accept Warners' offer, knowing full well that, given the current situation of the cinema, it was unlikely that such a opportunity

John Boorman directs Linda Blair (shooting *The Heretic*).

would come my way again – the opportunity, for example, of reconstructing landscapes in the studio.

Between the ideal project and the final result, every film encounters material obstacles which sometimes alter it considerably. The Heretic *was no exception to the rule – quite the reverse!*

A number of problems were due to the fact that it was a sequel. For example, Lee J. Cobb, who played the detective in *The Exorcist*, was an important character in Goodhart's original screenplay. But Cobb died before shooting began, which meant that we had to find an alternative solution. Curiously, certain functions of his role were assumed by Kitty Winn who, in *The Exorcist*, had played a secretary without making any particular impression. In the end, it was evident that she was going away, that she had had enough and that she had no intention of returning. But we needed someone and, with Rospo Pallenberg (who at this stage was working with me on the script), I met Kitty Winn and was struck by her extreme nervousness, her tension and vulnerability – in short, by a neurotic quality she had, as though she were permanently on edge. I was quite disturbed by that. We therefore decided to include this character, as she seemed an ideal means of conveying the strangeness of someone grazed by the shadow of evil. Frankly, it also enabled me to solve the problem posed by Linda Blair, who's physically attractive and has a real screen presence but lacks spirituality. And, as that was the film's subject, it was Kitty Winn, her friend, who would communicate the sensation of fear, of a strange form of spirituality.

Another problem was that I wanted a young man for the role of the priest; and when Jon Voight, who was my initial choice, finally turned it down because we couldn't agree about the character, I had to find a replacement. The only actor of that age who I felt would be convincing in the role was Christopher Walken; but the producers were reluctant to cast an unknown, which was quite understandable. The idea that he'd be a young man attracted me, because of the relationship which might develop with Regan. Ted Ashley, of Warners,

In *The Heretic*, as always in Boorman's work, the white man emotionally sterile, is enriched and revitalized by contact with other races. Here, Father Merrin in the heart of Africa (Max von Sydow and Joey Green).

1

2

1 Walker and the black nightclub singer in *Point Blank* (Lee Marvin and Stu Gardner).
2 The American pilot and the Japanese sailor in *Hell in the Pacific* (Lee Marvin and Toshiro Mifune).

1 Leo and the Jamaican inhabitants of his cul-de-sac (Marcello Mastroianni, Calvin Lockhart and Glenna Forster Jones in *Leo the Last*). **2** The American engineer and the Tupi Indians (Rui Polonah, Powers Boothe, Dira Paes and Tetchie Agbayani in *The Emerald Forest*).

was very keen on Burton, who, in his opinion, could carry the film. Burton, to be sure, was a very persuasive, very powerful actor – he was totally credible. But the choice immediately posed new problems, since a middle-aged man would behave in a quite different fashion. As a result, we had to make changes both to the character and the scenes in which he appeared. Many people, reading a script, say that they can't

imagine anyone but such and such an actor playing a particular role. And they're often right. But what they fail to realize is that it's not so much the actor who appropriates the role as the screenwriter and director who bring the role closer to what the actor is and what he can do. In this particular case, we gradually changed Lamont from a passionate, impulsive priest to the disillusioned Jesuit he is in the film.

Originally, the psychiatrist was a man. You ended by casting Louise Fletcher, which makes the plot far more complex, as a woman is usually associated with emotions and intuition, whereas here she represents science. And Lamont now finds himself confronted with three women: Sharon, Regan and Tuskin.

We didn't manage to find a suitable male actor for the role; and I was stimulated by the decision to cast Louise Fletcher. Naturally, we revised the character, which considerably affected the film. All these changes meant that the film was very different from what had originally been planned and it's a pointless exercise speculating on whether it might otherwise have been better. It certainly wouldn't have been the same, which only goes to show how flexible and plastic a film is. I particularly like the scenes which we were able to develop between Sharon and Tuskin; they really come alive and there's a tension between the two women, notably when Tuskin enters the McNeils' apartment and Sharon tells her that Regan is on the roof.

Another casting problem concerned Max von Sydow, who plays a minor but essential role, since he is the link between the two films and his struggle with evil is a basic theme of *The Heretic*. But he had no desire to play in the film, his opinion of *The Exorcist* being rather negative. He condemned it from a moral point of view, and found it heavy-handed and emphatic. Though he loathed the idea of playing the same character again, he realized that I shared his feelings about *The Exorcist* and I convinced him that he now had a chance to heal the wounds inflicted by the first film. For him, the success of *The Exorcist* derived from the fact that it aroused in audiences a latent hatred of children, which he believed was an unconscious reaction to the problem of overpopulation. Formerly, children were loved and pampered; today they're regarded as a threat and people took pleasure in watching a child being tortured on the screen. Finally, I persuaded him to help me and take part in the film.

Why from the beginning did you decide not to film in Africa?

The action was set in the Coptic churches of Ethiopia, which are found in inaccessible mountainous regions. In addition, the civil war, then at its height, and the frequency of epidemics, made filming there practically impossible. During the preparation, while I was rewriting the script and also scouting locations – that crucial period when one is trying to find a visual style – I spent a lot of time in search of an art director. That was a major decision. I met a lot of American art directors but could never agree with them on this particular project, since

1 Regan in front of her bedroom wall (Linda Blair and Katrine Boorman's drawings in *The Heretic*).
2 Father Lamont in front of the Coptic paintings (Richard Burton in *The Heretic*).

their approach was basically naturalistic and so quite unsuitable for the visionary quality I hoped to achieve. I particularly wanted there to be a link between the interiors in New York and the African scenes. That puzzled them; it was as though I were speaking in a foreign language. I had the good fortune to be able to use Richard MacDonald who, though English, had been allowed to work in Hollywood. He understood perfectly what I was aiming at and was very excited at the idea of having complete control in the studio. He was even more radical than I, and regarded any filming in exteriors – which is to say, nine days out of seventeen weeks! – as a kind of defeat. Thanks to the fact that we filmed in the studio, I was able to obtain a visual coherence, particularly where the colour was concerned. We used a very limited range of colours. We excluded blues and greens, which are reassuring colours, ones we associate with nature, with the sky, with trees, and concentrated rather on amber – the colour of the desert – and similar shades, such as chestnut, red and ochre, in order to create a certain disquet. I also noticed that, when film people look for locations, they've no hesitation in choosing the weirdest landscapes, since they have a strangeness that is both exciting and sanctioned by reality. In the studio, however, they become so preoccupied with creating an illusion of reality that they grow cautious and tend to aim for blandness. With MacDonald, I opted for the imagination.

Not only did we want the African forms and the New York settings to resemble each other, we also tried to evoke the theme of the locusts in other visual elements: in aeroplanes, for example, or the clinic, which is shaped like a hive with cells and glass partitions, further isolating characters who are already rather solitary creatures, capable of communicating only with the synchronizer. In addition, the theme of the mirror finds its correlative in the skyscraper which reflects Louise Fletcher and Kitty Winn, fragmenting their personalities and their universe. We devoted a lot of thought and work to the film's visuals; and it was a point on which William Goodhart and I disagreed. He thought that, because of the visionary element in the African episodes, the New York sequences ought to be prosaic, banal, 'realistic', from a visual point of view. In his script, for example, the clinic was a simple psychiatrist's surgery. It was my opinion that, on the contrary, as so much of the film was set there, it would have been impossible to cut from the Ethiopian scenes to a single, drably-designed room without creating a sense of anticlimax, without lowering the tension. What was important, rather, was to 'elevate' reality, to give it another dimension in order to create

Glass and reflections at the top of a New York skyscraper (Linda Blair and Kitty Wynn in *The Heretic*).

1

2

The journey of Father Lamont (Richard Burton in *The Heretic*).
1 To Brazil.
2 To New York.

To Ethiopia.

a sort of correspondence. That's why we thought of this clinic, with its infinite reflections and its strange children in the background – a complex space which would also serve to symbolize, through its technology, the scientific aspect of the conflict. As for the patients imprisoned in their separate cells, what made the situation so poignant was that, despite their efforts, neither science nor religion could reach them. And when Regan succeeds in communicating with a little girl and cures her, in the simplest possible manner, the fact that it happens in such a context makes it all the more forceful.

How did you film the shot in which, without any optical tricks or break in continuity, Max von Sydow is in a corner of the room, then we move to the décor of the temple?

It's the kind of shot I hope will succeed in baffling my colleagues. In fact, von Sydow lay down on the floor of the Georgetown house, then stood up again. When back on his feet, he finds himself in the Ethiopian church, at which point the camera tracks back and we can't see the room any more. We had a corner of the room specially constructed, about a metre high, and placed it in the church. The wall was painted a colour that gradually shaded into that of the church; and it was so cleverly done that the wallpaper served as a fade and thereby made the transition invisible. The corner of the room was attached to wires, so that, later, when the camera drew back, we were able to yank it out of shot.

It was very exciting to direct, as was the opening sequence, in which we see the young girl's hair burning around her face. For that we used a sheet of plate-glass and were able, by means of its reflecting surface on a black background, to superimpose her face on a black, bewigged polystyrene head. The two faces coincided exactly; she was able to act the character's responses and the camera to photograph them without any optical tricks.

How did you work on the film's storyboards with Richard MacDonald?

I've always used storyboards. For those scenes which are technically very complex, I have a storyboard designed for me, since it enables me to communicate with the crew and convey what I'm looking for. Such was the case, for example, with the destruction of the house. It was built entirely on a hydraulic system and each transformation had to be gauged exactly. MacDonald is an amazing man who had a tough time contending with studio bureaucracy, since they really couldn't understand anyone as imaginative as he is. He's a hard worker, with an extraordinary power of concentration. I remember that, when he came to my home in the evening, I'd describe each shot to him and, with his eyes closed, he'd sketch it out like some practitioner of Zen. For the scenes with actors, I consider a storyboard too constricting, even though I believe one of the worst things a director can do is allow an actor too much freedom within a scene. The actor knows it, since he has to make certain movements in relation to the camera; it's a technical problem and he expects you to be precise. Of course, once the indications have been given, in the composition which has been decided upon, he can then add his contribution.

There are many scenes in which you employ a highly mobile camera – from the very beginning of the film.

I used a new camera which had just been perfected by Gareth Brown, the Steadycam. Pazuzu, the spirit of evil, is personified by a subjective camera movement which gives the impression of flight. The Steadycam is harnessed to the cameraman and is very supple and fluid; it isn't mechanical in the way a crane or dolly is. It's half muscle, half machine, and has a floating, drifting quality which I wanted for the flight across Africa, for example, as well as for the scene in which Regan jumps on to the train. It enabled me to suggest the point of view of Pazuzu. The Steadycam is balanced like a frisbee, which makes it extremely light.

How did you film the scenes with the locusts?

The theme was gradually developed as we rewrote the script, to the point where the presence of the locusts became necessary at the end of the film. Showing clouds of locusts destroying a house created a number of difficult technical problems: it also took up a great deal of time, which was one of the reasons we shot it in the studio. We added back-projection film of real locusts flying against a blue screen on which were superimposed shots of locusts imported from California. Oxford Scientific, which had worked on *Zardoz*, supplied some footage – in particular, the shot of the outsize insect representing the spirit of evil. As soon as a locust no longer touches the ground, it automatically starts to beat its wings and fly. All we had to do, then, was suspend it on a wire, place it in front of the blue screen (a variation on back-projection) and move the camera to create the impression of flight. It wasn't easy, but after a number of attempts we succeeded. Similarly, for the attack on the house, I filmed only two shots a day for a fortnight. In fact, we shot so little that the first rough cut of the film lasted only two hours and twelve minutes; and I subsequently reduced that to just under two hours.

You constantly set up visual counterpoints: Regan's drawings in her room, Mantegna's fresco in the Vatican (which is, in fact, his 'Crucifixion' in the Louvre), the paintings in the Coptic churches, the diorama in the Museum of Natural History.

It's something which has always fascinated me. The diorama, in particular, a kind of petrified Africa in the very heart of New York, was very evocative for me – the idea of having travelled and returning to find onself confronted with an atrophied continent. It's not unlike the Vatican, which in the film represents a dead religion. We had lots of discussions about the type of painting we could use for the scenes in the Vatican. The second scene there begins with the fresco; then the characters appear in the image. The fresco serves as a kind of landscape and the figures of the actors in the foreground seem to become part of its perspective. And if we chose Mantegna, it was because of his sense of depth. In addition, the fresco conveyed a feeling of aridity, whereas the paintings of later artists have a sensuality which would have been unsuitable.

With your Catholic education, did you see the synchronizer and its therapeutic value as an equivalent to confession?

What Lamont is going through is the kind of crisis which many priests today experience. He feels spiritually 'blocked'. He's afraid that God might be dead. He's looking for alternative paths to a transcendental experience, and he believes he's found one in science. It's perhaps a difficult idea to convey in a 'thriller' like *The Heretic*, but what we have is a priest who, by the intervention of a psychiatrist, attempts to establish spiritual contact with the young heroine. The synchronizer has a historical origin. In the thirties, there was a scientist who developed a system of mutual hypnosis in which the hypnotist shared the patient's visions. I myself attended hypnosis sessions before making the film and it was extremely interesting. Some people claim that, under hypnosis, we see only what we want to see; but that's a falsely reassuring interpretation. It seems, on the contrary, that a number of mysterious assassinations, like that of John Kennedy, might have been carried out under hypnosis; and that it's possible for the murderer, after his act, to censor what he's done, which eliminates every trace of the crime.

What are your feelings about the occult?

Hypnosis interests me a great deal, as does extra-sensory perception; and it's a field I've studied quite thoroughly. What's more, I believe that the occult and the cinema are natural companions. What we experience while watching a film is comparable to the occult in its atmosphere and in the illusion that is created. My interest in Jung also reflects these preoccupations.

But the occult interests me more in the cinema than in literature. I'm thinking, in particular, of certain moments in Hammer films, even if they're sometimes formally crude and badly acted. I recently saw *Countess Dracula*, which is, in my opinion, eerily brilliant, very well directed and based on a very powerful idea. The price paid by the heroine for rejuvenating herself with the blood of virgins, in order to enjoy a night of beauty, is to find herself even older the next morning. And, of course, the German Expressionist films were a great influence on me.

In an interview, the painter Matta proposed that it would be from the African continent that the next great cultural innovations would arise; that, in fact, it was a privileged continent insofar as it contained the whole history of humanity; and that, in the conflict between homo sapiens *and electronic cerebration, the African soul might be capable of discovering a new form of rationality in the magnetic field of such a*

The wise man Kokumo isolates the 'good' locust (James Earl Jones and Richard Burton in *The Heretic*).

Parallel space and time.

1 While Father Lamont (Richard Burton) is stoned in Ethiopia . . .

2 . . . Regan (Linda Blair) collapses in a theatre in New York (*The Heretic*).

1 Regan (Linda Blair) drives off the locusts in the Georgetown house . . .

2 . . . just as Kokumo (Joey Green) had driven them off, years before, on the African plains (*The Heretic*)

confrontation.[208] *That's an idea which is also dear to you and which can be found in* Leo the Last*: regeneration through a primitive culture. It's what* Zardoz *says, too, through the medium of the Brutals.*

Teilhard de Chardin posed the same questions – on the origin of man, the moment at which he acquired spirituality, a moment which occurred in Africa. There was a conversation between Lamont and Edwards, the pilot of the aircraft, which I finally cut and which concerned the same problem. When Lamont asked him how he happened to take up his profession, Edwards replied: 'Ex-priest, ex-pilot, I'm still trying to believe, I'm still trying to fly.' And he added: 'It was I who introduced those plaster Madonnas into darkest Africa. And one day, in exchange, I'm going to steal an African soul and put it into this empty shell.' He ended the sentence by beating his chest and, with the other hand, throwing the statue out of the aeroplane window. The idea was that Edwards was a disillusioned priest who was desperately searching in Africa for the relationship with spirituality which he'd lost. We're all profoundly nostalgic for a kind of unity, hints of which we sometimes catch in art or in love or in inspiration. And it's in Africa that the quest for this unity is taking place.

From that point of view, Kokumo is the film's central character, simultaneously attracting and repelling the locusts.

He has found a way of fighting evil. Ted Ashley felt that, in the script, Kokumo's significance was expressed in too indirect a fashion; that, for example, he didn't speak to Lamont when the latter visited him. It's true that he doesn't utter a word, but there's an 'experiment' between them, a test. In addition, he's a living example of the fusion of two roles, the magical and the scientific. Finally, he presents him with the parable of the good locust as the key to what the young girl represents. When Lamont returns, Regan asks him what Kokumo has revealed to him and the priest gives her an unsatisfactory answer: he simply tells her that good and evil are in conflict within her. There we have the poignant aspect of the situation: an ordinary, simple young girl and a man who has understood what's happening to her, but is incapable of explaining it to her. She understands enough, however, and knows what to do; she knows that, through the synchronizer, they have to make their way to this other world. In the balcony scene with Dr Tuskin, she reacts like Kokumo; she realizes that the frontiers of time and space no longer apply when one is synchronized and that she can help Lamont. She has learned to live with a new concept.

The final sequence of *The Heretic*: Doctor Tuskin in the wreck of the taxi in Georgetown (Louise Fletcher).

What is your feeling about the film after all the obstacles you encountered?

The film represented an enormous amount of work, a struggle that never seemed to end. In particular, I tried to remain faithful to our original ambitions, to remain personal within the context of a big-budget, mass-audience Hollywood movie. The crew imagines that you're being terribly self-indulgent when you insist on eliminating certain colours or when you spend time on details that strike them as unimportant. And yet you have to insist, if you don't want to be swallowed up in the terrifying logistics which such a project represents. Then there's the pressure on you of the fact that a film of this dimension costs two thousand dollars an hour. It's like commanding an army; and though the shoot lasted twice as long as usual, I actually had less time to spend on the camera and the actors.

In addition, I fell seriously ill, was taken to hospital and almost died. The film came to a halt for five weeks and I was mortified, since I'd never been ill before. It happened because of some poisonous fungus growing in the soil which we'd brought into the studio for the African desert scenes. Then my wife had an ulcer and one of my daughters had a tumour! After the completion of the film, I was absolutely furious at having subjected myself to such an ordeal. I'd inflicted all that suffering on myself. No one had forced me to make the film. Also, instead of taking the easy way out, I had decided to set myself a number of challenges so that I might overcome them. And you end by wondering what's going on in your head the moment you make such a decision. I've always been struck by the fact that the only free act in the creation of a film is the decision to make it. After that, you become a slave for a year or two, and you simply can't escape. Each time I finish a film, I want the next one to be very straightforward; for some reason, though, I begin creating complications for myself all over again. My critics – who include my wife – say that I avoid confronting the emotional situations in my films by multiplying the technical problems to be overcome, by making them ever more complex and labyrinthine. Well, maybe it's true. On the other hand, an artist never really has any control over his creative mechanism. You can be conscious of your limitations but, when you begin shooting, you take just the same path as before. In any case, for better or worse, that's the way I work. *The Heretic*, and the reception it was given, was a traumatic experience for me. It forced me to question my relations with the public and with my own films; it forced me to question myself on the future.

Regan standing in front of the ruined house (Linda Blair in *The Heretic*).

1981

The cycle of the Arthurian legends: Merlin hands the magic sword to Uther Pendragon (Nicol Williamson and Gabriel Byrne in *Excalibur*).

Excalibur

The Sword and the Dragon

Excalibur, Boorman's eighth film, may be described as a culmination. By directly addressing himself to the cycle of Arthurian legends, he brings to a close twenty years of reflection on the interrelated themes of the Grail and the quest with which all of his work has been embued. What immediately strikes one is the sheer magnitude of the project: it is, in effect, the complete cycle that the director has appropriated, from the saga of the Knights of the Round Table by way of the romantic triangle of Arthur, Guinevere and Lancelot to Perceval's search for the hidden Chalice. Each of his previous films was the tale of an initiatory journey undertaken by a protagonist in search of his own identity. *Excalibur*, however, can claim not one, but two heroes: Arthur, first of all, whose life is recounted from birth to death; but also Perceval, who appears halfway through the film to 'relieve' Arthur when the ailing monarch surrenders his power. And it is Perceval on whom the hope of a new world is based: a 'child of nature', he defends the Queen's honour in the tournament, he crosses the heath, he survives an encounter with Death, he discovers the Grail, he revives himself in the waters of the Lake, he heals Arthur, he watches over the King's death agony and his subsequent departure for Avalon. It is he, too, who casts Excalibur into the Lake – so that, perhaps, the Lady of the Lake might one day offer mankind the possibility of redeeming itself.

But what this epic encompasses is nothing less than the history of the world. *Excalibur* begins in chaos and obscurity,

The romance of Arthur and Guinevere (Nigel Terry and Cherie Lunghi in *Excalibur*).

out of which flits the shadow of Merlin, as he hands the sword to Uther Pendragon. For a brief moment, chaos gives way to order. In alliance with the Duke of Cornwall, Uther inaugurates a reign founded on reason and justice. But his desire for Igraine, the Duke of Cornwall's wife, plunges humanity into further violence and anarchy. It is once more through the sword, wrested from the stone by Arthur, that peace and civilization are reinstated; this restoration of unity finds its emblem in the castle of Camelot. Yet the apparent harmony is deceptive – its gold and silver walls enclose a void. Here, as in *Zardoz*, a Utopia harbours the seed of its own destruction, since, being a pure product of reason, it fatally omits to account for either nature or spirituality. Arthur dreams of instituting the best of all possible worlds, one in which friction and dissension would be dissolved in law and civilization; but such an idealistic construction, such a futile attempt to smooth out human contradictions, cannot hope to survive. His desire to re-establish a Golden Age marks the end of the first, ascendant, movement of the film. It will be Perceval's role to set out in search of spiritual values – a movement towards interiorization which will affect all the other characters.

In *Excalibur*, the characters are ruled, and harmony is destroyed, by passion: Uther's physical passion for Igraine, Launcelot's romantic passion for Guinevere, Morgana's vengeful passion for her stepbrother Arthur, whom she seduces, and for Merlin, whom she immures in a block of crystal. In a universe governed by betrayal, the power of sexuality can only be destructive. Igraine is betrayed by Uther, who assumes the physical features of her husband, the Duke of Cornwall. From their adulterous union is born Arthur. Arthur is betrayed by Lancelot, his dearest friend, who becomes Guinevere's lover. Arthur is sexually abused by Morgana, his stepsister, who as a child had witnessed the primal scene: Uther's seduction of their mother. From their incestuous union is born Mordred, who in his turn betrays his father. Merlin, too, is betrayed by Morgana, whose charms are deployed to neutralize his power.

Lancelot (Nicholas Clay in *Excalibur*).

But passion is also an evolutionary force. It destroys, but it may also rebuild the world. By that unity of opposites which has informed Boorman's work since *Zardoz*, passion is the noblest form of indiscretion and therefore a guarantee of progress. Its power, moreover, remains beyond Merlin's understanding, even if it is he who pulls the strings of the narrative. He refers to it as 'a crazy humour affecting beggars no less than kings'. *Excalibur* was originally to have been titled *Merlin Lives!*, and we are aware of the importance in Boorman's films of the character of the manipulative, godlike puppeteer. Merlin hopes that, through the sword and its magic, the world will acquire wisdom; he even believes, mistakenly, that he can control human nature. His character is diametrically opposed to that of Arthur, his former pupil. The magician is ageless and ubiquitous; he has been emancipated from time and space, whereas Arthur is a prisoner of both. Merlin realizes, nevertheless, that he must eventually disappear. To Morgana – a malevolent witch to whom his goodness and wisdom are anathema – he declares: 'Our days are numbered. The one God chases out the many gods, and the spirits of wood and stream fall silent. So goes it, it is a time for men and their ways.' And the age, too, of a dissociation of culture from nature, with which the world has lived since the end of the Middle Ages. Merlin is inseparable from the idea of an earthly paradise – the true Golden Age, not the artificial Eden of Camelot. It is there, among the lizards and owls and serpents, that he teaches the young Arthur . . . a moment suspended in time which will never be repeated, save, briefly, when Lancelot and Guinevere enjoy a night of love in the forest.

He is also linked to the dragon, the emblem of life and goodness, the personification of that key to wisdom, the union of opposites. When he leads Morgana through the creature's innermost recesses, he reveals to her that it contains the source of his power. 'Here everything is possible. Everything meets its opposite. The future and the past. Desire and regret. Knowledge and oblivion.' Change is the only law of humanity. The

Uther Pendragon's death (Liam O'Calloghan and Gabriel Byrne in *Excalibur*).

sword is its embodiment, as is the dragon, and both are linked to Merlin. They can also be compared to the unconscious, to everything that lurks, repressed, just beneath the surface and one day arises to reawaken our dreams and desires. Like the unconscious, Excalibur is neither 'good' nor 'bad': it depends on the use to which it is put.

It is the women of the legend who, with Merlin, can claim a privileged relation to the sword: the Lady of the Lake as its keeper; then, during Arthur's illness, Guinevere as its guardian. As was first true of *Zardoz*, then of *The Heretic*, *Excalibur* assigns a major role to the feminine characters, who were much less prominent in Boorman's earlier films. Guinevere, who differs from Igraine and Morgana in being childless, is a kind of earthly divinity and the incarnation of sovereignty: after her adultery, for example, the King is no longer capable of exercising his authority. Guinevere and the Lady of the Lake are objects of veneration and sources of hope. They are also the only characters unrelated to the theme of blood. For blood flows freely through *Excalibur*: Uther Pendragon, Arthur, Lancelot, Morgana and Perceval all shed their blood. It is the blood of the Grail which heals the Fisher King. And if, from the sterile Utopia that Camelot becomes, blood is absent, it is because it is the instrument of change.

As should be clear, the symbolism of the elements, a recurring motif in Boorman's work, has never been so brilliantly deployed as in *Excalibur*. The dragon is the most immediately obvious example, representing as it does air, earth, water (which is where it comes from) and fire (which it spits out). In his study of the film's texture, Alain Masson has shown how the water which both opens and closes the film is combined with fire to create mist.[175] The horses' breath visible during the first battle between Uther Pendragon and the Duke of Cornwall parallels the fog conjured up by Morgana which is responsible for the death of her son Mordred in his final battle against his father. The symphony of elements is harmonized with that of the seasons. The cold and lifeless universe through

In *Excalibur* the women have a major role to play. The idyll of Lancelot and Guinevere (Nicholas Clay and Cherie Lunghi).

which the Knights ride in search of the Grail yields to the luxuriant rebirth of spring, with flowers bursting open in speeded-up motion as though in honour of their return.

But the splendour of the film's visuals cannot be divorced from the energy of its narrative. It is fire, the sign of passion, that governs the crosscutting between Uther's orgasm (as he penetrates Igraine) and Cornwall's death by impalement during a nocturnal encounter in the forest. Similarly, the fact that the idyll of Lancelot and Guinevere is intercut with the meeting of Merlin and Morgana hints at the underlying sexuality of the latter relationship. In *Excalibur*, Boorman explores an extraordinary variety of styles, moods and techniques, from the rhythm of nature to the different ages of man, from the epic to the tragic, from the elegiac to the comic. Rigorously constructed, yet leaving room for the irrational, the film can therefore be seen as developing the director's reflections on the necessary and complementary duality of reason and magic.

Morgana le Fay (Helen Mirren).

Igraine's dance (Katrine Boorman).

Interview

The Arthurian legends have always interested you and this film is an early project of yours.

It goes back quite a way, as far as *The Quarry*, which I directed for television. Even before making my first film, I'd written a script vaguely inspired by John Cowper Powys' *A Glastonbury Romance*, a novel which itself represented, in the early thirties, a reformulation of the Arthurian legends in a modern context. At the age of eighteen, I was very influenced by Powys, by those immense novels of his which are whole continents in themselves: you can get lost in them and can only read them when you're young and have the time! I was struck, at that period of my life, by the power of the Arthurian resonances, which I rediscovered in Eliot's *The Waste Land* and numerous other works. It was as though, with almost everything I read, I'd find myself confronted with the Grail cycle. And then, via Eliot, I read Jessie Weston's fascinating book, *From Ritual to Romance*, a commentary on the legend which I don't always agree with, but which is nevertheless stimulating. Later, I became interested in Jung, who was drawn to the stories but who – to my great regret – never really wrote on the subject, as it was the province of his wife Emma and he didn't want to encroach on it. The allusions to it in his work, though, are quite fascinating. He speaks, in his autobiography, about a stone in the garden of his house near a lake and how he wanted to carve on it the phrase 'Merlin's cry', the cry heard in the forest after the magician's disappearance. He always said his work on the unconscious was the continuation of that undertaken by Merlin. Merlin's cry, in other words, is the cry of the unconscious. Merlin's ambiguity, the fact that he is both more and less than a man, his capacity to intervene in human affairs,

Opposite John Boorman directs Nigel Terry (shooting *Excalibur*).
Above The meeting of Lancelot and Perceval (Nicholas Clay and Paul Geoffrey in *Excalibur*).

albeit in an erratic and irrational fashion, and the gift he possesses of seeing into the future and understanding the past, make him a representation of the unconscious. For the unconscious contains a kind of magic and even, if you like, the notion of the dragon that one finds in Merlin's story. The dragon is the prehistoric creature, the reptile, in all of us, the id rising out of the depths of the swamp, with all the terror which that supposes. For Jung, in effect, the unconscious has to be confronted, since it represents the past of both the individual and the race. But travelling through the unconscious is a terrifying enterprise and may end with the destruction of the ego. The Middle Ages, according to Jung, was a period which, like the unconscious, we ought to study in order to gain a better understanding of ourselves.

For a century now, we've been rushing headlong into the future; we've made a cult out of progress and we've forgotten our former selves, our former patterns of behaviour, whose origins can be traced to the Middle Ages. We no longer have any roots; and today, in particular, when we contemplate the possible destruction of our planet, there's a thirst, a nostalgia for the past, a desperate need to understand it. We are attracted to the legend of the Grail because it speaks to us of a period when nature was unsullied and man in harmony with it.

This neo-medievalism is not only a phenomenon of popular culture. In recent years, it has also surfaced in intellectual milieux, among historians, philosophers and mythologians.

That's very true. But, as you know, in America there is a disturbing tendency to pay little heed to history – even the most recent history. Americans rarely ask themselves where the can of meat they've just bought at the supermarket comes from. It's dangerous to cut yourself off from the sources of what you use and eat: I consider it a healthy attitude, rather, to ask about where things come from. The Middle Ages also represented a long period of stability – superficially, at least – compared with the acceleration of history during the Renaissance, the Industrial Revolution and the present day. I repeat, however, that what we've lost above all is our understanding of nature, our knowledge of plants, our capacity to *make* things, which every community used to assume. Everyone was concerned about the soil.

When you are faced with a cycle as rich as that of the Arthurian legends, you must feel submerged by the volume of material. How did you choose from among the extraordinary quantity of books and studies, a quantity which leaves you with greater freedom than would a single work closed in on itself, but which, on the other hand, forces you to take some drastic decisions?

For a long time, it's true, I felt overwhelmed. My intention was always to find an epic form rather than select a single one of the episodes of the legend, which would certainly have been more reasonable. But I also wanted to retain the whole scope of the story and cover in depth the period from Arthur's birth to his death: which is to say, the relationship between the boy Arthur and Merlin, the founding of the Knights of the Round Table, and the quest for the Grail.

Preceding pages Father and son in mortal combat (Nigel Terry as Arthur and Robert Addie as Mordred in *Excalibur*).

'Merlin is a representation of the unconscious'
(Nicol Williamson in *Excalibur*).

1

2

The fruits of adultery.
1 Queen Igraine and Uther Pendragon with the child Arthur (Katrine Boorman and Gabriel Byrne in *Excalibur*).
2 Morgana le Fay and her son Mordred (Helen Mirren and Robert Addie in *Excalibur*).

The seasonal cycle.
1 Winter: the battle in the forest (*Excalibur*).
2 Spring: the Knights of the Round Table (*Excalibur*).

That created certain problems of dramatization. In the first place, when Arthur sends his Knights in search of the Grail – to atone for the sins which had been committed – he ceases to play an active role. Second, Merlin also disappears at a certain moment in the story. And, third, there was the sheer profusion of episodes. Finally, in 1975, I wrote a scenario for Warner Bros which would have been a four-and-a-half-hour film. It had been constructed as a series of flashbacks centred on the character of Perceval, and that of Merlin when he emerged from the cave in which Vivian had held him prisoner. (At that stage, I hadn't yet amalgamated the characters of Vivian and Morgana.) I can't say that Warners were very enthusiastic, particularly in view of the film's running time, but I didn't see how I could have explored the theme in fewer pages. I'd encountered the same problem fifteen years before, when Rospo Pallenberg and I adapted Tolkien's *The Lord of the Rings*, for which the Arthurian legends were also a primary source of inspiration. Though we'd failed to convince a studio, I thought again of Rospo (who had just rewritten *The Heretic* for me) because of the relation between the two screenplays; I asked him to see if he could condense that of *Excalibur*. He reorganized the material and he had, in particular, two terrific

ideas. The first was to tell the chronological story with major gaps between each stage: between Arthur's birth and his youth; between Arthur's first meeting with Guinevere and their reunion after he has been victorious in battle; between the child Mordred and the adult Mordred. It allowed us to cut out Arthur's childhood, which forms the core of T. H. White's marvellous book, *The Once and Future King* (the origin of the musical *Camelot*). It also made Arthur's meeting with Lancelot more dramatic, since we move in a single shot from Arthur as an adolescent to the mature, bearded, armour-clad king seated on his throne. In the same way, Mordred's mother kisses her young son and, in the following shot, he's ten years older. These leaps forward in time give the story a dynamic narrative power. Pallenberg's other brilliant idea was the scene in which Uther Pendragon inserts the sword Excalibur into the stone, for it's nowhere explained how it got there.

Pallenberg's intervention was therefore crucial to the project, in that it enabled me to continue working on the scenario. One way of making the character of Arthur more present in the final section of the story was to make him also the Fisher King. Fusing two characters in this way (as also with Morgana and Vivian) helped to create a far greater simplicity. When you perform this kind of transformation, when you find such a solution to a dramatic problem, you feel you've discovered a fragment of the legend which had been lost. In any event, it's in the nature of myths to be so powerful, so indestructible, that you can change them and modify them, and yet they remain essentially the same. It's like a movie star who can play several different characters and yet it's always the same person you're watching.

There is no single reference text to the Arthurian legends. Which of the works most inspired you?

Oddly enough, I was more interested in works deriving from the legend, such as White's *The Once and Future King*, which really marked my childhood. Then, at school, it was *Idylls of the King*, the Victorian version which Tennyson wrote as a favour to the Queen. But I'd never studied the original texts. It was later that I came to them, and I was extraordinarily impressed by them: Malory's *Morte d'Arthur*, the works of Chrétien de Troyes and, especially, the most fascinating and modern of them all, Wolfram von Eschenbach's *Parsifal*. There are the three great books, English, French and German, in which our respective national cultures are inscribed. Malory leads directly on to T. H. White, Chrétien de Troyes to Bresson and Rohmer, von Eschenbach to Wagner.

And there is, in the character of Merlin, the nostalgia for a lost unity.

Yes, he speaks of it in connection with Excalibur, which was 'forged when the world was young, when the birds, beasts and flowers were as one with man and death was but a dream'. I also changed the final reference to Excalibur to make it more explicit when Arthur tells Perceval to cast the sword into the water. There is in *Morte d'Arthur* a very beautiful phrase which can also be found in the film. Arthur asks Perceval what he saw at the Lake and the latter replies: 'I saw nothing but the wind on the water.' I wanted Excalibur to be associated more with the world of Merlin, who represents the past; and when the sword returns to the Lake, it's also returning to the world of the unconscious. The image of the sword emerging from the Lake in a woman's hand had a very powerful charge for me. It connects with the shot in *Deliverance* in which a hand surfaces from the river and the one in *Zardoz* where Zed's hand, at the beginning, rises from the corn holding his gun.

The story of the Grail deals with people who are trying not to discover themselves, but their place in the world, a much more humble attitude. What they strive to learn is their destiny, the universe to which they belong and their relations with their fellow men. That's really what generates the narrative, and it strikes me as far healthier than an endless quest for self.

Is the moral of Merlin that too much knowledge is dangerous; that, by his desire to know too much, man is heading for destruction?

No. For me, what is implied is that knowledge in itself is not

A story of a family . . . Igraine and her daughter Morgana (Katrine Boorman and Barbara Byrne in *Excalibur*).

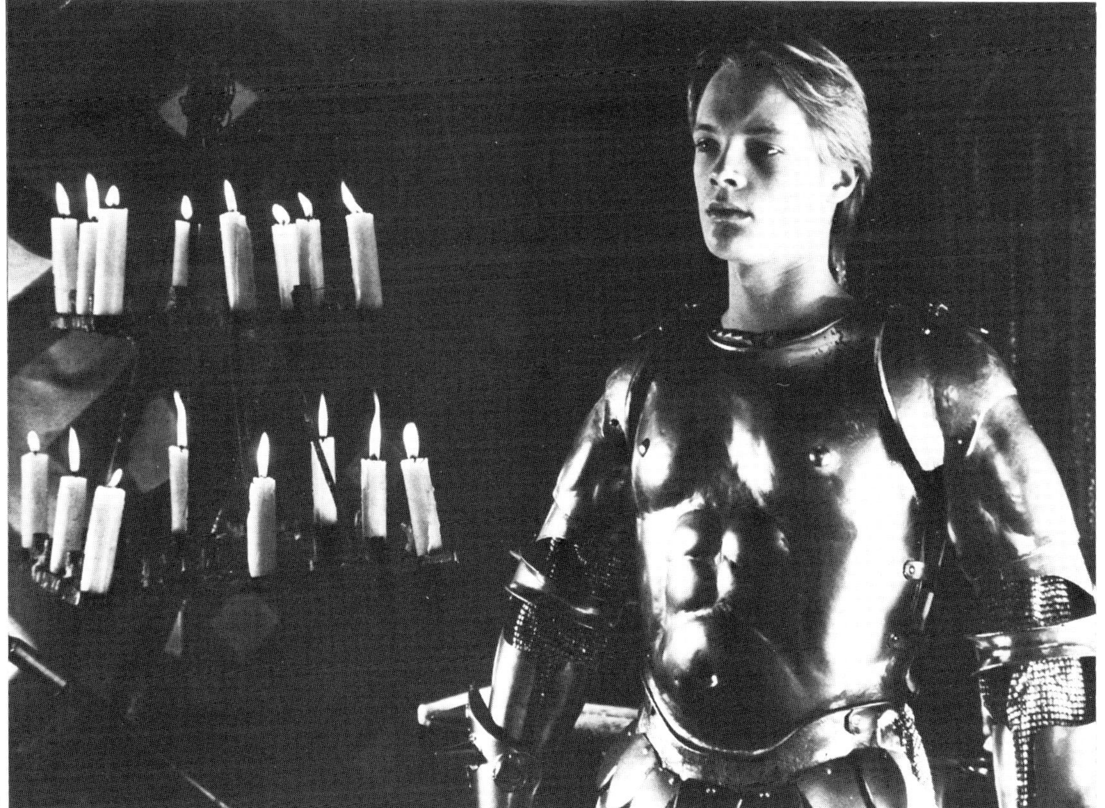

1 Morgana and her son Mordred (Helen Mirren and Charley Boorman in *Excalibur*).
2 Mordred grown up (Robert Addie in *Excalibur*).

1

2

3

Nigel Terry (in *Excalibur*).
Charley Boorman (in *The Emerald Forest*).

1 Lee Marvin (*Point Blank*).
2 Jon Voight (*Deliverance*).
3 Sean Connery (*Zardoz*).

enough. It's what is expressed in the scene where the young Arthur asks him to read the future and he is simultaneously offered a cake. Merlin says to him: 'Look at the cake, it's like predicting the future. When you look at it, what do you really know? And when you taste it, it is too late.' Knowing the future can't in any case replace the fact of living it. Merlin can predict what's going to happen, he can change the future with his magic, but he can't anticipate what the repercussions might be. He's like a chess player who can make a brilliant move, but cannot anticipate what's going to happen seven moves later. I realized also that Merlin was afraid of both the sword and the Lady of the Lake. That's what the scene reveals: there are always hidden forces, different levels of power. It makes the film more dramatic; for, often, when you have a magical character, you tend to believe he's going to be able to solve everything, which removes most of the suspense. With Merlin, it doesn't happen like that. You really can't count on him!

Given that the legend of the Grail was written over a period of four centuries from the eleventh to the fifteenth, which precise period served as a reference for you?

The risk – most notably, with a contemporary approach – would be to subject it to a political interpretation, explaining the story in terms of the political void which existed in England following the departure of the Romans, of the need to find a new leader. That isn't, in my opinion, where the real interest of the story lies, the historical facts striking me as of rather minor importance. What is at stake is the myth. The other dilemma is that much of the legend is associated with a twelfth-century setting, with knights in armour and jousting and so on; the poets who wrote about it incorporated the values of their own period. *Morte d'Arthur*, for example, was very much influenced by the Norman invasion and the establishment of a system of laws. I don't think one can go against that – the context is too deep-rooted, too familiar. What I had to do – with my set designer, Tony Pratt – was include the iconography and, at the same time, play with it by creating a 'Middle-earth', in the sense intended by Tolkien in *The Lord of the Rings*: which is to say, a parallel world, similar to our own but somehow different, with numerous allusions to the Middle Ages. When you recount a legend, you find yourself speaking more about your own period than you think. It belongs to the unconscious, so that I wouldn't be capable of saying what I put in it from that point of view. But I know that Malory spoke of the fourteenth and fifteenth centuries and T. H. White of the Edwardian era. What is essential, then, is not to refute the myth, but to refresh it.

What visual solutions did you find for the film?

To begin with, there's a development. The prologue corres-

The child Mordred and the hanging tree (Charley Boorman in *Excalibur*).

ponding to Uther's period is very dark. It's the Germano-Celtic era. For these sets we were influenced by an artist like Frank Frazetta, who knows how to create an elemental, primitive feeling. Then we shift to an intermediate period, that of the young Arthur, which corresponds to a more bucolic, perhaps more 'conventional', image of the Middle Ages. Then we arrive at Camelot, in which imagination runs riot, with a castle all in gold and silver, with gleaming armour, with a high degree of stylization in sets and costumes. There is, finally, Arthur's death and the decline of chivalry, in which, in a sense, we return to the atmosphere of the beginning.

The fact that your crew was British – the cast included – must have added to the authenticity of the shoot.

Absolutely, and I insisted on such a unity. I also spent a lot of time imagining how the characters would express themselves. In this kind of film, the danger is that, in eliminating familiar idioms, we fall into a kind of pseudo-Shakespearian style, particularly if you have actors who've played Shakespeare in the theatre and tend to become too dependent on that experience. I tried to avoid standard English as far as possible, and to distinguish each character with a regional accent, Scottish, Irish or Welsh. It gives them a special richness and density. I realized, when making tests, that the actors who were able to project the most, who were able to make the dialogue come alive, were those who had what you might call a spiritual comprehension of, and a profound intimacy with, their characters. They were the ones I chose. Most of them had never worked in the cinema – though some had appeared on television – and came primarily from the theatre. The stage had given them a sense of discipline, which was very important for a shoot as gruelling as ours. Several months before shooting began, they had to be trained in the medieval martial arts; they learned to ride and wear armour, the latter being particularly difficult as it was made out of real metal. That fostered the sense of belonging to a group, it brought them closer to each other and, I think, resulted in some very fresh and lively performances. As the story covers a very lengthy period, and contains a large number of characters, each one of them had to fight for his existence, each one of them had to make his mark in a very brief period of time, by rapidly fleshing out his or her character; and I believe all the actors managed to make their first appearances so memorable that the public was immediately able to identify them.

What creative problems are posed by a shoot as large-scale as that of Excalibur?

When you direct a film in which there's an abundance of elements – different sets and costumes, extras, horses, wigs, armour – it takes a considerable time to assemble and control

Uryens and Mordred in the forest (Keith Buckley and Robert Addie in *Excalibur*).

Above The marriage of Arthur and Guinevere (Nicholas Clay, Nigel Terry and Cherie Lunghi in *Excalibur*).

Opposite Merlin in his cave (Helen Mirren and Nicol Williamson in *Excalibur*).

them. Even if you have twenty weeks of shooting instead of the six or seven for a modestly budgeted film, ninety per cent of your time is spent preparing shots, not directing the actors on camera. As a result, you have in fact far less time to shoot intimate scenes than in an inexpensive film, where the director is better able to focus his attention on that essential aspect of his work. That's why, in so many epics, the performances are often stiff, whereas the rest may be brilliantly filmed. The fact is, quite simply, that the director hasn't had time to concentrate on them. When you film a scene as simple as the one in the convent between Arthur and Guinevere, there are 150 crew members waiting for you to finish, which represents an enormous pressure on both your work and the actors'. Everyone is conscious of how much time is passing and how much each minute is costing.

You were already thinking, during the shoot, of Trevor Jones for the soundtrack score, but you also used extracts from Wagner's operas.

I saw *The Ring* at Bayreuth in Patrice Chereau's production and was deeply impressed by it; my impressions have stayed with me undiminished, ever since. Wagner's music served as a guide in the early stages of my work. I didn't think of actually using it at the beginning but, little by little, in agreement with Trevor Jones, I decided that it would be suitable for certain passages; it was very well integrated into Jones's own score. Together, we selected extracts from 'Siegfried's Death' in *Götterdämmerung*, the prelude to *Tristan and Isolde*, for the love story, and the prelude to *Parsifal*, which I've always adored, with those ineffable chords that raise the spirit up and, in the film, become the motif of the quest for the Grail.

You succeeded in combining a sense of reality by means of some very natural settings – rivers, forests, clearings, etc. – with highly stylized shots, such as the one of Mordred being murdered by Arthur in a painted set, with a crimson moon and a clutter of suits of armour.

That came from our desire – after the convent scene – to move from a concrete reality, which was essential for the spectator to feel at ease in the story, on to a more magical, mythical level. The characters are in the process of becoming legends; and the misty twilight of the final battle expresses the level of other-worldly transcendence at which the tale has arrived. At the same time, however, in order that the context remain completely credible, it was necessary for Modred's agony to be all the more ghastly, for the sword to plunge into his body and blood to spurt out of it.

The darkness which swathes the film at the end is very different from that which opens the narrative. It's no longer a pagan, but a spiritualized, darkness.

What we wanted, at the beginning, with all those sombre colours and forests and suits of armour, was to express the reptilian nature of man. This is man emerging from nature. The end, by contrast, denotes the final stage of an evolution. The story becomes complicated after Mordred's birth at the height of the storm, with the waste land, the quest for the Grail, the leaps forward in time and, simultaneously, the compression of time. This complexity has a direct relation to the adventures of the knights whose concern is to advance beyond the medieval conflict between the material and the spiritual. It's therefore normal for the spectator to feel, on occasion, the absence of many of the usual spatio-temporal guidelines. He has been struck by the horror, the blackness, of the opening scenes; then he has been seduced, enchanted, by the sunnier scenes at Arthur's court, by the romantic elements and also by Merlin's sense of irony; and I hope that, when he reaches the deepest waters of the quest, he won't any longer be able to resist, he'll allow himself to be carried along, even if, sometimes, he may lose his footing.

The masks are linked to the theme of deception which permeates the film.

The masks, and also the armour. The armour both expresses and conceals the characters who wear it. It's very mysterious.

Uther Pendragon (Gabriel Byrne in *Excalibur*).
Lancelot in old age (Nicholas Clay in *Excalibur*).

Mordred's mask, of course, bears a strong resemblance to those of *Zardoz* – perhaps there was a lack of imagination on our part! Or there may be a much deeper reason of which I'm unaware. But it did enable us to achieve one rather striking effect when, behind this golden mask, we discover the disturbing features of a child, then jump forward in time, with the grown-up, and almost naked, Mordred speaking to his mother. And when, once again, he dons his mask, what is now being expressed is his power; removing it in his father's presence, he becomes vulnerable again.

When you wrote two parallel scenes – like that in which the young Arthur runs into the forest and that in which he re-emerges accompanied by Merlin – did you already have the idea of the double tracking shot which follows them?

My directorial methods are related to my concept of each scene. I really don't see how a director can be consistent and not write his own scripts, or at least collaborate on them, even if he isn't officially credited in the film's titles. The relation between the script and the shoot is a necessarily organic one. I wanted to express Arthur's arrival in the innermost depths of the forest, exactly where Merlin's power resides, and the ordeal which his meeting with the magician represents. Initially, I'd envisaged an even more lyrical, almost operatic, scene, in which Merlin would initiate Arthur into the world of nature and he would become an insect, a fish, a bird. But it would have harmed the film's tone and I finally decided on this simple form, on the tracking shots which you see in the film and which describe Arthur's submersion in the forest, followed by his return to the clearing and to civilization. I wanted to show, in a very brief, single sequence, Merlin's education of Arthur – which is the subject of a whole book like *The Once and Future King*. And, in the Middle Ages, a forest was a place to be conquered, it represented nature's resistance to culture; it was a place of terror but, also a place of profound knowledge and essential truth. For Jung, trees were the thoughts of God.

'What we wanted, at the beginning, with all those sombre colours and forests and suits of armour, was to express the reptilian nature of man' (*Excalibur*).

1985

Tomme and Kachiri (Charley Boorman and Dira Paes in *The Emerald Forest*).

The Emerald Forest

The Eagle and the Jaguar

As *Leo the Last* was followed by *Deliverance*, and *Zardoz* by *The Heretic*, so, by the system of alternating 'American' and 'British' works, *Excalibur* is followed by *The Emerald Forest*. At the core of each of them, however, is the same problematic – notably that of culture.

In Boorman's films, there is a double relationship with culture. Vertical and diachronic, it links the past with the present by an exploratory movement encompassing the Coptic churches of Ethiopia and the Vatican frescoes (*The Heretic*), the poetry of T. S. Eliot (*Leo the Last*) and the Arthurian legends (*Excalibur*), until what is at stake is the totality of our artistic heritage (*Zardoz*). Horizontal and synchronic, it proposes instead a confrontation of cultures: between the white clients and the black singer of the nightclub in *Point Blank*; between the American pilot and the Japanese sailor in *Hell in the Pacific*; between the exiled prince and his Jamaican neighbours in *Leo the Last*; and between Father Merrin, first, then Father Lamont and the Ethiopians and African blacks in *The Heretic*. In each case, the 'other' culture enriches and fructifies the barren, atrophying Western world; and this confrontation becomes, in *The Emerald Forest*, the predominant theme. In the Amazonian depths is enacted a drama of abduction – abduction from a *culture* – known to us from westerns. The child Tommy, son of an American engineer, is raised into adolescence by an Indian tribe and refuses to return to the white civilization. By casting, in the role of the father, a television actor with fairly average, typically American features, Boorman underlines the cultural shock. Bill Markham, a builder of dams, believes in the virtues

Tommy as a child with his father and sister (William Rodriguez, Powers Boothe and Yara Vaneau in *The Emerald Forest*).

of technology and the values of his society. Through his adventure, he will come to understand that other points of view may be just as valid, and acknowledge his own responsibility (the dam has destroyed the region's ecology, starting tribal wars and forcing the Fierce People into an alliance with white traffickers in arms and women). As in all of Boorman's films, the hero's pilgrimage is essentially one of self-transformation: between the first and last shots of *The Emerald Forest*, the distance covered by the protagonists is immeasurable. The Bill Markham who, in the end, returns to the United States is a changed man, one now enriched by contact with a *living* culture.

As always with Boorman, the narrative is structured around the notion of a quest, of which this film offers a new variation. Until *Zardoz*, that quest was personified by a single character. *The Heretic* described two parallel descents into the past, of Father Lamont and Regan, sharing their point of departure (the clinic) and ultimate destination (the Georgetown house). In *Excalibur*, Perceval renews the quest for the Grail first undertaken by Arthur. In *The Emerald Forest*, the quest is doubled: that of the father for his son (from the town to the jungle) is succeeded by that of the son for his father (from the jungle to the town).

As in *Deliverance*, the dam is a threat; it also objectifies the conflict between nature and culture. As in *Deliverance*, again, nature effects its revenge. But the change which Boorman's vision of the world has undergone since *Zardoz*, towards a positive affirmation, is confirmed by *The Emerald Forest*. Instead of the pessimism of a grisly weekend in the hills of Georgia, the film proposes the tempered optimism of the Tupi communities, the appeal of whose primitive way of life countless Westerners, from Rousseau to Gauguin, have been unable to resist. Boorman's libertarian temperament is attuned to these stateless, politically uncoercive societies, which do not impose order through any ideology or authority but generate it within the group by the propagation of living myths and their celebration in rituals and feasts. Similarly, there is no God, as in theocratic societies; the supernatural, however, plays a significant role in the social organization.

Western man maintains an uneasy relationship with culture: too much has estranged him from the elements and the cosmos. In primitive societies, by contrast, the relationship is physical, perceptible, tangible, and reaffirmed on a daily basis. The white man is oppressed within a technocratic society; the Indian has succeeded in controlling his natural environment. For Boorman, the answer to Marx's question is simple: the advent of the lightning-rod and the telegraph has not quashed the mythic creations of the imagination. In this sense, the

The world of technology . . . (Powers Boothe in *The Emerald Forest*).

closed community of *The Emerald Forest* is the first in Boorman's work to hold out the possibility of growth rather than destruction, precisely because it is *not* Utopian, because it accepts mythopoetic forces as integral to its existence, and because it has established a vital harmony. The circular form of the shabona is not, as was the Round Table of *Excalibur* or the Vortex of *Zardoz*, a confining structure but rather an opening on the world.

In Boorman's previous works, the closed societies brought about their own destruction, by rejecting the course of history (the secret society presided over by Laszlo in *Leo the Last*), by denying the existence of death (the Eternals of *Zardoz*) or by pursuing an inaccessible goal (*Excalibur*). In *The Emerald Forest*, the Invisible People have successfully warded off the threats of nature by integrating it into their culture. They live outside History; and it is when History makes an appearance, in the guise of the white man, that the drama erupts. One of the first, and most powerful, images in *The Emerald Forest* is that of branches being slowly drawn apart to reveal, in front of the white child, the painted faces of the Invisible People – archetypal images, familiar from countless westerns, in which are invested all our irrational fears of otherness. The film's concern, however, will be that we first understand, then accept, these painted bodies and what they signify. Here body paint fulfils the same function as the masks in *Zardoz* or *Excalibur*. (The mask is virtually unknown among the South American Indians.) These embellishments reveal as much as they conceal; they are a means of apprehending reality, a more obscure, more profound reality than that of appearances. For Boorman, fascinated as he has always been by the theme of the double (and its correlates: mirrors, still or moving images), masks and body paint are not only the signs of an authentic culture but instruments through which one enters into contact with nature. As Michel Thevoz noted, 'The tegumentary inscriptions of primitive peoples, and more particularly facial paintings, thoughtlessly bring into play the very thing we exhaust ourselves trying to avert: the dissociation of the body, the fragmentation of the physiognomy, the influence of partial instincts, the disintegration of the self – in short, all those pathological virtualities to which the Western adult is forever capable of regressing.'[214] By his initiation, Bill Markham will take the same path as his son and accept values which were once alien to him. The Oedipal relationship is taken over from *Excalibur*, but inverted. Mordred, the bastard son, wished only for Arthur's death. Tomme, the 'wild child', conducts himself on the contrary like a child who is 'father of the man' (though in a very different perspective from that intended by Wordsworth), and guides his own father towards enlighten-

. . . and the primitive world (Rui Polonah in *The Emerald Forest*).

ment. Like the young Arthur, Tomme has been snatched from his family, raised in the forest by a shaman (Wanadi = Merlin the magician) and initiated into the secrets of nature. And, like Arthur, Bill Markham is the Fisher King. Carried into the shabona by Tomme and Wanadi, he comes close to dying. Whereupon he is reborn and, with his son, metamorphosed.

The Emerald Forest, in which man is reconciled with himself and the world, is Boorman's least violent film. In *Point Blank*, *Hell in the Pacific* and *Deliverance*, Boorman's heroes appeared for a time to accept the failure of their lives. No longer is this the case, however, since the energy expended here by his characters results in an inner victory, a form of rediscovered serenity.

The forest has always haunted Boorman, because, in a sense, it represents the unconscious; by its ambivalence, too, as

both a haven and a threat. From *Hell in the Pacific*, by way of *Deliverance*, to *Excalibur*, his films have captured its shifting nature; and now it actually figures in the title of his latest. When, a few moments after the disappearance of his son, Bill Markham desperately tries to clear a path through the matted vegetation, the camera rises up to encompass an impenetrable jungle stretching away as far as the eye can see. One is reminded of Claude Lévi-Strauss's description, in *Tristes Tropiques* (*A World on the Wane*), of this same region in Brazil where these same Tupi Indians live: 'Seen from the exterior, the Amazonian forest resembles a mass of congealed bubbles, a vertical accumulation of green blisters; one would say that some pathological ailment had afflicted the whole of the fluvial landscape.'[206]

From that first scene, Boorman will set about exploring the landscape from the *inside* (and not, as in many films, exploiting it merely as a setting, as a backdrop), as though to illustrate from within the description of the same traveller–ethnologist, who continues: 'But when one bursts the skin and moves inside, everything changes: seen from the interior, this confused mass become a monumental universe. The forest ceases to be an earthly disorder; one might take it for some new planet, as rich as our own, which it had replaced.'

Jacareh, the chief of the Fierce People (Claudio Moreno in *The Emerald Forest*).

Tomme and the ritual of the Invisible People (Charley Boorman in *The Emerald Forest*).

The Indians and whites meet.
1 Chico Terto (left) (*The Emerald Forest*).
2 Atilia Iorio (*The Emerald Forest*).

Boorman's attitude to the forest is akin to an Indian's: following an initial gesture of apprehension and fear comes a gradual acceptance and the urge to reconsider one's own way of life and thinking. *The Emerald Forest* therefore constitutes a decisive stage in its director's aspiration towards a cosmic cinema – cosmic in the sense of nature reverberating through the artist and the film itself becoming a rustling, quivering landscape.

From its ceremonial ants to its frogs whose croaking precedes the storm which will burst the dam, *The Emerald Forest* contains a fabulous bestiary. But I shall consider only the eagle and the jaguar since it is with these animals, respectively, that the son and the father have identified. Traditionally, in Amerindian culture, the eagle is to the jaguar what a celestial power might be to an earthly power. The eagle outstares the sun: 'It is the symbol of intellective strength.'[199] And it is interesting that Jung should have interpreted the eagle as a paternal image of virility and potency, since, in *The Emerald Forest*, in a sense, maturity and wisdom are the qualities of Tomme. The flight of the eagle which opens and closes the film makes possible the discovery of the emerald while Tomme is in a trance during his initiation (and the bird traverses all four elements), then helps the young man locate his father's house in the centre of a modern town (in a sequence which recalls Father Lamont's flight on the wings of Pazuzu in *The Heretic*). In both cases, it is Tomme's body paint which facilitates the (initiatory, shamanic) 'journey', which is to say, as Michel Thevoz has pertinently remarked, 'the evolution towards the inhuman, towards the animal, towards the Other undergone by the officiant of the ritual'.[214] As for the jaguar, it represents the gift of clairvoyance, the ancestor, the civilizing hero. (Already, in *The Heretic*, the witchdoctor Kokumo turned himself into a leopard.) As in all of Boorman's films, then, the physical ordeal becomes a mental discovery. Likewise, the Indian's arrow is, at the same time, the expression of a desire, of a tension and the symbol of knowledge. Passion, for a Romantic, creates its own universe.

Boorman's characters, each in his own fashion, are genuine 'heroes', driven on by an atavistic will to live, to satisfy which they will confront every conceivable obstacle and defy even death. The will-power which they personify makes of them, in a sense, a projection of the artist who conceived them and who himself is driven on by a creative impulse whose ultimate goal is nothing less than immortality. Like *Hell in the Pacific*, *The Emerald Forest* is based on a true story (in the first case, the survival of Japanese soldiers on Pacific atolls after the end of the Second World War; in the second, the kidnapping of children by Amazonian Indians). But the factual status of the original events does not mean that these films are different from *Point Blank* or *Excalibur*: as always, that creative impulse operates between the real and the imaginary. Boorman's cinema can therefore claim both the weight of reality that is conferred upon it by fire, water, air and earth and that free, airy space which can only be created from the reveries of a poet.

1

2

1 Atilia Iorio, Powers Boothe, Patricia Prisco and Isabel Bicudo in *The Emerald Forest*.
2 Atilia Iorio and Gabriel Archanjo in *The Emerald Forest*.

1

2

The forest is sometimes a threat . . .
1 Ned Beatty, Burt Reynolds, Jon Voight and Ronny Cox in *Deliverance*.
2 The Exterminators (*Zardoz*).

1

2

. . . sometimes a shelter.

1 Merlin and the education of Arthur (Nicol Williamson and Nigel Terry in *Excalibur*).

2 Wanadi at the ritual of his adopted son (Rui Polonah in *The Emerald Forest*).

Interview

Were you inspired by a true story?

Yes. It was brought to my attention in 1972. Rospo Pallenberg sent me an article which had just appeared in the *Los Angeles Times* and which fascinated me. But, at the time, I had no thought of making a film out of it, as I had just directed *Hell in the Pacific* and *Deliverance* and had more or less exhausted my interest in this type of relationship with nature. All the same, the experience I had when shooting *Hell in the Pacific* on the island of Palau, and my contacts with the local tribes, had had a profound effect on me, since it didn't correspond to anything I'd read on the subject. From that moment, I began to reflect on tribal life; it has never ceased to haunt me and I've always wanted to understand it better. It seemed to me to represent the past. Even when described by anthropologists, it's viewed from the outside, as something essentially primitive, whereas for me it served as a kind of support, a way of life which I found complex, subtle and emotionally satisfying. In short, I put the newspaper cutting to one side, and from time to time Pallenberg and I would talk about it, particularly when we were writing the screenplay of *Excalibur*. After that film, I had numerous projects, including *The Double* and *Broken Dream*, which I haven't as yet been able to set up; and when I was once again discussing this Amazonian subject with Pallenberg in Los Angeles in 1982, I decided I wanted to film it. I did the rounds of the Hollywood studios to see what their reactions would be. They were all negative – which led me to believe that we might have an interesting idea!

What was the original anecdote?

An engineer, working in Peru on a mining project, was picnicking one day with his family on the edge of a forest, and his little boy suddenly disappeared. They searched in vain for him, and realized that he had been kidnapped by Indians. Years passed, and every vacation he'd return to try and find him; and, ten years later, he succeeded. The child had become a member of the tribe, he had been initiated into it, and his father decided to leave him there. He returned to the city, but the adolescent, who remembered his father's gun, came looking for him to ask for his help when the tribe was attacked by its neighbours. His father and elder brother gave him their support; then, their task

John Boorman (shooting *The Emerald Forest*).

accomplished, they left him once more with the Indians. What is interesting is that there are still tribes in Amazonia which have never had any contact with the white world and others whose contacts have been very intermittent. In the Andes, for example, there's a tribe which, once every generation, makes a raid on the city, steals knives and axes and returns to the hills. And that's been going on for two hundred years. But, of course, the majority of the tribes which have come into contact with whites have been decimated by alcohol and disease, and have seen their wives sold into prostitution. The dam at Tukurui where we filmed paralleled our story very closely. The tribes around it had been dispersed, uprooted, forced to hunt in alien territories, with all the friction that would ensue, and the women had been forced into prostitution.

In the Xingu, where the Indians are protected and where I myself went to live with a tribe, there are Indians who dress Western-style, commute betweeen the cities and their homes and, in general, live astride the two cultures. Some of them perform in *The Emerald Forest* and they're fascinating people. I didn't want to engage Indians who'd had no contact with the whites, since it would have had a destructive effect on them, setting in motion a process of aculturation. In fact, we did the opposite. Many Indians who, in the film, play the 'Fierce People' and the 'Invisible People' were retribalized by us. A few of them, in addition, were half-breeds. We set them in a camp in the middle of the jungle so that they might become reaccustomed to living naked, hardening the soles of their feet by walking shoeless and rediscovering all the rituals and patterns of tribal life.

Why did you change the action from Peru to Brazil?

It was unimportant so long as we remained in the rain forest. On the other hand, we needed a dam, a variety of landscapes and also, because of the shooting difficulties, an infrastructure on which we could depend. Brazil seemed to us more suitable. To return to the story itself, and the effect it had on me, what fascinated me, as a father, was the fear all parents have of losing a child, of seeing him disappear into a crowd, when he's still very young. I remember leaving my first daughter, Telsche, in a locked car while I went shopping. When I returned, I was in

Jacareh, the chief of the Fierce People (Claudio Moreno in *The Emerald Forest*).

Above Marcus Tuantagno, Charley Boorman, Aloisio Flores and Rui Polonah in *The Emerald Forest*.
Opposite Powers Boothe in *The Emerald Forest*.

despair to find that she was no longer there. Then I discovered a car identical to mine had been parked nearby. I was intrigued by what might happen between a couple and how long they would continue to search for the child, trying to discover the truth. That's the human, or elementary, reaction to the story. More mysterious, however, was the father's decision not to bring his son back. We therefore depicted the character of the American engineer as someone who wasn't prepared to confront this kind of dilemma. He possesses his own system of values, he isn't assailed by doubts as to the validity of his actions: razing the forest and constructing a dam. He believes in progress, he sees himself as an agent of civilization and he never questions the morality of his role. But when he discovers the tribal life which his son has come to know, and that it could be more beneficial than the existence which he himself can offer him, it brings about such a change in his view of things, it creates such a distance between him and his wife, that he's incapable of explaining to her on his return. He lies to her, he tells her that Tommy is dead, which pains him. In fact, Tommy has indeed, in a certain sense, died: he's become a man living in another world.

Did you think of developing the opposition between the technological world such as exists in modern Brazil – in Belém, for example – and the primitive life, an opposition which can be found in Zardoz *and* The Heretic*?*

At certain stages of the screenplay, we certainly thought of it, but that kind of contrast rapidly becomes too predictable. And we considered it preferable to explore such themes strictly in relation to the characters. What Markham, the engineer, represents in society by his work is itself enough to produce such an opposition. Besides, the image of the dam which interferes with the course of nature, as also that of the jungle edging on to the city, is so strong that any further visual commentary would have become redundant.

Did you spend any time among the Indians before writing the screenplay?

No. As I told you, my experience of tribal life goes back to my sojourn on the Pacific Islands during and after the shoot of *Hell in the Pacific*. When we began writing the screenplay, Rospo Pallenberg had read a great number of books on the subject. But he didn't visit any tribe. The dialogue between us was therefore very constructive: his extensive knowledge was drawn from works of anthropology and my experience was more direct. Then, after the first version of the script, I began to visit Amazonia and got to know the life of the Indians; and it was really on my return, when we set about rewriting the story, that everything started to come to life. I learned, for example, about the Indians' concept of nudity when they told me that I couldn't attend a ceremony naked even though I was wearing clothes. For them I was naked because I wasn't painted. And, in the film, the turning-point of the story is when Markham is painted by the Indians. He is then integrated into their world and starts to understand the meaning of this life for his son. Many similar images came to me from the

1

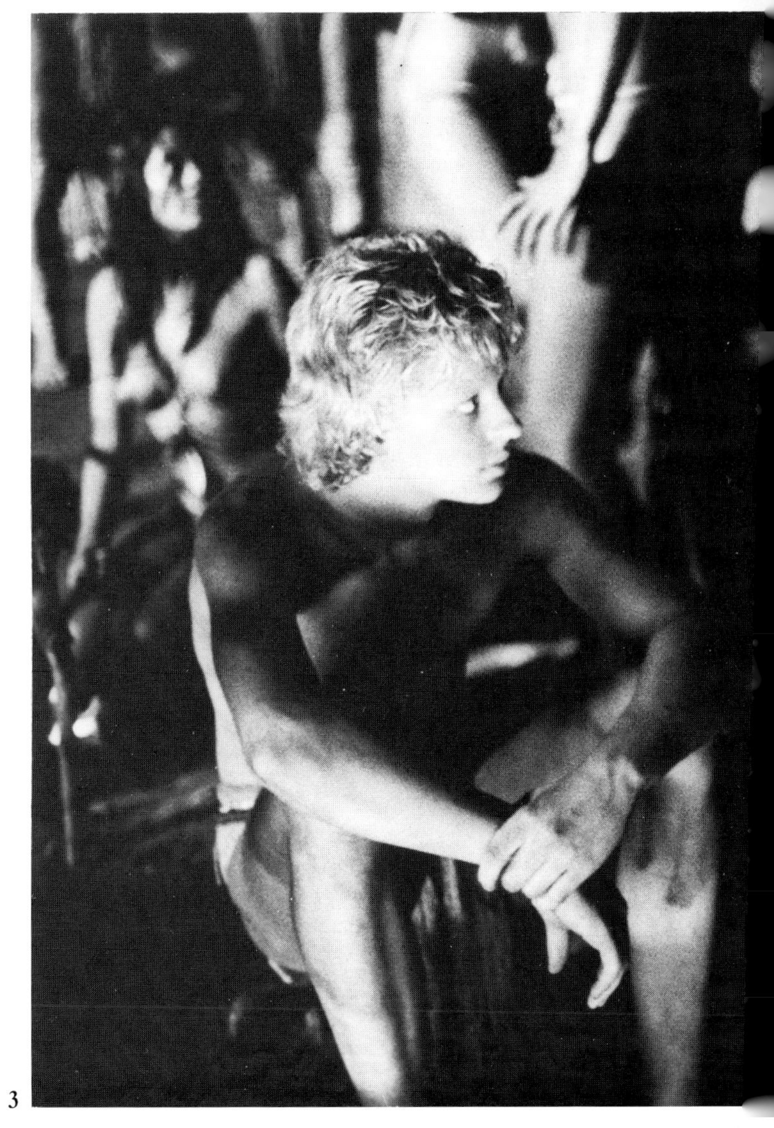

3

1 Paulo Vinicius and Charley Boorman in *The Emerald Forest*.
2 Tetchie Agbayani and Dira Paes in *The Emerald Forest*.
3 Charley Boorman and Powers Boothe in *The Emerald Forest*.

2

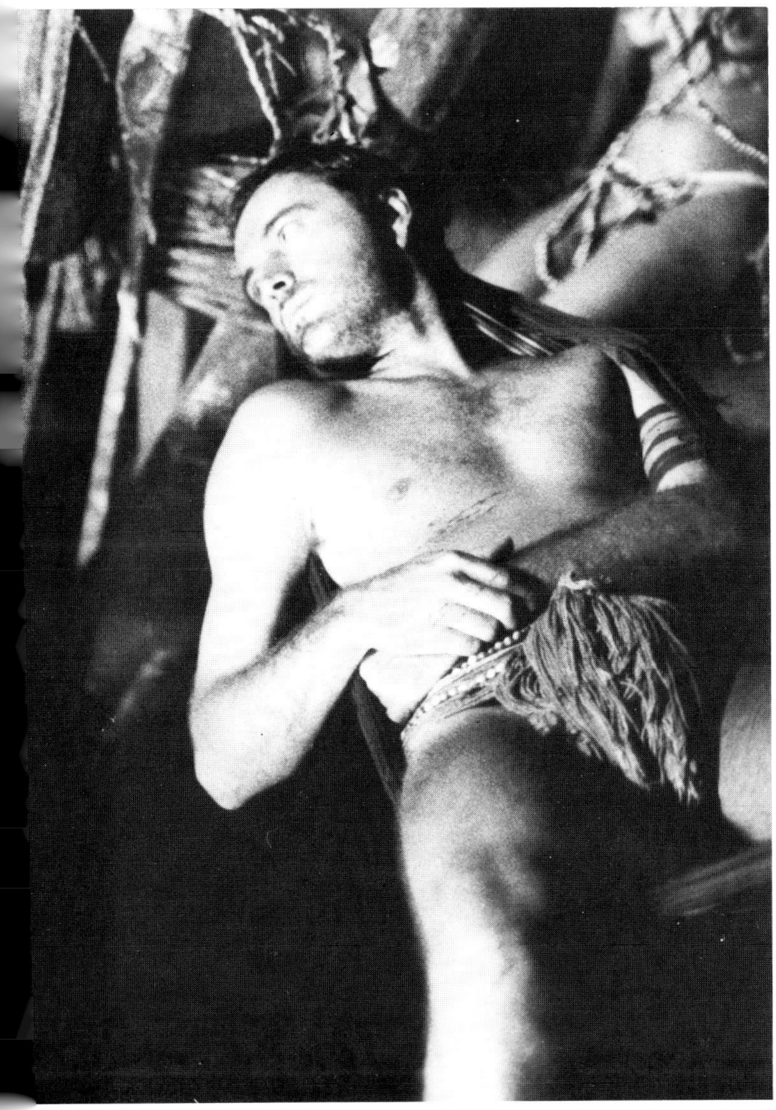

period I spent in the jungle: the one, for example, of the young girls drying their hair in the shabona after their morning bathe by beating it against their shoulders.

Do the ceremonies in the film refer to real ceremonies which you attended?

I didn't attend all of them, but they're all authentic. That of the initiation with the ants, for example, is very widespread. That of the wedding, I was witness to, as well as the hallucinogenic ones, of which there are many variations. The Indians will inhale tobacco smoke until they vomit and then start again, to the point where they begin to go into a trance. Johannes Wilbert, one of my advisers and an expert on the subject, told me a great deal about the remedies used by Indians to cure diseases. We invented two different tribes which don't actually exist, yet every element of their communal life is based on authentic customs which I either observed for myself or was informed of by anthropologists.

What struck me, from my first contact with tribal life in Polynesia, was that every man and every woman knows all there is to know about his or her world, so that each family unit is completely independent and self-supporting: they gather fruit, hunt and fish, cultivate the soil, build their own homes and perform their own rituals. Only the shaman possesses knowledge which they don't have, knowledge of a visionary kind, the ability to see into the future and discover remedies for every kind of disease, We Westerners, by contrast, are totally dependent on thousands of people whom we'll never meet. Primitive man, moreover, has the support of his tribe, whether for the education of his children or for his defence. There's something very attractive about that for us, since it's an experience we've never really known. When you think about it, though, humanity lived a tribal existence for the greater part of its history, until only a few thousand years ago. We abandoned that kind of life without a backward glance even though, if you carefully study the way in which businesses, universities and sports clubs function, you'll discover a kind of subconscious desire to reconstruct the patterns of tribal life. It's for that reason that it seems to me important to have a better understanding of how primitive societies live. I'm very fortunate to have shared the life of these communities, the more so as, in twenty years or so, they'll probably have ceased to exist. I consider it to have been a privilege and one of the most profound experiences of my life.

I remember, for example, when I was doing research, managing to persuade Orlando Villas-Boas – who has done so much to protect the tribes – to authorize me to enter the Xingu, a region as large as Denmark, a hunting-ground for the Indians and therefore out of bounds to outsiders, except for very precise reasons, whether medical or ethnological. I was able to go only if invited by one of the tribes, an invitation obtained for me by Villas-Boas when he realized that the film would serve the Indian cause. I lived with a shaman named Takuma, who has an immense reputation throughout the country because of his healing powers. We got on wonderfully well together and, when we left each other, he told me I was his brother, which was a singular honour. We had lots of

1

2

1 Gaya watches over Bill Markham during his illness (Tetchie Agbayani and Powers Boothe in *The Emerald Forest*)
2 Kachiri and Gaya as prisoners of the Fierce People (Dira Paes and Tetchie Agbayani in *The Emerald Forest*).

From the dam . . . (Powers Boothe in *The Emerald Forest*).
. . . to the feast (Dira Paes and Charley Boorman in *The Emerald Forest*).

discussions, but only in the evening; apart from a few shared jokes, there's no conversation during the day, since everyone is busy at his chores. Takuma asked me what I did and I realized how difficult it was to explain what the cinema was to somone who'd never seen a film or television screen in his life. I described the abrupt shifts from one scene to another, the way editing enables one to move back and forward in time and space; and he suddenly seemed to understand, telling me that it was like the experience of a dream, where you change from one place to another, from one person to another. When I added that my work was creating illusions, he declared that we had the same magical activity, scaring people and perhaps curing them.

What I tried to express in the film about tribal life – and the thing that so impressed me – was that there's no distinction between the material and the spiritual world, between reality and dreams. Everything is connected. The Indians are capable of devoting themselves to some extremely practical activity, which then gradually turns into a ritual. I would ask them what was going to happen that afternoon or the following day, and they'd stare at me in astonishment, since no one had the slightest idea! It reminded me a little of how moods shift at a party. When you arrive, everything seems awkward, you hardly know what to say; and suddenly you look around and all kinds of things are going on, someone starts to sing, others to dance, and groups begin to form among the guests. Well, tribal life is a bit like that.

Even more than in your other films, there is a rich bestiary in The Emerald Forest: *ants, toucans, an eagle, a jaguar, frogs . . .*

Animal life is organically linked to the film. There's an animal intermediary for each of the Indians' actions. In the same way, for them, every human being enjoys a privileged relation with some animal; and the knowledge he must first of all acquire is that of his own animal identity. When Tomme is initiated into the tribe and given his hallucinogenic drug, he still doesn't know by which animal he is to be represented, not until he sees the eagle flying over the shabona. Similarly, Markham, during his initiation, becomes a jaguar, which Jacareh, the chief of the Fierce People, foresees when he tells him that he has the heart of a hungry jaguar. When you visit Amazonia, you're amazed

Powers Boothe and Charley Boorman in *The Emerald Forest.*

by the profusion of animals, by the incredible tumult of insects, birds and beasts sharing the vegetation. It's what I was trying to convey in the film.

Is there anything exceptional about the news item which you propose at the beginning?

During our research, we discovered that the kidnapping of children by the Indians is a relatively common occurrence. More than five hundred cases have been recorded between North and South America. Frequently, it's an act of vengeance. Two years ago in Brazil, for example, after a region had been deforested and hunters had killed some Indians, the latter, as a reprisal, kidnapped a child; and the Brazilian Department of Indian Affairs, the Funai, organized an expedition to bring him back. There may be other reasons for a kidnapping. When an Indian woman loses her child, her husband promises her he'll replace it. In general, he steals one from another tribe or, which is easier, leaves the jungle and kidnaps one in a white township. Sometimes, too, there's a dispute between two families as to which of their children will be raised to become the chief of the tribe; and the shaman, to keep

Joao Mauricio Carvalho in *The Emerald Forest*.

Body paint and the relationship with nature. Marcos Tuantagno and Charley Boorman in *The Emerald Forest*.
Opposite The rite of passage to manhood: Tomme covered with ants (Charley Boorman and Joao Mauricio Carvalho in *The Emerald Forest*).

the peace, goes looking elsewhere for a child, which also allows for the introduction of new blood.

How did you imagine the opposition between the two tribes, the Fierce People and the Invisible People?

We started with an idea that later proved too theoretical. One of the tribes was to represent aggression, territorial expansion, the other would represent peace, creation and poetry. Little by little, the Invisible People also became warriors, while the Fierce People, though very violent, turned out to be extremely beautiful. Their body paint was, of course, quite different. That of the Fierce People resembled the Urucu red and black paint, from the Xingu tribe among whom I'd lived. As for the Invisible People, they believed they couldn't be seen by their enemies and had therefore made themselves invulnerable. We tried to create a body paint composed of green and yellow, thereby suggesting such invisibility. Of course, there's a paradox which is impossible to resolve: demonstrating their invisibility by visual means, rendering it visible to the spectator! I think I achieved it once or twice, as in the scene of the kidnapping, where we glimpse them, without really seeing them, submerged in the jungle.

The shoot must have posed a lot of problems.

Many and varied. First of all, the humidity and the heat are absolutely exhausting. Then there was the threat of disease, particularly malaria; and we were constantly being attacked by insects. The actors also had a number of dangerous scenes to perform, and I've always been afraid, when shooting my films, of the possibility of an accident. It's an enormous responsibility. I've often wondered whether I'd be able to complete a film if a member of my crew were to die while doing his job. I've had difficult locations in my life but, thank God, there's never been a major incident.

Did you, from the beginning, decide not to have any stars in the film, and to choose unknowns?

We thought – with Goldcrest, the original production company – that a film of this kind, necessitating a large budget and a difficult shoot, didn't really need a star, since the story itself would be the star; and that the money would be better spent on making the best film possible rather than on paying for a handful of famous actors. The other reason is that few stars would be prepared to spend five months in the jungle! Experience has taught me that the more you pay an actor, the less work he's prepared to do to earn it! I spent a long time looking for someone to play Markham and I finally chose Powers Boothe, who had won an Emmy for his performance as Jim Jones, the evangelist murderer of Guyana. I'd also been very impressed by him in *Southern Comfort*. He comes from Texas, and his cultural and social origins corresponded to those of my engineer. He hasn't been contaminated by Hollywood and, in ten minutes, I'd made up my mind.

What prompted you to choose your son Charley for the role of Tomme?

The choice of actor for that character was by far the most difficult. In fact, at one point, I almost abandoned the idea of the film as I hadn't succeeded in finding anyone. I interviewed hundreds of teenagers, both in England and the States. I knew what the major problem was: how do you make convincing a young Westerner living in a primitive tribe? The more tests and auditions I held, the more actors I watched moving and speaking, the more insoluble it seemed to me. I was determined that he'd really be sixteen or seventeen years old – not merely that he could pass for that age – that he'd possess a certain innocence and be in that crucial stage between childhood and manhood. One of the film's themes is how one becomes a man, how one grows into assuming responsibilities. When Tomme returns to the town and sees his mother again, we have, expressed in a single scene, all the difficulties a mother experiences in letting her son go. In tribal life, there exists a ritual for each of the important transitions in human life – birth, leaving the family unit, marriage and death. I always had Charley in mind, because he had already acted and had a kind of authenticity which suited the role. I'd even tested him – but had decided against casting him because of the pressures it would bring to bear on us both, especially with a production of such dimensions. To have the whole project rest on the shoulders of my own son seemed to me too heavy a burden – something of which Charley himself was aware. Finally, when I'd found no one else and was ready to abandon the film, I chose Charley because I knew I could rely on him and that he'd be capable of assuming all those physical hardships for months on end. It wasn't easy, especially to start with. And, curiously, what happened to Tomme and Markham was reflected in my relationship with Charley during the shoot. At the beginning, I coddled him like a child; then, gradually, he acquired a certain self-confidence, he matured and, about the middle of the film, he began to have his own ideas, to discuss them with me and become more independent. And, at the end, he decided to leave home!

Charley Boorman in *The Emerald Forest*.

1 The Fierce People of *The Emerald Forest*.
2 Powers Boothe and Eduardo Conde in *The Emerald Forest*.

John Boorman (shooting *The Heretic*; in the background, Richard Burton).

Projects

Like all film-makers, John Boorman has worked on a number of projects which, for one reason or another, he has not been able to set up. I have endeavoured to date them (sometimes approximately), and questioned him about the most important ones – those, at least, which reached an advanced stage of preparation.

1 A Film about Captain Cook (circa 1960)

'When I was in Southampton, working in television, I wanted to tell Cook's life story and show how such a man of humble origins could have become a great navigator. I read his diaries and went looking for locations in the South Pacific. He was very different from the explorers of the period and totally non-violent in his relations with the natives, who regarded him as a god. The idea of greatness, and the state of grace which it implies, has always interested me. I should have liked to direct a series of films on the great individuals of history, a little like those made by Rossellini at the end of his life. Among those to whom I was drawn, apart from Cook, were Isaac Newton, Doctor Johnson, Isambard Brunel, the Victorian engineer, and Sir Walter Raleigh. I should also have liked to make a film about the relationship of Freud and Jung.'

2 A Film about Christopher Isherwood (circa 1965)

'I'd just read his latest novel, *A Single Man*, about a homosexual marriage in which, after the death of his companion, the "widower" finds himself alone in Los Angeles. I was doing some research for my film on Griffith and I paid Isherwood a visit. I should have liked to make a filmed portrait of him in his relationship with Los Angeles, as I think what he's written about that city is just as lively and accurate as his descriptions of Berlin in the thirties. I wanted to understand why he settled there, attracted by Aldous Huxley, as well as his interest in Hinduism. Finally, I made *Point Blank* and abandoned the project, but we've remained good friends.'

3 The Diamond Smugglers (circa 1965)

'After *Catch Us If You Can*, David Deutsch suggested that I adapt this Ian Fleming novel, which George Willoughby wanted to produce. He was eager to exploit the success of the James Bond cycle, but it was of course very different, almost documentary-like. The book explained how diamonds were smuggled out of South Africa, and the way in which the black miners would swallow them in order to pass the X-ray tests at the end of their working day. The stories were all true; and they ended by giving a very precise idea of South African society and the problem of apartheid. But the producers wanted to add some fictional scenes and we never came to an agreement.'

4 The Patriots (circa 1967)

'This was a marvellous screenplay by Charles Wood, a bit too long and rambling, as is usually the case with him. It was a very tough, realistic story about two soldiers during the Second World War which Alex Jacobs hoped to produce.'

5 Sanctuary Man (circa 1968)

'The idea came from Michael Croucher, with whom I'd worked in television in Bristol. With Alexander Jacobs – who was writing *Hell in the Pacific* with me – I developed a medieval theme: if a man had committed a crime, he could claim sanctuary inside a church, where he was protected. He'd then be offered either trial or exile. If he chose exile, he had to reach a port within a given time and find himself a ship. If he didn't succeed, his enemies could kill him. It was the story of a man in love with a young girl who is engaged to the son of the richest man in the village. He kills his rival, seeks refuge in a church, then chooses exile, followed by the girl and the victim's family and friends, who are out to kill him. Alex Jacobs fell ill; moreover, we disagreed about the screenplay of *Hell in the Pacific*; our friendship cooled somewhat and we abandoned *Sanctuary Man*.'

6 The Americans (circa 1968)

'This project proved to be too rich for the blood of American film companies. I wrote it with Griffith's *Intolerance* in mind. In a sense, it was a western, with four stories unfolding simultaneously. I wanted to make a film about what really happened to the Indians, but I realized that the myth was so much stronger than the reality and that, if I were to show the reality to the public, the myth would intervene. I therefore had to show both myth and reality. One episode dealt with an authentic incident in the Indian Wars and I wanted it to be totally honest. The second concerned a film being made in Hollywood on a theme similar to the first, except that, given the number of earlier remarks, it was only a pale shadow of the original. The subject of the third would have been the degenerate survivors of the tribe living on a reservation. The fourth would have shown a group of hippies trying to live like the Indians. Finally, the four episodes would have come together: the film company visits the reservation to shoot some sequences of the film; the hippies also go to try and live there; and the whole thing ends farcically with a battle during which the Indians kill the film crew.'

7 Rosencrantz and Guildenstern Are Dead (1968)

'Since my Bristol days, I've been very friendly with Tom Stoppard and we'd spoken of several projects together. Aboard the *Queen Mary*, on which I was travelling to America to prepare *Hell in the Pacific*, we discussed the possibility of adapting his play, which was going to be produced in New York. I proposed the idea to MGM, who wanted to work with me again after *Point Blank*. But the play's huge success on Broadway resulted in the agents setting an enormous sum for the rights (200,000 dollars, I believe) – which made the budget too high, as we knew the film was bound to have rather a limited audience. We'd done a lot of rewriting on the play. Tom had added new scenes and there were more extracts from *Hamlet*. I'd found locations in Dubrovnik, as well as in Denmark and Sweden; and I was thinking of Tom Courtenay and Albert Finney for the title roles. I'd also made a test with John Hurt. After the success of *M*A*S*H*, Donald Sutherland and Elliott Gould wanted to make it with me; at the time, however, I couldn't follow it through, as I was working on *Deliverance*.'

8 I Hear America/Labour of Love (1968)

'After *Point Blank*, I wanted to make a film about America. I did some exploratory work with the journalist Tom Wolfe, as I admired the way in which he observed his native land. We travelled together, and spoke of the film as telling the story of the United States through its music. That didn't amount to very much. Later, in 1970, I returned to the idea when I proposed a few projects to United Artists. 'I hear America' is, of course, a quotation from Walt Whitman. It was a completely musical story, with the music of the blacks who had come from Africa, tap dancing, which had come from Ireland, then jazz, swing and finally pop. Bill Stair worked with me on a complementary story, about an American movie director and an English editor who are making this film and have an affair together. *Labour of Love* added another level to *I Hear America*.'

9 The Last Run (1970)

'This screenplay – by a Scottish writer, Alan Sharp – was offered me by a friend who worked at MGM. Sharp was really talented and had the knack of breathing new life into Hollywood's classic stories: when you scratched its surface, however, this particular story proved to be rather shallow. It was the traditional theme of a former criminal, now retired (in this case, in Spain), who's approached to pull off one last job. We wrote several versions of the screenplay, but weren't satisfied with any of them. MGM sent one version to George C. Scott, who liked it a lot and wanted to act in the film just as it was. I wasn't too keen on the idea and, with Bill Stair, I drafted a new version, one that was completely crazy and turned all the situations inside out. MGM detested it and I had to withdraw from the film. Finally, John Huston began shooting, then was replaced by Richard Fleischer.'

10 The Lord of the Rings (1970)

'After *Leo the Last*, I proposed to United Artists a screenplay centred on Merlin the magician, but they suggested instead that I adapt Tolkien's novel, whose rights they owned. Not only did I know it well, but it had been a great influence on me for the manner in which it succeeded in revitalizing myths by appropriating certain Arthurian legends. The story is set in 'Middle-earth' and has a vague, undefined medieval quality to it. There are elves and dwarfs. The Ring, which represents power, is coveted equally by the forces of Good and Evil; and the only means of preventing it from falling into the hands of the latter is to destroy it. But, with its destruction, the two poles of Good and Evil are also destroyed, and from then on there's good and evil in everyone. It's a little like the death of God. It's a wonderful book, a metaphysical fable as well as an adventure story. I thought it was impossible to adapt to the screen, but United Artists were so insistent that I allowed myself to be persuaded; it was so very tempting. I asked Rospo Pallenberg to help me. He was an architect who'd studied in Rome and designed one of Wall Street's finest skyscrapers. I admired his cast of mind, his intelligence and the original outlook he had on life. It was a colossal undertaking, one very difficult to bring off, and I think I would have aimed for something close to Max Reinhardt's *A Midsummer Night's Dream*. I began to correspond with Tolkien, who refused to have illustrations in his book and, above all, was terrified that a cartoon film would be made of it! He finally authorized my adaptation. Subsequently, there was a change of management at United Artists, my relations with them turned sour and I had to abandon the project. With hindsight, I realize that the preparation of *The Lord of the Rings* greatly helped me with *Zardoz* and *Excalibur*. Tolkien died before Ralph Bakshi's animated film appeared.'

11 Hoover Blues (1972)

'This was a project, suggested by Fox, which dealt with farming during the Depression – a period that witnessed the final rupture of Americans with the soil. It seems to me that the old frontier values have been lost and there's been nothing to replace them. One of America's problems is that its citizens no longer have any roots and so are only romantically, nostalgically linked to the soil. It's also the theme of *Deliverance*, which I was to direct not long after: something fundamental has been lost. *Hoover Blues* dealt with the struggle of three young people to raise melons on a smallholding. I played with the idea of the film and worked on a script; but I never really succeeded in making it something of my own.'

12 Dr Frankenstein (1972)

'With Don Bachardy, his companion, Christopher Isherwood had written a version of *Frankenstein* for Universal, the studio which owned the rights. It was a wonderfully powerful scenario which went back to Mary Shelley's original and was innovatory in that the monster was very handsome. I wanted Jon Voight for the role of the monster and Isherwood agreed. But I was determined to direct it for the cinema; the TV department of Universal, which had commissioned the scenario, however, refused to let us make a film of it for theatrical release.'

13 Naked Without a Gun (circa 1975)

'I was keen to work with Tom Stoppard again. Together we collaborated on an adaptation of David Hare's play *Knuckle*, which we both greatly admired. It was the story of an extremely wealthy, powerful Englishman and his son, who rejects both him and the whole ethic of English snobbery. What he does is go to the States, invent a new identity for himself, in the style of a movie gangster, and become an arms trafficker. He returns to England to find his sister, who has opted out and become a member of a terrorist group. The young man, who meanwhile falls in love with an actress, doesn't rest until he has destroyed his father. I'd thought of Laurence Olivier, Jon Voight and, in the role of the actress, Kate Nelligan.'

14 Interview With a Vampire (circa 1978)

'This was another project with Jon Voight, from the novel by Patricia Reiss. The story, a fascinating one, centred on the destiny of a vampire in the Deep South, from the early nineteenth century to the present day.'

15 Broken Dream (1979)

'Claude Nedjar, the French producer, drew my attention to Daniel Odier's *Les Voyages de John O'Flaherty*. I asked Neil Jordan, a young Irish writer whose short stories I admired, to collaborate with me. Every day for three months we worked on the screenplay in an office at Ardmore studios.

'The world is apparently coming to an end. A young magician and his girlfriend are travelling across the country. His father, also a magician and now blind, has finally discovered the ultimate trick of making objects disappear. He teaches it to his son, who becomes expert at it. Finally, the father asks the boy to make *him* disappear. He announces that he's going to the place where the vanished objects are in order to prepare the way for others. It's a story about magic and imagination, about the inner life of objects, about families and love. It is, above all, a comedy.

'We completed the screenplay in 1979 and it was refused by several major studios, who found it rather disconcerting. The problem is that it isn't a "blockbuster" and yet is quite expensive to make. I still have hopes of raising the necessary finance and I refuse to believe that its title, "Broken Dream", applies to the project itself.'

16 The Double (1982)

'I wrote this story in 1982. It's a version of the *Doppelgänger* myth which I set in the "sun belt" of contemporary America. Robert Garland, who works with Sydney Pollack, collaborated with me on the screenplay.

'As the father of twins, I'm fascinated by the strange manner in which two people can appear identical. What is it, in fact, that defines identity, particularly in a world where people are less and less distinguishable, more and more alike with each passing day?

'It'll be a very black comedy.'

17 Autobiographical stories (1985)

'Among a number of minor projects, I wanted to direct for television a series of films on my past experiences – it would be more interesting than writing my memoirs! One – for which I've written a detailed script – would be devoted to my childhood memories during the war. Another, to my National Service days. The third, to my mother and her three sisters, who are all over eighty. It would partly be a documentary – they'd speak about their lives – but there'd also be episodes with actors. The idea came to me when I saw some snapshots of them, as children, on an old boat in Shepperton, snapshots which had been exquisitely coloured in by my aunt Billy (they all have masculine Christian names, Bobby, Billy . . .). When they were fifty, all four of them had clambered into a similar boat, with the same sailors' costumes, and had had themselves photographed again. I'd love to take the same photograph today. My three daughters and my sister's daughters would play the roles of their grandmother and great-aunts as young girls. In this way, I could conjure up a whole vanished era.'

Recollections

Marcello Mastroianni, Actor

Leo the Last

John Boorman asked me to play in *Leo the Last* after seeing me in Mario Monicelli's *The Organizer*. He came to Rome with his proposal. I have to say that I never go to the cinema and Boorman's name meant nothing to me; but I immediately took to him, which, for me, is very important. Of course, personal empathy is not the only thing that counts – so I made a few enquiries and finally he screened *Point Blank* for me. I was dazzled by it; I was fascinated by its extraordinary rhythm. As I also liked the man himself – the fact that he could not have been further from the conventional image of the cold, phlegmatic, slightly snobbish Englishman, that he was on the contrary as friendly as an Italian film-maker, and that the screenplay impressed me as interesting and original – I accepted, even though I didn't at that time speak a word of English. I therefore embarked on this 'adventure'. For that's what it was for me: I had never acted in an English-speaking film before; I had never worked in England and I didn't know the language, which was a problem in view of the fact that the film was not post-synchronized, as is the custom in Italy.

The complete absence of stiffness in Boorman's temperament – unlike that of many Northerners – his humour and his patience helped me a great deal, and every evening I would learn my lines with the aid of an interpreter. Because of his influence, there was a precision and a professionalism among the crew to which I was unaccustomed. He would put me at my ease; he would reassure the sound engineer, who occasionally worried about the unintelligibility of my accent, by telling him that such and such a word could be re-recorded during the dubbing. I well remember – for I was extremely touched by it – his saying to me one day: 'Forget the interpreter and look me straight in the eyes. I'm certain you understand me.' And, it's true, his powers of expression and his kindness were such that I was able to grasp what I was supposed to be playing. My work in the theatre enabled me to enter the imaginary world of both the film and my own character. And my experience as a foreigner in London, being constantly taken by surprise and not understanding what people were saying, no doubt also contributed to my ability to play Leo from the inside.

Boorman makes his actors participate in his work. He's a very open person. On the first day we met to read the screenplay and pass comment on it, a practice I had never known in Italy. I remained silent, of course, as I couldn't speak a word! I also remember a scene in which I was to take refuge in a church, pursued by my entourage, my mistress and my doctor, then clamber into the pulpit. I said: 'John, what if I were now to bark like a dog, like an animal tracked down by hunters?' And he told me to go ahead.

I am very proud of having been in the film, because I consider it a very fine one, even if it was not commercially successful. I had a very pleasant stay in London, in great part thanks to John. Knowing that I was alone, and being the extremely kind and thoughtful person he is, he would often invite me to his house for the weekend, with his wife and children. I know that people generally exude compliments when asked to pass judgement on someone with whom they have worked, but Boorman is a wonderful director. He has an amazing eye, a true film-maker's eye, and he invests each image with a rare visual beauty and nobility.

Opposite John Boorman with Marcello Mastroianni (shooting *Leo the Last*).
Above 'I took refuge in a church' (Marcello Mastroianni and Alba in *Leo the Last*).

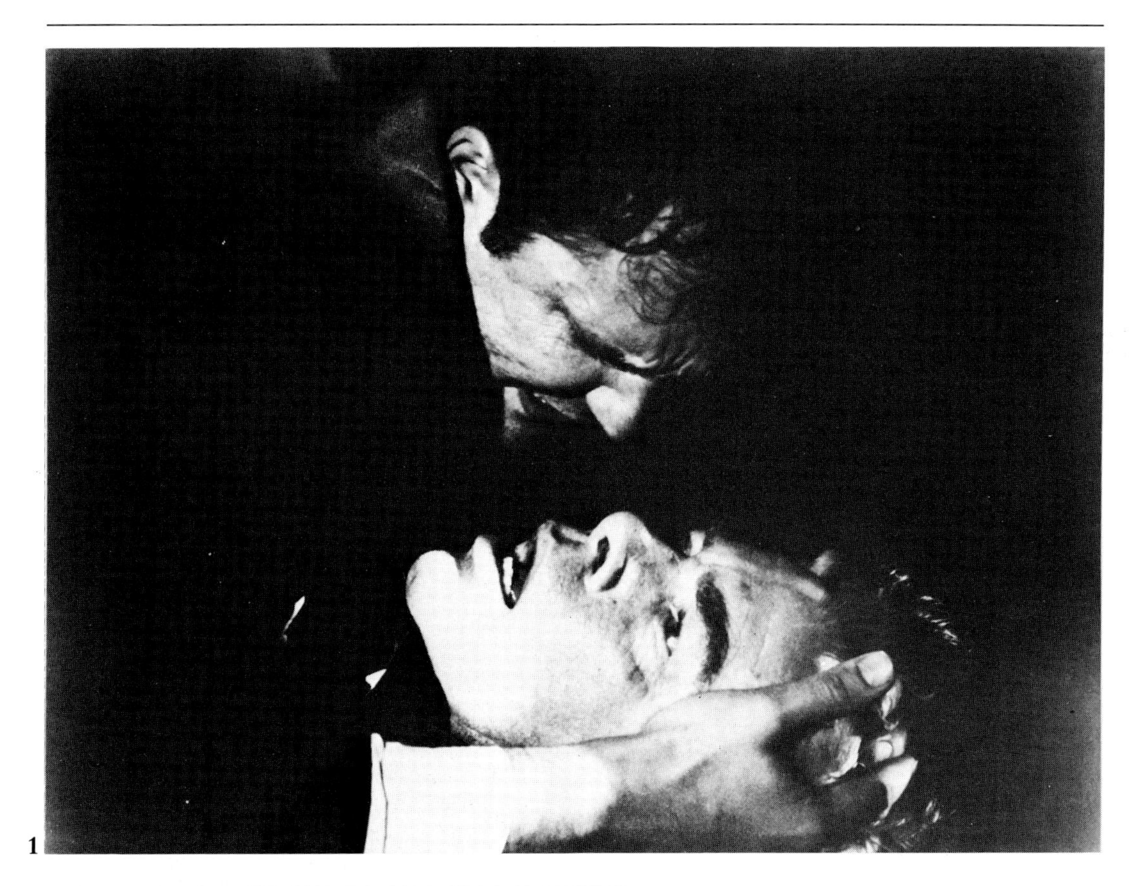

1

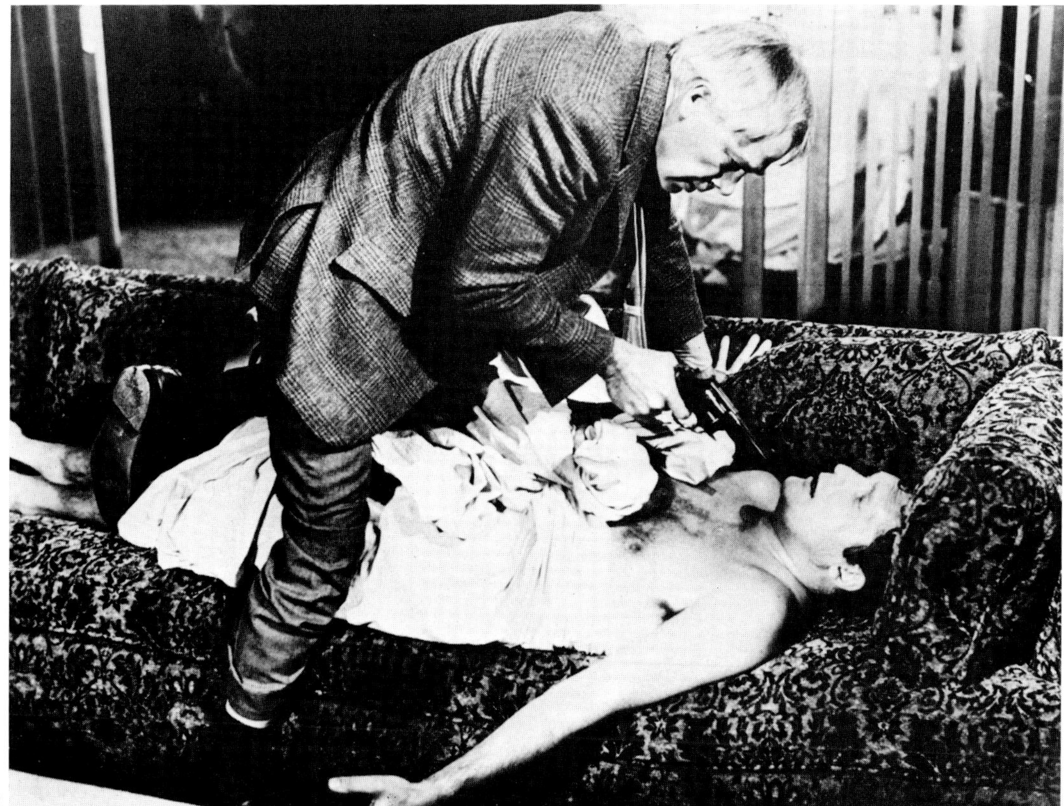

2

1 'One day we prepared the scene where I roll on the ground with John Vernon during a party' (*Point Blank*).
2 Another encounter between Lee Marvin and John Vernon in *Point Blank*.

Lee Marvin, Actor

Point Blank, Hell in the Pacific

I was filming *The Dirty Dozen* in London when I met John Boorman for the first time. A young producer, Judd Bernard, wanted me for one of his projects, the adaptation of a thriller that was to become *Point Blank*. Boorman came to my home several times and we immediately got on to the same wavelength. We'd talk about emotions, about mythologies . . . It was one of those chance meetings that evolve into a friendship. Later, I suggested we make the movie together. We had a good relationship, on both a personal and an intellectual level. We swapped ideas on Zen Buddhism, on war, on the movie's visuals. I think that, during these conversations, he realized he could make *Point Blank*, with my image as its starting- point.

I more or less based the part of Walker on my own movie image, the same one I've had for a number of years now. We simply created variations on my screen personality. My father was a shooting champion and, in 1936, he'd beaten the world champion with a .45 automatic. A film was made of him where you see him in slow motion. That's what gave me the idea of slow motion when Walker goes into his wife's bedroom; the whole movie was made out of memories and dreams.

Our producers were very supportive, especially as MGM didn't understand the movie at all. One day the studio bosses wanted to meet John. They asked him to tell the story and, because he was evasive, they treated him like a punk. I told them I wouldn't allow my director to be spoken to that way! John just didn't know how to handle American producers. He's not the kind of guy who'll recite a script to you, scene by scene; what he does is film it! He's an individualist who isn't going to beg you to understand him.

Saturday afternoons we'd meet at my place to discuss the screenplay; and Sundays, late into the night, we'd rehearse with the other actors. One day we prepared the scene where I roll on the ground with John Vernon during a party, a very homosexual scene. Vernon was nervous. After discussing it for about an hour, I told him to roll on the ground with me. But he shied away from any kind of physical contact. So I pulled his pants down and kicked him in the ass, literally. That was at my place. He was horrified, he looked at John with tears in his eyes and he said: 'John, he's beaten me.' The next week we shot the scene. It was necessary, though, to understand what it meant for the two characters.

Physically, it was a very tough shoot, but also a very amusing one, since we never stopped inventing and improvising. My memories had an important part to play, whether sensual or emotional ones, because the character's state of mind was something I'd known at first hand. All I had to do was track it down in the file of my memory.

When we were preparing *Hell in the Pacific*, I was lounging about on a porch near a beach in California, and I spotted a raft near a buoy. It reminded me of a World War II ace I'd known, who'd shot down twenty-six enemy aircraft and been taken prisoner by the Japs. I also used my own experiences as a Marine between the ages of seventeen and twenty in the Pacific war. I was wounded, and later had time to think about how scared I'd been and about how much I admired the Japanese . . . Since then I've matured; and I wanted, with this movie, to make up for my ignorance as a kid and get straight with myself. I loathed *The Bridge on the River Kwai*, where the British soldiers, whistling and marching about, kill those cretinous Japs without the slightest effort. I wanted to show moviegoers that those little bespectacled monkeys who couldn't shoot straight had in fact decimated us and that the Marines who'd been in combat with them had suffered a helluva lot.

Hell in the Pacific was also a tough movie to make. To tell the story, we had nothing but water, sand, the jungle and the skill of our own hands. There were lots of problems with local atmospheric conditions. We all lived on a large boat rented out of Hong Kong. The Chinese crew was led by a Captain Tsung, who didn't speak English; Boorman can barely speak American; the Japanese contingent had an interpreter; and there were also American technicians and the inhabitants of Palau. We had to coordinate five different languages. I made *Hell in the Pacific* with my heart and soul, to rid myself of certain bad feelings I had about myself. *Point Blank* represented more of a discovery of myself and my own way of thinking.

Boorman's very good at speaking with actors; for some of them, he can even be too intellectual. Working with him isn't easy; but for me that's a compliment, because he forces you to think. When you begin a day's shooting under his direction, you know that by the evening you're going to be worn out by the demands he makes on you. And that's his right. I've worked with other directors – Ford, Lang, Hathaway – but they belonged to the old school and they never addressed a word to you.

Boorman knows everything there is to know about the movies, from the editing down to the choice of a colour scheme. He's also got a terrific sense of humour. Whenever I visit him in his house in Ireland, I let him choose the subject of conversation. Because if I do, and it's something that interests him, I know he'll take the discussion so far I'll come out of it dead beat! Another of his qualities is that he's able to look at America with a fresh eye. Americans are so used to their own country, they don't know how to see it any more.

He wanted to cast Marlon Brando and me in *Deliverance*. I said to him: 'John, we're too old. In circumstances like these, I wouldn't hesitate to kill a guy. Yet this is a story about guys who hesitate to kill.' Later, he offered me a part in *Perceval*, one of the versions he'd written of the quest for the Grail and that afterwards became *Excalibur*. When I look at the movies he's directed and I haven't acted in – movies I love, like *Deliverance* and *Leo the Last* and *Excalibur* – I can relax, I can let myself be carried away by the story, because I don't know any of the problems he had in making them!

John Merritt, Editor

Zardoz, Excalibur

I first met John Boorman in 1962 in Bristol, where he had come to produce a weekly magazine programme for television called *View*. This started off as a mixture of live TV studio material, together with filmed documentary sequences, the longest of which ran about ten minutes . . .

I joined the team of editors working on this programme around the middle of 1962 and, as the months went by, the proportion of filmed material gradually increased until, by the beginning of 1963, the whole programme consisted of a filmed half-hour documentary.

To call them documentaries, however, would not really do them justice, as they were very far from being the conventional newsreel type of 'reportage' that the word 'documentary' implies, certainly at that time, in the early sixties. Nor were they essays in 'cinéma-vérité', a technique much in use at that period, but one that lacked the freedom needed for John's creative instinct to operate, as illustrated by his comment in one newspaper interview that being a film director 'was the next best thing to being God.'

John always had an eye for the dramatic core of a story – sometimes a purely visual one, in others some unusual aspect of its content, but one that he always spotted and brought to the fore in the choice of shots and locations that he used to illustrate it.

In other words, he thought like a film-maker and not like a journalist when constructing his filmic essays. This was very stimulating for those of us working on his programmes, as one could sense the vision of someone who thought in terms of filmic construction; and so his material was capable of being moulded into a far more exciting shape than anything conceived of by a conventional documentary producer.

I worked with John at the BBC for some four years, with his films becoming more ambitious and closer to his concept of cinema feature films. One of his last films for the BBC was an early exploration of the Arthurian legend (in modern dress), which was called *The Quarry*. In it he was able to employ many

Sean Connery in *Zardoz* (edited by John Merritt).

of the images and ideas that were later to appear in his films for the cinema.

Working with John Boorman, one had the excitement of treading new paths with an intrepid and determined explorer of the cinematic world. We technicians were encouraged to aid him in his exploration, and he welcomed any ideas that we could offer if he felt that they added anything to the final result. If they did not, he would quickly perceive the weak points and make one think again, in a way closer to his own original conception.

When he left the BBC to start his feature-film career, our ways parted for a few years, as he left for Hollywood and the promised land. On his return to England, he asked me to work on *Leo the Last*; but on that occasion I was unable to leave the BBC to do so. My chance came in 1973, when he started work on *Zardoz* and asked me to join him as editor on the film, a chance I was only too ready to accept.

John's insistence that every element in a shot should be perfectly orchestrated meant that, with some of the more complex set-ups, much time and many rehearsals were necessary to achieve the result he desired. It also meant, towards the end of the schedule, that some of the scenes had to be shot before the paint was even dry on the sets and that the coverage of the action was kept to the absolute minimum possible, as the limit of the budget was approached. A sad decision, I felt, as *Zardoz* was a picture which needed the luxury of a large budget to achieve its aims.

Again, as in his time at the BBC, he gave me a very free hand in the initial editing of the film, but was always ready to suggest alternative methods of assembling the shots if he felt that I was not really expressing the essence of a sequence.

I felt very honoured to be asked to work on *Excalibur*. And, as an example of John's determination to get the utmost out of his material, I should like to mention how he asked me to make two entirely different opening sequences for *Excalibur*, to be quite certain that the most effective combination of shots was used to obtain the maximum effect.

As an instance of the rapport he desired and expected of all his technicians, I should also like to refer to the occasion when I heard him remonstrate with the camera 'grip', whose job it was to move the camera in a tracking shot. In this particular shot, he felt that the 'grip' had started moving the camera too late. 'But,' said the grip, 'you didn't tell me to move any earlier.' 'Ah!' said John, 'I shouldn't have to *tell* you. What I pay you for is to be able to read my mind.'

Nigel Terry and Helen Mirren in *Excalibur* (edited by John Merritt).

Peter Nichols, Screenwriter

Catch Us If You Can

In 1965, I was living in Bristol, where I'd been born nearly forty years before. I was earning a sort of livelihood writing plays for television, but not all of them were accepted and I was not only broke, but deeply in debt to my agent and those friends who could afford to lend me money. John Boorman lived nearby, busily making factional films for the BBC West Region television service. Both of us had small reputations as interesting workers in our fields. We both felt we'd been 'promising' long enough and were overdue to deliver. The chance came when a producer called David Deutsch, who had spotted John's promise, asked if he'd care to make a feature film on any theme he fancied, with guaranteed distribution here and in the States. There was only one condition – the stars had to be a pop group called The Dave Clark Five. This was, after all, the Swinging Sixties, as American journalists were always telling us. John, knowing how much I needed money, asked if I'd like to provide an original script. I in turn asked him who were The Dave Clark Five. He hardly knew and didn't seem to think it mattered.

'Listen, Peter, this is your chance to pay off your debts, put a quid or two in the bank and buy the time to write that stage play.'

'And what's in it for you?'

'A Hollywood contract.'

He said it without his usual boyish smile. He was in earnest, I could see, and his seriousness carried me along.

We went to meet the 'star' – John, David and I – at his new mock-Tudor home in a suburb of north London. Here, over coffee supplied by his Mum, we discussed the sort of subject he envisaged for his movie debut. It was a weird encounter, typical of the period. Three middle-aged men smiling and nodding at a shrewd, good-looking man of twenty-two who'd struck lucky and was able to call the tune, even if he couldn't play it. I'd bought one of his records by now and marvelled at his good fortune. After the meeting, I tried to say it wasn't for me, but John pointed out that I had no alternative.

I undertook to deliver an original screenplay within a month. John and I met in each other's houses and strung together half a dozen episodes set in locations we both knew, from London through Salisbury Plain, Bath and Somerset to south Devon. He was always clear that he wouldn't shoot in studios. The theme was immensely pretentious, a distorted reflection of the moment we'd first met Dave Clark. He and the other four were to play stuntmen who run away from the middle-aged entrepreneurs who are exploiting them, are pursued across the country and finally trapped by the Big Brother figure who's anticipated their every move. It was romance with pseudo-psychological overtones, but it served the purpose, which was a stage play for me and a Hollywood contract for John.

When I told David Deutsch that I couldn't promise the script would be good in the time, he replied with the story of the composer asked to do a full score for a movie by the following Wednesday who told Samuel Goldwyn he couldn't do good music in the time. Goldwyn said: 'I don't want it good, I want it Wednesday.'

I delivered on time and shooting began as planned. As long as Dave and the other four appeared and some of their music was played on the sound-track, the American distributors would be happy and the drive-in movie-houses would have something to show the kids. On the first day of shooting, I went down with the only bout of real 'flu I've ever had. It kept me in bed for two weeks and by the time I was able to rejoin the unit, I'd lost all authority. The rest of the work on *Catch Us If You Can* was a miserable humiliation. I don't blame John. He had worked mostly in documentary and didn't respect the writer's contribution. He'd had no experience of actors and didn't respect them, either. His five stars were untalented amateurs and couldn't learn the lines. Clark himself knew something was wrong and tried to get his own way. A second unit was formed to shoot some of the sequences he wanted (a fox-hunt, a motorcycle scramble), though no one ever intended to use this footage in the final cut. New dialogue was improvised each day by John; and others, including the lighting cameraman, who was wrong for the job, resigned; he was re-engaged on terms which apparently entitled him to rewrite the script. The producer's assistant (also a script re-writer) punched Dave Clark in the face and had to be fired. In the midst of it all, my father died. It's all in my diary and makes

Dave Clark and Barbara Ferris in *Catch Us If You Can* (script by Peter Nichols).

funny reading now, but at the time it was awful.

Like my script, the film was delivered on time. And John was right – I earned the time to write my play, he got a Hollywood contract. The film is sometimes shown on Saturday morning TV, which is where it belongs. I can't look at it, but it has its followers. Dave Clark, living now in affluent retirement, thinks it was ahead of its time. Bryan Forbes says it's underrated. Ken Tynan reviewed it and found it promising, but blighted by overcute scripting.

John rang me when the reviews came out and said that we seemed to have survived. Considering our motives, that was surely the most we could expect. More surprising, our friendship survived as well, though only just. We now admire each other's stuff at a distance, but have never worked together since. As well as some of his films, I respect his courage, his vigour, his humour, his quick intelligence and his loyalty to friends.

John Boorman directs Dave Clark in *Catch Us If You Can* (script by Peter Nichols).

Rospo Pallenberg, Screenwriter

The Heretic, Excalibur, The Emerald Forest

I met John in 1969. At the time I was practising architecture in New York, and a year before I had seen *Point Blank*. The film impressed me to the extent that I thought two things: that's the way to make a movie; I could work in pictures also. I set about to meet John, and a year later I succeeded. We hadn't talked for more than ten minutes, when he offered me the possibility of working on the screenplay of Tolkien's trilogy, *The Lord of the Rings*.

That was our first collaboration.

It is very easy to work with John; and difficult.

Easy, because John is highly intelligent, clever, resourceful, generally well-informed, relatively patient, and tolerant of the idiosyncracies of others; difficult, for the very same reasons – you can't fool him and it's hard going to contradict him, but ultimately worthwhile, to him and to yourself.

Writing together was a lot of fun; I would say that thirty-five per cent of the time we spent together had to do with matters unrelated to the project. I believe the collaboration worked on a distribution of attitudes: John, classical and centripetal; me, baroque and centrifugal; although at times the roles were reversed. If I wanted to try something audacious, it fell to him to be cautious, and vice versa; or at a more prosaic level, if I was distracted, it fell upon John to be more focused. Writing alone (*Excalibur*) was much more challenging, in that I had to imagine his potential responses, overcome phantom objections, without the stimulation of his company – artistically rewarding but ultimately tedious and gruelling.

Working as a creative associate (*Deliverance, The Heretic*) was very simple – there were standards, spoken and unspoken, that I had to live up to. The title encompassed all sorts of activities, from casting to location scouting, from designing to making shooting suggestions and shooting second unit, from working on the set to coordinating the music, with a degree of freedom that ranged from the minimal to the maximal. John doesn't like to relinquish authority, but when he sees the wisdom of it, he does it enthusiastically.

John Boorman (left) directing *The Heretic* (artistic collaboration by Rospo Pallenberg).

Shooting *The Heretic* (artistic collaboration by Rospo Pallenberg).

Anthony Pratt, Art Director

Hell in the Pacific, Zardoz, Excalibur

I first met John Boorman at the house of an art director, Tony Woollard, who had done *Catch Us If You Can* and went on to do *Leo the Last*.

Several years later, I went out to America to work on a western, *Blue*, as a sketch artist and met John Boorman again. He was then working on *Point Blank*.

Months later I received a call from John, who was preparing *Hell in the Pacific* at that time. He asked me if I was interested in working in collaboration with a Japanese art director (who was, incidentally, very good and experienced) on the project.

I was naturally delighted to be offered such a position for what was, in effect, my first job as an art director. Previous to this, I had mainly worked as a draughtsman, assistant art director and occasional sketch artist.

I later went on to work with John Boorman on *Zardoz* and *Excalibur*.

The point I would like to make straight away about working with John Boorman from an art director's point of view is the immense visual input he gives to a film.

Certainly, in my case, he has virtually designed the films I have worked on for him. He has tremendous visual ideas and the art director's problem is being able to do them justice by translating them into concrete form, such as sets, etc.

It is perhaps this aspect which accounts for the fact that, while I always feel invigorated and stimulated at the end of working on one of his films, I also feel depressed because his vision has not been adequately achieved.

I would suggest that he is among a relatively small group of directors, such as Kubrick, Fellini and Lean, who give enormous attention to all technical aspects of a production and thus stamp their work with their own individuality and personality.

This also has the effect of making lighting cameramen, designers, editors and so forth produce their best work when working for such a director.

John Boorman virtually lives in the art department during the pre-production period and his help, guidance and approachability are of enormous value.

There was one incident during the filming of *Zardoz* which I remember vividly. I had to show John a new set while he was filming the Renegade dance hall set, which was built in the Bray Studios canteen. The new set, the 'crashed head of Zardoz', was on a path which wound down a hill outside the canteen.

As we were returning along the path to the canteen, we were met by the actor, John Alderton, his face grotesquely disfigured by make-up in the part of Friend, who informed us that the set had fallen down. I received a particularly icy stare from John Boorman and hurried back up the path to see what had transpired. Fortunately, as it turned out, the aged extras had just been called to a tea-break moments before the set had collapsed.

John Boorman very quickly sized up the situation, took the crew outside and quite happily played football with them while the construction crew hastily rebuilt the set under my nervous supervision.

His pragmatic approach to this problem took the pressure off me, as he occupied all the crew during what was a time of acute embarrassment for an art director.

To sum up, he is an eternal optimist who decides to do something first and finds the means to achieve it afterwards, rather than not attempt something until he has all the means to achieve it.

Drawings by Anthony Pratt for *Zardoz*.

apple green
velvet trousers
with decorated
bottoms

Tom Priestley, Editor

Leo the Last, Deliverance, The Heretic

I promise to tell, certainly not the whole truth, and possibly anything but the truth. Everything is relative. It is much easier to talk about someone, and chat about past experience, to let the ideas provoke each other, and to answer loaded questions with devious answers, gliding round the truth, using an actor's technique to confuse and influence the interrogator. But to write it means a whole process of editing has already taken place; much will be missing, for reasons of forgetfulness as much as delicacy.

I was invited to meet John Boorman towards the end of a gruelling stint editing Karel Reisz's bruised masterpiece, *Isadora*. Curiously enough, neither John nor I knew much of the other; I vaguely remembered some of his earlier TV films, but had never seen any of his feature films. I am slow-speaking at the best of times, and at that moment was exhausted; over a year of difficult editing had reduced us to tranquillizers and sleeping pills, just to keep going, and after our meeting John questioned his associates about my ability. Anyway, he could not find anyone else, so I got the job as editor on *Leo the Last*.

Leo the Last was a delightfully independent film. They had taken over a derelict street only a mile or two from where I live in Notting Hill Gate, and virtually all the exteriors and most of the interiors were shot there. For offices, dressing rooms, etc., they put up portable huts in a nearby street. We took over an old school as cutting rooms, with the assembly hall as a screening room. I could walk there in a gentle fifteen minutes. It was a sunny time; I gave up smoking, ate fruit nervously and grew fat.

John expects the best from his collaborators and can seem harsh, even inconsiderate, at times, because totally unwilling to accept other people's foolishness; he has a low boredom threshold and will decline into gloom in the face of ordinariness. On the other hand, he enjoys eccentricity and the foibles of those he trusts and likes. And this sense of enjoyment is often expressed with a kind of boyish glee which is the exact reverse of a black grimness when things are not going well. Then the sparkle of his eyes puckers into a frown, the smile becomes a grimace and his lower lip protrudes.

If John trusts you, he will allow you the freedom to make the maximum contribution. I sense that, of all aspects of film-making, he is least interested in the details of editing and relies on his editor to take care of that without prompting. It's worth noting that on his last five films he has used only two editors, one of whom goes back to his BBC days.

Leo the Last was largely created in the cutting rooms. We took one hour out of the first cut, which meant losing several scenes. The songs were all added; a rough version was recorded and picture cut to fit this, then the final songs recorded precisely to match the cut film.

The notion of using voices as an integral part of the soundtrack, and sometimes blended with the sound effects, only emerged during editing. All that John relished. He enjoys the sound-mixing stage of film-making as a more relaxed kind of shooting, when much can be changed and improved.

Deliverance was again a very independent film, shot one hundred per cent on location, far from the studios, far enough from California for the American crew to feel more strange in North Georgia than we Europeans. The setting, the place and the people were very much part of the total experience; it was a voyage of discovery for everyone.

There were two unusual features about the making of *Deliverance*. First, all the music was recorded at the start of shooting, when we laid down the playback for 'Duelling Banjos'. This was to avoid having to return to the USA during post-production. We had to guess at the permutations of 'Duelling Banjos' which we would need to accompany different scenes. The story of the battle which John had with Warners to get them to issue a record of the music (which, when issued, became a best-seller) should be told by him.

The second unusual feature was that the film was almost entirely shot in sequence, as they followed the story down the river. This meant that we could pretty well keep up with the editing; and, most importantly, it meant that, before the crew and cast left the location, we could do some necessary pick-up shots to cover gaps in the story, where the physical difficulties of shooting had sometimes got in the way of the narrative. For instance, we did an extra shot in the gorge to show the moment that Ed (Jon Voight) realized that he had to take over if they were to survive.

John always admits that narrative tends to be the weakest part of his films. Visually, he is always strong, because he has a great command of the camera, and takes a lot of trouble to get the right 'look' for his films – quasi-black-and-white for *Leo the Last*, with colour only showing in the skin tones, and desaturated colour for *Deliverance*, marrying black-and-white with colour to produce a wonderfully sinister darkness in the river.

Deliverance was a pleasure to edit – a strong story, well shot and plenty of cover. The big river scenes were put together like a mosaic and gently trimmed into a final shape which combined action with emotion. The big debate scene, which follows the death of the mountain man and takes place round his body, was shot in a series of elaborate camera moves, difficult to put together; yet it worked so well that it became our show reel during shooting, and remained little changed from first cut to finished film. I am proud of my Academy Award nomination, and glad to have worked on such a fine film.

I was unable to edit *Zardoz* because of other commitments, but returned to John on *The Heretic* towards the end of shooting, when my colleague had to withdraw. It was a very different kind of film – no longer the freedom and independence of the maverick Boorman of the earlier films: this was very much the big time, a large-scale studio picture. But the studio was clogged up with television work, so there was a shortage of skilled people and facilities. Getting it finished in time to meet the almost impossible deadline became a nightmare: administrative problems overshadowed creative problems.

There were many experimental scenes with no proper time to try once and fail, and then try something different. John and I seemed to spend less time together than on the previous films. Perhaps one great advantage of location work is that everyone is available most of the time.

Because of the complexity of many of the scenes – elaborate sets and difficult camera moves, never mind the enormous set-piece stunts – there was less cover than on the earlier films, and therefore less opportunity to use the editing creatively, and never enough time. Sadly, once the film had been released, it was clear it was not working properly with audiences, so John had to supervise an amended version. It was a shame that we had not been allowed the time to finish the film properly in the first place, and to stand back and review it critically. Experiments must be allowed to fail.

Ned Beatty and Burt Reynolds in *Deliverance* (edited by Tom Priestley).

Philippe Rousselot, Lighting Cameraman

The Emerald Forest

Shooting in an equatorial forest poses problems such as few film-makers have ever been faced with. Rather than film on location, most of them have preferred to reconstruct it in the studio – and not only during Hollywood's 'golden age', even quite recently (e.g. *Greystoke*).

On the one hand, the problems of administration, transport and climate, plus the risk of illness or accident, have done much to discourage producers; on the other, a rather unexpected discovery: the jungle bears only a faint resemblance to our image of it, the fantasy jungle of adventure books and films.

When you enter a rain forest for the first time, it's very disappointing: a dark green, monochromatic mass, with neither shape nor perspective, rarely and feebly lit by the sun. The eye fails to distinguish any sense of order and soon grows tired of such a dusty entanglement of greenery; one's overriding feeling, after even a short while, is that of being blind, of there being nothing to see.

There was absolutely no reason why the camera should see any better, or anything else, than we ourselves did. We had therefore to impose some order on a visual chaos and rediscover not merely the jungle of our imagination, but that of the Amazonian Indians, who, accustomed to living and surviving in this unusual environment, see in the forest's forms and paths a whole landscape informed both by their daily existence and their mythology.

John already had some experience of the jungle while making *Hell in the Pacific*, and he came up with a number of solutions which, when systematically applied, proved highly effective.

Each shot required the setting to be virtually reconstructed (as would have been the case in the studio), either by removing or (more often) adding plants, creepers, branches, even enormous pre-fabricated polystyrene trees.

Numerous scenes were shot with artificial mist, so that the vegetation would be clearly silhouetted against the background. The foliage in the foreground was washed with the aid of fire-engine pumps, which also lent brilliance and colour to the vegetation.

As far as lighting a shot is concerned, you cannot hope for nuances in a rain forest: either the sun filters through the trees forty or fifty metres above the ground, in which case the landscape is lit by thousands of little metallic sparks in the middle of an inky blackness, a somewhat unreal effect which reinforces the impression of mist; or else the sun doesn't break through at all and the flat, rather sad light makes the landscape appear terribly drab. There is nothing to distinguish dawn from dusk, a clear day from a cloudy one; there is nothing to indicate the passage of time. So that scenes supposed to be taking place at dawn or dusk were shot at noon – with better results than if we had respected the correct hour of the day.

The light changes very quickly, either because of the endlessly variable weather or because the sun has shifted away from the narrow openings in the vault of the treetops. Which

means that, from one hour to the next, the same little corner of the forest has completely altered its appearance, making the matching of consecutive shots extremely tricky.

The whole shoot consisted, therefore, of trying to catch the sun, between showers and cloud movements, and we employed as much back-lighting as possible, since it creates sharper outlines, and attempted to relight the shadows with powerful projectors and large swathes of white silk stretched over frames.

As a director, John prepares his films very carefully and long in advance. Just as, during the preparation, he's willing to devote his time to the people around him, so, while shooting, he adopts a strict working routine, dispensing with pointless chatter, rehearsals and any kind of trial-and-error.

We had long conversations together during the six months before shooting began (indeed, I was rather taken aback when John invited me to attend rehearsals with the actors, where I had nothing to do), and hardly any during the shoot itself. It was as though, after a long period of initiation and apprenticeship, things had to take their own course on the set without there being any need to go back over what had already been said.

My relations with Simon Holland, the film's art director, were of the same type – an unspoken agreement and no further words wasted between us.

John and Simon had spent some time with an Indian tribe – a journey back into the Stone Age which absolutely enthralled them. The way they described it greatly helped me in my conception of the lighting of the shabona, much more so than all the photographic documents I was able to find.

Something else I enjoyed was that John really knew about light and the problems of lighting, so that I felt constantly reassured by his viewpoint, knowing that there wouldn't be any unpleasant surprises during the rushes, and that he would be able to warn me whenever I strayed too far from what he wanted.

To be sure, the shoot was difficult and sometimes painful, because of the climate and the nature of the locations. But, even at the worst moments, John would display an extraordinary capacity for adaptation; he knew how to turn difficulties and even disasters to advantage. We had a single day's interruption, when rain caused a river to overflow, destroying one whole set and blocking the equipment trucks, which were enmired on a runway. On the same day, the royal eagle, a trained bird flown out from France, was poisoned and died within a few hours.

John, in my opinion, was the only one of us who truly *liked* the Amazonian forest and refused to believe that it could be dangerous: he would brush off poisonous snakes as though his mind were elsewhere and he even went as far as to claim that the heat was pleasant, the rain refreshing and that the mosquitos never stung him (which was untrue). What he seemed to be saying was that it wasn't such a difficult film to make after all, and he actually got the rest of us to believe him. He was always the first to dive into the icy rivers, the first to venture along the most difficult paths, on the principle that what he could do the actors and technicians could also do. Even more than physical courage and strength, he took a genuine pleasure in working in such conditions, a pleasure that became contagious and enabled us to perform all kinds of feats and prevented more than one accident.

Gale Tattersall, Philippe Rousselot and John Boorman (shooting *The Emerald Forest*).

Bill Stair, Screenwriter

Leo the Last, Zardoz

I have worked in various design and writing capacities with John over the years . . . I came to collaborate with him early in his career, more by chance than design, as an artistic adviser on a *Monitor* programme of his, *The Quarry*.

He is a very dynamic individual and works extremely hard throughout the production, from its inception to the very end, and likes to be in charge at all levels.

With my background of fine art, illustration and the like, I was able to give him an overview which his other distinguished helpers could not perhaps do, as they are *specialists* in their fields, the very nature of film being to create such specialists even at directorial level. Film was and is for me something more than a job of which I do a part. I always like to have a look at the whole problem and, furthermore, to see it right through to the end, rather than doing my bit on one section of the production line (which is the fate of most film workers because of the nature of commercial cinema). I would hasten to add that I don't then think of myself as a generalist, but rather as someone who was able, when working with John, to bring him many allied and related views, so that I could, for example, help with the overall style of a film as well as contribute to the script as such (I've always felt that films are visual first and verbal second). I suppose my credit on *Zardoz* was a fair one also, that of Story and Design Associate.

I think John is a supreme optimist. I remember jumping on a speeding, full train with him once. We had no tickets and were obviously in for a deal of trouble with rail officials, as we had run round barricades, failed to stop on shouted commands, etc., etc. John's view of the situation was, however, quite clear: 'Look at it this way, Bill . . . we are at least ON THE TRAIN!'

I feel that John has always continued in this way. Get *on* the train (film, problem, whatever) and work it out from there. Invariably, it works out fine. In the example given, the train *wasn't* full, we *weren't* arrested, everything went well. He is always 'at least on the train', usually an express.

Billie Whitelaw in *Leo the Last* (collaboration on the screenplay by Bill Stair).

Sean Connery in *Zardoz*.
Jessica Swift in *Zardoz* (collaboration on the screenplay by Bill Stair).

Alex Thomson, Lighting Cameraman

Excalibur

I had never worked with John Boorman before *Excalibur*, but I had been recommended to shoot some tests for him in Black Park, a wood next to Pinewood Studios.

John was at that time looking for a 'Perceval' and testing several suits of armour at the same time. It was an extremely dull winter's day, with low exposure values, but when one saw the silver armour glowing in the grey light reflecting the black branches, one got the impression of how the picture could and should look.

Naturally, I was rather hoping to do the picture – every cameraman in the world would have given a great deal to work with John Boorman – so that when eventually the call came I was highly delighted. I didn't come immediately, however – another lighting cameraman had been engaged to do the picture. But, after a series of tests and three days' shooting, it was obvious it wasn't going to work out; it was then that I was asked to take over.

This sort of situation is always a little tricky, because it can go one of two ways. In the first instance, the director can lose heart, in that his first choice – the person he's been talking to for weeks, probably, trying to hammer out a style – hasn't come up with the goods and he will settle for mediocre results as long as it goes smoothly and quickly. In the second instance, he becomes over-anxious and interferes with whoever has taken over the job, in the fear that they, too, might not give him what he wants. John, in fact, did neither of these things.

It was fortunate in that there was a three-day break for the Easter holiday, when in fact Ireland closes, which allowed John, Tony Pratt, the production designer and I enough time to sit down and talk, to 'walk' around the locations, to see a couple of sets which were ready and for me to read the script.

Obviously, the first week of any picture is pretty nerve-

Arthur and Lancelot in combat at their first meeting (*Excalibur*).

wracking when you haven't worked with the director before especially when he looks as balefully at you as John sometimes does (which I subsequently found out was generally when he was preoccupied with another problem).

He keeps a watchful eye on what is going on and, because he is such a skilful film-maker, seems to know at any time what is happening or what if anything we are waiting for. If we *are* waiting for something, and it seems to take longer than is necessary, then he will want to know in specific terms why, and the answer had better be good.

He works very closely with the camera crew and will spend a lot of time on the framing and composition of a shot. And, whilst he will listen to suggestions, he will only accept them if they are an improvement on his original conception. He gives time equally to all departments and is constantly talking to and rehearsing the actors; but I have the feeling the most important thing for him during the shooting of a film is the camera and what it records. And yet, maybe this is the strength of John: that he makes you feel that way. Perhaps, if one talked to any other person on the unit, they would say the same thing about their department.

Excalibur was one of those pictures where everybody knew it was going to be good and was proud to be working on it. Yet we had an absolutely foul summer. It rained almost every day and matching problems were bad. The bleaker the weather became, it seemed, the happier John was. There's something about a challenge that he enjoys. We had some trouble with a horse at one time during the beginning of the fight between Arthur and Lancelot when they first meet. The horse was supposed to gallop towards the camera and exit as close as possible. What with the fact that the rider was holding a sixteen-foot lance, and that the horse definitely didn't like us or the camera, the boys were having a bit of trouble with it. It was decided by the horsemaster that we would have to change the horse, which involved waiting until another of the same colour and build could be brought forward, have its tack changed and be rehearsed. John, whether because he was the film's producer or because he liked the challenge, got up on the horse, grabbed the lance, rode away to the start position, wheeled round, came back to camera at full gallop, passed the camera with about a foot to spare, got off the horse and said, 'Why can't we shoot it?'

Nigel Terry and Nicholas Clay in *Excalibur* (photographed by Alex Thomson).

Tony Woollard, Art Director

Catch Us If You Can, Leo the Last

I first met John Boorman in 1965. He interviewed me with regard to designing his first feature film, *Catch Us If You Can*, which had a script by Peter Nichols and starred Dave Clark with his band.

I had taken along a large portfolio of sketches from previous projects and was excited to find he was looking at each sketch carefully, then asking detailed questions; I could tell immediately that John would be an interesting, visually aware director to work for.

John gave me the job and straight away was prepared to discuss each character in great detail, which helped me visualize their settings accurately. He was very pleased to receive new ideas, not scripted, and would incorporate them if he felt them right.

The film had gone well and I had high hopes of working with John again; so I was more than delighted when, a few weeks after shooting, he asked me to design the lettering for the title sequence. With this encouragement I have gone on to design the title sequences on most of the films I have made – it's what John and I call total design.

After the film, John returned to Bristol, where he lived, but it was not long before he settled in London. He liked our house in Putney and bought one in the same square. Our children were the same age; thus the families grew close together.

It was an exciting time, discussing scripts he was receiving from Hollywood and England. From my point of view (as I had no green card to work in Hollywood), I was hoping he would make *The Rose Lounge* for David Deutsch here in London.

But, as we all know now, he made the right decision; I was with him the day he decided; it was to be Hollywood and *Point Blank*. He would move his whole family out and live there.

He asked me if I would be interested in going over there with him as adviser, not designer. What a fool I was not to accept! (One looks back afterwards in wonder at the mistakes one makes.)

We saw John many times when he returned to England after his success with *Point Blank* – he had not sold his house in London and the children loved meeting each other again.

I was unable to join John on *Hell in the Pacific* because of prior engagements, and we did not work together again until he asked me to prepare a film of Tom Stoppard's great play, *Rosencrantz and Guildenstern Are Dead*.

I set to with great gusto, charging around Europe to find a suitable castle for Hamlet's Elsinore. On my journeys, I read the play carefully and discovered that, because of the very nature of the Elizabethan stage, Shakespeare had never conceived a long shot of the castle: that is, of a shape. The shape of the castle was immaterial to him, and I considered it a mistake to establish it: Shakespeare wanted Elsinore to be the sum total of the all the people who inhabited the castle, not an exterior shape with particular national characteristics, but just a King and Queen within a setting that could be anywhere, just huge stone walls such as Olivier had used years before. We could shoot the film anywhere. In fact, a studio would have been better.

John loved this theory of mine, and I came home from my search to design a much more intimate film.

To my surprise, within a few weeks John was back in London from Hollywood to make a film entitled *Black Comedy*. I was to drop my work on *Rosencrantz* for the moment, since it was to be shelved until after the new project. As we all know, it was never made (a pity, I think) and *Black Comedy* developed into *Leo the Last*.

I enjoyed designing this film. The idea of shooting in colour with sets, props and costumes in black-and-white came from the early location surveys, where we had selected houses and squares in London that were inhabited.

I pointed out the enormous difficulties we would have shooting such a long and complicated film in locations that were not under our complete control; and another important fact for me was the problem of colour control. I showed John that if we shot on doors and windows and real interiors with the bright, gaudy colours that existed in those types of locations, they would look, when framed by our cameras, like colour supplement pretties – which was not what we were trying to say in the film. So I painted an interior location setting in blacks and whites to shoot some tests. John loved the effect and we selected new streets which were completely uninhabited, which we could paint entirely black.

The style of the film was set – I mean to say, who has ever seen a supermarket full of goods with no colour, just black and white?

The success of the colour effect came from the fact that the only warm colours on screen were those of the actors' faces and hands, so that one's eyes were drawn straight to them.

I loved the film and the effect; it was great to be shooting with John again. I found that he loved us to bounce ideas off him and he in turn would bounce ideas off us. John makes you feel very much part of the whole creative unit. Nobody is on the outside – even my wife was brought in by John to design the costumes for *Leo*.

This aspect of John's way of working has grown, until now his whole family, his wife and children were drawn into his filming, action, editing and designing of *Excalibur*.

Leo the Last (designed by Tony Woollard).

Vilmos Zsigmond, Lighting Cameraman

Deliverance

Boorman is a very visual director, if not to the point of usurping the responsibility of his lighting cameraman for the photography, as is true of some film-makers! He works very closely with you, often looking into the viewfinder; at the same time, however, he knows enough to let you get on with your work alone if he trusts you. Yet one has to give him credit for the visual side of his films, since the role of his cinematographer is basically to respect his wishes and follow his guidelines. English film-makers tend to communicate directly with their framers, which isn't the case in the States, where the framer works exclusively with the lighting cameraman. With me, Boorman's task was simplified since, having worked in Hungary, I'm used to being actively involved in the framing, which was important for a film like *Deliverance*, particularly in the scenes on the river where there might be all kinds of unpredictable movements which we had to be able to catch.

We were so far removed from any civilization that there wasn't a single passable road. We got around in a jeep, to and from the landing-stages. There, we had only two canoes and two motor-boats for the actors, a couple of cameramen (myself and another), two assistants, Boorman himself and two or three technicians. It was a drastically reduced crew and sometimes we had to carry our food supplies with us. At the beginning, in the scenes on the rapids, we thought of using stuntmen. There were to be four weeks of shooting with a second unit and a few stand-ins. Finally, we had only two days with the stuntmen, and practically all of that footage ended on the cutting-room floor. In fact, the actors gradually became real pros and insisted on doing everything themselves, which lent a greater weight of reality to the narrative: you can see them in close-up performing a number of difficult acts.

We experimented a great deal. Choosing the colours was an important job. We decided to use only greens, blacks and whites, eliminating reds, yellows and blues. When the weather was fine, we had to wait for the sky to cloud over. That's why, in the film, it's either white or black. We also desaturated the colours in the laboratory.

The nocturnal scene in which Jon Voight clambers up a wall

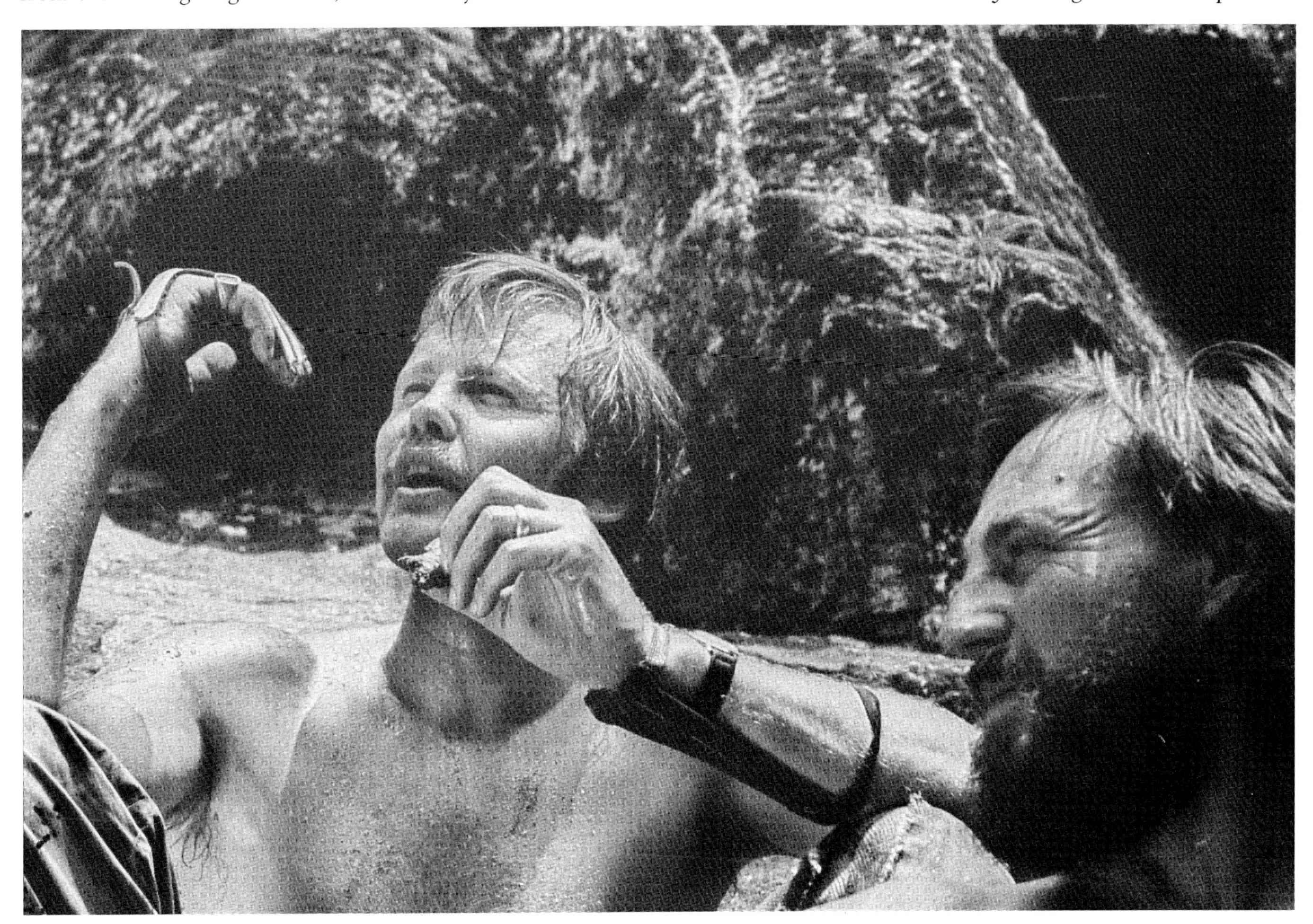

Jon Voight with Vilmos Zsigmond, the lighting cameraman of *Deliverance*.

of rock was shot in day-for-night. It would have been impossible any other way, as we wouldn't have been able to light the mountain at night. I'm fifty per cent satisfied with the result, except that the laboratory didn't really know how to treat the image. The effect remains very unreal, as we wished: there's moonlight at the same time as the sky is pitch black.

The underwater sequences were actually shot in a swimming pool in Clayton, Georgia. We poured milk into the water and added some earth to make it look grubby, as the river wasn't supposed to be limpid. These shots were filmed by Boorman himself. I'd never done any underwater filming and there was no time to learn. John took the oxygen bottles, he dived in and he himself operated a hand-held camera.

We used anamorphic lenses and lots of long focals, zooms from 50mm to 500mm. Sometimes we even went up to 1000mm. The zoom was more flexible: we were able to follow the characters along the river. John likes to use all kinds of lenses, a 25 for long shots, then a 100 for close-ups. For the big discussion scene in the forest after the murder, there wasn't enough light for the zoom; so we used a 180, which was our favourite lens.

Few film-makers with whom I've worked are as visual as John. He's familiar with every problem concerning photography and lighting. He never exerts pressure on you, he gives you all the time you need, since he knows how much work is involved in setting up a shot. In fact, he's an expert in just about everything.

He's also a wonderful man. He'd rented a large house to be able to invite everyone to it, not only the actors. During the shoot, there'd be about fifty people at his dinner table. It was our only amusement. There was neither the cinema nor television. We were really cut off from civilization. The only distraction we might have found was to be beaten up by the locals. So John had movies flown in and screened them in the house, he organized ping-pong tournaments and installed hi-fi equipment. We were like one big family. His personality is such that everyone is made to feel at home, which is how he gets the best out of us all.

These recollections were written for this book at the author's request, with the exception of those by Lee Marvin, Marcello Mastroianni and Vilmos Zsigmond, which were recorded on tape.

Jon Voight, Vilmos Zsigmond, John Boorman and Burt Reynolds (shooting *Deliverance*).

Delivrance
WARNER BROS A Warner Communications Company
présente
un film de JOHN BOORMAN
WB
JON VOIGHT · BURT REYNOLDS dans " DELIVRANCE "
NED BEATTY · RONNY COX · PANAVISION TECHNICOLOR · Scénario de JAMES DICKEY d'après son roman · Produit et mis en scène par JOHN BOORMAN
Distribué par WARNER COLUMBIA FILM

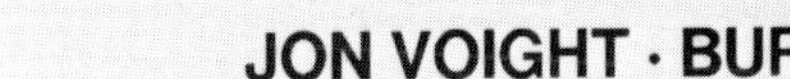

Filmography

Television

Between 1956 and 1964, as editor, director or producer, in London (ITN), Southampton (Southern TV) and Bristol (BBC West), John Boorman was involved in the making of several hundred programmes. I have not indicated these credits here, but discuss, in the chapter 'From Shepperton to Griffith', his principal activities in television. I felt it necessary, however, to provide such information on the last of Boorman's television productions, between 1963 and 1965: these are important in that they already offer evidence of his artistic personality and anticipate his work in the cinema.

1963 **Citizen 63**
(a series of six 30 min programmes, three of which were directed by Boorman: the portraits of Barry Langford, Marion Knight and Frank George).
Dir.: John Boorman. *ph.*: Arthur Smith. *ed.*: John Merritt. *mus.*: Tony Desmond. *sd. rec.*: Clifford Voice, Howard Smith. *sd. mix.*: Jack Robottom. A BBC West Region feature.

1964 **The Newcomers**
(a series of six 30 min episodes).
Dir.: John Boorman. *prod.*: John Boorman. *ph.*: Arthur Smith, Jim Saunders. *ed.*: George Inger, John Merritt. *mus.*: David Lee. *sd. rec.*: Howard Smith. *ass. prod.*: Michael Croucher. *l.p.*: Alison Kennedy, Arthur Smith (*themselves*). A BBC West Region feature.

1964 **The Quarry**
Dir.: John Boorman. *sc.*: John Boorman. *ph.*: Jim Saunders. *ed.*: John Merritt. *art. cons.*: William Stair, Ernest Pascoe. *mus.*: Brian Fahey. *sd. rec.*: Robin Drake. *sd. mix.*: Jack Robottom. *assistant to prod.*: Barbara Harrison. The works of the mentally ill provided by the Adamson Collection of Schizophrenic Art. The works of children provided by the *Sunday Mirror*. BBC West. *l.p.*: John Franklin Robbins (*Arthur King*), Sheila Allen (*Ruth*), Alexandra Malcolm (*Jean*), Ingrid Hafner (*Ursula*), David de Keyser (*Doctor*), Alexander Cranfield Abbott (*Journalist*), George Tute (*Jim*), Catherine Rodgers (*Rebecca*), Richard Howard (*Photographer*).

1966 **The Great Director**
Assembled, produced and directed by John Boorman. Research: William K. Everson. Commentary written by John Lloyd and spoken by Clive Swift. With the cooperation of the Griffith Estate and the Museum of Modern Art, New York. BBC.

Cinema

1965 **Catch Us If You Can**
(US title: Having a Wild Weekend)
Great Britain. *Cert*: U. *dist.*: Warner-Pathé/Anglo Amalgamated. *p.c.*: Bruton Film Productions. A David Deutsch Production. *p*: David Deutsch. *Assoc. p*: Basil Keys. *Assistant to p*: Alexander Jacobs. *p. manager*: Donald Toms. *assistant to d*: Michael Blakemore. *assistant d*: David Tringham. *sc*: Peter Nicholas. *ph.*: Manny Wynn. *ed*: Gordon Pilkington *production designer*: Tony Woollard. *m.d.*: Dave Clark. *m. played by*: The Dave Clark Five. *sd*: Arthur Ridout *sd. rec.*: Robert Allen. *sd. re-rec*: Len Abbott. *cost.*: Sally Jacobs. *l.p.*: Dave Clarke (*Steve*). Barbara Ferris (*Dinah*), Lenny Davidson (*Lenny*), Rick Huxley (*Rick*), Mike Smith (*Mike*), Denis Payton (*Denis*), David Lodge (*Louis*), Robin Bailey (*Guy*), Yootha Joyce (*Nan*), David de Keyser (*Zissell*), Robert Lang (*Whiting*), Clive Swift (*Duffle*), Ronald Lacey (*Beatnik*), Michael Gwynn (*Sponsor of meat ad.*), Hugh Walters (*Grey*), Michael Blakemore (*Officer*), Marianne Stone (*Mrs Stone*), Julian Holloway (*Assistant Director*), Peter Nichols (*Photographer*). 8,190 ft. 91 mins.

Steve, Lenny, Rick, Mike and Denis, freelance stuntmen who make films in winter and teach skin-diving in Spain in summer, are working on a television commercial for meat in London when Steve and the star of the show, Dinah 'the Butcha Girl', decide to get away from it all, and drive off in the white E-type Jaguar that they're using as a prop in the film. Heading for an island that Dinah hopes to buy off the coast of Devon, they encounter a group of beatniks and become involved in an army exercise that results in the destruction of their car. A predatory middle-aged couple, Guy and Nan, give them a lift to Bath, where they offer them hospitality in their elegant home. The advertising firm, on the instructions of the executive Zissell, who is fascinated by Dinah, has issued a story to the effect that Steve has kidnapped her. Guy and Nan persuade their visitors, who now include the rest of Steve's group, to attend the Arts Fancy Dress Ball, where Zissell's henchmen and the police also converge upon the scene. Eluding their pursuers, the youngsters make for a farm run by Louis, former leader of their London youth club. Steve is disillusioned to see that all his one-time hero cares about is publicity for himself and his so-called ranch. On Dinah's equally disappointing island, Zissell himself is waiting for them. Worse still, he has walked there, for at low tide it isn't an island at all. Refusing to play a part in the press stunt that Zissell has lined up, Steve leaves Dinah to face the photographers alone.

1967 **Point Blank**
USA *Cert*: X. *dist*: MGM. *p.c.*: MGM. A Judd Bernard-Irwin Winkler Production. *p.*: Judd Bernard, Robert Chartoff. *p. manager*: Edward Woehler. *assistant d*: Al Jennings. *sc*: Alexander Jacobs, David Newhouse, Rafe Newhouse. Based on the novel *The Hunter* by Richard Stark. *ph.*: Philip H. Lathrop. Panavision. *col*: Metrocolor. *col. consultant*: William Stair. *sp. ph. effects*: J. McMillan Johnson. *ed*: Henry Berman. *a d.*: George W. Davis, Albert Brenner. *set dec.*: Henry Grace, Keogh Gleason. *m*: Johnny Mandel. *Song*: 'Mighty Good Times' by Stu Gardner. *sung by*: The Stu Gardner Trio. *sd*: Franklin Milton. *sd.-mx.*: Larry Jost. *cost.*: Lambert Marks, Margo Weintz. *make-up*: William Tutt, John Truwe. *l.p.*: Lee Marvin (*Walker*), Angie Dickinson (*Chris*), Keenan Wynn (*Yost*), Carroll O'Connor (*Brewster*), Lloyd Bochner (*Carter*), Michael Strong (*Stegman*), John Vernon (*Mal Reese*), Sharon Acker (*Lynne*), James Sikking (*Gunman*), Sandra Warner (*Waitress*), Roberta Haynes (*Mrs Carter*), Kathleen Freeman (*1st Citizen*), Victor Creatore (*Carter's Man*), Lawrence Hauben (Car Salesman), Susan Holloway (*Girl Customer*), Sid Haig, Michael Bell (*Penthouse Lobby Guards*), Priscilla Boyd (*Receptionist*), John McMurtry (*Messenger*), Ron Walters, George Strattan (*Two Young Men in Apartment*), Nicole Rogell (*Carter's Secretary*), Rico Cattani, Roland LaStarza (*Reese's Guards*). 8,254 ft. 92 mins.

While stealing a fortune in loot from a helicopter run operated by a rival gang, Walker is double-crossed by his partner, Mal Reese, who shoots him and leaves him for dead in the deserted island prison at Alcatraz before running off with his faithless wife Lynne. Walker miraculously survives and swims to the mainland. Two years later, he is approached by a mysterious man called Yost, who offers to help him have his revenge and regain his money from 'the Organization' for which Reese now works. Acting on a tip from Yost, Walker goes to Los Angeles and confronts Lynne, now deserted by Reese. She commits suicide. With the help of Lynne's sister Chris, and more information from Yost, Walker gets to Reese, who falls to his death over a parapet while the two men are struggling. Still seeking his money, Walker threatens two Organization bosses, Stegman and Carter, who are both killed in a trap set for Walker by Brewster, the Organization's second-in-command. At gunpoint, Brewster agrees to take Walker and Chris to Alcatraz, where large sums of Organization money still change hands. There, Brewster is shot by Yost, who reveals himself to be Fairfax, the Organization's top man. Accompanied by a professional gunman, he challenges Walker to emerge from his hiding-place in the shadows and collect his money. Walker does not move.

1968 **Hell in the Pacific**
USA *Cert*: U. *dist*: CIRO *p.c.*: Selmur Pictures. *exec.p.*: Selig J. Seligman, Henry G. Saperstein. *p*: Reuben Bercovitch. *p. manager*: Lloyd E. Anderson, Harry F. Hogan, Isao Zeniya. *assistant d*: Yoichi Matsue. *sc*: Alexander Jacobs, Eric Bercovici. *story*: Reuben Bercovitch. *ph*: Conrad Hall. Panavision. *col*: Technicolor. *ed*: Thomas Stanford. *a.d.*: Anthony D. G. Pratt, Masao Yamazaki. *set dec.*: Makato Kikuchi. *sp. effects*: Joe Zomar, Kunishige Tanaka. *technical adviser*: Masaaki Asukai. *l.p.*: Lee Marvin (*The American Marine Pilot*), Toshiro Mifune (*The Japanese Naval Officer*). 9,249 ft. 103 mins.

Towards the end of the Second World War, an American pilot and a Japanese naval officer find themselves stranded on a tiny Pacific atoll. Facing each other on the beach with the only weapons they have, a knife and a bamboo spear, they circle each other warily before retreating, baffled. Neither speaks the other's language, and some desultory mutual harassment follows, until finally the Japanese overpowers the American and ties him to a yoke. Before long the American reverses the situation. Then suddenly, irrationally, he frees the puzzled Japanese. A state of wary truce follows, the days pass in idle, childish pastimes, and the Japanese starts building a small, pathetically unseaworthy raft. At first scornful, the American becomes interested, and together they build a raft which carries them, after a nightmare voyage, to a group of small islands. These prove to be deserted, but amid the ruins of bombed Japanese and American installations they find various stores, including cigarettes and a bottle of sake. Washed, shaved and in clean clothes, they celebrate. But half-drunk, and upset by pictures of the war in a magazine, they let their old enmity flare up again, and stride angrily away in opposite directions.

1969 **Leo the Last**
Great Britain. *Cert*: X. *dist*: United Artists. *p.c.*: Char/Wink/Boor. *p.*: Irwin Winkler, Robert Chartoff. *p. manager*: James M. Crawford. *assistant d*: Allan James. *sc*: William Stair, John Boorman. Based on the play *The Prince*, by George Tabori. *add. dial.*: Ram John Holder. *ph*: Peter Suschitzky. *col*: DeLuxe. *Ed*: Tom Priestley.

production designer: Tony Woollard. *sp. effects*: John Richardson. *m/songs*: Fred Myrow. *sung by*: Ram John Holder, The Swingle Singers. *sd. ed*: Jim Atkinson. *sd. rec*: Ron Baron. *assistant to d.*: Allan James. *cost.*: Joan Woollard. *l.p.*: Marcello Mastroianni (*Leo*), Billie Whitelaw (*Margaret*), Calvin Lockhart (*Roscoe*), Glenna Forster Jones (*Salambo*), Graham Crowden (*Max*), Gwen Ffrangcon-Davies (*Hilda*), David De Keyser (*David*), Vladek Sheybal (*Laszlo*), Keefe West (*Jasper*), Kenneth J. Warren (*Kowalski*), Patsy Smart (*Mrs Kowalski*), Ram John Holder (*Negro Preacher*), Thomas Buson (*Mr Madi*), Tina Solomon (*Mrs Madi*), Brinsley Forde (*Bip*), Robert Redman, Malcolm Redman and Robert Kennedy (*Madi Children*), Phyllis McMahon (*Blonde Whore*), Princess Patience (*Negro Whore*), Bernard Boston and Roy Stewart (*Jasper's Bodyguards*), Lucita Lijertwood (*Wailing Lady*), Ishaq Bux (*Supermarket Manager*), Doris Clark (*The Singing Lady*), Lou Gossett, Alba, Marcia Redman, Billy Russell. 9,360 ft. 104 mins.

Leo is an alienated, atrophied aristocrat who comes to a London cul-de-sac to convalesce. His entourage includes Margaret, who wants to marry his money, and Laszlo, who is organizer of a group of exiles bent on reinstating the prince in his now defunct monarchy somewhere in Europe. All Leo wants is to watch birds through his telescope. His hobby leads him to take an interest in the poor slum-dwellers on whom he spies and with whom he shares the street. His realization of the plight of Salambo's family, black and almost starving, is accelerated by three events. A Polish shopkeeper is constantly trying to rape Salambo, and her boyfriend, Roscoe, is imprisoned after beating him up. Secondly, her father dies – 'killed by kindness' – the day Leo sends the family a huge stock of food. And Salambo becomes a ward of Leo to protect her from Jasper, the street pimp, and a life of prostitution. Leo recognizes that self-realization must come by destroying his own mansion, and with the local population behind him, he effects a 'firework revolution', sending his house up in flames, spoiling the aspirations of the wealthy hangers-on, and giving the street to the poor.

1972 **Deliverance**
USA *Cert*: X. *dist*: Columbia-Warner. *p.c.*: Warner Bros./Elmer Enterprises. *p*: John Boorman. *p. manager*: Wallace Worsley. *asst. d*: Al Jennings, Miles Middough. *sc*: James Dickey. Based on his own novel. *ph*: Vilmos Zsigmond. Panavision. *col*: Technicolor. *2nd Unit ph*: Bill Butler. *ed*: Tom Priestley. *a.d.*: Fred Harpman. *sp. effects*: Marcel Vercoutere. *m*: 'Duelling Banjos' arranged and played by Eric Weissberg, with Steve Mandel. *sd.ed*: Jim Atkinson. *sd. rec*: Walter Gross. *sd. re-rec.*: Doug Turner. *creative assoc.*: Rospo Pallenberg. *technical advisers*: Charles Wiggin, E. Lewis King. *cost.*: Bucky Rous. *make-up*: Michael Hancock. *l.p.*: Jon Voight (*Ed*), Burt Reynolds (*Lewis*), Ned Beatty (*Bobby*), Ronny Cox (*Drew*), Billy McKinney (*Mountain Man*), Herbert 'Cowboy' Coward (*Toothless Man*), James Dickey (*Sheriff Bullard*), Ed Ramey (*Old Man*), Billy Redden (*Lonny*), Seamon Glass (*1st 'Griner'*), Randall Deal (*2nd 'Griner'*), Lewis Crone (*1st Deputy*), Ken Keener (*2nd Deputy*), Johnny Popwell (*Ambulance Driver*), John Fowler (*Doctor*), Kathy Rickman (*Nurse*), Louise Coldren (*Mrs Biddiford*), Pete Ware (*Taxi Driver*), Hoyt T. Pollard (*Boy at Gas Station*), Belinha Beatty (*Martha Gentry*), Charley Boorman (*Ed's Boy*). 9,802 ft. 109 mins.

Driving to a ramshackle village in the Appalachian mountains with three city friends – Ed Gentry, Bobby Trippe and Drew Ballinger – Lewis Medlock pays two local inhabitants, who are full of forebodings about his plans, to drive the party's cars downriver to Aintry. A fanatical believer in the need for man to come to terms with nature if he is to survive, Lewis has persuaded his friends – of whom only Ed, admiring but sceptical, has any non-urban skills – to join him in a weekend away from work, canoeing down the uncharted and possibly dangerous river before it and the entire valley disappear in a new dam project. The first day, as they learn to handle their two canoes and shoot their first rapids, is pure exhilaration. But on the second day, landing ahead of the other two, Ed and Bobby are held at gunpoint by two men in the forest, one of whom sexually assaults Bobby. Ed watches helplessly, awaiting his own fate, until, with mingled relief and horror, he realizes that Lewis has come to the rescue by shooting one man dead with an arrow. The other vanishes. Partly because they fear a prejudiced jury if the case is tried locally, partly because Bobby doesn't want the story spread, Lewis proposes to bury the body where it will soon lie forgotten under new waters. A vote is taken and, with Drew insisting that the law should be respected, Lewis's plan prevails. As they press on and approach new rapids, Drew, already distracted, mysteriously vanishes overboard. The two canoes tangle and capsize, and by the time they struggle ashore, Lewis is crippled by a broken leg, Drew has vanished, and they have only one canoe left. Certain that Drew was shot from the cliff-tops, Ed assumes the leadership, manages to scale the cliff, and next morning, using an arrow, kills a man lurking there. After disposing of the body, and not entirely sure that it was the same man as the one who ran away, they are horrified to come across Drew's body wedged against rocks in mid-stream. Unable to determine whether he was really shot or not, they sink the body with stones in accordance with a concocted story designed to conceal what really happened to ensure that no bodies are found, and reach Aintry after safely negotiating the worst set of rapids yet. There Lewis is hospitalized; the sheriff, though suspicious, is unable to shake their story or find any evidence; and they are allowed to go home – Ed to be haunted by a nightmare of a dead hand rising from the waters.

1973 **Zardoz**
Great Britain. *Cert*. X. *dist*: Fox-Rank. *p.c.*: John Boorman Productions. For 20th Century-Fox. *p*: John Boorman. *assoc. p*: Charles Orme. *p. manager*: Seamus Byrne. *asst. d*: Simon Relph. *sc*: John Boorman. *story associate*: Bill Stair. *ph*: Geoffrey Unsworth. Panavision. *col*: DeLuxe. *ed*: John Merritt. *p. designer*: Anthony Pratt. *design associate*: Bill Stair. *set dec*: John Hoesli, Martin Atkinson. *sp. effects*: Gerry Johnston. *m*: David Munrow. 'Symphony no. 7' by Ludwig van Beethoven, played by the Amsterdam Concertgebouw Orchestra. *cost*: Christel Kruse Boorman. *make-up*: Basil Newall. *sd. ed*: Jim Atkinson. *sd. rec*: Liam Saurin. *sd. re-rec*: Doug Turner. *l.p.*: Sean Connery (*Zed*), Charlotte Rampling (*Consuella*), Sara Kestelman (*May*), Sally Anne Newton (*Avalow*), John Alderton (*Friend*), Niall Buggy (*Arthur Frayn*), Bosco Hogan (*George Saden*), Jessica Swift (*Apathetic*), Bairbre Dowling (*Star*), Christopher Casson (*Old Scientist*), Reginald Jarman (*Death*). 9,360 ft. 104 mins. *Original running time* – 105 mins.

2293. Since the collapse of industrial society in 1990, most of the earth has been a polluted wasteland, known as the Outlands. The tribes of Brutals who till its recalcitrant soil worship Zardoz, a giant flying godhead made of stone, which periodically descends among them to relieve them of their grain and issue their overseers, the Exterminators, with weapons. Alone among the Brutals the selectively bred Exterminators are permitted to reproduce. During one of Zardoz's descents to the Outlands, the Exterminator Zed stows away inside a consignment of grain. Once Zardoz is in flight, Zed shoots its controller and 'voice', Arthur Frayn, who falls overboard. Eventually the head lands in a verdant valley, and Zed discovers the existence of the Vortex, a 300-year-old commune of scientists and intellectuals, a repository of all human knowledge, protected from the outside world by a gravitational force field. The community is governed by an elaborate consensus system, a combination of sophisticated technology and spiritual meditation. Its dominant members, the Eternals, are perennially youthful and beyond sexual desire. Less fortunate are the Apathetics, reduced to a near catatonic state by the strain of immortality; and the Renegades, condemned to senility for persistent offences against the group will. Only death is denied to all. Zed is swiftly captured by the Eternals; and although the idealistic Consuella is convinced that he should be destroyed immediately, the geneticist May is authorized to keep him for one week as a subject for research. Between sessions with May in the Brain Room, where his fragmented memories appear as images on a large screen, Zed is shown around the Vortex by the cynical Friend, whose attitude to the outside soon has him condemned to Renegade status. As the hour of his death approaches, Zed – whose virility has already aroused ambiguous feelings among the lady scientists – determines to save his own life and to liberate the Brutals from their servitude. Hunted by the Eternals, he hides among the Renegades; with a magic leaf donated by the prophetess Avalow and riddles supplied by the resuscitated Arthur Frayn (who has masterminded Zed's revolt to free the Vortex from its burden of immortality), Zed eventually locates and penetrates the secret of the Tabernacle, a network of crystals designed by the Vortex's now senile founder. As the Exterminators overrun the Vortex and mow down its grateful inhabitants, Zed escapes with Consuella to a cave. Here they mate, grow old and die, while their son grows to maturity.

1977 **The Heretic**
USA *Cert*: X. *dist*: Columbia-Warner. *p.c.*: Warner Bros. *p.*: Richard Lederer, John Boorman. *assoc. p*: Charles Orme. *p. managers*: John Coonan, William Gerrity (New York). *location manager*: John James. *2nd Unit d/creative associate*: Rospo Pallenberg. *asst. d*: Phil Rawlins, Victor Hsu. *sc*: William Goodhart. Based on characters created by William Peter Blatty. *ph*: William A. Fraker. *col*: Technicolor. *2nd Unit ph*: David Quaid, Ken Eddy, Diane Eddy. *sp. locust ph*: Sean Morris, David Thompson (Oxford Scientific Films). *sp. ph. effects*: Albert J. Whitlock, Van Der Veer Photo. *process consultant*: Bill Hansard. *ed*: Tom Priestley. *assoc. ed*: Alex Hubert. *p. designer*: Richard MacDonald. *a.d.*: Jack Collis, Gene Rudolf (New York). *set dec.*: John Austin. *scenic arts*: Ron Strang. *Regan's drawings*: Katrine Boorman. *sp. effects*: Chuck Gaspar, Wayne Edgar, Jim Blount, Jeff Jarvis, Roy Kelly. *m/m. d*: Ennio Morricone; 'Lullaby of Broadway' by Al Dublin, Harry Warren. *choreo*: Daniel Joseph Giagni. *cost*: Robert de Mora. *sp. make-up*: Dick Smith. *make-up*: Gary Liddiard. *titles*: Dan Perri. *sd. rec*: Walter Gross. *sd. re-rec*: Arthur Piantadosi, Les Fresholtz, Michael Minkler. *sd. effects*: Jim Atkinson. *sync effects ed*: Russ Hill. *African technical consultant*: Fiseha Dimetros. *hypnosis consultant*: Dr Kenneth Fineman. *entomologist*: Steven Kutcher. *continuity*: Bonnie Prendergast. *Steadicam oper.*: Garrett Brown. *l.p.*: Linda Blair (*Regan MacNeil*), Richard Burton (*Father Philip Lamont*), Louise Fletcher (*Dr Gene Tuskin*), Max von Sydow (*Father Merrin*), Kitty Winn (*Sharon Spencer*), Paul Henreid (*Cardinal Jaros*), James Earl Jones (*Older Kokumo*), Ned Beatty (*Edwards*), Belinha Beatty (*Liz*), Rose Portillo (*Spanish Girl*), Barbara Cason (*Mrs Phalor*), Tiffany Kinney (*Deaf Girl*), Joey Green (*Young Kokumo*), Fiseha Dimetros (*Young Monk*),Ken Renard (*Abbot*), John Joyce (*Monk*), Hank Garrett (*Conductor*), Lorry Goldman (*Accident Victim*), Bill Grant (*Taxi Driver*), Shane Butterworth, Joely Adams (*Tuskin Children*), Vladek Sheybal (*Voice of Pazuzu*). 9,223 ft. 102mins. *Original running time* – 117 mins.

Father Philip Lamont, who fears his own faith to be weakening, is investigating the case of Father Merrin, who died while exorcising the ancient Assyrian demon Pazuzu from young Regan MacNeil in Georgetown, Washington DC. At the psychiatric institute where Regan, now an apparently normal adolescent, is still being monitored by Dr Gene Tuskin, Lamont witnesses a deep hypnosis session in which Dr Tuskin, linked to Regan by a machine called a 'synchronizer', is overwhelmed by a vision of the Georgetown exorcism and has to be 'rescued' by Lamont. Shaken but fascinated by this experience of evil, and by his feelings in the now deserted Georgetown house (which he visits with Regan's guardian, Sharon Spencer, who is still haunted by what happened), Lamont joins Regan in a second 'synchronizer' session, and is whisked away by Pazuzu on a frightening visionary journey to the time in Africa when a young Father Merrin exorcised a boy, Kokumo, who had great healing powers and strength to fight the dreaded locust swarms (Pazuzu appears in the form of a locust). Believing that Regan has similar powers, and that this has drawn the evil to her, Lamont defies his superior, Cardinal Jaros, to go to Africa to find the adult Kokumo. Despairing in his search, Lamont loses faith and calls on Pazuzu's help; he is rewarded with a vision of Kokumo as a priest of unholy arts, before meeting him as a researcher into the control of locusts. Returning to New York, and more than ever drawn to Pazuzu, Lamont rushes with Regan to the Georgetown house (pursued by Dr Tuskin and Sharon), where he is confronted both by locusts and Pazuzu in the form of a seductive Regan. Lamont dies fighting the demon as the house splits asunder; swayed by the evil, Sharon sets fire to herself; but Regan uses her spiritual strength to subdue the evil manifest in the locust swarm.

1981 **Excalibur**
USA *Cert*: AA. *dist.*: Columbia-EMI-Warner. *p.c.*: Orion Pictures. *exec. p.*: Edgar F. Gross, Robert A. Einstein. *p*: John Boorman. *assoc. p.*: Michael Dryhurst. *p. manager*: Jack Phelan. *location manager*: Kevin Moriarty. *2nd Unit d*: Peter MacDonald. *asst. d*: Barry Blackmore, Ted Morley, Andrew Montgomery, Robert Dwyer-Joyce, David Murphy, John Lawlor. *sc*: Rospo Pallenberg, John Boorman. Based on *Le Morte d'Arthur* by Thomas Malory. *adapt*: Rospo Pallenberg. *ph*: Alex Thomson. *col*: Technicolor. *2nd Unit ph*: Peter MacDonald. *camera op*: Bob Smith. *sp. ph. effects*: Oxford Scientific Films. *sp. optical effects*: Wally Veevers. *ed*: John Merritt. *p. designer*: Anthony Pratt. *a.d.*: Tim Hutchinson. *set dec.*: Bryan Graves. *scenic artist*: Mervyn Rowe. *sp. effects*: Peter Hutchinson, Alan Whibley, Gerry Johnstone, Michael Doyle. *models*: Anthony Freeman. *m/m.d*: Trevor Jones. *m. extracts*: Prelude to *Parsifal*, Prelude to *Tristan and Isolde*, 'Siegfried's Funeral March', from *The Ring*, by Richard Wagner, performed by the London Philharmonic Orchestra, conducted by Norman Del Mar, 'O Fortuna' from *Carmina Burana*, by Carl Orff, performed by the Leipzig Radio Symphony Orchestra and Chorus, conducted by Herbert Kegel. *choreo*: Anthony Van Laast. *cost*: Bob Ringwood. *wardrobe*: Daryl Bristow, Janet O'Leary. *make-up*: Basil Newall, Anna Dryhurst. *titles/opticals*: General Screen Enterprises. *sd. ed*: Ron Davis. *sd. rec.*: Doug Turner, Tom Curran. *m. rec.*: John Richard, Richard Lewzey. *sd. re-rec.*: Delta Sound. *creative consultant*: Neil Jordan. *p. assistants*: Beryl Harvey, Marie McFerran. *stunts*: Ken Byrne, Dominic Hewitt, Paul Kelly, Chris King, James MacHale, Ed McShortall, Donal O'Farrell, Bernard O'Hare, Peter Spelman, Alan Walsh. *riders*: (sup.) Michael Rowland; Philip Bernon, Richard Collins, Seamus Collins, Joe Cullen, Daithi Curren, Tony Doyle, Donal Fortune, David Gavaghan, Eddie Kennedy, Bronco McLaughlin, Michael O'Farrell, Ray O'Toole. *fight arranger*: William Hobbs. *armourers*: Peter Leicht, Steve Tidiman, Nick Fitzpatrick. *armour*: Terry English. *jewellery*: Liberty's. *l.p.*: Nigel Terry (*King Arthur*), Helen Mirren (*Morgana*), Nicholas Clay (*Lancelot*), Cherie Lunghi (*Guinevere*), Paul Geoffrey (*Perceval*), Nicol Williamson (*Merlin*), Robert Addie (*Mordred*), Gabriel Byrne (*Uther Pendragon*), Keith Buckley (*Uryens*), Katrine Boorman (*Igraine*), Liam Neeson (*Gawain*), Corin Redgrave (*Duke of Cornwall*), Niall O'Brien (*Kay*), Patrick Stewart (*Leondegrance*), Clive Swift (*Ector*), Ciarin Hinds (*Lot*), Liam O'Calloghan (*Sadok*), Michael Muldoon (*Astamor*), Charley Boorman (*Young Mordred*), Mannix Flynn (*Mordred's lieutenant*), Garrett Keogh (*Mador*), Emmet Bergin (*Ulfius*), Barbara Byrne (*Young Morgana*), Brid Brennan (*Lady in Waiting*)

Kay McLaren (*Aged Morgana*), Eammon Kelly (*Abbott*). 12,645 ft. 140 mins.

The Dark Ages. In return for the gift of the magic sword Excalibur, Uther Pendragon promises his necromancer Merlin that he will make peace with his enemy, the Duke of Cornwall. The promise is broken as soon as Uther lays eyes on the latter's wife Igraine, and he persuades a reluctant Merlin to help him enter Cornwall's castle, in the guise of the Duke, to make love to Igraine (watched balefully by her small daughter, Morgana). Nine months later, Merlin arrives to collect his fee: Uther's first-born, Arthur, whom he entrusts to the poor knight Ector. Uther dies in an ambush, first planting Excalibur in a stone from which Merlin predicts it will only be removed by a true king. Some years later, now squire to Ector's son Kay, Arthur startles everyone by easily extracting the sword. Advised by Merlin, Arthur then subdues the squabbling knights, who refuse to accept him as king, marries Guinevere, and finds a champion in Lancelot. When the land is pacified, Arthur cements the fellowship of his knights by building the Round Table. But his half-sister Morgana, now a budding necromancer, begins to spread dissent. Gawain accuses Guinevere of being unfaithful with Lancelot, and the latter nearly dies after a joust to disprove the charge. Saddened to see the fellowship breaking up, shocked to learn that his queen and his champion *are* lovers, Arthur launches the quest for the Holy Grail to restore their sense of purpose. Morgana meanwhile tricks Merlin into revealing the 'charm of making', and seduces Arthur in the guise of Guinevere, conceiving a child by him in order to supplant him. Of the questing knights, only Perceval holds true, and eventually returns to Camelot with the secret of the Grail: that Arthur and the land are one. Arthur leads his knights into regenerative battle with Morgana's son Mordred, while Merlin, recalled to the world of men by Arthur's love, tricks Morgana with a spell that takes away her youth and lays down a fog to Arthur's advantage. Lancelot returns to the fellowship at the height of battle and dies; Arthur and Mordred mortally wound each other, and Perceval, the sole survivor, is instructed by Arthur to return Excalibur to the Lady of the Lake. At first reluctant to cast away such power, he at last complies.

1985 **The Emerald Forest**

USA *p.c.*: Embassy Pictures. *exec. p.*: Edgar F. Gross. *p.*: John Boorman. *co-p.*: Michael Dryhurst. *asst.d.*: Barry Langley. *sc.*: Rospo Pallenberg. *ph.*: Philippe Rousselot (Eastmancolor, Technicolor, Panavision). *a.d.*: Simon Holland. *set design*: Marcos Flaksman, Ian Wittaker, Monica Castro. *m.*: Junior Homrich, Brian Gascoigne. *m. consultant*: John Merritt. *ed.*: Ian Crafford. *s.ed.*: Ron Davis. *tribal chor.*: José Possi. *make-up*: Peter Frampton. *cost. design*: Christel Boorman, Clovis Bueno. *wigs*: Jaime Rodriguez Oliveira. *ph. location*: Lucio Kodato. *cameraman*: Gale Tattersall. *stunts*: Marc Boyle. *spec. eff.*: Raph Salis. *trainer*: Joe Camp. *eagle trainer*: Etienne Garde. *tech. cons.*: Prof. Charles F. Bennett, Dr Eduardo Vivairos de Castro. *l.p.*: Powers Boothe (*Bill Markham*), Meg Foster (*Jean Markham*), William Rodriguez (*Tommy as a child*), Yara Vaneau (*Heather as a child*), Charley Boorman (*Tomme*), Dira Paes (*Kachiri*), Eduardo Conde (*Uwe Werner*), Ariel Coelho (*Father Leduc*), Peter Marinker (*Perreira*), Mario Borges (*Costa*), Atilia Iorio (*Merchant*), Gabriel Archanjo (*Merchant's Right-Hand Man*), Gracindo Junior (*Carlos*), Arthur Muhlenberg (*Rico*), Chico Terto (*Paulo*). THE INVISIBLE PEOPLE: Rui Polonah (*Wanadi, the Chief*), Maria Helena Velasco (*Uluru, one of his Wives*), Tetchie Agbayani (*Gaya*), Paulo Vinicius (*Mapi*), Aloisio Flores (*Samanpo*), Isabel Bicudo, Patricia Prisco (*Kachiri's Cousins*), Silvana de Faria (*Pequi*), Alexandre Fontes, Antonio Japones (*Warriors*), Ana Lucia Dos Reis, Elidia Moraes (*Women*), THE FIERCE PEOPLE: Claudio Moreno (*Jacareh, the Chief*), Antonio Rodriguez Neto, Coluene Kodwel, Denilto Gomes, Fernando Pires, Guto Macedo, Iran Magalha Magalhaes (*Warriors*). 10,220 ft. 113 mins.

Bill Markham, an American engineer, is working on a dam in Brazil on the fringe of the Amazonian forest. He lives in a modern town with his wife Jean, his son Tommy, aged seven, and his daughter Heather, aged five. One day Tommy, attracted by Indians at the jungle's edge, disappears with them. Ten years later, after numerous searches, Bill has still not despaired of finding his son, even as he supervises the completion of the dam. During this period, Tommy has been raised by Wanadi, the chieftain of the tribe of the Invisible People, with his three wives, Uluru, Gaya and Pequi. Bill, accompanied by a German named Werner, travels deep into the jungle and confronts the tribe of the Fierce People, the enemies of the Invisible People, and its chief, Jacareh. Wounded, he encounters his son, who leads him to his own tribe. 'Tomme' – who now has a wife, Kachiri – refuses to follow his father back into the world of the whites. Bill is initiated, participates in the rite, is identified with the jaguar and returns to his wife. Meanwhile, Jacareh, taking advantage of the absence of Wanadi and Tomme, organizes a raid against the village of the Invisible People and abducts the tribeswomen (including Kachiri) to sell them as prostitutes to the whites. In the ensuing battle between the two tribes, Wanadi is killed and Tomme leaves to enlist the aid of his father, who possesses a gun. He finds his family, before returning to the jungle with Bill, freeing the prisoners and saving his tribe. Tomme then confesses to his father that he intends to destroy the dam, since it represents a source of great hardship for the region. He invokes supernatural powers for a storm and a torrential downpour to wreck the dam, though his father believes it to be indestructible. The dam bursts without anyone knowing who was responsible – whether Tomme or Bill, who is now on his son's side. Markham returns to the town; and, as he departs for the States with his wife and daughter, the forest begins to come alive again.

Forged by a god.
Foretold by a wizard.
Found by a King.
EXCALIBUR
ORION

1965-85

1

2

1 Shooting *Catch Us If You Can.*
2 Shooting *Hell in the Pacific.*

Directing

1

2

1 Shooting *Excalibur.*
2 Shooting *The Emerald Forest.*

1 Shooting *Deliverance*.
2 Shooting *The Heretic*.

1 Shooting *Excalibur.*
2 Shooting *The Emerald Forest*.

International
Film Quarterly
SIGHT AND
SOUND
Autumn 1973
35p $1.50

CINEMA
Deliverance
Morrisey
Leisen
Tennessee Williams
VOL. 8 NO. 1 ISSUE NO. 33 SPRING 1973 $2.00

film
directions
Vol. 4, No. 15
50p

American Film
Magazine of the
Film and Television Arts
March 1981
$2.00
EXCALIBUR
GAMBLING ON
CHIVALRY
INTERVIEW WITH
ROBERT DE NIRO
HOW WE CREATED
A HIT TV SERIES
by Richard Levinson and
William Link

Bibliography

This already considerable bibliography is limited to texts published in France, Britain and the United States; and, for the most part, in magazines. A succinct Italian bibliography can be found in Adriano Piccardi's book, cited below. With a few exceptions, I have not included the numerous articles, some of them of undeniable interest, which have appeared in daily or weekly newspapers, as their numbers would make classification impossible within the scope of this book.

Texts by John Boorman

(See also under 'Films')

1 'Enterprise', *Manchester Guardian*, 31 January 1955
2 'The Cabbage Kings', *Manchester Guardian*, 14 February 1957
3 'In the City, on Sundays', *Manchester Guardian*, 23 October 1957
4 'The Crisis We Deserve', *Sight and Sound*, Autumn 1970
5 'The Americans', (film project), *Positif*, nos. 200–201–202, December 1976–January 1977
6 'The Un-person' (review of *Chaplin, Genesis of a Clown*, by Raoul Sobel and David Francis, Quartet), *Irish Press*, 22 December 1977
7 'Jon Voight, Dedicated Idealist' and 'Lee Marvin, a Dying Breed', *Close-Ups, the Movie Star Book*, edited by Danny Peary, Workman Publishing, New York, 1978
8 'Sean Connery', introduction to *Sean Connery, His Life and Films*, by Michael Feeney Callan, W.H. Allen, London, 1983

General interviews with John Boorman

9 Barnes (Michael) (up to and including *Zardoz*), *Film Direction*, nos. 3 and 4, Autumn and Winter 1975
10 Braucourt (Guy) (up to and including *Hell in the Pacific*), *La Revue du cinéma*, no. 232, November 1969
11 Ciment (Michel) (up to and including *Hell in the Pacific*), *Positif*, October 1969
12 Du Cane (John), Elliot (Tony) (up to and including *Deliverance*), *Time Out*, 29 September 1972
13 Farber (Stephen), 'The Writer in American Film' (up to and including *Hell in the Pacific*), *Film Quarterly*, Summer 1968
14 Gow (Gordon), 'Playboy in a Monastery' (up to and including *Deliverance*), *Films and Filming*, February 1972
15 *IFT News*, no. 6, October 1968
16 Lightman (Herb) (up to and including *Zardoz*), *American Cinematographer*, March 1975
17 Waddy (Stacy) (up to and including *Leo the Last*), *The Guardian*, 31 May 1969
18 Yakir (Dan) (up to and including *Excalibur*), *Film Comment*, May–June 1981

Book

19 Piccardi (Adriano): *John Boorman*, Il Castoro Cinema, no. 100, La Nuova Italia, Florence, 1982

General studies of John Boorman's work

20 (Anonymous): *John Boorman, Le cinéma*, vol. 8, pp. 2138–40. Atlas
21 *BFI Bulletin*, June 1979 (Boorman retrospective at the NFT)
22 Brown (John Lindsay), 'Islands in the Mind', *Sight and Sound*, Winter 1969–70
23 Cluny (Claude-Michel), 'John Boorman', in *Dossiers du cinéma*, Les cinéastes, vol. III, Casterman, Paris 1974
24 Dunne (Aidan): 'A Language of Vision', *Film Directions*, vol. 2, no. 7 (1975)
25 Elley (Derek), 'John Boorman, Director of the Year', in *International Film Guide* (ed. Peter Cowie), pp. 15–21, Tantivy Press, London 1974
26 Legrand (Gérard), 'Homage to Boorman', *Positif*, no. 157, March 1974
27 Legrand (Gérard), 'John Boorman', in *Cinémanie*, pp. 183–7, Stock, Paris, 1979
28 Lovell (Alan), 'John Boorman, Of Myth and Modernism': *The Movie*, vol. 8, pp. 1835–7, Orbis, London, 1981
29 Mathieu (Martine), 'The Unconscious in John Boorman's Work': *Positif*, no. 203, February 1978
30 Rosenbaum (Jonathan), 'John Boorman', in *Cinema, A Critical Dictionary* (ed. Richard Roud), Secker and Warburg, London, 1980
31 Sineux (Michel), 'A Herald of Our Time', *Positif*, no. 247, October 1981
32 Thomson (David), 'John Boorman', in *A Biographical Dictionary of the Cinema*, Secker and Warburg, London, 1975
33 Walker (Alexander), in *Hollywood, England*, pp. 383–7, Michael Joseph, London, 1974

The television work

Interview

34 Smith (A.C.H.), interview with John Boorman, *Observer*, 21 June 1964

Articles

35 Burgess (Anthony) (on *Citizen 63*), *The Listener*, 5 September 1963
36 Hill (Derek), 'The new naturalists' (on *Citizen 63*), *Observer*, 1 September 1963
37 Purser (Philip) (on *The Newcomers*), *Sunday Telegraph*, 3–17 May 1964
38 Vas (Robert), 'Bristol Breakthrough' (on *Citizen 63*), *Contrast*, Winter 1963

The films

Catch Us If You Can (*US title: Having a Wild Weekend*)

Interview

39 Tremois (Claude Marie), *Télérama*, 11 October 1969

Review

40 Bean (Robin), *Films and Filming*, August 1965
41 Kael (Pauline), in *Kiss Kiss Bang Bang*, pp. 348–9, Bantam Books, New York, 1969
42 [E.S.], *Monthly Film Bulletin*, vol. 32, 1965
43 Tessier (Max), *Cinema*, 'Are you going or staying?', no. 139, September–October 1969

Point Blank

Book

44 Stark (Richard), *The Hunter*, Pocket Book, New York, 1969. *Point Blank!*, Hodder, London, 1967

Reviews

45 Austen (David), *Films and Filming*, March 1968
46 Bates (Dan), *Film Quarterly*, Winter 1967–8
47 Bory (Jean-Louis), in *La Nuit complice*, pp. 187–8, collection '10–18', Paris, 1972
47(a) Buache (Freddy) in *Le Cinéma américain 1955–70*, p. 551, L'Age d'Homme, Lausanne, 1974
48 Ciment (Michel), 'An American Dream', *Positif*, no. 96, June 1968
49 Clark (Arthur B.), *Films in Review*, October 1967
50 [J.A.D.], *Monthly Film Bulletin*, February 1968
51 Farber (Stephen), 'The Outlaws', *Sight and Sound*, Autumn 1968
52 French (Philip), *Sight and Sound*, Spring 1968
53 Gregory (Charles), 'Living Life Sideways', *Journal of Popular Film*, vol. 5, no. 3–4, 1976
54 Gross (Larry), 'Film après noir', *Film Comment*, July–August 1976
55 Lacombe (Alain), *Elia Kazan, John Boorman, and the redistribution of American myths*, Imprimerie Espic, Toulouse, 1971
56 Martin (James Michael), *Film Quarterly*, Summer 1968
57 Ross (T.J.), 'A Stalker in the City', *Film Heritage*, Autumn 1969
58 Sarris (Andrew), in *Confessions of a Cultist*, pp. 320–21. Simon and Schuster, New York, 1971
59 Shadoian (Jack), in *Dreams and Dead Ends*, pp. 308–25. MIT Press, Cambridge, Mass. 1977
60 Silver (Alan) and Ward (Elizabeth), in *Film Noir*, pp. 225–30, Secker and Warburg, London, 1979
61 Tessier (Max), 'Point of no return?', *Cinéma*, no. 128, August–September 1968
62 Thomson (David), in *America in the Dark*, pp. 183–5, William Morrow, New York, 1977
63 Toback (James), '*Bonnie and Clyde, Point Blank: style as morality*', in *Violence, Causes and Solutions*, a Laurel original, Dell, New York

Hell in the Pacific

Interview

64 Cohn (Bernard), *Les Lettres françaises*, 20 August 1969

65 Gilles (Edmond), *L'Humanité*, 3 September 1969

Reviews

65(a) Buache (Freddy) in *Le Cinéma américain 1955–70*, p. 551, L'Age d'Homme, Lausanne, 1974

66 Farber (Stephen), *Film Quarterly*, Summer 1969

67 Heard (Colin), *Films and Filming*, July 1969

68 Kluge (P.F.), 'The Hollywoodization of Palau', *Micronesian Reporter*, vol. 16, no. 2, second quarter, 1968, Saipan Marcana Island

69 Legrand (Gérard), 'No Way Out', *Positif*, no. 109, October 1969

70 Milne (Tom), *Monthly Film Bulletin*, March 1969

71 Tessier (Max), *Cinéma*, 'A Duel without Seconds', no. 139, September–October 1969

72 Wilson (David), *Sight and Sound*, Summer 1969

Leo the Last

Interview

73 Ciment (Michel), *Positif*, no. 118, Summer 1970

Reviews

74 Bory (Jean-Louis), in *L'Écran fertile*, pp. 90–2, collection '10–18', Union Générale d'Editions, Paris, 1974

75 Ciment (Michel), 'The Melancholic Observer', *Positif*, no. 118, Summer 1970

76 Gow (Gordon), *Films and Filming*, September 1970

77 Miller (Logan), *Films in Review*, June–July 1970

78 Sand (Luce), *Jeune cinéma*, no. 48, June–July 1970

79 Steele (Llord), *Los Angeles Free Press*, 7 August 1970

80 Strick (Philip), 'White man's burden' (article on the film shoot), *Sight and Sound*, Summer 1969

81 Strick (Philip), *Sight and Sound*, Summer 1970

82 Tessier (Max), *Cinéma*, no. 147, June 1970

83 Wallington (Michael), *Monthly Film Bulletin*, August 1970

84 Walsh (Martin), *Monogram*, no. 3, 1972

Deliverance

Books

85 Dickey (James), *Deliverance, a novel*, Houghton Mifflin Co, New York, 1970; Hamish Hamilton, London, 1970

86 Dickey (James), *Deliverance, a Screenplay*, Southern Illinois University Press, Carbondale and Edwardsville, 1982

Interviews

87 Braucourt (Guy), *Écran*, no. 9, November 1972

88 Ciment (Michel), *Positif*, no. 157, March 1974

89 Grisolia (Michel), *Les Lettres françaises*, 19 October 1972

90 Lightman (Herb A.), 'On Location with *Deliverance*', *American Cinematographer*, August 1971

91 Malcolm (Derek), *Guardian*, 5 October 1972

92 Strawn (Linda), *Action*, November–December 1972

93 Volmane (Véra), *La Croix*, 8 October 1972

Reviews

93(a) Aigner (Hal), *Film Quarterly*, Winter 1972–3

94 Allombert (Guy), *La Revue du cinéma*, no. 265, November 1972

95 (Anonymous), *Le Cinéma*, vol. 8, p. 2136–2137, Editions Atlas, Paris, 1984

96 Armour (Robert), '*Deliverance*: four variations of the American Dream', *Literature/Film Quarterly*, Summer 1973

97 Beaton (James F.), 'Dickey down the river', in *The Modern American Novel and the Movies*, edited by Gerald Peary and Roger Schatzkin, pp. 293–306, Ungar Film Library, New York, 1976

98 Benoit (Claude), and Prédal (René), 'Two Americas Face to Face', *Jeune cinéma*, no. 76, December–January 1972–3

99 Bleikasten (André), 'Anatomy of a Bestseller', RANAM, no. 4, 1971, Strasbourg, Université des Sciences Humaines

100 Bory (Jean-Louis), 'Fleeing Nature', in *La Lumière Ecrit*, pp. 351–5, Coll. 10–18, Paris, 1975

101 Buckley (Peter): *Films and Filming*, October 1972

102 Ciment (Michel), 'Journey to the End of Night', *Positif*, no. 143, October 1972

103 Dempsey (Michael), 'Boorman-Dickey in the Woods', *Cinema*, no. 33, Spring 1973

104 Dunne (Aidan), 'A Labyrinth of allusion', *Film Directions*, vol. 1, no. 4, 1978

105 McGillivray (David), *Focus on Film*, no. 11, Autumn 1972

106 Milne (Tom), *Monthly Film Bulletin*, September 1972

107 Renaud (Tristan), *Cinéma*, no. 170, November 1972

108 Samuels (Charles Thomas), 'How not to film a novel', in *Mastering the film and other essays*, pp. 194–7, University of Tennessee Press, Knoxville, 1977

109 Strick (Philip), *Sight and Sound*, Autumn 1972

110 Tessier (Max), *Écran*, no. 9, September–October 1972

111 Watts (Tony), *The Movie*, vol. 8, pp. 1838–9, Orbis, London, 1981

112 Willson (Robert F.): '*Deliverance* from novel to film. Where is our hero?', *Literature/Film Quarterly*, Winter 1974

Zardoz

Book

113 Boorman (John), with Bill Stair, *Zardoz*, Signet Book, New American Library, New York, 1974; Pan Books, London, 1974

Interviews

114 Ciment (Michel), *Positif*, no. 157, March 1974

115 Douin (Jean-Luc), *Télérama*, 16 March 1974

116 Lachize (Samuel), *L'Humanité Dimanche*, 6 March 1974

117 Strick (Philip), *Sight and Sound*, Spring 1974

118 Tessier (Max), *Écran*, no. 23, March 1974

119 Volmane (Véra), *La Croix*, 10 March 1974

Reviews

120 Allombert (Guy), *La Revue du Cinéma*, no. 283, April 1974

121 Avery (William), *Films in Review*, March 1974

122 Bory (Jean-Louis), in *L'Obstacle et la gerbe*, pp. 275–9, collection '10–18', Union Générale d'Editions, Paris, 1976

122(a) Buache (Freddy), in *Le Cinema américain 1971–83*, pp. 379–80, L'Age d'Homme, Lausanne, 1985

123 Champlin (Charles), 'Look Back: John Boorman's *Zardoz*', *Millimeter*, October 1976

124 Ciment (Michel), 'Boorman and James Bond?' *L'Express*, 6 August 1973

125 Dawson (Jan), (on the film shoot), *Monthly Film Bulletin*, April 1974

126 Duval (Bruno), *Téléciné*, no. 188, May 1974

127 Gallo (William), *Film Heritage*, Summer 1974

128 Garsault (Alain), 'The adventure story and the metaphysical fable', *Positif*, no. 157, March 1974

129 Gay (R.), *Cinéma Québec*, April–May 1974

130 Goimard (Jacques), 'The poetics of science fiction', *Positif*, no. 162, October 1974

131 Goldberg (Stephanie), 'Boorman's metaphysical western', *Jumpcut*, no 3, September–October 1974

132 Gow (Gordon), *Films and Filming*, April 1974

133 Jameson (Fredric), 'History and the death wish: *Zardoz* as open form', *Jumpcut*, no. 3, September–October 1974

134 Kael (Pauline), in *Reeling*, pp. 276–80, Little, Brown and Co., Boston, 1976

135 Kinder (Marsha), *Film Quarterly*, Summer 1974

136 Matthews (F.), *Cinema Papers*, July 1974

137 Renaud (Tristan), *Cinéma*, no. 186, April 1974

138 Strick (Philip), *Sight and Sound*, Spring 1974

139 Tessier (Max), *Écran*, no. 23, March 1974

140 Thirard (Paul-Louis), 'Reading the reviews of *Zardoz*', *Positif*, no. 160, June 1974

The Heretic

Books

141 Boorman (John), Goodhart (William) and Pallenberg (Rospo), *Exorciste II: L'Hérétique*, *L'Avant-scène cinéma*, no. 201, Paris, 1 February 1978

142 Pallenberg (Barbara), *The Making of Exorcist II: The Heretic*, Warner Books, New York, 1977

Interviews

143 Behar (Henri), *La Revue du cinéma*, no. 326, March 1978

144 Ciment (Michel), *Positif*, no. 203, February 1978

145 Le Pavec (Jean-Pierre), and Rabourdin (Dominique), *Cinéma*, no. 231, March 1978

146 Paranagua (Paulo Antonio), *Rouge*, 1 February 1978

Reviews

147 (Anonymous), 'Speaking in tongues', *Monthly Film Bulletin*, October 1977

149 Ciment (Michel): 'Boorman's Genius', *L'Avant-scène cinéma*, no. 201, 1 February 1978

150 Ciment (Michel): 'Boorman's Heresy', *L'Express*, 5 December 1977

151 Combs (Richard), *Monthly Film Bulletin*, October 1977

152 Edelman (Rob), *Films in Review*, August–September 1977

153 Garec (Alain) and Mérigeau (Pascal), *La Revue du cinéma*, no. 326, March 1978

154 Kané (Pascal), *Les Cahiers du cinéma*, no. 286, March 1978

155 Lepoute (F.), *Lumière du cinéma*, no. 11, January–

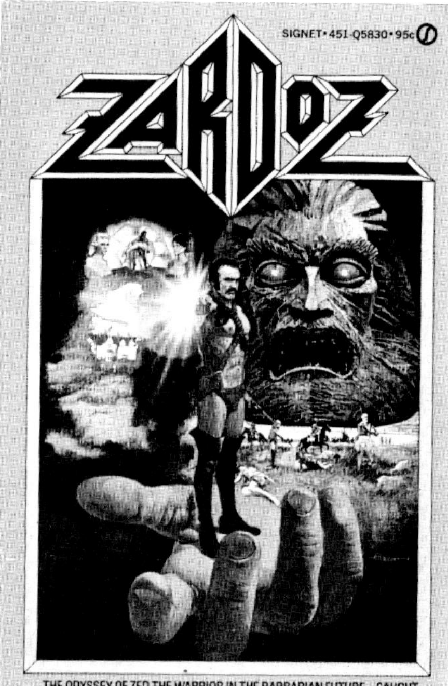

February 1978
156 Lofficier (Jean-Marc), *L'Écran fantastique*, no. 3, First Quarter, 1978
157 McCarthy (Tod), 'The Exorcism of *The Heretic*', *Film Comment*, September–October 1977
158 Renaud (Tristan) and La Fuente (Leonardo), 'Two Points of View', *Cinéma*, no. 231, March 1978
158(a) Scorsese (Martin), 'Guilty Pleasures' *Film Comment*, September–October 1978
159 Tarratt (Margaret), *Films and Filming*, December 1977
160 Tessier (Max), *Écran*, no. 63, November 1977

Excalibur

Interviews

161 Ciment (Michel), *Positif*, no. 242, May 1981
162 Heymann (Danièle), *L'Express*, 22 May 1981
163 Kennedy (Harlan), 'The World of King Arthur According to John Boorman', *American Film*, March 1981
164 Open (Michael), *Film Directions*, vol. 2, no. 15, 1981
165 Strick (Philip), 'John Boorman's *Merlin*' (on the film shoot), *Sight and Sound*, Summer 1980
166 Stringer (Robin), *Daily Telegraph*, 29 June 1980
167 Tessier (Max), *La Revue du cinéma*, no. 363, July–August 1981

Reviews

168 Assayas (Olivier), 'Kitschy Grail', *Les Cahiers du cinéma*, no. 326, July–August 1981
168(a) Buache (Freddy), in *Le Cinéma américain 1971–83*, pp. 380–1, L'Age d'Homme, Lausanne, 1985
169 Ciment (Michel), 'The Knights of King Boorman' (on the film shoot), *L'Express*, 5 July 1980
170 Combs (Richard), *Monthly Film Bulletin*, June 1981
171 Domecq (Jean-Philippe), 'Sword and Heath', *Positif*, no. 242, May 1981
172 Gow (Gordon), *Films*, July 1981
172(a) Kael (Pauline): 'Boorman's plunge', in *Taking It All*, pp. 182–7, Holt-Rinehart-Winston, New York, 1984
173 Kennedy (D.), *Cinema Papers*, September–October 1981
174 Markal (Jean), '*Excalibur*, or the impossible masterpiece', *Positif*, no. 247, October 1981
175 Masson (Alain), 'Geoliad Gwad'. *Positif*, no. 247, October 1981
177 Prédal (René), *Jeune cinéma*, no. 136, July–August 1981
178 Rabourdin (Dominique), 'In the land of myths', *Cinéma*, no. 270, June 1981
179 Ruiz (Raoul), 'Three remarks', *Positif*, no. 247, October 1981
180 Tessier (Max), *La Revue du cinéma*, no. 362, June 1981
181 Ventura (Michael), 'In the arms of the dragon, parts I and II', *Los Angeles Weekly*, 19 and 26 June 1981

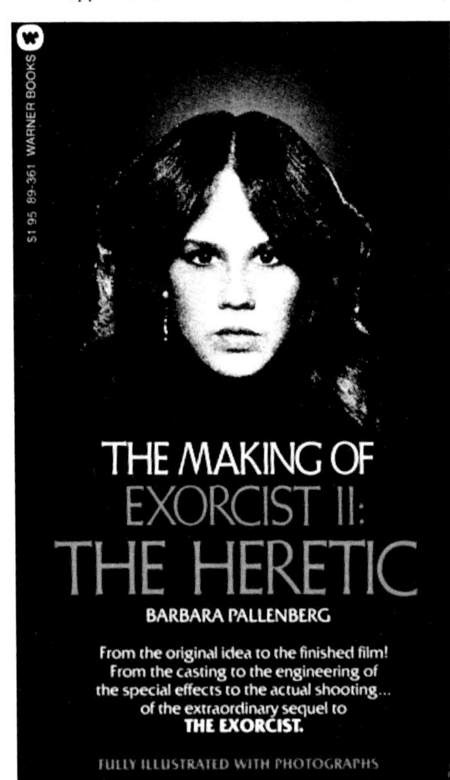

The Emerald Forest

Book

182 Boorman (John), *Money Into Light*, Faber and Faber, London 1985

Collaborators

183 Burke (Tom), 'Conversations with Jon Voight', *Esquire*, January 1972
184 Farber (Stephen), 'An interview with Alexander Jacobs' (on *Point Blank* and *Hell in the Pacific*), *Film Quarterly*, Winter 1968–9
185 Guy (Rory), 'An interview with Toshiro Mifune', *Cinema* (Los Angeles), vol. 5, no. 1, 1969
186 Gow (Gordon), 'A secretive person: an interview with Sean Connery', *Films and Filming*, March 1974
187 Jacobs (Alexander), Letter to *Positif*, no. 118, July–August 1970
188 Lightman (Herb A.), 'The photography of *Exorcist II, the Heretic*: and interview with William Fraker', *American Cinematographer*, August 1977
189 Macklin (F. Anthony), 'An interview with Vilmos Zsigmond', *Film Heritage*, Spring 1977
190 Maltin (Leonard): 'Interview with Conrad Hall' in *Behind the Camera: the cinematographer's art*, pp. 185–216, a Signal Book, New American Library, New York, 1971
191 Norman (Geoffrey), 'An interview with James Dickey', *Playboy*, 1972
192 Stair (Bill), 'Working with Boorman', *Positif*, no. 157, March 1974

Various

193 Bachelard (Gaston), *La Poetique de l'espace*, PUF, Paris, 1958
194 Blake (William), Poems
195 Breton (André), *Manifestes du surréalisme*, Jean-Jacques Pauvert, Paris, 1962
196 Broch (Hermann): 'Hoffmannstal and his period', *Gesammete Werke*, Zurich, 1952–9
197 Buraud (Georges), *Les Masques*, Club des Editeurs, Paris, 1961
198 Char (René): *Oeuvres complètes*, 'La Pléiade', Gallimard, Paris, 1983
200 Eliot (T.S.), *Collected Poems 1909–62*, Faber and Faber, London, 1963
201 Flaubert (Gustave), *Correspondance*, vol. 2, 'La Pléiade', Gallimard, Paris, 1980
202 Jauss (Hans Robert), 'Littérature médiévale et théorie des genres', in *Poétique*, no. 1, Le Seuil, Paris, 1970
203 Jung (C.G.), *The Undisguised Self*, Routledge and Kegan Paul, London, 1974
204 Jung (C.G.), *Psyche and Symbol*, Anchor Books, Doubleday, New York, 1958
205 Lapouge (Gilles), *Utopie et civilisations*, Weber, Paris, 1973
206 Lévi-Strauss (Claude), *A World on the Wane*, Hutchinson, London, 1961
207 Lévi-Strauss (Claude), *La Voie des masques*, Skira, Geneva, 1975
208 Matta (Roberto), 'Interview with Peter de Francia', in *Hayward Gallery Exhibition Catalogue*, London, 1977
209 Montagnon (Rosemary Gordon), 'Jung, rebellious son or prophet?', in *Carl G. Jung*, Cahiers de L'Herne, no. 46, Paris, 1984
210 Pasquier (Marie-Claire), Rougier (Nicole), Brugière (Bernard), *Nouveau théâtre anglais*, Armand Colin, Paris, 1969
211 Paz (Octavio), *El Arco y la lira*, Mexico, 1956
212 Paz (Octavio), *Points de convergence*, Gallimard, Paris, 1976
213 Starobinski (Jean), *L'Oeil vivant*, Gallimard, Paris, 1961
214 Thevoz (Michel), *Le Corps peint*, Skira, Geneva, 1984
215 Valéry (Paul), 'Degas, danse, dessin', in *Pièces sur l'art, Oeuvres*, vol. 2, 'La Pléiade', Gallimard, Paris, 1960
216 Valéry (Paul), *Les Principes d'anarchie puré et appliquée*, Gallimard, Paris, 1984

VIDEOGRAPHY

(Betamax – VHS/VH)

Point Blank RCV (Pan and scan)
Hell in the Pacific Thorn-EMI (Pan and scan)
Deliverance Warner Home Video
Zardoz CBS-Fox
The Heretic Warner Home video
Excalibur Warner Home Video

DISCOGRAPHY

Deliverance: Warner Bros Records BS 2683
The Heretic: Warner Bros Records BS 3039
The Emerald Forest: Varèse Sarabande STV 81244

Index

Page references in italic refer to one or more illustrations.

Acknowledgements

The preparation of a book on the cinema often presents insoluble problems of documentation, iconography and the mere possibility of re-viewing films. For having helped me solve these, I should like to thank:

Daniel Bouteiller; Roger Dagieux; John Kobal; Michelle Snapes, Markku Salmi (The BFI stills archive); Mary Corliss (The Museum of Modern Art stills archive); Marc Bernard, Denise Breton (Twentieth Century-Fox); Michèle Darmon, Marie Hélène Février (Warner Bros, Paris); Julian Senior (Warner Bros, London); Michèle Abitbol, Caroline Decriem (CIC); Alain Roulleau (United Artists); Agnès Chabot (Gerick Distribution); Yvonne Decaris, Micheline Daguinot (Mac-Mahon Distribution); Claude Beylie, Jean-Paul Török (Cinemathèque universitaire); Gillian Hartnoll (BFI Library); Marie McFarren, Norma Paulsen (John Boorman's production secretaries).

I should also like to thank the *Monthly Film Bulletin* for the plot synopses (with the exception of that for *The Emerald Forest*) which appear in the filmography; and the journals *Positif*, *L'Express* and *L'Avant-Scène cinéma* for having consented to my reprinting certain critical texts and interviews which were originally published, in a less complete form, in their pages.

Finally, I owe a special debt to the collaborators of John Boorman who allowed me to publish their recollections of him; Christel Boorman for her generous hospitality; John Boorman himself, who expended both time and effort in his assistance to me; Alain Oulman of Calmann-Lévy publishing company for the confidence he showed in me; Bernard Père, a gifted layout artist and a shrewd cinéphile with whom it is always stimulating to work; and my wife Jeannine, who shared my discovery of Boorman's work and helped make this book possible.